Renegade Love

by

Donna Fletcher

Cover art
http://thekilliongroupinc.com/
EBook Design
http://www.athirstymind.com/

Visit Donna's Web Site
www.donnafletcher.com
http://www.facebook.com/donna.fletcher.author

Table of Contents

Prologue

1818 – California

"*Madre Dios*! You've come home." Alejandro Cesare stared at his son as though he was an apparition, a ghost returning from the dead.

"Am I welcomed home, Father?" Esteban asked.

Alejandro continued to stare, watching the way his son gripped the reins, ready to command the stallion he straddled if the answer should provoke. His deep voice was that of a stranger. There was no resemblance of the young, carefree boy that had been forcibly removed from his family sixteen years ago.

"You hesitate, Father."

He spoke without sentiment and Alejandro nearly shivered from the chill of his icy demeanor. "You are more than welcomed home, my son, of that there is no doubt. The shock of your sudden return but catches my tongue and my senses. I have searched so long and hard for you and now... here you are."

"No longer the fourteen year old boy who was torn away from you."

That was obvious. Esteban was far from the skinny, young boy whose limbs had been too long and lanky for his thin frame. And who had born no trace of a manly chest, though he had strutted around in front of the young ladies as though he had.

No, that young embolden boy was gone as were the lanky limbs replaced now by sheer muscle. He could strut now if he wanted to, his black shirt spread tight across a lean chest defined with muscles. While his appearance certainly impressed and stirred apprehension, it was his features that startled Alejandro the most.

Esteban had sent the young *senoritas* hearts fluttering at an early age and Alejandro had only imagined what maturity would bring. However, Esteban had grown more handsome than Alejandro could have ever imagined, though he was not prepared for the cold hardness that accented his son's stark, breath-catching features.

His child, though child no more, who had laughed and smiled so often appeared completely devoid of emotion. What had happened to him? What had stolen his humanity?

"It has been too long, my son," Alejandro said aching to reach out and hug him tightly, so grateful was he that his son had finally come home. "I thank God you are home."

Esteban's dark brows drew together in a scowl. "Let us see if you feel that way after you hear the details of my life these last sixteen years."

Sharp anger stung his words and Alejandro could not blame him. He, himself, had dealt with the never-ending guilt for not having protected his son the way he should have—and worse—for not having been able to find him all these years, though not for lack of trying.

Alejandro stood tall, his shoulders drawn back, a lingering ache persisting in his right one. Age was creeping up on him. He'd be sixty in less than three years. He had prayed he would see his son before death took him and God had answered his never-ending prayers. He wanted to know all his son had suffered. But mostly he wanted to help heal him and see him laugh and smile again.

"I want to hear everything," Alejandro insisted.

"Then I will tell you, Father," Esteban said. "And you can tell me then if you truly welcome me home."

Chapter One

Rosalita Mendez pulled with all her might to retrieve the water bucket from the community well. Her arms ached as did her back. She felt the stretch of each muscle with every yank of the rope, the sweltering heat making the laborious chore that more difficult.

"Blisters again," she sighed as the hemp line slid roughly along her hands.

"Rosa, you complain when your job is so easy?" Marinda Chavez teased with a hearty laugh.

A sad smile graced the delicate features of Rosa's face. And even with wisps of her silky brown hair falling along her brow and a trace of perspiration touching her slender neck, her natural beauty still shined through.

Marinda shook her head and spoke half in jest and half truthfully. "I hate you for being so beautiful."

Rosa opened her mouth to protest.

"Don't bother to deny it. Every woman in St. Lucita comments on your lovely face. And every man cannot keep their eyes off you. Your skin is clear and perfect like the angelic carved statues in the church and your body..." Marinda shook her head again. "What I wouldn't give to be petite and slender like you."

"You are far from fat and besides Paco loves you just the way you are," Rosa said after hefting the heavy water-filled bucket to sit on the edge of the well.

With the mention of her new husband, Marinda beamed. "He tells me that I am a beautiful goddess who he will worship forever."

This time a happy smile appeared on Rosa's face. She was truly pleased that her friend had found love. Paco Chavez had followed Marinda around like a love-starved puppy for months, claiming that he would wait for her forever. Forever hadn't been long away. Paco's irresistible charm had swept the robust Marinda off her feet, and they had wed two months ago.

Marinda looked around the well at the other women. She waited until some of the older women walked away, their water jugs full, and the few younger women who lingered were deep in conversation before she whispered to Rosa, "I'm glad Paco wed me when he did. The search still goes on."

Rosa involuntarily shuddered. "Don Cesare has still not found a wife for his son?"

Marinda shook her head and kept her voice low. "Who would want to marry Esteban Cesare, handsome though he may be?" Marinda crossed herself for protection before continuing. "It is said he had done unspeakable things during his sixteen years with Pacquito's band of renegades."

Rosa could not help but feel a twinge of sympathy for Esteban Cesare. "It was not his fault that he was captured by renegades when he was fourteen years old."

"No, it wasn't," Marinda agreed. "But why did he stay with them these many years. Why didn't he return as soon as escape was possible?"

Rosa kept her thoughts to herself. She understood what it was like to be in a position where although escape seemed possible... it wasn't.

"I have heard that no decent family will accept Don Cesare's generous marriage offer for his son. All the wealthy haciendas have closely guarded their daughters since his return and that now Don Cesare looks to the peasant people for a suitable wife."

Rosa raised her brow in question. "Don Alejandro would allow a peasant woman to marry his son?"

"The gossips say he is desperate for his son to return to a normal life, marry, have children, and help run the wealthy Cesare lands. I suppose he hopes it will help bury his son's sinful past and he would once again be accepted into their world."

"His son needs to heal... to forgive before he can forget."

"Forgive who?" Marinda asked always curious by Rosa's strange responses.

"Himself, of course," Rosa answered as though it was common knowledge and everyone understood.

Marinda's voice dropped so low that Rosa had to lean closer to hear her. "Forgive himself for what... for all the vile things he has done?"

"No," —Rosa shook her head— "forgive himself for the strength it took him to survive. Few people would have such courage."

Audible, shocked gasps drew both their attentions and they looked up to see what had caused the startled cries.

Don Alejandro and his son Esteban were riding in an open carriage through the center of St. Lucita at a slow pace. The shiny black and silver trimmed conveyance glittered in the morning sun. Don Alejandro waved and called out to friends, his smile broad, pleasant and sincere.

Esteban sat straight and stiff as though prepared to battle any ill wind that blew his way. His demeanor was arrogant and unapproachable. But his handsome features caught the women's breathes and sent their hearts beating rapidly.

From the size of him compared to his father sitting beside him, he had to be several inches over six feet. And from the fit of his garments his body was well-honed. His black-as-night hair shined and was pulled back and tied with a leather string at the nape of his neck.

The carriage neared Marinda and Rosa.

"Don't look into his eyes," Marinda warned before lowering her head.

But Rosa could not take her eyes off the handsome man that had had tongues wagging since his return and besides he looked straight ahead, as if he wasn't the least interested in those around him.

Don Alejandro waved to her, which she had

expected since on several occasions business had brought him to the home of the family she resided with. Rosa smiled and waved recalling the older man's warmth and friendliness.

Esteban's head turned then with a sharp snap and caught her eyes in such an intense grip that Rosa was held spellbound. It was as though his eyes penetrated her and she could feel the heat and fury contained within him as he stayed his glance, his head turning slowly to hold it there as the carriage continued on. It wasn't until the conveyance disappeared around the end building that she was free of him.

The breath, she hadn't realized she had been holding, came out in a short gasp. Her knees turned so weak that Marinda grabbed her arm and helped her to lean against the well wall.

"I warned you not to look at him," Marinda scolded. "Now that you have cast your eyes upon evil, you will pay."

Rosa trembled from Marinda's dire prediction or from Esteban's potent look, she couldn't be certain. She knew one thing though. She would not look upon his dark sinful eyes ever again.

~~~

"The young woman interests you?" Don Alejandro asked shortly after the carriage pulled away from the St. Lucita Mission. As usual Esteban had refused to enter the church and Padre Marten had not encouraged him to do so. Until Esteban confessed his sins, the scared ground of the church was no place for him.

Receiving no immediate answer Alejandro asked again, "The young woman... she interests you?"

Esteban did not look at his father when he spoke. "I have no intentions of marrying... ever."

"It is your obligation as my son to marry and produce an heir," Alejandro reminded patiently for what he felt must have been at least the hundredth time.

Esteban turned his head slowly as his brow knit together in a frown and he spoke in a tone that always managed to send a chill through Alejandro. "I will *not* marry."

Alejandro stirred uncomfortably in his seat. "We will discuss—"

"We have discussed enough!" Esteban snapped. This ridiculous idea his father had must be put to rest immediately. Marriage was not now or ever part of his life. "I have not taken another man's orders for several years. You will do well to remember the things I have told you, Father, and cease this senseless search for a wife for me."

Alejandro gave a gentle shrug as though it was no burden. "Your mother and I only wish your happiness."

The one corner of Esteban's mouth rose but a fraction. Alejandro had learned quickly that this slight, almost undetectable expression was what passed as a smile for his son. And laughter? He had heard none from his son since his return and it made him wonder if Esteban was even capable of ever laughing again.

"I am happy, Father," Esteban said not all convincingly.

Alejandro could hold back no longer. "*Happy*? You barely speak to anyone. You never smile or laugh. You distance yourself from your mother whenever she approaches you. This is what you call *happy*?"

Esteban had remained stoic throughout his father's brief scolding. Even now no emotion clouded his face. "I have changed. If you and Mother find my change too difficult to accept, perhaps I should leave."

Alejandro's hand flew to his chest, his heart skipping several beats and his breath catching. He could not lose his son a second time. He would be devastated not to mention his dear wife Valerianna's reaction. It was unthinkable. He shook his head slowly, his expression sad. "Your mother and I love you and would be heartbroken if you were to leave us. We want only what is best for you."

"What is *best*," Esteban emphasized, "is to *leave* me be."

Don Alejandro simply nodded in response and watched with little interest as the carriage turned onto Cesare property. His generous wealth laid spread around him. Vineyards of fresh grapes, orchards abundant with fruit, livestock enough to feed the entire valley, yet it all seemed unimportant at the moment. The only thing that concerned him was his son.

"Rosalita Mendez is a sweet *nina* and talented."

Esteban stiffened considerably, and it brought a pleased smile to Alejandro's lips. He had finally touched an emotional chord in his son, or perhaps Rosalita had.

"She was so very delighted and grateful when I presented her with drawing charcoals and papers that she insisted on drawing a portrait of me. Your mother contended that Rosalita had captured my true nature, especially around the eyes."

Alejandro stopped, disappointed that he wasn't holding his son's attention. He recalled what best stirred a man's interest in a woman. And smiled as he said, "Many of the young men fancy Rosalita."

That did it.

Esteban turned with a snap to glare at his father. His voice remained controlled but his tone was hard. "And does she enjoy their favors?"

Alejandro refused to allow his son's caustic remark to disturb him. "She is a good girl and keeps them at a respectable distance."

"She wears a gentle smile," Esteban said although Alejandro felt certain it was more a spoken thought not meant to be shared.

"She is gentle and kind, truly a good woman," Alejandro assured and tempted fate further with his next words. "Would you like to meet her?"

Esteban remained silent as the carriage pulled into the circular entrance of the courtyard of the Cesare hacienda and stopped beside the fountain spurting water to the heaven.

He stepped down out of the carriage and with deliberate slowness turned back around to catch his father's hopeful look with his potent one. "She fears me. I can see it in her eyes, and she has good reason to," —Esteban raised his hand to stop his father from interrupting— "*good reason*, Father."

Esteban loosened the black slim tie at his throat and opened his shirt down to his waist, as if shedding the image of Don Cesare's respectable son and returning to who he had been forced to become... a wild, merciless renegade. And his words proved it. "The moment I laid eyes on her I wanted her. My blood fired with uncontrollable lust, my groin throbbed and I thought of nothing more than stripping her naked and taking her like a wild stallion would take a mare."

Alejandro paled considerably.

"I see that you needed reminding of what I have become. Keep the *gentle nina* away from me or she will suffer badly." Esteban turned and walked away grumbling.

Alejandro barely caught the last of his son's words—*she deserves better*— and that gave him a ray of hope.

He would contact Roberto Curro, Rosalita's guardian, immediately. He was certain that the man would be most cooperative. It was well known that Roberto was more interested in coin than people. That was the only reason Roberto and his wife Lola had taken the twelve year old girl in seven years ago. Rosalita's parents had passed away when fever had struck the town. There were whispered rumors that a padre from a nearby mission had paid Roberto to take the child in and care for her.

Alejandro would offer a substantial amount for Rosalita. One that Roberto surely would not refuse, although he might demand more. But Alejandro was willing to pay a king's ransom to buy his son a wife, especially one his son had found some interest in. He shuddered recalling his son's sinful words from moments before. Esteban was not the barbarian he painted himself to be. Somewhere inside him was the respectful and caring son that he had raised and perhaps Rosalita could help set him free.

He shook his head absentmindedly as he finally climbed down out of the carriage. Esteban would not hurt Rosalita. Never would he surrender to such wicked thoughts. *Never.*

"Rosalita will make Esteban a good wife," Alejandro murmured, as if saying it aloud would make it so. "She will help heal him."

Alejandro walked toward the door, his step a little lighter, but he stopped suddenly just before entering the house and crossed himself. "Please, *Madre Dios*, let it be so."

Chapter Two

Rosa was frightened. Usually, she kept fear at bay. The last time she could recall the bone-chilling feeling was when she had been twelve and had watched her parents' plain wooden coffins being lowered slowly into the ground to rest atop each other. She hadn't known what would become of her then. Her small hand had clung tenaciously to Teresa, her mother's best friend. Her eyes had been swollen from crying. Fear had caused her to shiver uncontrollably. There was no one left to take care of her... no one left to love her.

That same helpless emotion now attacked her full force. It started as a small tingle of alarm as soon as she had spied Don Alejandro's elegant carriage in front of the adobe ranch house where she lived with Roberto and Lola Curro.

Rosa managed to convince herself that Don Alejandro was merely here to do business with Roberto, perhaps arranging the purchase of a horse. But when she attempted to enter the three room house Lola had quickly ushered her away with a strong shove, informing her that Roberto was discussing an extremely important matter with Don Alejandro and she was to wait outside until summoned.

Every minute that crawled by escalated Rosa's

concerns. She stood braced against the cool adobe wall in the back of the house, hoping to catch at least snatches of conversation. She heard only whispers, and the hushed, secretive voices sounded even more foreboding to her ears.

"What are you doing lolling about," Lola barked, moving her heavy bulk slowly through the open doorway.

Rosa moved away in haste from the woman. Too often she had felt the sting of her large hand as well as her harsh words of criticism.

Lola shook her head, her eyes narrowed with disgust. "Lazy that's what you are. You never work hard enough. You—" She stopped abruptly and smiled while wiping at an egg stain, left from the morning meal, on her white blouse.

It was a strange almost dismissive gesture as though in brushing off the offending stain, she was brushing away Rosa.

Rosa shivered to the tips of her small toes.

In a more gentle tone than Rosa thought possible, Lola ordered her to prepare green beans for supper, then wash up and change into her church clothes and wait in the cookhouse until summoned.

"Be quick about it," Lola snapped in her usual waspish tongue. "I'll make sure you work hard, as you should, until the very *end*."

Lola turned in haste bumping her ample shoulder against the door frame, and cursed it and Rosa, as she entered the house.

Rosa had had a mind to ask until the end of

what. But she would have only received a slap to the head for being inquisitive. So she had reluctantly, though wisely, held her tongue. Besides, she had a sinking feeling that she truly wouldn't want to know.

It was an hour later that Rosa was summoned by a smug Lola to the front room that was kept strictly for business visitors.

Don Alejandro's generous smile did little to alleviate her apprehension. And Roberto's gruff voice and manner only added to her nervousness.

"Come over here, *nina*. Now!" Roberto ordered sternly.

Rosa obeyed without question, fearful of the leather strap he often used on her without compunction. Several fading bruises on her arms and hips attested to the fact. She approached him slowly and stopped a safe distance from his reach.

"She may be small, but she's strong," Roberto boasted.

"And lazy," Lola added, "it's a heavy hand you'll need with her."

Rosa, for an instant felt a fleeting sense of relief, thinking that Don Alejandro was purchasing her services for his hacienda, but Roberto's next words quickly squashed that hope.

"Her husband will decide how heavier a hand he will use on her. And she will obey him as she does me. She is trained well, Don Alejandro."

Don Alejandro nodded, well aware that Roberto intended for this arrangement to succeed. Alejandro had no intentions of losing Rosa as a bride-to-be for his son. He would have paid any price Roberto had asked. He had actually thought Roberto had settled for far too little for the sweet-natured, young girl.

Don Alejandro turned his attention to Rosa and smiled, hoping to ease her obvious apprehension. "I'm certain that Rosa will do fine, though I would like to discuss the arrangement with her."

"That's not necessary," Roberto argued and shifted his weight uneasily in the wooden chair. "She will do as she is told. She has no say in the matter."

Don Alejandro's posture grew rigid. He was an imposing figure with his silver hair and intense dark eyes. "I wish for Rosa to understand the circumstances and the arrangement."

Roberto was no fool and was already spending, in his head, the large sum of money he was getting for the puny, useless girl. "As you wish, Don Alejandro."

Alejandro crossed his arms and relaxed back in the chair, then nodded for Roberto to proceed.

"Rosa," Roberto said his tone stern. "I have arranged a most generous marriage for you. In two weeks, you will wed Don Alejandro's son Esteban."

Rosa stood in shocked silence. She had remained quiet, as proper, listening to their exchange and assuming the worse, and she had been right. Marinda's words drifted back to haunt her.

You have looked upon evil and now you will

pay.

She recalled Esteban's dark, brooding eyes that had felt as if they reached down deep into her soul and tainted it. How could she marry such a man? The villagers whispered his name, they feared him so. The women blessed themselves and hid their daughters when he was near. She could not marry this man—this heartless soul—she couldn't.

Her words stuck in her dry throat and when she finally managed to speak, her voice sounded odd to her own ears. "Two weeks? But there will not be enough time for the banns to be read in the church."

Don Alejandro stood and slipped his arm around her, so worried was he that she would faint. All color had drained from her lovely face and her hands trembled even though she held them folded together. He directed her to a chair beside his and sat her down before sitting himself. "I have arranged everything with the church, and my wife is already busy planning the wedding festivities."

Rosa looked with desperation into the older man's eyes. She wanted to scream out her refusal to wed Esteban Cesare. But it would do little good. Roberto held the power to sign her over into marriage to whomever he wished, and there was no one who would pay near as handsomely for her as Don Alejandro.

Alejandro patted Rosa's folded hands. "You will be happy at the hacienda. Life will be easy there for you."

Rosa nodded slowly, knowing with each

reluctant nod her fate was sealed. Don Alejandro had not said she'd be happy with his son, only that she'd be happy at the hacienda and that thought sent a shiver of fear through her.

"Roberto," Don Alejandro said, turning to the large man. "You and your wife will bring Rosa to the hacienda this evening for supper."

"It will be my pleasure," Roberto said with a huge grin and a puffed out chest.

Rosa shuddered and Alejandro once again patted her hands, but offered no words of comfort. What words could he offer her? He had no idea how Esteban would treat her, and he prayed most fervently that his decision to arrange this marriage had been the right one.

~~~

"You what?" Esteban yelled at his father.

"I've arranged a marriage between you and Rosalita Mendez," Alejandro repeated calmly, although his heart raced at an alarming rate.

Esteban paced in front of his father's wide desk, glad that it separated them from each other, for he had an uncontrollable urge to reach out and strangle him. "I have told you repeatedly that I would not marry—and yet—you arrange a marriage against my wishes?"

"I do not need your permission," Alejandro reminded him.

Esteban stopped pacing. "I take orders from no man, Father."

Alejandro lowered his head a fraction in defeat,

though he had no intentions to surrender. He rubbed at his forehead, hoping to ease the throbbing pain, and his voice muffled as he spoke, "You have a duty, my son. You must marry and produce an heir so the Cesare name and land will continue to prosper."

It was partially the truth, though what Alejandro prayed for most was that Rosa would help restore Esteban to his old self, erase his hurtful past and that they would share a happy life together. His son deserved it after all the suffering he had been made to endure.

Esteban braced his hands flat upon the desk and leaned forward toward his father. "Believe me, Father, when I tell you that no good would come of this marriage. You do the innocent girl an injustice by forcing her upon me."

"Rosa seems pleased with the arrangement," Alejandro lied and silently offered a quick prayer of contrition.

Esteban stood straight. "Why?"

Alejandro scrunched his brow confused. "What do you mean?"

"Why should she agree to marry me in only two weeks? Does she need a husband?"

Alejandro caught his son's insinuation immediately. "Rosa is a good girl as I have told you. There is no need for her to marry quickly. Why I doubt she has ever been kissed."

Esteban found his blood racing at the idea of one so innocent. To taste such purity would be a mistake. It would only leave an insatiable appetite for more and once started he would not stop, and then—she would be innocent no more—and by the time he was done... she would be full of sin.

"Find another woman, Father, she will not do."

Esteban's calm response puzzled Alejandro. "I cannot do that. The papers have been signed and the money paid. She will be shamed if you back out of the arrangement."

"Better shamed than to spend the rest of her life in hell," Esteban spat.

Alejandro's expression betrayed the sadness he felt for his son. Why did he insist on torturing himself over the past? It was over and finished. Nothing could be done about it.

Esteban casually lowered himself to the wooden chair a few feet in front of his father's desk. "How many fathers in the valley have turned down your offer of marriage before you were forced to turn to the peasants?"

Alejandro cleared his throat. "Let me think on that."

"There's no need to think, Father. You know the answer, but allow me to remind you. Every hacienda that has a daughter of marriageable age turned you down."

"Rosa is the best choice anyway," Alejandro defended.

Esteban loosened the restricting tie at his throat. He hated wearing it and the memories of confinement it brought him. "She is the only choice... is she not?"

Alejandro stared at his son, watching as his

long fingers spread the stark white material of his shirt away from his neck. He recalled Esteban's words when he first returned to the hacienda. They were meant to shock, but they hurt Alejandro much more than his son would ever know.

A rope was kept around my neck for Pacquito to lead me around like a captured animal.

"Are you listening, Father?"

Alejandro shook away the heartbreaking image of his young son's suffering. "I'm listening and yes, she is the only one, but the best one and that is no lie."

Esteban stood and stared at his father, his dark eyes disquieting in their blank stare and his sharp angled features boldly handsome as he spoke in defiance. "I will not marry her."

"Perhaps if you meet her you will change your mind," the soft voice suggested from behind.

Esteban turned to find his mother, Valerianna entering the room. Her beauty never failed to touch his heart. She looked almost as she did fourteen years ago. Only a few lines and wrinkles touched her face, though didn't distract from her attractiveness and her dark hair bore not a trace of gray. Her figure was still trim and fit, her stance regal, making her appear taller than her six inches over five feet. He loved her dearly and that was why he found it so difficult being around her. She was a lady and he was no longer a gentleman.

"It matters not, Mother, I will not marry her," Esteban said and walked away from her to stand behind the desk near the window.

Dona Valerianna's smile turned sad and Alejandro's heart went out to her. She had tried so hard since their son's return to recapture the closeness they had once shared. But Esteban had rebuffed all attempts. And his obvious rejection had cut deeply.

"I think this marriage would be good for the both of you," Dona Valerianna said, bringing a smile to her husband's lips. He loved her stubborn nature and was glad the years hadn't diminished it.

Esteban looked from one to the other. "I will not marry. And tell me have you arranged for a marriage for my sister as well." His sister, Crista, had been only two years old when he had been captured. He hadn't been surprised to learn that she had been sent to Spain when she was ten to be educated, though what she would be taught in a Spanish convent would do her little good here.

"Crista has been schooled well and will do her duty when the time comes," Alejandro said. "And I will do my duty as a father and see her wed to a good man as I see you wed to a good woman. Now, I have signed the papers. You are committed to this marriage." Alejandro looked to his wife for support.

"He's right, Esteban. It is done. The arrangements have been made. You will wed Rosa Mendez here on Saturday, out in the garden, the ceremony to be performed by Padre Marten."

Alejandro took a deep breathe to deliver the final blow. "You will be introduced to her and her guardians this evening. They are joining us for supper."

Esteban's portentous glare pinned first his father and then his mother to where they sat and sent shivers through them. He walked from the room without uttering a word, his silence being far more potent than words.

Dona Valerianna dropped her head until her chin almost touched her chest. She brought her slim fingers up to her mouth to help hold back the choked sobs caught in her throat.

Alejandro hurried to his wife's side. He took her hands in his and lifted her chin. The unshed tears pooling in her eyes tore at his heart. "Do not worry, my dear. This marriage is right for him. I know it. I can feel it in my heart. Rosa will be good for him.

Dona Valerianna's smile was weak and her words barely a whisper, "But will he be good for her?"

~~~

The swinging strap caught Rosa's arm and she winced as she braced herself not to fall.

"I told you to wear your hair up like a proper engaged woman should," Roberto screamed, his face red with fury. "You look the whore with your hair loose and free. Now pin it up and back and behave as you should. I will not be shamed by your thoughtless actions tonight."

Lola added her own rebuke. "And that dress looks shabby, though I suppose it must do. You can't wear your church clothes, the blue skirt and white blouse are too plain for such a grand occasion."

Rosa rubbed her arm and felt the welt already beginning to rise beneath the lace of the pale blue dress she wore. I'll see to my hair."

"And make it quick," Lola snapped. "We don't want to be late."

Rosa went to her room, a small shack behind the house. She was close to tears, uncertain if it was from the Curro's cruelty or the ordeal she was about to face. The dress had belonged to her mother, and although the lace had faded to the palest of blues, Rosa always thought of it as lovely. It hugged her small frame perfectly, accenting her large breasts and trim waist. The lace ran high up over her chest to cup her throat and ran down her arms to fall gracefully along the back of her hand in a series of graduated ruffles.

Her mother had worn it for special occasions and her appearance would always bring a broad smile to her father's face. She brushed at the few tears that spilled from her eyes. Now was not the time to lose control. She needed her wits about her tonight.

She combed her hair back, twisting it up, and secured it tightly in the back with two dark combs. The severe effect of the style brought out her innocence and natural beauty, highlighting her flushed cheeks, damp eyes, and generous lips tainted a soft pink from the berries she loved to eat as she picked them.

She was ready. She could delay no longer the

night's event rushing to meet her. She glanced at the wooden cross hanging on the wall above the chest that held her few meager possessions and blessed herself, bringing her folded fingers to her lips as she prayed, "Please, *Madre*, please help me."

Chapter Three

"Perhaps you should finish dressing," Dona Valerianna suggested to her son. "The Curros and Rosalita will be here shortly."

Esteban swirled the dark red wine in the crystal glass he held firmly in his right hand. He kept his eyes on the swirling liquid as he answered his mother. "I am dressed."

Dona Valerianna sent her husband, impeccably outfitted in dusty gray, a pleading look. He shook his head and frowned, a signal that advised her not to pursue the matter.

"If my appearance shames you, I can beg to be excused for the evening," Esteban said well aware of the silent exchange that had passed between his parents.

Dona Valerianna was conciliatory. "No, not at all. Your attire is adequate."

Esteban raised his glass in a salute. "Thank you, Mother."

Dona Valerianna attempted a smile, though not successfully. It barely reached her lips before disappearing.

Alejandro swallowed the remainder of his wine and poured another. This was going to be a difficult evening. Even though Esteban looked splendid in his black, tight-fitting pants and bolero jacket, his white linen shirt remained open at the throat, an obvious impropriety and one Esteban had no intentions of correcting. And if either Alejandro or Valerianna pursued the matter, Esteban would take his leave.

Alejandro hoped that his son's improper behavior would not be the center of village gossip the next day, though knowing the Curros, he held little doubt that their tongues would remain silent.

"Excuse me, Don Alejandro, the guests have arrived," Dolores, the Cesare's longtime housekeeper announced from the doorway.

Esteban remembered Dolores well, and though she had aged and grown a bit plumper, she still wore her usual vibrant smile and delicious scents still clung to her. He had visited her often in the kitchen when he was young and she would always have his favorite sweet treat ready for him. He had not visited her there since his return, but she had not forgotten his penchant for sweet cakes and cookies. Every night when he returned to his quarters a plate of his favorite sweet treats waited on the table beside his bed. And he was more appreciative of her thoughtful gesture than she would ever know.

Dona Valerianna hurried to stand and straighten pale pink layers of lace that draped softly from her waist to her feet, while pink linen completed the top portion of the dress. She brushed back the sides of her dark hair to make certain no strands had fallen loose from the intricate braid fastened at the back of her head.

"Ready?" she asked, her cheeks flushed with anticipation and concern.

"Ready," Alejandro said walking over and holding out his arm to her.

She greedily grasped hold of it for support.

Esteban stared with angry eyes at his parents, then stormed past them and out of the room.

"Alejandro what are we to do?" Valerianna clutched his hand.

"We will do our best as always, my dear," he said. "I'm sure Esteban will realize his rudeness and join us, extending an apology for his lateness.

Dona Valerianna didn't even attempt a smile this time. Her son might decide to join them, as to whether he would offer an apology, she had her doubts, though she did have hope.

~~~

Rosa stood in awe of her surroundings. She had heard of the Cesare's wealth, though thought the gossip fanciful tales to entertain. The stark white-washed walls were graced with gorgeous tapestries depicting various places in Spain. The chest, chairs, and tables were dark, richly polished wood. The candle stands, some over five feet tall, were of intricately designed metal shapes. The tall narrow windows, six in all, opened out to the courtyard, abundant with a variety of flowers, their fragrant scents drifting throughout the room.

A jab to her ribs brought her wandering attention back.

"Mind your musings," Lola scolded.

Rosa nodded and respectfully lowered her eyes along with her head. Footsteps on the tile floor outside the room ran a shiver through her. She had feared this moment for hours. She did not wish to look on Esteban Cesare's empty, brooding eyes again.

"I am so pleased that you could join us this evening," Alejandro said entering the room. "Please allow me to introduce my wife Dona Valerianna." After he introduced her to Roberto and Lola, Alejandro introduced his wife to Rosa.

Rosa brought her head up slowly and was surprised when Dona Valerianna reached out and took her hand.

"It's such a pleasure to meet you, my dear. I know you will find much happiness here with us."

Rosa forced a brief smile. Dona Valerianna was a beautiful, gracious woman who appeared sincere in her welcome, though Rosa could not help but notice that again a reference was made to her finding happiness here... but not with their son Esteban. *Madre di Dios*. What was she getting herself into?

"Where is this son of yours who is lucky to be getting our Rosalita as his wife?" Roberto asked his smile curious.

"Right here."

The foreboding voice had everyone turning hastily, except Rosa. She turned reluctantly and kept her eyes downcast.

Esteban stepped out of the shadows in the corner of the room and Valerianna smiled at him.

He had fastened his shirt at his throat. The simple, kind act brought a tear to her eye. She quickly wiped it away not wishing to display her emotions in front of her guests.

Esteban offered no apology or reason for not being there to greet them. He accepted Roberto's hand and Lola's smile with an indifferent nod.

"This is my son, Esteban," Alejandro said proudly and placed his hands on Rosa's shoulder to gently guide her to stand before her future husband. "Esteban, I'm pleased to have you met Rosalita, your soon-to-be wife."

Rosa raised her eyes slightly, not enough to see his face only his neck, slim and kissed by endless hours in the sun. She stared at a spot just above his collar that pulsed slightly and the more she focused on it the faster it pulsed, as if something inside him beat to a heated rhythm. She felt a blush rise and quickly lowered her eyes. She kept her hands straight at her sides and buried in the folds of her dress, so he would not reach out and take them in his.

The room remained silent and Rosa held her breath waiting for him to speak. She focused on the scuffed tips of his black boots as they remained steady and only a mere inch from the hem of her dress. The strain of the awkward situation had her eyes misting, and she took a moment to close them hoping to clear the unease so no one would suspect her of crying. Otherwise she would suffer Roberto's hard hand when they got home for embarrassing him.

She was not sure of the proper manners in such a situation and wondered how to react to his silence or if she should.

She opened her eyes and no scuffed boots brushed the hem of her dress. He was gone. She raised her head slightly noticing all in the room stared at Esteban as he filled a glass of wine for himself at the sideboard spread with crystal wine bottles and platters of cheese and freshly cut fruit.

The wide-opened mouths of Roberto and Lola told Alejandro that the news of Esteban's rudeness would be all over the village by the next day. And he fought to correct his son's error. "A good idea, Esteban, a toast to the new bride."

Dona Valerianna sighed softly with relief and quickly joined her husband to ward off the embarrassing moment. "Come and let us raise our glasses."

Dolores quickly had servants fill all the glasses and Alejandro didn't wait, he immediately raised his glass high, offering a toast. "To the young couple, may their marriage be happy and fruitful."

Rosa's hand shook so badly that she barely got the glass to her lips without spilling the red wine. She had not thought of their marriage as being fruitful. She had not thought at all on her wifely duties, though the obligation struck her now, and hard. She would lay with this man as his wife and he would have the right to do as he wished. The thought made her ill. She casually made her way to a chair and sat, only half listening to the conversation going on around her.

Esteban watched Rosa's every movement. It was obvious that she didn't wish this marriage. She had no desire for him to be her husband, to share their lives together, and she definitely didn't want to share his bed. Why she paled at the mere mention of fruitfulness. She even feared looking at him. She had a weak nature and not an ounce of strength.

"The meal is ready," Dolores announced and moved to the side to allow them entrance to the dining room. Esteban didn't waste a moment, he went directly to his mother and offered her his arm.

Once again Dona Valerianna was shocked by his rudeness in ignoring Rosa, his intended, but his chilling stare warned her to take his arm or else, and she did.

Alejandro rushed to Rosa's side to escort her, fearing the girl would be upset and rightfully so. But it wasn't distress he saw on her pale face, but rather relief and that alarmed Alejandro. This meeting was not going as he had hoped it would. He patted Rosa's hand that rested on his arm as they followed behind Valerianna and Esteban, worrying that this was only the beginning of the many hurts Esteban would inflict upon the poor girl.

Roberto and Lola looked at each other, smiled, hooked arms, and trailed behind Alejandro, their greedy minds busy counting the tidy sum of money that would be turned over to them on Rosa's wedding day.

The meal was terribly frustrating for all but

Roberto and Lola, who ate with gusto. Alejandro and Valerianna attempted to keep up a lively conversation. Rosa remained completely silent, barely touching her food. Esteban drank his wine, ignoring his food and the conversation going on around him. Near the end of the meal his eyes remained steady on Rosa, while hers continued to remain downcast.

"It will be a lovely affair," Dona Valerianna said. "The wedding will take place out in the garden. The flowers are in their height of bloom and will serve as a beautiful surrounding to such a special occasion."

"The wedding will not take place in the church?" Roberto asked aware, as was the whole village, that Esteban was not welcomed there since his return and refusal to take confession.

"The church will not hold the amount of guests that have been invited," Alejandro explained annoyed by the man's lack of manners.

"Yes, many will attend, won't they?" Lola asked a sweet, though false smile wide upon her face.

"Of course they will. None would be so rude as to refuse Don Cesare's invitation to his son's wedding," Dona Valerianna said with an air of superiority that warned the woman to tread carefully.

"Naturally," Lola remarked more thoughtfully after receiving a sharp kick beneath the table from her husband. "It will be the event of the year."

"No one would dare miss such a splendid

celebration," Roberto said attempting to lighten the tense situation.

Esteban sat disgusted with the whole matter. The Curros were interested in only one thing... the hefty dowry money this union would bring them. And he had no doubt that his father had to pay a large sum to buy his son a wife. At least his father and mother had their son's best interest at heart or so they thought, and as for Rosalita?

He had been watching her for a while. Her eyes remained focused on her plate where her food sat untouched. She was smaller in size and gentler in appearance than he had first thought. She was certainly no match for him. His wife would require bold strength to defend against the vicious gossip that would surely surround them. Her unwillingness to look him straight in the eyes, clearly showed how easily she could be intimidated.

Her beauty was another matter. It sparked something hot and primal in him that he was having a hell of a time ignoring. At the moment he was sorely tempted to ruffle her delicateness. Why he wasn't certain, though perhaps it was to catch a glimpse of her eyes.

"I wish to speak with Rosa alone," he found himself saying, instantly silencing those around him.

It brought the desired reaction from Rosa... her head shot up. He caught her eyes with his before she could look away. Dark and wide with fright, they glared at him and he grew annoyed with himself that her fear should stimulate him even more. But then he craved control, had to have it in every aspect of his life. Never—never—would he allow anyone to control him ever again.

"A walk in the garden," he announced, as if it had already been decided and allowing no room for her to refuse him. He stood and walked around to stand behind her chair, placing his hands firmly on the back to assist her.

Rosa sat numb. She knew he waited for her to rise so that he could pull the chair back, but she found herself unable to move. She did not wish to be alone with him. He frightened her more than she cared to admit. Though lean, you could tell by the cut of his clothes that his body was taut with muscles, which no doubt gave him strength that she would be hard pressed to defend against. And his sinfully handsome features sent tingles over her entire body every time she looked at him, which she did as little as possible, and then there was his open rudeness. She simply did not know how to deal with it.

The chair was suddenly slid back with her in it, which alarmed her even more since it only served to impress upon her just how strong her future husband was. She stood abruptly, almost toppling to the side if it wasn't for his hand that reached out and grabbed her.

She winced softly as his hand gripped the spot where Roberto had earlier taken the strap to her. He released her instantly.

"Come," Esteban ordered sternly and stepped

back away from her. He was annoyed at her reaction to his touch. Was she so fragile that his touch had caused her pain or had she been disgusted by his touch?

Rosa walked around the chair and moved quickly past him, not waiting for him to offer his arm in assistance.

Esteban shot his father a look that warned that this was not over yet before following Rosa.

Alejandro could do nothing but say a silent prayer that his decision had been a wise one and that this marriage would be good for both his son and Rosalita. He maintained his smile and returned the conversation to the impending wedding.

Esteban was amazed that for one so small and delicate Rosa could walk with such haste. She was down the garden's stone path before Esteban entered the garden. She obviously didn't care to be in his presence, which served to blacken his already dark mood even further, and so he hurried after her.

When he caught up with her, he reached out and grabbed her arm. She winced again, though more dramatically this time and pulled away from him.

"Which is it?" he demanded with a biting fury. "Do you abhor my touch or is my touch too strong for your delicate nature?"

His arrogant assumption irritated her and she opened her mouth to protest and then thought better of it. She quickly shut her mouth and lowered her glance. What good would a retort do?

It would only serve to anger him further and perhaps cause him to strike her as Roberto always did when she annoyed him or found the courage to speak her mind. Besides, she had felt the strength Esteban possessed when he had grabbed her.

"Look at me," he demanded sharply, his tone brooking no disobedience.

Rosa raised her head slowly, biting her bottom lip and wishing she could speak her mind but knowing that she would suffer for it.

"Don't ever cast your eyes down away from me again," he ordered, his words a dire warning to be heeded. "I assume this marriage is as much against your wishes as it is mine."

Rosa nodded, trying to ignore the way the moonlight played off his face, causing his imposing features to standout even more. The women in the village had been right when they had said that his sinfully handsome face stole a woman's breath, for right now Rosa felt her breath catch at the sight of him in the moonlight.

"I suppose you cannot refuse this marriage contract?" he asked less harshly.

"I haven't the right." Rosa's response was soft and sorrowful since she couldn't help but think of the beating Roberto would serve on her if she refused to honor the agreement.

Esteban stood silent, her softly gentle voice firing his insides to burning, which irritated him even more. "Go," he snapped, "return to your guardians and my parents."

Rosa hesitated, though she would have liked

nothing better than to flee his presence, she understood that his absence would be questioned. "You are not returning?"

Esteban took a sharp step toward her and she hastily stumbled back away from him. "Don't ever question me."

Rosa was accustomed to apologies and so she gave one quickly. "I meant no disrespect, Senor Cesare."

"Do not call me that," he said with a bitterness that caused Rosa to shiver. "You know my name, use it."

Rosa nodded afraid to speak.

"Use it now!"

"Es—Esteban."

"Again."

"Esteban," she said more clearly.

"Now go," he ordered, not offering any excuse as to why he would not be returning with her.

Rosa turned and walked down the stone path, relieved with each step she took that he wasn't beside her.

"Rosa."

The voice sounded as though it came from directly behind her. She turned around swiftly and was startled to see Esteban right there in front of her. She had not heard the crunch of the stones beneath his feet to warn of his approach. How had he managed to come up behind her without her hearing a single footfall? The thought of such skill alarmed her.

"You never answered my question," Esteban

said.

Rosa titled her head slightly and frowned trying to recall his question.

Esteban was taken by her obvious confusion and the sheer beauty of her frowning face. The soft wrinkle of her dark eyes, the puzzling pucker of her tempting lips, the warm flush to her high cheekbones, they were all too appealing... much too appealing.

"My touch," he snapped sharply annoyed with himself for allowing his thoughts to stray where they shouldn't. "Do you abhor it or are you too delicate for my strength?"

Rosa jumped, startled by his bark and in her nervousness answered honestly before thinking. "Neither."

"Neither?' Now he was confused.

Rosa realized too late her error. How was she to explain the bruise on her arm?

She hesitated too long and he demanded, "I'll have a truthful answer now."

Rosa had no way out of this. She had confessed to no one except Marinda the abuse she suffered at her guardians' hands. There was no point in complaining, nothing would be done about it. She unwittingly raised her hand to rub at the welt left by the strap Roberto loved to wield.

Words were not necessary, Esteban clearly understood her actions. He pushed her hand aside, surprising her, then turned her toward the moonlight. He ran his hand slowly up and down her lace-covered arm almost as if he was caressing it, and it sent a tingle rushing through Rosa.

He stopped when he felt the welt, his fingers carefully exploring the width and length of it. "Who took a strap to you?"

Rosa grew fearful. Never had she heard such savagery in a voice before. "It is nothing."

"Who?" His tone was menacingly low.

"It was my own fault. I did not obey his orders fast enough."

Esteban heard and felt her quiver of fear. It brought back painful memories. Memories he longed to forget, though he doubted he ever would. Anger boiled inside him and he took hold of Rosa's hand, and it was all she could do to keep up with his powerful strides.

The dining room was empty when they entered and Esteban went straight for the parlor where his father would be having his best after dinner wine served. He stopped abruptly in the doorway, Rosa 's small frame bumping into his side from his sudden halt. His eyes scanned the room and when he spotted Roberto, he dragged Rosa alongside him over to the man.

He swung her to the side and released her hand only to swiftly grab a startled Roberto by the neck and slammed him against the wall, squeezing the breath from him.

Esteban heard his father shout for him to stop, but he paid him no heed. "Listen well," he said so menacingly that the whole room turned silent. "Raise your hand or a strap to Rosalita again and I will silt you from throat to groin and watch you die like the pig you are. Understood?"

Roberto could barely breathe, but he managed to nod.

Esteban released him and the man choked to regain his breath as he sunk down on a chair. He then turned to Rosa. "Anyone who dares to lay a hand on you or speaks disparagingly to you will die." Esteban looked to his father and then pointed to Roberto. "Do not dare apologize to that pig for my actions, he got what he deserved." He then stormed from the room, leaving shocked silence in his wake.

Chapter Four

Marinda blessed herself for the third time. "I don't believe this. I don't believe this. Didn't I tell you not to look upon him?"

Rosa couldn't prevent the yawn or shiver that overtook her simultaneously. Marinda's words upset her and her lack of sleep last night was fast catching up with her. The Curros had hurriedly made excuses to leave last night after Roberto was nearly choked to death by Esteban. Lola had berated her during the whole trip home for having made Esteban believe she was being abused. Didn't she understand, stupid girl that she was, that she had deserved every abuse she had suffered at their hands. Lola reminded her again and again what a lazy sot she was and if it wasn't for their strict discipline she would not be prepared to be wife to such a powerful man. She should be grateful and thank them. Rosa had remained silent, her thoughts lost on how Esteban had immediately and without question defended her. No one had done that since her parents had died.

Marinda poured her friend another cup of strong black coffee. "I don't blame you for being unable to get an ounce of sleep last night. Actually, I don't know how you will be able to function until the wedding. I would be a mess."

Bright sunlight spilled through the open front door and one window warming the two rooms of Marinda's small adobe house. It was sparsely furnished but clean and colorfully decorated. Bright colorful blankets hung on two walls, clay pottery filled with fresh flowers lined the roughhewn mantel above the fireplace and baskets dyed in various colors added to the wealth of care and happiness that Marinda obviously gave to her home.

Such would not be the case with Rosa, and she made no attempt to hide her disappointment and sorrow from her friend.

Marinda reached out to rest her hand over Rosa's, offering her what comfort she could. "Perhaps," Marinda began, though hesitated as if unsure of her next words, then fixed a firm smile on her face and continued. "Perhaps this marriage will be good for you."

"Good for me?" Rosa repeated surprised that her friend could suggest such a thing.

"Yes, think about it, Rosa. What kind of life do you have with the Curros? Lola takes her hand to you often and Roberto thinks nothing of using the strap on you. You work like a dog day after day and what do they say to you... you're a lazy sot." Marinda shook her head. "They care nothing for you. Life would be easier for you as the wife of Esteban Cesare."

Rosa noticed that Marinda's voice dropped to a bare whisper when she spoke his name, almost as if she feared evoking some evil.

"You will have servants to wait on you." Marinda turned Rosa's hand over in hers and patted the blisters on her palm that were healing. "And you will have these no more. Your hands will become like the rich ladies of the haciendas, soft and pretty."

Rosa tossed her head back and laughed. "And you will come to visit me and the servants will serve us. We will not lift a finger."

Marinda joined in the merriment, glad she had been able to bring her friend out of her sorrowful mood. "And we will take our wine outside and sit in the garden enjoying the lovely flowers."

"Yes," Rosa agreed joyously. "The garden off the dining room is beautiful. We shall walk the stone path together and admire the variety of flowers."

Marinda beamed with enthusiasm. "We will take our children there to play..." Her words trailed off as she watched Rosa's face turn a deathly pale. "What's wrong?" she asked with concern.

Rosa shook her head, although it wasn't the only part of her that shook, the rest of her shivered as though the room had suddenly turned stone cold. "Marinda," her voice quivered, "I—I'm frightened."

Marinda grasped her friend's hand tightly. "Your wedding night frightens you?"

Her response was a sharp squeeze to Marinda's hand.

"It's not as bad as the old women wish us to believe," Marinda said with a giggle. "I actually like making love. Paco is a wonderful lover, kind and considerate..." Once again her words trailed off. She suddenly realized what truly frightened her friend. "Oh, Rosa, I did not think. I thought you fearful of the act itself."

"No, Marinda, it's not the act itself. You well know that I am not ignorant of it, you and I having giggled and teased each other often enough about the secrets of the marriage bed. I had looked forward to sharing such intimacy with the man I loved and wed. But..." This time Rosa's words drifted off as if she could not bring herself to speak them.

"But you don't love Esteban, nor does he love you," Marinda finished for her.

"And..." Again Rosa was unable to finish.

"And you fear he will not be gentle in bed."

Rosa nodded slowly.

"You think of the things he did to women when he was with Pacquito's band of renegades, don't you?"

"How can I not? You've heard the stories." Rosa shuddered and crossed herself.

"You can't believe all you hear."

"Don't try to console me with lies," Rosa said wearily

"I don't know what else to offer you," Marinda said honestly, holding back the tears she wished to shed for her friend.

"He is rough in his manner."

"Perhaps he knows no other way. After all he spent many years with the renegades."

Rosa sighed, as if her burden was growing too heavy for her. "But how do I help his tortured soul?"

"By being who you are, a kind and gentle soul. He will learn and change."

"Until then?" Rosa asked, hoping for an answer.

Marinda crossed herself once again. "You survive."

Chapter Five

"I grow weary of telling you that I will not marry Rosa," Esteban said, walking with his father toward the stables.

"And I grow weary of hearing it," Alejandro said. "The arrangements have been made and finalized. You will marry Rosa next week and that is my last word on the matter."

Esteban stopped abruptly and turned to his father with controlled calmness, yet fire blazed so out of control in his dark eyes that it made the older man's blood run cold. "I have taken a knife to many a man who dared to dictate to me, but you are my father and deserve respect. I will give it to you, though only so much so watch your tongue. I will not be told what to do, I am not a boy. I am a man who has done things that would make you turn away from me in disgust. I am far from a gentleman and sometimes far from human. Is this the fate you wish for the innocent Rosa?"

"Somewhere in you still lurks that young boy who was filled with compassion and love," Alejandro said hoping to reach that part of his son. "That ounce of humanity would never allow you to hurt Rosa."

Esteban pulled off his jacket and tossed it to the ground, the dry dirt sending up a plume of dust.

He yanked his tie from around his neck and threw it to land on top of the jacket. He ripped his shirt open baring a good portion of his muscled chest, the defiant act casting off his gentleman's façade. "You are a fool, old man, if you think that." His fists clenched at his sides. "These clothes cannot hide who I am... a man with no remorse, no heart... no soul."

Fear had Alejandro stepping back away from him. His skin suddenly dampened and he paled at the thought that the renegade bastards could have possibly taken all that was left of his son's humanity. He quickly recited a prayer that it not be so.

"That's better, *Father*." Esteban's smile was cruel, his voice mocking. It was as if he enjoyed seeing the fear on his father's face. "Forget this farce of a marriage. I will be captive to no man— or woman—ever."

Esteban walked away, his strides firm and powerful.

Alejandro let out the breath he had not realized he had been holding. His hand went to his chest, his heart racing wildly

"Alejandro, are you all right?" Valerianna asked, rushing up to him. The deathly pallor of her husband's face alarmed her and she reached out to him.

Alejandro grasped his wife's hand and squeezed his eyes shut against his own trembling. "For a moment, just a moment, I thought Esteban would harm me."

"You can't mean that, Alejandro."

Alejandro continued, needing to voice his doubts. "Have we misjudged our son's nature? Has his years with the renegades actually turned him into a cold and uncaring savage?"

"Stop! Please stop," Valerianna begged, hearing her own misgivings expressed aloud and feeling as though she betrayed her son.

Alejandro slipped his arm around his wife. "I worry for Rosa. I pray she will help him and that this marriage will be good for him."

"It will. It will," Valerianna insisted, her head nodding with each word as if she was trying hard to believe her own words.

"But Rosa is young and inexperienced," Alejandro said with worry.

"Esteban would not harm one so innocent."

"The Esteban we knew would not, but what of the Esteban who has returned to us?"

Valerianna held her tongue, for in all honesty she could not answer truthfully.

~~~

Esteban rode in the direction of the village. He had made a point of keeping his distance from Rosa. Her few visits to the hacienda to be fitted for her wedding dress had been planned and so he was able to avoid her.

His father and mother remained steadfast in their determination to see him wed. No amount of talking or threatening seemed to do any good, though he had struck a chord—a fearful one—in his father moments ago.

The idea that he had frightened his father upset him. He had thought himself in control of his emotions, what emotions he still possessed. His unacceptable reaction reminded him just how much of a renegade he had become. His total disregard for his father's concern and love offended him. He was offering help, a way of keeping him at the hacienda surrounded by those who cared and would help heal him.

No one could heal him. No one. Not even Rosa.

Esteban slowed his horse as he entered the village, the animal snorting and holding his head erect, displaying as much fierceness as his master. Several women hurried their children into their homes, while others crossed themselves and turned their heads away from him.

Padre Marten, standing with two older men, offered a blessing or perhaps the slow, methodical way he made the sign of the cross was meant more to ward off evil.

Rosa followed Marinda out of her house and caught the padre's action. Marinda followed it with a blessing of her own and Rosa grew angry. The padre had no right to condemn Esteban so blatantly. If the church would not forgive and accept him, how could the people of St. Lucita?

The cruelty and injustice of the situation disturbed Rosa. It wasn't fair. There was no one to defend or protect him just as there had been no one to defend or protect her when she had been turned over to the cruel Curros. But this man who sat his horse so proudly even when being scorned by the people of the village, who had once held him in high esteem, was going to be her husband and he had defended her last night. So fearful or not, she would give him what he had given her... she would defend and protect him.

"Rosa don't," Marinda warned grabbing Rosa's arm as she took a step forward.

"He seems so alone. Would you not offer help to a lost soul?"

"He's not alone, he's indifferent. And perhaps his soul is far too lost or too evil to save."

"Perhaps," Rosa said weighing her friend's words, "but he is to be my husband and I have a duty to him. It is not right of me to standby and do nothing."

Marinda's voice softened. "You are right, perhaps then he will look kindly upon you."

Esteban, in a savage way, had shown her kindness last night, and she would do the same for him. Besides, her thoughtful nature would not allow her to abandon him.

Her steps were quick in fear of her courage deserting her. And desert her it almost did when she drew close. Turbulence marked his dark eyes. His black-as-night hair, usually tied back, fell loose, the ends skimming the top of his broad shoulders. His torn shirt allowed for a clear view of his chest defined with muscles. His disheveled appearance made him appear more renegade than aristocrat.

The frightening thought turned her legs weak

and almost faltered her steps, but somehow she managed to keep walking without a misstep.

"Rosa!"

She jumped from the strength of his voice and looked up at him perched on his saddle. A chill ran down her arms from his icy stare.

Esteban leaned down toward her. His words were direct yet spoken low for her ears alone. "Obedience, I like that in a woman. You come and I don't even call. I wonder... will you come so quickly and obediently to my bed?"

Her gasp was audible and caused many eyes to widen, she in turn looked at their questioning faces embarrassed that they may have heard his improper remark.

Esteban immediately reached down, grabbed her chin and forced her to look up at him. "Don't ever take your eyes from mine when I speak with you unless I give you permission."

Nothing ever changes. Here she thought to defend him and what does he do? Demands obedience. Her life would be no different from what it was or perhaps it would be worse. Either way what did it matter, her life was not her own. It never would be. "As you say, Esteban."

Her easy acceptance of his orders irritated him. No fire fueled her blood, her nature much too passive. She would obey all his commands without question as a good wife should. Why did that irritate him? She would do as she was told, which meant she would leave him alone if he so ordered.

He released her chin with a gentle shove and,

without a word, turned his horse and rode out of the village, leaving Rosa standing in the road alone.

Marinda went to hurry to her side, but stopped when she saw Padre Marten approach.

"Come with me, my child," Padre Marten said, holding his hand out to Rosa. "It is time we talked."

Rosa walked in silence beside the padre. The early afternoon found the adobe church empty and the echo from their sandals slapping the stone floor as they entered appeared an intrusion upon the holy silence.

With a hand to her elbow, Padre Marten directed her into a pew near the front, close to the altar.

Rosa crossed herself and slipped into the pew. Her nervousness increased when the padre sat beside her. Padre Marten was strict and stern in his religious beliefs. The parishioners followed the law of God and the church, and one did not falter from that law. If he did, he must seek forgiveness in confession and perform penance. This was expected from all, with no exceptions.

"You will marry Esteban Cesare Saturday," Padre Marten said, as if it were already done. "Are you prepared to accept him as your husband?"

Accept him as her husband. She was just beginning to realize the depths of what that meant and the fact that nothing would change it. She would marry Esteban Cesare whether she wanted to or not. She nodded and felt as if she finally acquiesced to her fate.

"Good, child, good," the padre praised. "And as his wife it will be your duty to see that he attends church services."

Rosa held her tongue, though her eyes turned wide.

"It is your duty as a daughter of God," the padre warned sternly.

"Rosa will serve only one master, Padre... me!"

Padre Marten stumbled to his feet. He grabbed the back of the pew, steadying himself as he turned to face Esteban. Rosa remained frozen in her seat.

"Your presence on holy ground offends," Padre Marten said, "unless you are here to take confession."

"I am here to collect my intended." Esteban extended his hand to Rosa in a silent command.

The padre moved to block his path. "I am speaking with her."

"No, Padre, you are finished speaking to Rosa."

The padre's face contorted in anger. "You deny this young woman access to her church and priest?"

Esteban took a quick step forward as his hand shot out, causing the padre to step aside in alarm. Esteban grabbed Rosa by the arm and yanked her right passed the startled padre. He positioned her in front of him, her back braced against his chest while his hands took firm hold of her shoulders. "Rosa will attend church only when I give her permission to do so."

The padre opened his mouth to protest.

Esteban didn't give him a chance. "As my wife, her obedience is to me."

"You are riddled with sin and will pull this innocent girl into the depths of your hell to suffer your wickedness. Repent your sins. Save your soul and hers as well before it is too late," the padre warned.

Rosa watched as the padre's face suddenly drained of all color and his eyes widened until she thought they would pop from his head. She could not imagine the threatening expression that Esteban had fixed on him to cause such a fearful reaction. And she did not want to, especially when the padre hastily blessed himself and mumbled a quick prayer.

"I see no words are necessary, Padre," Esteban said releasing Rosa only to grab her hand tightly in his.

The padre shook his head, not in defeat but sorrow. "One day you will call upon God for help, Esteban, I only hope it won't be too late for him to hear you."

Silence hung so heavy in the church that for a moment Rosa actually thought that the padre, in some small way, affected Esteban. She discovered the affect was far different than she had imagined when she heard his sharp response.

"I already have and He didn't hear me, Padre. No matter how desperate my cries, God never heard me."

Rosa shivered from the pain in his voice. His

hurt ran deep, so deep, that she wondered if he would ever be able to heal. The sorrowful expression on the padre's face told her that his thought mirrored her own.

No further words were spoken. Esteban led Rosa from the church. Once outside he stopped to take a deep breath needing to cleanse himself of the painful memories. But it lingered like a shadow, refusing to go away, refusing to leave him in peace.

"I'll take you home," Esteban said, not glancing at her.

She followed along beside him, knowing there was little else she could do. His free hand reached for the reins draped around the post, and he directed his horse away from the church to walk her home.

It was a short and silent walk and when he stepped toward the front door she gave his hand a gentle tug to stop him. "I do not live in the house."

"Show me where you reside."

It was a command and she wondered if that was the only way he knew how to speak... in commands. She nodded and he followed as she walked around to the back of the house and to the small rundown shack that was her home.

Esteban stopped and stared at it for a moment, then with swift steps he opened the door and looked inside. He stepped out just as quickly, the space having been so small he could take the whole room in with a simple glance.

"You live in this hovel?"

She watched fiery anger grow in his eyes and she could have sworn he looked as he had when he had lost his temper and attacked Roberto. She didn't need to suffer another of Lola's tirades.

Rosa's hand quickly flew to rest on his bare chest. The warmth of his hard muscles stung her palm and she thought she felt his heart beating wildly. She spoke softly, hoping to make him understand. "It may not seem like much, but it is my sanctuary and if you say anything to them I will have more chores heaped upon me, and I can barely finish the ones I already have."

He understood all too well, thinking back to how he had been made to live like an animal and the endless days of backbreaking labor he had been made to endure until the squalid sleeping pallet that had greeted him at night became his sanctuary.

It seemed that they both had endured hardships, but no more. "I will not have you suffer these unbearable conditions. I will see you moved to the hacienda right away." He stepped away from her and mounted his horse, the animal pawing the ground anxious to be on his way. "Pack your things. I will send someone to collect you before this evening."

Rosa watched as he rode off, her hand that touched him tingling and sending a shiver through her.

Chapter Six

Rosa stood in the small alcove waiting. It was a beautiful day, the sun bright, the breeze warm, and the hacienda gardens fragrant with new blooms. And yet she felt chilled. In a few minutes she would enter the garden where it seemed the whole town waited to see her wed to Esteban Cesare. She would walk to the arbor plump with red grapes, stand beneath it, beside Esteban, and with a few spoken words she would become his wife... forever.

She shivered at the thought. If only Esteban had convinced his father to have Rosa become a servant at the hacienda rather than become his wife. Esteban had been true to his word and a wagon had come to collect her and her few belongings that day he had told her that he would no longer allow her to live with the Curros. That evening she had taken a stroll through the gardens and had heard Esteban and his father arguing. Esteban thought it more appropriate that Rosa live and work at the hacienda away from the cruel Curros.

His suggestion had ignited a spark of hope in her, though it never flamed to life. Don Alejandro insisted that the marriage would take place, the arrangements having been finalized and the money paid to the Curros.

She had been bought and paid for, but far worse was what Esteban had said after that.

You will regret giving one so innocent to one so evil.

She had run to her room then, her hands over her ears trying desperately to stop the repeated toll of his words in her head. His remark continued to haunt her, more so yesterday when her few possessions were moved to his quarters on the opposite side of the hacienda away from Don Alejandro and his wife's quarters. No one would be able to hear her cry out.

She shuddered as she heard the guitars being tuned. Soon she would walk alone to meet her fate. She grasped the white lace that flowed in layers from her hips. Her bodice was white lace as well, hugging her slim waist and dipping much too low across her breasts, though she did favor the long sleeves. They hid the fading bruises on her arms.

Her dark hair had been drawn severely up and away from her face and a lovely ivory comb had been secured at the top of the chignon, with a waist length, white lace mantilla draped over it.

Dona Valerianna had seen to all the details of the wedding dress and the styling of her hair. When the servants had finished with her, Dona Valerianna had fastened four strands of pearls around her neck. The pearls hugged her neck tightly and from the center hung a single strand of small pearls that attached to a good-size pear-shaped pearl that rested just above the crevice of her breasts. She had seen such expensive jewels on the hacienda women and thought them beautiful, though they were not for her. She coveted no such gems. She would have much preferred to be free to make her own choices, to live her life as she pleased.

The soft strands of the guitar music interrupted her musings and sent a shiver through her. It was time for her to meet her fate.

She didn't know how she did it, but she got her feet moving and kept them going even though her legs trembled, and she thought for sure that she would collapse at any moment. They grew weaker when she saw that the people wore no broad smiles of happiness for her, but stared at her as if she was some poor soul being led to the gallows.

Her steps almost faltered when she caught sight of Esteban. He wore all black except for a red sash that wound around his waist. His hair even appeared darker, drawn back away from his face, though left unbound. His dark eyes glared in anger and his lips was set firm, as if he fought to keep from speaking.

Run before it's too late.

The words tolled like a warning bell in her head. Where would she run to, back to the abusive Curros? There was no place for her to go. She had no choice but to face her fate.

Rosa took her place dutifully beside Esteban, her hands trembling and her mouth so dry she worried that she would not be able to recite her vows.

Esteban leaned over, close enough so that his warm whispered breath faintly brushed her cheek as his warning echoed her own. "Run before it's too late."

Even if she wanted to Rosa could not move, her legs trembled too badly. She so worried that she would crumble right there beside him that she reached over and rested her hand on his arm.

She thought for a moment that she caught a brief look of shock on his face, but it was so sudden that she couldn't be sure that she saw it at all.

Padre Marten cleared his throat, catching their attention, and began the ceremony.

Rosa barely whispered her vows, while Esteban recited his with depth and clarity. When the ceremony finished, the padre declaring them husband and wife, silence filled the garden.

Esteban turned to Rosa. "Now for our first kiss."

Rosa's mouth dropped open.

"Eager to taste me, *wife*?" Esteban said as his hand shot out, grabbed the back of her neck and claimed her lips with a force that had Rosa grabbing hold of his arms as his tongue rushed into her mouth.

She wasn't sure what to do, and then she realized that though his kiss had seemed forceful, it was more commanding. And the dance of his tongue with hers, the warmth of his strong hand at her neck, and the feel of his powerful lips all served to turn her body powerless to his will.

He pulled his mouth away so abruptly that she experienced a sense of loss, her thoughts cloudy, and her legs growing weaker, as if she was about to collapse. She clamped on tightly to his arm for support.

He brought their kiss to an end and eased his arm around her, then asked, "Are you all right?"

It took her a moment to nod, since she wasn't certain how she felt. His kiss wasn't at all unpleasant and the concern in his voice for her sounded sincere. Did he actually care how she felt?

Don Alejandro was soon upon them with a broad smile, offering congratulations and stating how proud he was to have her as his daughter. Dona Valerianna joined him, expressing her own joy over the marriage and soon the guests were cheering and stepping up to congratulate the newlywed couple.

The guests were shown to another garden where food and drink waited in abundance. Music played and wine began to flow and the festivities began.

Rosa soon found herself alone, Don Alejandro having commandeered a most reluctant Esteban to meet with some of the other dons. She had been surprised that Esteban had remained by her side and been cordial, if a nod and a scowl could be called cordial, to all who had approached them. However, now that everyone had dutifully wished them well, the guests had drifted off to talk amongst themselves, leaving her feeling a bit isolated from the festivities.

She noticed that her friends, the peasants she had grown up with, were cordoned off by a low row of hedges, as if a line had been drawn between the two groups. Marinda caught her eye and beckoned her to join them. She didn't think twice, she hurried over to her friends.

They drank the fine Cesare's wines, talked, and laughed. Esteban had yet to return to her and she had not spied him since he had left her side. Surely her friends had noticed his absence, but none were so rude as to remark on it.

The night wore on and Rosa was beginning to think that Esteban had purposely fled the festivities or perhaps it was her that he wasn't interested in being around. Could he be averse to claiming his husbandly rights? She wasn't sure if she was relieved or troubled by the thought. She got it in her head to retire to the room that had been assigned to her when she had first arrived a few days ago. The idea took root quickly enough and helped to relieve the nervousness in her stomach, allowing her to eat, drink, and enjoy the wedding festivities.

Guests began taking their leave and she politely thanked each one for attending.

When Marinda approached, Rosa threw her arms around her friend. "Thank you for sharing this day with me."

Marinda returned the hug and whispered, "You were wise in drinking much wine. It will make the night easier for you."

Rosa hadn't realized she had drunk that much

wine, though she did feel a slight dizziness in her head. With one last hug to Marinda and a wave to Paco, Rosa turned to attend to the few guests who lingered. She poured herself another glass of wine and strolled amongst the near empty tables that had been set up for the occasion. The few lingering occupants smiled at her, though none extended an invitation for her to join them, whereas her friends had welcomed her with open arms.

She looked over across the hedges and saw that the tables had been cleared and were being removed. All her friends had left, the celebration was waning and soon it would be time for her to retire. She hoped her plan of sneaking off to her room was successful, and she would be spared the night with her new husband.

An hour later, her head spinning a bit more and fatigue creeping up on her, she finally bid farewell to the last few guests.

"Make sure that you behave and do your duty to your husband," Roberto ordered as he approached her, Lola following close behind. "I want people to know that I taught you well."

Rosa didn't know if it was the years of abuse by the Curros or the wine that gave her the courage to speak, but something did for the words spewed from her mouth before she could stop them. "What duty did you do by me? You took a frightened young girl who had just lost her loving parents into your home and treated her like a servant, raising your hand to her at whim. Never once did you care for me. You used me at every chance you got, especially now when you sold me and committed me to hell for a hefty dowry price."

She knew with her last words that she was about to suffer for speaking her mind, but she didn't care if Roberto raised a hand to her. It would be the last time. She would never see the pair again and at least she would have her say. A bruise or two was a small price to pay for the satisfaction of telling the couple what she thought of them.

Roberto's face grew bright red and he sputtered and spit as he tried to speak. "How dare you—" he raised his hand and Rosa did not turn away or cower. She braced herself and held her chin high.

Rosa was shocked at the speed in which Roberto disappeared before her eyes and when she saw that Esteban had him planted against the wall, his one hand at his throat and the other holding a knife, she paled.

"I told you that if you ever touched her again I'd kill you," Esteban said and in a flash moved his hand away from the trembling man's throat and pressed the point of a knife against it.

"Esteban!" his father shouted

Rosa reacted without thought. She hurried to her husband's side and placed her hand on his arm. "Please, Esteban, I beg of you, do not spill blood on our wedding day."

Esteban turned to her and glanced at her hand on his arm. She had a gentle touch, and he had not known gentleness in a long time. He lowered the knife and stepped back, though turned a heavy scowl on Roberto.

"You are not welcome on Cesare land ever again and do not dare speak to my wife when in her presence or next time—no one—will stop me from killing you."

Roberto nodded and hurried off, Lola hugging close to his side.

Don Alejandro turned on his son as soon as they left. "Whatever is the matter with you acting so barbarically on your wedding day?"

Esteban went to take a step toward his father but Rosa's hand stayed him, though didn't prevent him from responding. "What else would you expect from a barbarian, Father?"

"You are not a barbarian and not need act as one," Alejandro scolded.

"You don't listen very well, Father, or should I once again remind you what has made me one?"

"You wouldn't be so crude to do such a thing in front of the women," his father chided.

Before Esteban could challenge him, he felt Rosa squeeze his arm and he looked down at her. She was as pale as the white lace gown she wore. She didn't need to say a word, he knew she was about to be ill. With a firm arm around her waist, he rushed her outside, her feet never touching the ground. He got her to the bushes and ripped the mantilla from her head just in time to bend her over his arm so that she could retch.

When she finished, she dropped back against him and moaned.

He unbound the red sash from around his waist, and then gently lifted her into his arms. She weighed hardly anything and her petite size irritated him. How could she defend herself against anyone? He walked over to the small wall fountain spewing water from the widespread mouth of a man with sculpted leaves for hair. He sat on the bench beside the fountain keeping Rosa on his lap to rest against his chest while he wet and rinsed the sash in the basin that caught the running water and then, with care, wiped her face.

She moaned again.

"Was the thought of fulfilling your wifely duties so difficult to accept that you drank yourself drunk?"

She pushed away from him, but found it a mistake, her head spinning and quickly rested it on his shoulder once again. "I intended to sleep in my room tonight."

"And you thought I would approve of this?"

Though she was feeling ill, she still had a modicum of courage left from the wine. "You did not wish to wed me, why then would you want to bed me?"

"Because you are a beauty and have a luscious body and I am a man with needs."

The thought that he would take her to only satisfy himself left her feeling sick all over again. Her stomach rumbled and he once again took her to the bushes where she retched until she could retch no more.

This time however he did not return to the fountain. And Rosa had no doubt where he was taking her and a few minutes later she was proven right. He entered his quarters bolting the latch behind him.

When he eased her down on her feet, she dared ask, "Will a servant come help me undress?" her head still spun and she knew she'd never be able to get out of her wedding dress without assistance.

"No," he said bluntly. "I'll undress you."

Rosa wasn't sure if it was the shock of his words or the wine finally taking its toll, but suddenly everything began to fade away into the distance, as if she was falling down a hole and she wondered what would happen when she hit bottom.

Chapter Seven

Rosa didn't want to wake from her dream. The bed was much too soft as was the blanket she snuggled under and the scent intoxicating, though she couldn't quite recall it. Once she opened her eyes the dream would be gone and she would wake to find herself in her narrow bed with its straw stuffing and threadbare bedcovers.

She clamped her eyes tightly shut hoping to hold onto her dream for a bit longer, and then her memory began to return. She no longer lived in the rundown shack that had been her home. She had been moved to the Cesare hacienda and yesterday she had been wed to Esteban Cesare. And worst of all, she had drunk too much at the wedding celebration and Esteban had been the one to come to her rescue. He had brought her to his room and was about to undress her when... her eyes popped wide and she lifted the blanket to peer beneath.

Good lord, she was naked.

"It wasn't easy getting you out of that much lace, especially since you were passed out."

Rosa pulled the blanket over her head, her cheeks burning bright. Esteban had undressed her, had seen her naked, and had touched her. What else had he done to her?

The blanket was suddenly ripped from her

hands and pulled down below her neck. Her eyes remained wide and her cheeks continued to flame as she stared at him. He didn't gloat or smile, he just stared with those cold, angry eyes that frightened down to the bone and sent a chill through her, or perhaps the chill came from the fact that he stood naked to the waist, his chest defined with such muscle that he appeared sculpted by a master artist.

"You don't need to drink yourself into a stupor or cower beneath a blanket for fear of me claiming my husbandly rights. I have no intentions of touching you now... or ever. I will move into the adjoining room, you will have these quarters all to yourself."

Rosa didn't know what to say. She was pleased that he would not share a bed with her or was she? What kind of life would it be to have a husband and yet not have a husband? And what of children? She had always wanted several. Children brought joy and laughter to a home, something that she had noticed was sadly missing from the Cesare hacienda.

He turned and reached for a white shirt on the chair, and she gasped at the sight of the numerous thin scars that crisscrossed his back. He didn't turn around until he reached the door.

"As you can see the whip was used on me often, don't make me use it on you. Your skin is far too soft and beautiful to bear such ugly scars."

Rosa jumped when the door shivered shut from the slam. And she did the same... shivered. Would he forever send a chill of fear through her? She sat up holding the blanket over her breasts, in case he should enter again, and stared at the door. She thought of last night when he had tended her while she retched and how he had gotten her out of layers of lace and undergarments and put her to bed. Were those the actions of a man who would raise a whip to her?

She shook her head. Her new husband was a puzzle. He protected her against harm and yet he threatened her with harm. It made no sense and it made her curious. Everyone gossiped about how barbaric Esteban had become running with the renegades. But no one, not one, ever gave thought to what he had suffered. And that was something she wanted to find out about, though she had no doubt that it would not be an easy task. It was, however, one she felt compelled to tend to.

She was relieved to spy a silk white robe lying across the foot of the bed and quickly reached for it and slipped it on. She knotted the soft belt as she got out of bed and walked over to the dark wood wardrobe. Two gowns hung inside, though neither suited her. She much preferred a simple skirt and blouse and her comfortable sandals. Her hair she usually wore either unfretted or braided.

She stared at the gowns. Each day since she had been moved to the hacienda Dona Valerianna had done her best to instruct Rosa on her responsibilities as Esteban's wife. One of them was dressing appropriately. The thought of being stuck in a fancy gown all day was not at all to her liking.

And the way Dona Valerianna had servants waiting on her was something Rosa would never want or grow accustomed to. She hadn't even started her new life yet and she was already missing her old one... somewhat.

At least here though, no one raised a hand or strap to her.

Don't make me use the whip on you.

Was she foolish in believing that he would not do such a thing? Should she truly fear him?

She fumbled around in the bottom of the wardrobe until she finally found the bundle she searched for. In the bundle was all she possessed. She took out her mother's faded blue lace dress and hung it on one of the many pegs in the wardrobe. She then unfolded her faded orange skirt and pale yellow blouse. They might not be fancy but she had kept her garments mended and clean. She also retrieved her sandals, near to threadbare from constant wear. Lola had warned her that once the sandals wore through that she would not be given another pair. And while most of the women went barefoot, she did not like the way the dry dirt collected between her toes and so she chose to wear her sandals more often than she should have.

Rosa glanced between the fancy dresses and her skirt and blouse. She did not wish to spend most of the day inside as Dona Valerianna often did. Dare she break the mundane routine and explore the various gardens that surrounded the hacienda and perhaps stroll through the orchards and enjoy fruit picked fresh from the trees?

The thought was too inviting to ignore and besides who would worry about her whereabouts. Don Alejandro and Dona Valerianna would not dare venture into their son's bedchamber and Esteban made it clear that he wished nothing to do with her. So the day belonged to her and the thought of such freedom filled her with joyous anticipation.

She hurried to slip into her peasant garb and hoped that perhaps she could sneak to the kitchen, gather a basket of food for herself and be off before anyone spotted her and could bear witness to her departure.

Once her sandals were on and her hair quickly braided, she rushed from the house to the kitchen in no time, pleased that she met no one along the way. It was earlier than she first thought and it appeared as if the hacienda was just stirring to life, though she doubted that, the vaqueros no doubt had been up and working since before sunrise.

The kitchen was empty but the delicious scents let her know that Dolores had already been busy cooking. She had made a friend of Dolores and knew well her routine. She was probably at the hen house collecting eggs and she wasted no time in gathering bread and cheese, careful not to take too much. She would add the fresh fruit she picked to it and picnic by the stream she had discovered that ran not far from the hacienda. She grabbed a cloth from the stack neatly folded on a narrow table under the lone window in the kitchen, draped it over the modest meal she placed in a basket, and then once again hurried off before anyone saw her.

The day was hers to enjoy and the decadent thought had her blessing herself as she hurried her steps, eager to taste freedom. She made her way through one of the many hacienda gardens, though didn't stop to admire the numerous beautiful flowers. She was anxious to reach the orchards and find a fat orange or lemon and of course she could not resist the red plump grapes that beckoned from several arbors scattered throughout the various gardens, not to mention the ones in the vineyards.

Rosa dropped her head back to allow the warmth of the sun to kiss her face. It was a beautiful day and being free of chores and obligations, if only for this day, made it all the more beautiful.

Her stomach grumbled and she patted it. "Be patient, we soon feast." She laughed and hurried into the orchard to pick an orange or two.

~~~

"They have missed breakfast and now they don't show up for the noon meal," Dona Valerianna said with a worried frown.

Don Alejandro attempted to soothe his wife, though he too fretted over Esteban and Rosa's absence.

"Do you think she is all right?" Dona Valerianna asked with a whisper.

Don Alejandro patted his wife's arm. "They are getting to know each other. This is good." He wanted to believe his own words, but he had doubts that haunted, though he tried not to feed them. Rosa was a good girl and would be good for his son. He had to hold on to that hope. Otherwise, he feared there was nothing that could save his son.

"Perhaps we should have food taken to them," Dona Valerianna suggested.

"Who is too lazy not to get food for themselves?" Esteban asked striding into the dining room and taking a seat at the table.

Dona Valerianna smiled at her son, half relieved to see him, but concerned that Rosa wasn't with him.

Alejandro looked to the door, his concern more obvious than his wife's. And he was quick to say, "Why you and Rosa of course. You both missed breakfast and we worried you would miss the noon meal as well, but here you are. Will Rosa be along soon?"

Esteban sat straight up in his chair. "I have not seen her since early this morning."

"Either have we," Dona Valerianna said with a hint of alarm.

Esteban bolted out of his chair and hurried out of the room without a word. When he reached his bed chambers and saw that Rosa was not there his heart began to hammer against his chest. He saw that the wardrobe was open and that her dresses hung there, so what had she worn.

He returned with a rush to his parents. "She is not in my room."

Dona Valerianna grew pale with fear. "Could she have run off?"

"Why do you think that, Mother?" Esteban asked accusingly. "Do you think I ravished her so badly that she has run away?"

Dona Valerianna gasped and Alejandro chastised her son. "Do not speak so rudely and crudely to your mother. She worries for you and your wife and wants only happiness for you both."

Esteban wanted to remind his parents that that would never be, but the sadness in his mother's eyes had him holding his tongue and silently cursing himself for having spoken so improperly to her. He was worried himself about Rosa, but he didn't want his parents to know. They would assume that he cared for the petite peasant woman, when it was nothing more than his husbandly duty to protect and keep his wife safe... or so he told himself.

He refused to pay heed to the haunting images of her naked in his arms last night. No soon as he attempted to scatter them with a shake of his head, then they would return full force. As would blatant images of what he ached to do to her.

But that had nothing to do with love. It was lust that taunted him and kept him aroused, and if he didn't satisfy it soon he would find himself mounting his wife like a wild stallion after a mare in heat, just as he had done to the willing woman in Pacquito's band of renegades.

"I do not think Rosa would run away," Don Alejandro said. "She has nowhere to go and she is a dutiful woman and would not abandon her responsibilities."

"She is obedient, I will give her that," Esteban said annoyed, wishing that she had some fire to her nature. He had seen a spark of it last night when she had bravely spoken up to Roberto. She had even braced herself for the blow she had known would come, but then the wine had given her courage. She also had had the courage to stop him from killing Roberto, and he had had every intention of splitting the man from throat to groin as he had promised he would do if he dared to raise a hand to Rosa again.

He hadn't been sure what had stopped him. It could have been her gentle touch or the pleading look in her eyes. Whatever it had been, he didn't know, though he had warned himself to be cautious, somehow she had affected him and no one had done that in a long time.

Dolores entered the dining room and Esteban was quick to ask, "Have you seen my wife?"

"No, senor, I have not, though..." Dolores hesitated.

"Tell me," Esteban ordered sharply.

Dolores hurried to obey. "I noticed that a basket and some food, not much, were missing from the kitchen when I returned from collecting eggs. The items taken would barely feed one person."

"Thank you, Dolores, you may leave now," Don Alejandro said.

"Rosa seeks some solitude," Dona Valerianna said with relief.

"But she did not seek permission from her

husband," Alejandro reminded her. "It is not wise of her to wander off on her own. Our land spreads wide and there is no telling who lurks about."

Esteban felt his whole body grow taut and his heartbeat that had calmed, now once again slammed in his chest. He had wandered off on his own one day and it had taken him sixteen years to return home. He rushed out of the room, alarming his mother.

Alejandro laid a comforting hand on his wife's arm and smiled. "This is good; he worries about her."

Dona Valerianna sighed heavily. "But what will he do to her when he finds her?"

Chapter Eight

Rosa sat under the shade of a large oak tree, content after having a fine meal of bread, cheese and the plumpest orange she had ever seen. She was however worried that perhaps she should not have gone off on her own without telling anyone. It wasn't that she was trying to be defiant, she had simply wanted... what? What had she wanted? Had she snuck away because she was fearful of facing Esteban again? Just thinking about him sent a shiver through her. How was she to learn about him if she kept her distance from him?

She wondered if anyone had noticed her absence by now and would it matter to anyone. The Curros had been on her every minute of every day. She had barely had a free moment to herself, so today was a gift of sorts and while she thought it might be wise to return to the hacienda, she also didn't want to relinquish this precious free time afforded her.

No doubt she would have duties as Esteban's wife, though from what she had seen of Dona Valerianna's duties they appeared minimal, nothing close to what she had been accustomed to. Actually, Rosa thought that Dona Valerianna's task was to always look beautiful and be there for her husband whenever he needed her. And then there was her stitching. Dona Valerianna was quite talented with a needle, creating the most beautiful embroidery pieces that Rosa had ever seen.

Rosa scrunched her brow. Was that thunder she heard? She looked up, shading her eyes from the sun with her hand. The sky was a clear blue, not a threat of a storm in sight.

The thunder grew louder until Rosa jumped to her feet, finally realizing that it wasn't thunder at all but a fast approaching rider. She turned almost in a full circle before she saw him in the distance. And there was no denying who it was.

The urge to run gripped Rosa like a tight hand squeezing the breath from her and yet she found herself frozen. She couldn't move, couldn't do anything but watch her husband approach at a fast gait. The closer he got, the more clearly she could see how angry he was and the sudden thought of his warning rang in her head.

Don't make me take the whip to you.

He no soon as brought the mighty stallion to a stop than he bolted off the horse and raced toward her, his face tight with anger

Rosa reacted instinctively, she backed away from him until her back hit the old oak tree and she could go no further. Her eyes turned wide as he kept coming toward her and she braced herself, for what she didn't know.

She tensed as he slapped his hands against the tree on either side of her head, trapping her. Esteban didn't say a word, he just stared at her, but then he needed to calm himself before he spoke or did something he would regret. His muscles were tense and ready to strike, ready to protect Rosa. He worried that he would find her embroiled in a dangerous situation, though more worried that he wouldn't find her at all. When he had seen her in the distance, it had set his heart to hammering more wildly, though with relief this time. Then his anger sparked again.

He brought his face down inches in front of hers. "*Never, ever*, go off anywhere without my permission."

She nodded rapidly.

He could see her fear and sense it, but what caught his attention the most was her plump moist lips and the sweet scent of oranges that drifted off her. His groin suddenly tightened and the urge to kiss her overpowered him. If he didn't back away from her now, put a good distance between them, he would surrender to the urge and he wasn't sure if he would stop at just a kiss.

"*Never again*," he repeated. "*Understand*?"

She nodded again and the tip of her tongue darted out to lick the center of her lips before darting back in and taking her lips with her, snagging them tightly closed as if locking them away from him.

The thought irritated him, though he doubted she did it on purpose, but it definitely was instinctive, as if she was protecting herself against him... her husband.

Turn away. Walk away. Far away.

He didn't listen to his warning. It seemed he

wasn't able to. He was too caught up in the closeness of their bodies. Her hard nipples poked at his shirt. All he had to do was lean a bit closer and they would poke his chest.

Get away from her!

Again he didn't heed the warning. Instead he dared to lean closer and she shrank back away from him, though there was no place for her to go. And when his chest crushed against her breasts, she startled, her eyes turning wide.

He thought to remind her that she was his wife and he could do as he wished with her, but that was not a reminder that he needed to know. It stiffened his already hardened groin. He didn't realize that his lips had drifted close to hers and pulsated with such a desire to kiss her that it startled him.

Get away now!

This time he listened. He tore himself away from her, turning and stepping away. He'd be a fool to kiss her, for then he'd want to touch her, slip his hand beneath the peasant blouse she wore and caress her soft skin, and then...

He swerved around, his arm snapping out as he approached her and coiled around her waist to yank her hard against him, and then his mouth claimed hers.

Rosa was too shocked to respond. She remained stiff in his arms. Her own arms spread out to her sides, while he kissed her with a hunger that she didn't know was possible. And it wasn't long before her body responded to his need or was it her need?

Her hands drifted to his shoulders and rested there as she let instinct take control and she began to respond to his demands. She didn't know when her hands slipped around his neck or her fingers drifted into his soft hair or when her body pressed against his, she only knew that she was enjoying this intimate moment with her husband.

He groaned while he continued to devour her senses with his kiss. She moaned at the unexpected pleasures that were beginning to consume her. How could she be frightened of her husband and yet feel such pleasure?

She didn't know what was happening and there was a part of her that didn't care. Oddly enough she felt safe in his arms and for some reason she felt that he wouldn't hurt her.

He suddenly grabbed a handful of hair at the back of her head and yanked it back, forcing their kiss to end. He pressed his lips to her exposed neck and mumbled, "I want to sink myself into you."

And the next thing Rosa knew she was down on the ground on her back and his hands were shoving her skirt up. When his fingers plunged between her legs, she cried out shocked at the intrusion and surprised at the unexpected tingle of pleasure.

He was off her in an instant, turning away as he ordered, "Gather your things, we leave now."

Rosa wondered what she had done wrong, though she didn't hesitate to obey him. She pushed her skirt down as she stumbled to her feet and hurried to get her basket. He didn't have to tell her to follow him to the stallion that was grazing contentedly nearby.

Esteban turned and grabbed her around the waist lifting her onto the saddle in one swift motion. He then mounted behind her, his arm going around her waist while his hand took command of the reins.

He directed the horse in a tempered gallop and after a few silent moments he pressed his cheek to hers and said, "I am a savage. I have taken women with only thought to my pleasure. Keep your distance from me or I will do the same to you."

Rosa didn't respond, she didn't think he expected her to. Not even one day wed and he had warned her twice to stay away from him, and made certain she knew that he was not a gentleman, yet he had come in search of her. Why? If he was such a savage, why would he care?

He didn't say another word to her. When they reached the hacienda he dismounted, and then reached up and swung her down off the horse.

"Go dress as befitting my wife and do not insult me by dressing in peasant clothes again."

Rosa was taken aback, upset that he should think that she had dressed to insult him. "I am sorry, I meant no disrespect."

Her apology annoyed him all the more since he had been the cause of it. After all what did he expect her to do... argue with him? That would only fuel his already fiery blood and have him wanting to finish what he had started under the oak tree.

Without a word, he turned away from her, mounted his stallion, and rode off. He didn't look back at her. He couldn't. He feared he would turn his horse around, snatch her up onto the saddle, and ride off with her to a secluded spot to have his way with her more than once.

He spurred his stallion into a hard gallop, but even after a hard ride, it didn't help. It wasn't the mighty stallion he wanted to ride. He wanted to ride his wife like no other woman he had ever ridden.

The problem was that she was a delicate, gentle soul and he was no gentleman. She had cried out in alarm when his fingers slipped inside her. What would she do when he was thick with arousal and entered her... faint?

The urge to find out haunted him and would not let go. He feared that sooner or later he would surrender to it, and then what? His wife would find out just how much of a savage he had grown to be.

Chapter Nine

Supper was a difficult affair that evening. Esteban was silent throughout the whole meal, no matter how many times his father or mother tried to engage him in conversation. They finally gave up and turned their attention to Rosa.

"Do you ride, Rosa?" Don Alejandro asked.

"Yes, do you ride, wife?" Esteban asked.

Rosa looked surprised at him since he knew that she had not shied away from his stallion earlier and had not shown any signs of never having ridden before. So exactly what did he mean?

Don Alejandro must have thought the same for he sent his son a scowl. Only Dona Valerianna seemed unperturbed by her son's question.

"I have known how to ride since I was young," Rosa said

"That's good, for I have a gentle mare that I think would suit you," Don Alejandro said.

"I'll decide who my wife mounts," Esteban said.

That brought a threatening glare from his father, though it didn't seem to affect Esteban in the least.

"I'm sure Angella is well suited for Rosa, she is such a gentle mare," Dona Valerianna said as if trying to convince her son.

"Perhaps it is not gentleness she needs in a mount," Esteban argued and received another glare from his father, though his mother unwittingly, or perhaps not, saved father and son from an argument by changing the subject.

"Invitations have already come in from various haciendas inviting Rosa and me to visit," Dona Valerianna said with a pleased smile, which Esteban managed to wipe away with a few words.

"Those women are interested in only one thing, to see how Rosa has fared being wed to me."

"That's not true," his mother said. "The women are eager to accept Rosa as one of us."

Esteban shook his head. "Do not be a fool, Mother, they will never accept a peasant as one of their own. They look to gossip."

"Esteban may be right about that, Valerianna," Alejandro agreed. "I would advise that you take Rosa to visit only your closest friends, ones you feel you can trust."

"No one is trustworthy," Esteban said, as if declaring it so.

"That is not true," Alejandro argued. "We have many trustworthy friends."

"And yet you had to go to the peasants to find a wife for me," Esteban said. "Not one of your trustworthy friends would even consider an arranged marriage with their dear friend's son."

"Lucky for you since Rosa is far more beautiful and thoughtful than any of the Dons' daughters." Alejandro said.

Rosa blushed at the compliment.

"That is finally something we agree on, Father," Esteban said raising his glass of wine and nodding at his wife. He watched her blush deepen and creep down along her neck to disappear into the crevice of her full breasts. He wondered how far it went. Did it taint all of her sun-kissed skin?

He shifted in his chair when he felt himself grow aroused at the thought and it didn't stop there. He couldn't prevent himself from imagining stripping her of her clothes and kissing every inch of blush.

He stood abruptly, his glass of wine toppling over. He didn't bother to right it; he left the room without a word.

"I'm sorry, my dear." Dona Valerianna turned to Rosa apologizing. "My son sometimes lacks manners."

"I can't imagine how very difficult it must be for him returning to a life that he had once known but has now become so foreign to him," Rosa said in defense of her husband's unmannerly actions. "It must be a constant struggle for him to be the man he once was when he is so much more familiar with the man he has become."

Don Alejandro and his wife stared at their daughter-in-law for several minutes before Dona Valerianna said, "I never thought that he waged a battle with himself, but you are right. It must be very difficult for him." She reached her hand out to rest it on Rosa's. "I am so grateful that he has you to help him."

Esteban stood outside the dining room listening. He had stopped abruptly after his hasty departure. He had known he had been rude, though he didn't care and that disturbed him as well. And when he heard his mother apologize to his wife for him, he grew angry and was about to return and warn her never to apologize for him again.

He stopped when he heard his wife's gentle voice not only defend him but understand him, almost better than he was trying to understand himself. She had been right. He was more comfortable with the savage he had become than the aristocratic boy that had been abducted years ago. The question was how did he reconcile the two? And could he?

He walked away shedding his jacket and opening his shirt, in a sense shedding the constraints that this life here placed on him. After many years with Pacquito's band of renegades he had found a certain sense of freedom and the taste intoxicated. He could never let anyone rule him nor could he follow rules. He had learned that rules could be broken and many were meant to be and with each rule he had broken, he swore he would never let rules dictate his life again.

The beautiful night beckoned and he answered its call. He had spent more nights under the stars than in the confines of the small hut that had been his so-called home. He followed the pebbled path to the garden just outside his quarters, looked up at the blanket of stars against the dark sky, took a deep breath and slipped his shirt off. He discarded it and his jacket to a nearby bench and rolled his neck around trying to loosen the tightness that bit at him there.

He thought about collecting his bedroll and sleeping under the stars tonight, perhaps then he would be able to sleep. Since his return home he had been haunted by nightmares that would wake him throughout the night. He wondered if he would ever be able to sleep soundly again.

He smelled her before he heard her footsteps and the corner of his mouth rose. She did have a penchant for oranges. He recalled their kiss and grew thick and hard in an instant. The problem was that he hadn't been with a woman since his return. While there were plenty of willing women in town, he couldn't bring himself to insult his parents by making use of the whores. He had seen to his own needs, but it was less satisfying than the pleasure he got between a woman's legs.

You have a wife, take her.

He grew harder at the thought, though shook it away and grew annoyed.

"Keep your distance, wife, or I will think you not adverse to me burying myself deep inside you and riding you hard." His words were meant to frighten, and they did.

Rosa gasped and took several steps back, though she was already a good distance from her husband. She had entered the bed chambers and had been surprised to see the patio doors open and Esteban standing outside in the small private garden.

She had stopped when she had spotted him and once again she had cringed when seeing the thin scars on his back. But this time she also took note of the corded muscles that ran across his shoulders and down his arms and how his waist narrowed and his firm backside rounded so nicely.

Heat rose to stain her cheeks at her sinful thought, especially since Esteban was the first man she had ever found physically appealing. But what woman wouldn't. He was magnificently beautiful, from his fine features to his sculpted body, though his soul was heavily scarred. And it seemed that those scars had yet to heal as good as the ones had on his back.

With his warning quite clear and not wanting him to get the wrong impression, she turned to leave.

"Come here."

Had she hesitated too long in taking her leave after he had warned her? Had he assumed that she had acquiesced by remaining there? She took cautious steps toward him.

"The stars are beautiful tonight, are they not?"

She stopped a short distance behind him and looked up at the night sky. "Yes, the stars twinkle brilliantly." When she brought her head down she was surprised to see how close he stood to her. That was the second time he had moved so silently that she hadn't heard him. And it was worrisome to know that he had such skill.

He reached up and ran one finger down along her temple, over her cheek and to her chin slipping it beneath and tilting her chin up a fraction. "You are far more beautiful than the stars and I would love to strip you naked, bend you over the bed and ride you good and hard."

This time Rosa was unable to gasp. She was too shocked by his words and the image they painted in her mind.

He grabbed hold of her chin pinching it between two fingers. "I had all kindness and gentleness whipped out of me. It is not a tender lover you would find in our bed if ever we were to consummate our vows." He gave her chin a slight shove as he released her and walked away.

Rosa didn't turn around for several long minutes. When she finally did, her husband was gone and she hurried into the room. How her trembling legs managed to get her to the bed, she didn't know, but she was relieved to sit. Why was he forever warning her? He had told her that he would never touch her, so why bother to make such a remark? Did he fear he would not be able to keep his word and so in frightening her, she would see to keeping her distance from him?

One full day of marriage and she already felt the weight of being Esteban's wife. But she had been burdened with difficult situations before and had done her best in adapting to them. What else was there to do when one's freedom was limited?

She stretched her arms along with her yawn and struggled out of her gown alone. Dolores had told her that a servant would be along shortly to help her undress and Rosa had stared speechless at the older woman. When she had finally found her voice, she had told Dolores that she would need no assistance. The woman had shaken her head and warned her that she was now a noble and needed to learn how to behave like one.

Rosa didn't feel that way. She was who she always was and would be, nothing would change that. She didn't want it to.

After seeing to brushing her long dark hair and stifling several yawns she gladly crawled into bed and was almost asleep when she sprang up in bed and cast a cautious eye at the door that separated her and Esteban. She would never hear him if he entered and she wondered if she should lock the door.

She gave it only a moment's thought, realizing that it would not bode well for her to lock her husband out of his own room. So she dropped back on the bed and after several more yawns, sleep finally claimed her.

~~~

Esteban bolted up in bed. He woke often during the night, though this was an abrupt awakening and that meant something, other than a nightmare, had woken him. His hand went for his knife beneath his pillow only to find that it wasn't there. It took him a moment to realize where he was... home. A weapon under the pillow wasn't necessary, though he did feel more comfortable knowing the weapon was in the wooden box that sat on top of the four-drawer chest next to his bed.

Another realization struck, he wasn't in his bedchamber, which meant he had no weapon.

He scanned the room, his eyes not only having grown accustomed to the darkness but almost able to see in the dark like the nocturne animals did. It was one of many skills he had acquired and was grateful for, another being a heightened sense of hearing.

With an animal like grace he slipped out of bed and stood naked in the dark room, and listened. He heard it then... a whimper. He didn't hesitate and he didn't bother to don a shred of clothing. He went directly to the door to his bed chamber, opened it, and walked in.

His wife was in the throes of a nightmare. She tossed her head from side to side, while her body twisted, as if trying to escape imaginary hands that held her prisoner and her whimpers turned to distressed cries.

He hurried to the bed and didn't think twice about his actions, he slipped beneath the blanket and eased her into his arms.

"You're safe," he whispered in her ear, his cool cheek pressed against her heated one. "I have you, nothing can hurt you now." His eyes narrowed and his temper flared. "And I will kill anyone who tries."

She squirmed, as if trying to break free from him, and he realized she needed soothing rather than words of retribution. "I'll keep you safe, Rosa, I'll let no one hurt you," he repeated softly over and over as his hand caressed her back.

It wasn't long before she calmed and settled contentedly in his arms. She pressed her cheek to his chest and snuggled closer against him, as if she had finally accepted his words and knew that she was safe.

What he hadn't expected was for her slim leg to insert itself between his two, almost as if she was attempting to lock herself to him so that he could not escape her. The problem was that her night dress had worked its way up and had left just below her stomach bare. With her leg tucked between his two, her soft thatch of hair fit snugly against his groin and he hardened in an instant.

He warned himself to be good, while another part of him reminded that she was his wife and he had the right to take her. He shut his eyes tight against his warring thoughts. He didn't want to take his wife like a common whore. And though many of the women he had been with had often praised his skills as a lover, he had no doubt they did so out of necessity. No one would dare say a bad word about Pacquito's men or he would kill them.

He glanced down at his wife sleeping peacefully in his arms and at his hands that rested on her soft, warm flesh. If she knew the blood that his hands had spilled, he wondered if she would want him to touch her.

A soft sigh escaped her lips and it felt as if she kissed his chest. She burrowed even closer against him, her bottom shifting as if searching for something to settle against. He silently swore as he reached down to settle her tormenting movement before he did something foolish like pushing her on her back and delving deep inside her.

His hand rested on her backside just as she settled, his arousal slipping between her legs. She sighed again as if she had found the spot she had searched for. He stilled, and though he warned himself to remain that way, he couldn't help but give her firm, round backside a light squeeze.

Her sigh was unexpected and of course it caused her lips yet again to brush his chest, as if in a kiss, which fired his blood and caused him to caress her derrière some more.

Damn, if he didn't ache to do more—much more—than simply caress her backside.

He tore his hand away, as if he had touched fire and in a way he had. If he didn't get away from her soon, he would plunge himself into the flames, though he feared that it would ignite them even more and he'd never be able to extinguish them.

How was he ever going to stay wed to his beautiful wife and never touch her? He had set himself an impossible task. Eventually, he would surrender to this burning need, and then what? Would she fear him even more than she already did?

He closed his eyes. He should have never returned. He should have stayed away, it would have been better for all. His father and mother had suffered and what of his sister Crista when she returned from Spain? What chance would his father have of arranging a good marriage for her with him being her brother?

Worst of all, this innocent young woman had been forced to wed him, committing her to a life of hell. Though if he was honest that wasn't the worst of it, he may have fought against their union, told himself it was wrong, it should never be... when all along he wanted Rosa as his wife. He wanted someone to share his torment with him. And it was only a matter of time before he dragged her down into the burning flames, into his depravity, into the depths of hell.

Chapter Ten

The pleasant scent tickled Rosa's nostrils and had her smiling. It was familiar, though she couldn't recall from where. And all she wanted to do was linger in it. Along with the intoxicating scent came the overwhelming feeling of being protected. Nothing could hurt her. She was safe and she hadn't felt this safe and protected since her parents died.

She snuggled closer to the warmth until she suddenly realized that she rested in someone's arms. And then she recognized the scent... it belonged to her husband.

Her eyes popped open and she stared at his naked chest. Her body was pressed against his and—good Lord—he was naked. And her leg was tucked between his two and to make matters worse her night dress had ridden up almost to her waist.

What was he doing in her bed—his bed—their bed. She didn't know what to do. Did she jump up and run? But where would she go? He was her husband and had every right to come to their bed.

She breathed a heavy sigh and her lips grazed his chest and—Lord forgive her—he was tasty. Whatever was the matter with her? She should be thinking of means of escape not how tangy his warm flesh tasted.

He hadn't moved, perhaps he was still asleep and she could slip out of bed, grab her clothes, and slip out of the room without waking him. Did she dare raise her head and look at him or slip carefully out of his arms?

She shifted a bit to see what would happen and when nothing did, she assumed he was asleep. She shifted again hoping she could work her way out of his embrace without disturbing him. When he continued to remain still, she continued her efforts until... she stopped moving.

She felt something poke her between her legs and suddenly her entire body flushed with a deep heat that she feared would set her on fire. Had her squirming aroused him? She had foolishly never considered the consequences of her actions.

Her friend Marinda and she would talk in whispers about sex, Marinda telling her things that made her blush, smile, and sometimes laugh. She had told Rosa once about how Paco always woke hard, ready for them to make love.

Her body stiffened. Was Esteban awake?

Now what was she to do?

She remained still and gave her predicament thought, and then an idea hit her. She could shift a bit more carefully again and stretch her way out of his arms and roll to her side, as if she was just drifting awake.

Courage, she warned herself, though it took her a few minutes to convince herself that it could actually work. With a thumping heart and trepidation, she moved slowly and began to work her arms up for a stretch when suddenly...

She was flat on her back with Esteban's naked body hovering over her. His hands were planted on either side of her head, his arms extended, the muscles taut so that his chest did not touch hers. His arousal however poked between her legs, the wet tip planted firmly against her.

A tingle sparked in her lower region and grew as he shifted against her, as she had done to him. He didn't say a word to her, though his dark eyes bore into her with such flaming heat that her spark began to burn brighter and stronger.

Esteban fought for control. He had woken shocked to find himself in bed with his wife and then he recalled why he was there. He had silently cursed himself a thousand times over for not having left after she had calmed, but she had rested so comfortably in his arms and he had... slept through the remainder of the night without waking. He had not done that since his return.

It had been his growing arousal that had woken him and he thought to face another morning of seeing to his own mounting need, when he woke to find his wife in his arms. He didn't know what overcame him when she went to move away from him. But his reaction was instinctive. He flipped her on her back and trapped her with his body.

He now could easily plunge into her and satisfy his need that was burning beyond control, beyond anything he ever felt before. He could smell her sweet scent and the thought that she was growing wet for him pushed him nearer to the edge of losing control. It would be quick, for he had been without a woman far too long, but he would have no trouble hardening again and taking her repeatedly. A quick image of him mounting her, had him cursing silently. He tried to shake it away. It wasn't right. He couldn't think of her like that. He had no need to claim her as his woman... she already belonged to him. She was his wife. He had returned to civilized society and there was no need to claim a woman the way Pacquito's band of men did by riding a woman for all to see.

He clamped his eyes shut trying to stop another memory from invading his mind, Pacquito with a gun to a young woman's head ready to shoot her if Esteban didn't claim her in front of the men. He had had no choice, take her or watch her die. She had had no choice either. He did what he had to do. Now he had a choice and he would not bring such filth upon his wife. She was thoughtful and kind and if he intended to seal their wedding vows he would need to take her with tenderness and consideration.

The problem was he didn't know if he was capable of either.

Get off her now!

The silent warning reverberated in his head until it pounded like a hammer against his temples.

Take her and be done with it!

He shook his head at the arguing voice that grew louder and louder in his head, until his eyes popped open and his mouth reached for hers.

Rosa didn't have time to grasp at the shock of

his kiss. The suddenness of it jolted her, but she found that she favored the way he kissed her. His commanding way forced her to respond in kind and share in the kiss. Otherwise, she might have been too nervous to respond at all.

She wasn't sure what was happening to her, but it felt good and oh so right. After all, he was her husband and they had the right to make love.

He tore his mouth away from hers suddenly and he seemed to hesitate for a moment, and then he lowered his mouth to her nipple, his tongue circling the already hardened nub before he took it into his mouth and suckled it.

She thought that she would die from pleasure.

Esteban had never tasted anything so exquisite and it sent his body reeling with passion. If he didn't stop soon he would take her and it wouldn't be just once. He would have her over and over and over.

He ripped his mouth away to rest his brow to hers, his breathing heavy as he said, "I'm a savage, and I will take you like a savage, innocent or not."

He jumped off her and strode out of the room.

Rosa watched her naked husband walk away and shivered, not from his words of warning, but from the empty ache that left her wanting... him.

She didn't believe her husband was a savage or that he would take her like one, or perhaps it was that she didn't want to believe it. What she did believe was that it would be inevitable... they would seal their wedding vows. Nothing would stop it. And surprisingly, she didn't want it to.

~~~

Rosa could see that Don Alejandro and Dona Valerianna were pleased with her appearance when she joined them for breakfast on the brick patio. She had fought the urge to once again don peasant garb and had dressed as was befitting her new station, that of Esteban's wife. She wore a pale yellow dress overpowered with lace. She would never get used to dressing as if she was forever attending a celebration. She wondered if perhaps she could have other garments made that more suited her, yet still pleased her new in-laws.

"You look lovely, my dear," Dona Valerianna said with an approving smile. "Of course you will need more garments, two dresses will not be enough. I will speak with the seamstress and have her start on a wardrobe for you."

Here was her chance and she took it. "You are so busy, Dona Valerianna, it would please me to see to the chore for you."

The woman smiled and seemed hesitant to speak. A nod from her husband, as if a command had her saying, "That is thoughtful of you. Lita is an excellent seamstress and will guide you wisely in design and what garments you will need."

So that was why she hesitated, the woman did not think her capable of the task.

"My wife will tell the seamstress what garments she requires and she will dress how she pleases and if that means she wishes to wear a peasant skirt and blouse then so be it," Esteban said joining them on the brick patio where breakfast was being served this morning.

Dona Valerianna paled while staring speechless at her son.

Rosa was surprised by his remark since he had ordered her to dress appropriately. Now he was saying she could dress as she pleased, upsetting his mother. No doubt she was worried that Rosa would embarrass the Cesare name if she were to prance around in peasant garb.

Rosa would never be so disrespectful, though with her husband's remark she could now see to having dresses made that better suited her without worry of repercussions.

Silence circled the table for a few moments before Don Alejandro cleared his throat to speak. "Esteban, I have documents that must be delivered to Padre Marten today. I thought perhaps you could deliver them for me and Rosa could accompany you so that she would be able to visit with her friend."

Esteban was well aware of what his father was attempting to do... force him to spend time alone with his wife. His sly tactics weren't going to work and Esteban was about to tell him just that when he caught the look of joy on his wife's lovely face. And his words died on his lips.

"That would be wonderful for then you could stop at the mercantile," Dona Valerianna added, "and see if there is any news from your sister. In her last letter she told us she would write before she left Spain and the drawing material I ordered for Rosa might have arrived as well."

Esteban might have refused—out of sheer stubbornness—his parents' request, but the way his wife's eyes turned wide at the mention of drawing material settled it. He would take her to town.

"As you wish, Father," Esteban said and both his parents' mouths dropped open, though they closed them fast enough and replaced them with joyful smiles.

Rosa was delighted and was about to ask Don Alejandro if it would be possible to take a couple of oranges to her friend Marinda when instead she looked to her husband. "Esteban, would it be permissible for me to take my friend some oranges fresh from the orchard?"

A bone aching chill raced through him at her request. It reminded him of all the times he had had to seek permission just to eat. And he'd be damned if his wife would be made to do the same.

"You need not ask permission for such a trivial matter. Take what fruit you want for your friend, the orchard belongs to you now as much as to me."

His father took the opportunity to remind his son. "And the land will pass to your sons, of I pray there will be many."

Esteban expected his wife to blush at the mere mention of children. After all they would have to consummate their vows for that to even be a consideration. So her words caught him by surprise and the fact that she did so with a smile and not the least bit of shyness.

"And daughters. It would be lovely to have a daughter or two." Rosa looked to Dona Valerianna who was also smiling. "You must miss your daughter."

"Very much, which is why I am eager for her to return home, but I also look forward to being a grandmother." Dona Valerianna's smile grew. "It would be wonderful to have the hacienda filled with children's laughter once again."

Esteban stared at his wife as she spoke with his mother. She sounded as if she not only would fulfill her duty and produce one child, but that she wished for more. Did that mean she wasn't opposed to his touch?

Damn, if the thought didn't turn him hard. Could there possibly be a chance for them to have a good marriage? To have children? To care for each other?

To fall in love?

A foolish thought he dismissed immediately. There wasn't an ounce of love left in him, Pacquito had seen to driving it completely out of him and replacing it with hate. Hate is what had helped him to survive and he feared he could never stop hating.

Esteban stood, having finished barely half of what was on his plate and looked to his wife. "We leave in ten minutes." He strode out of the room, his heart pounding, and his groin aching.

He fought the sinful images in his head that took hold as he walked through the hacienda. He was forever thinking of her naked and what he would do to her and in different ways and repeatedly. It was as if he couldn't get enough of her. He could almost feel himself slamming into her over and over and it wasn't cries of pain that escaped her lips but pleasure. In his thoughts she enjoyed everything he did to her and that made him grow even harder.

~~~

Esteban took the smaller of the carriages, the one he could drive himself. He wanted no driver listening to their private conversation, and then gossiping about it. Not that they had spoken since they had left the hacienda, which he was about to rectify.

But Rosa spoke before he could. "Marinda is going to be so happy when I give her these oranges." She smiled down at the basket filled with the plump fruit. "It was thoughtful of your father to have someone pick the oranges for me, though it wasn't necessary. I so enjoy doing it myself."

"He wasn't being thoughtful. He didn't want his new daughter picking fruit like a common laborer."

Rosa sighed. "I wondered if perhaps that was the reason."

Esteban looked over at her and it disturbed him that her smile had faded, though hadn't entirely disappeared. He liked when she smiled, it made him feel—damn—it actually made him feel. It was as if when he looked upon her smile he felt a bit of her happiness. And he could not recall the last time he knew happiness.

"I'll take you to pick fruit." He didn't know

what made him say it, though he didn't regret it, at least he hoped he wouldn't.

Her smile brightened once again. "That would be wonderful. Did you pick fruit when you were a young boy?"

He stiffened not wanting to recall his youth but he needn't worry, she went right on talking and he enjoyed listening.

"The Curros would have me go and pick fruit on the one day the haciendas would open their orchards to the townspeople. The fruits were the last before harvest, the ones not good enough to pick, though the people treasured the opportunity and picked the trees bare. Every now and then I would get lucky and find a good fruit. I would find a place where no one could see me and eat it." She laughed. "It would be the only fruit I would get since the Curros would not let me have any of the fruit I brought home."

Esteban turned to her stunned. "They didn't let you eat any after all the work you did?"

"Not a one," Rosa said without malice. "Roberto accused me of having my fill while I picked the fruit. Fruit he insisted belonged to them, so therefore I didn't deserve anymore."

"I knew I should have killed him that day."

Rosa didn't think twice about her reaction or response, her hand went to rest gently on his arm. "No, you are not that man anymore. You are free."

Free.

He had yearned for freedom these many years and he still did. He didn't feel free and he wondered if he ever would and yet—sitting here next to his wife—he felt somewhat content. Could being wed to her make a difference? Could she help him... or would he destroy her?

She squeezed his arm lightly. "So tell me did you pick fruit when you were young?"

"All the time," he said the side of his mouth lifting in a partial smile.

It warmed Rosa's heart to see that slight smile, though it faded too quickly. His brow knit and he appeared to drift off, no doubt into memories that were anything but pleasant. Dare she ask him? If she didn't, how could she even begin to understand him? She did not want to spend a lifetime fearing her husband. And there was too many times he put fear into her and that wasn't what she wanted in her marriage.

With her heart thumping and her stomach roiling, she took a chance and asked, "It must have been difficult for you being captured so young?"

"Young?" He sneered. "According to Pacquito I was a man and I deserved a man's punishment when I disobeyed him, which seemed to be a daily occurrence."

"How frightened you must have been," she said and wishing to comfort him, she gave his arm another gentle squeeze.

"I don't need your sympathy," he snapped and she pulled her hand away, as if he had slapped it. He cursed silently, having enjoyed the feel of her hand on his arm and the way she had squeezed it now and again to emphasis her words or perhaps her feelings.

Rosa contained the shiver that wanted to race through her. His abruptness frightened her, perhaps because when the Curros had spoken to her in such a fashion it had always been followed by the slap of a hand or the strap. She would immediately turn silent and obey them. But then hadn't Esteban experienced the same, only to a greater degree. She could not imagine surviving such an ordeal. Esteban certainly had proved just how much of a courageous man he truly was. And being he had defended her against Roberto, she felt the need to defend him against what Pacquito had created.

Refusing to surrender to her quaking limbs and nervous stomach, she spoke up, "It isn't sympathy I offer, but rather friendship. Can we not be friends and at least care for each other as such?"

I want more.

The thought startled him, though he didn't show it, nor did he understand it. It would do well to be friends with his wife and yet... he wanted more. What more was there? Love? A foolish, irrational thought.

"You wish to be friends with a savage?"

Her hand returned to his arm. "I wish to be friends with my husband."

The words were out of his mouth before he could stop them. "I want more."

Chapter Eleven

Rosa had no chance to ask him what he meant by more and she wondered if he had made the remark purposely so that she would not have a chance to respond since they had just entered the town and eased to a stop at the Mercantile, the first building on the right.

"Stay where you are," Esteban said. "I'll only be a moment."

Rosa watched as men moved out of his way and women would not even dare go near him. Two crossed the street and blessed themselves as they went. One woman grabbed her young son by his shirt collar to stop him from crossing Esteban's path. And two women rushed out of the Mercantile shortly after he had entered.

Her heart went out to her husband. He was treated as if he had some horrible disease that one could catch if they got too near him, though that wasn't true. At least they would have sympathy for such a person, his illness not being his fault. No, they feared Esteban, thought him the devil's own and blamed him for remaining with Pacquito as long as he had and not escaping.

Esteban walked out of the Mercantile and all eyes turned on him. Some men even followed him out to stare at him as if he was an oddity. Her husband stopped before stepping off the planked walkway and turned his head slowly to glare at each and every person who stared at him. They quickly averted their eyes, the men rushing back into the Mercantile and the men on the streets hurrying off.

He stood there a few minutes until everyone dispersed, and then he climbed into the carriage placing the wrapped package with sealed letters tucked beneath the string, under the seat.

They drove on passing several more buildings until they finally entered St. Lucita Plaza, the center of the small town and the gathering place for the peasants. It was busy this time of morning. The women were assembled at the well not only to collect water but also gossip. The men went about their daily chores, stopping occasionally to talk and barter.

It was a familiar scene to Rosa and one she missed. She was eager to see her friend Marinda and discover what news she had to share. Who had had babies? Who was falling in love? Who had taken ill? But the more she saw the way the people bowed their heads or averted their eyes not only at Esteban, but at her as well made her realize that things had changed. She feared that she was no longer one of them and that she would not be welcomed at the well to share gossip. She had felt homeless, adrift after losing her parents, not knowing where she belonged. She felt that way again now, the people she once called friends glaring at her as if she was a stranger just like at the hacienda. Where now did she belong?

To her husband.

She looked at him and saw how stiff he sat, his eyes straight ahead, acknowledging no one, as if he could not be bothered. Her posture had grown taut as well and she realized neither of them smiled. Don Alejandro had always greeted the townspeople with a smile when he rode through the Plaza. She, herself, had always had a smile for her friends. She had always looked forward to such pleasant exchanges, especially having to live with two people who offered only berating and not an ounce of pleasantry.

Would the townspeople believe her new life with Esteban difficult since she had yet to greet them with a smile? Would they think she too was as fearful of him as they were? The thoughts no soon as entered her head than a smile spread across her face and her hand went to squeeze her husband's arm as she said, "Please stop the carriage."

Esteban eased the horses to a stop, concerned that his wife felt ill. Before he could inquire, she was climbing out of the carriage, taking the basket of oranges with her. He watched her call out greetings to various people she knew and hurried over to a few children at play to give them each a plump orange. They smiled as Rosa ruffled their hair and they took the offered fruit without hesitation. She gave another orange to an old woman sitting on a bench, though not before peeling the skin off it for her. She then hurried over to her friend Marinda and the two women hugged like long lost sisters reunited. They spoke a few words, laughed, spoke a few more words, and then Rosa handed her the basket and what was left of the oranges.

He watched how stares turned to smiles as Rosa called out to people by name and asked how they were or asked about a family member that had been feeling poorly. Then before she reached the carriage she called out that she would light a candle for the sick and they all smiled and nodded.

Esteban jumped out of the carriage and a few men that stood close by scurried away. He went to his wife, took her hand, and assisted her into the conveyance. He then snapped the reins as soon as he returned to his seat and they proceeded to the mission.

Rosa continued to smile and wave at anyone they passed and when he brought the carriage to a stop in front of the mission he turned to her.

"Do you think to show the people that you have tamed the beast?"

"No," she said forcing her smile to remain and ignoring the tremble in her legs. "That I have survived the beast."

Esteban sat shocked as she climbed out of the carriage, though it didn't take long for him to respond. He bolted out of the vehicle to grab his wife's arm as she walked away from him and swung her around to face him. He was angry that she should think that she needed to survive him. That is what he had thought about his capture—he had needed to survive—no matter what he had needed to survive.

"So you think to survive me?"

"Isn't that what we both have done? Survive how best we could?" Her curiosity gave her the courage to seek an answer to his prior remark. "Or is there more you wanted?"

This time Padre Marten interrupted an answer. He spread his arms wide in greeting. "Welcome my children." He turned to Esteban, his glance settling with a scowl on the hand that grasped Rosa's arm. "Have you come for confession?"

"There aren't enough prayers in heaven to cleanse my soul, Padre." Esteban released his wife and returned to the carriage to grab the leather satchel. He handed it to the padre. "From my father." He reached into his pants pocket and retrieved a few coins. "My wife wishes to light some candles for friends."

Padre Marten accepted the coins and nodded to Rosa.

"Do not take long," Esteban said and walked over to the carriage. He would give her a few minutes to see to her task. He wanted to be on his way home. He preferred the solitude of the hacienda and he was beginning to enjoy time alone with his wife. He was aware that could prove dangerous, but he had decided to chance it.

Is there more you wanted?

Her question suddenly assaulted him, though it was his own words that she had tossed back at him. He did want more from her, so much more and it wasn't only about consummating their vows. He was beginning to see his wife differently than he had first thought. There was courage beneath her meek demeanor that was tempered by her kind heart. And he realized that while her courage had been stumped on by the Curros, they had been unable to rob her of her kindness.

He, on the other hand, had been robbed of every ounce of kindness he had ever possessed and he wanted to know how she had managed to hold on to her humanity while suffering such abuse.

Esteban glared at the mission doors that stood open. What was keeping her? He almost climbed down out of the carriage when he reminded himself that it hadn't been that long since she had entered the church. He would give her a few more minutes and if she didn't appear, he would go in and get her.

After barely a few minutes had passed Esteban lost his patience and hurried out of the carriage and into the church to collect his wife. He remained in the shadows when he saw that the padre was speaking with her. He moved closer with such silent steps that they did not hear him approach.

"It is good of you to light candles for your friends," the padre said standing to the side of the metal rack that held numerous candles.

"And for my husband, who is also my friend," Rosa informed him with a smile.

"Esteban is your husband, not your friend," the padre said sadly. "I doubt he knows what it is to be a friend. And a candle lit for him will do him little good if he doesn't attend confession."

Rosa softly blew out the flame at the end of the slim stick she had used to light the candles and replaced it in the glass holder along with the others to be used again. Her heart pounded and her hands trembled. She always got like that when she worried about speaking up and more often than not she kept her thought to herself. This time, however, she felt compelled to defend her husband.

"You are wrong, Padre. Esteban knows how to be a friend and is a good friend to me."

"You barely know him, my child."

Rosa raised her chin a notch. "I know that he has suffered and is deserving of compassion and forgiveness for the horrors forced on him."

"He need only attend confession to receive that."

"Perhaps, but shouldn't he be welcomed into the safety and sanctity of the church until that time?"

"There are rules—"

"That restrict rather than console an injured soul," Rosa interrupted.

"A sinful soul is far different than an injured soul."

"My husband is not sinful. He is a good man and good friend."

"And is he a good husband? Is he kind and proper in all his husbandly duties?"

Heat rushed to stain her cheeks apple red and she clenched her hands together tightly so the padre would not see how they trembled. She knew what he was asking, for without the consummation of their vows their marriage was not valid. But why would he question such a thing?

"Did you expect her to be bruised and unable to walk after I got done exerting my *husbandly duty*?"

Padre Marten gasped as Esteban stepped out of the shadows and extended his hand to his wife.

Rosa took it, relieved he was there, though as usual she was amazed that she had not heard him approach. He tucked her against his side, his arm going around her waist, and she rested there quite comfortably.

"A marriage can be dissolved if vows are not sealed," the padre said. "Do you want that, Esteban?"

Instinctively, Esteban eased Rosa closer against him. "I can assure you, Padre, I slept with my wife and I also can assure you that this marriage will never be dissolved."

Padre Marten nodded. "I accept your word, Esteban, for I do not believe you would lie to me in God's house. And it pleases me to see Rosa so happy. She deserves happiness. And think on the confessional, Esteban, for you will certainly want to attend the baptism of your first child and the many children that I am sure will follow. Bless you both." The padre made the sign of the cross in front of them. "Now I must go and administer to the sick." He turned and soon disappeared behind the altar.

Esteban took his wife's hand and led her from the church. He grabbed her around the waist and lifted her into the carriage, as if she weighed nothing, then he climbed in beside her and snapped the reins.

Rosa wasn't surprised when he directed the horse away not only from the mission but the town itself. This way would take a bit longer to get home, but it was apparent that he didn't want to ride through town again. She was glad she had gotten a chance to give Marinda the oranges and had told her that she would return another day to visit with her.

Her thoughts were far too concerned with the incident in the church to even consider a visit with her friend. She wished that she could discuss it with Esteban, but she worried that she had expended her courage for the day and would not fare well against his biting temper if unleashed.

So she sat in silence focused on the lovely day and the beautiful landscape, trying to forget that their marriage was not truly valid in the eyes of the church. The thought turned persistent and soon the landscape lost its appeal and all she thought about was... that she wasn't truly Esteban's wife and wouldn't be until... the image hit her hard.

She and Esteban naked in bed together and he kissing her while his fingers slipped between her legs and...

Her hand flew to her stomach where it felt as if thousands of butterflies fluttered inside her.

"Are you all right?" he asked, his hand quickly

covering hers.

His hand completely devoured her small one and she noticed how long his fingers were and once again the image hit and it was as if she could feel his slim fingers penetrating her. She pressed her hand to her stomach harder, hoping to ease the ache.

Esteban pulled the horse to a stop and turned to his wife. "What's wrong? Don't you feel well?"

What was she to say to him? *I'm thinking of you naked, kissing me and touching me.*

She shut her eyes against her wicked thoughts, though he was her husband so how could they be wicked? She hurried to say, "My stomach is a bit upset."

"Can you make it to the stream? It's not far and the cool water may help you."

She nodded thinking how she would like to dunk herself in the water and chase away the throb between her legs.

They were there in no time and Esteban helped her down out of the carriage and kept his arm around her waist until they got to the stream. He helped her sit near the bank, and then dunked his handkerchief in the water, rinsed it, and gently pressed it to her flushed cheeks.

"I would ask you if you were pregnant, but I know that is not possible. So why does your stomach trouble you?"

He had the most gorgeous sinful dark eyes she had ever seen. Marinda had been right when she had warned her that day not to look upon Esteban.

His eyes captivated and captured, never letting go, not that you wanted him to. You were lost once he had firm hold of you with one penetrating glance.

Penetrating. Damn, why did she have to think about that again?

She closed her eyes and shook her head trying to rid herself of the persistent image. Then she opened her eyes only to meet his eyes once again and feel her body continue to tingle with pleasure.

"You will tell me the truth," he said, as if she had no choice.

But how did she tell her husband that she had never expected to tingle at his touch or at the mere thought of it? She was too new to this marriage, yet to be sealed, to speak so intimately with him. And to outright lie to him was no way to start a marriage, especially after just coming from church.

So when she finally spoke it was the truth. "It upsets me to see how people treat you."

"They fear me," —he paused for a moment— "don't you?"

"Fear has no place in a marriage." And she surprised him with a generous smile. "My mother and father smiled, laughed, and hugged often. My father would tell me how rich we were, though it was not the type of wealth you could see. He told me that love—true love—grows and thrives and produces a harvest of happiness with each passing year."

"So you don't fear me?"

"I don't want to fear you. I want us to be friends."

"So you said."

"You said you wanted more."

"I do."

"What more do you want?"

"I want all of you," he said adamantly.

She wasn't sure if it was a tingle of fear or passion that ran through her, but since there hadn't been an ounce of menace in his voice she tended to believe that passion was the culprit for her reaction.

"As my wife you belong to me, but can you give every part of yourself to me, Rosa? Can you surrender yourself completely?"

The words were out of her mouth before she could stop them. "Can you do the same? Surrender yourself completely to me?"

He sprang to his feet. "It's time to go." He didn't offer his hand. He turned and walked to the carriage.

She stared after him for a moment, and then went to get to her feet. He was there before she realized it, his hands at her waist lifting her to stand. When she raised her head, she caught a spark of anger in his eyes.

"I surrendered myself once... I'll never do so again."

Chapter Twelve

Rosa watched her husband walk away from her, his strides unhurried, though determined. As soon as they had reached the hacienda, he had helped her out of the carriage, then turned and walked away. She couldn't help but feel as if he abandoned her. Was he walking away from their marriage? Their vows had yet to be sealed, so in the eyes of the church they were not truly married. Would it remain that way unless... she surrendered *completely* to him? Would he settle for nothing less?

She entered the hacienda, her mind troubled.

"Rosa."

She turned to see Dona Valerianna in the small parlor where the woman spent a good amount of time on her embroidery. Rosa joined her, though she would have preferred to go to her bed chamber and be alone.

"Was there a letter from my daughter?"

Rosa hadn't realized that she had the package and letter that Esteban had picked up from the Mercantile pressed to her chest. She had scooped it up just before he had scooped her out of the carriage.

She handed the package to Dona Valerianna.

"A letter from Crista," Dona Valerianna said

with excitement as she slipped it from beneath the thin rope tied around the package. "And the package I have been waiting for,"—she smiled and handed it to Rosa—"for you my dear."

Rosa stared at the package wrapped in brown paper. It had been so long since she had gotten a gift and the ones she remembered receiving had been small items that her father or mother had handmade.

"Take it, it's for you," Dona Valerianna urged and Rosa did.

Rosa carefully untied the string and peeled away the brown paper. Words eluded her as she stared at drawing paper, a tin of charcoals, and a tin of graphite sticks. Never had she imagined having such precious drawing tools.

Rosa turned to Dona Valerianna with tears pooling in her eyes. "I don't know what to say. Thank you doesn't seem adequate."

Dona Valerianna reached out and patted Rosa's arm. "You have a talent and you should have what you need to grow that talent. And I so want to display your drawings throughout the hacienda. I have also inquired about sending for an easel, paints, and canvas for you."

"That is too much," Rosa protested, already feeling the woman had overindulged.

"Nonsense, I hope one day you will do a portrait of the family so that we will all live on for future generations to know us."

Rosa did not believe herself that talented, though she would love to attempt such a painting, but first she would practice with these drawing tools and grow her talent as Dona Valerianna suggested.

"Now I must see what my daughter has to say," Dona Valerianna said breaking the wax seal on the letter. "Oh my, she'll be leaving Spain in the next week or so." Tears pooled in her eyes. "I have missed her so much and she is so happy to be returning home. I cannot wait to tell Alejandro."

Raised voices had both women jumping. Esteban and his father were arguing, not an unusual occurrence as Rosa had come to learn, but one that never failed to upset Dona Valerianna.

"Esteban and his father had such a wonderful relationship before... " Dona Valerianna turned her head, though not before Rosa caught the glimmer of tears in her eyes. "I was hoping they could once again... " She shook her head as if she knew it was not possible.

"Esteban is not a young, defenseless boy anymore," Rosa said. *And I am not a young, defenseless girl any longer.* The thought startled her, for she had felt defenseless when living with the Curros. And while there was a degree of obedience expected from her now, no one treated her badly... no one raised a hand to her.

"No he's not," Dona Valerianna agreed with a gentle shake of her head.

"It must be extremely difficult for Don Alejandro to deal with a full grown son when last he saw him, he was only a young boy. And to not have been part of guiding him into manhood must be heartbreaking for him as it is for you."

A tear poised at the corner of Dona Valerianna's eye and she smiled. "My son is fortunate to have you as his wife and I hope one day he realizes it."

"Perhaps with time Esteban and I will come to realize how fortunate we both are to have found each other."

The single tear spilled from Dona Valerianna's eye and rolled slowly down her cheek. "I pray that that be so, for I believe you are good for each other."

~~~

Rosa sat in the garden alone, twilight having settled hours ago and supper long passed, Esteban having been absent from the meal. She hugged herself, the night bringing with it a slight wind that chilled. She thought about the day and possibilities. Dona Valerianna felt they were good for each other and Esteban wanted more than friendship from her. And though she still had to get to know her husband, she was—to her growing surprise—attracted to him.

She sighed and cast a glance to the heavens and recited a long remembered prayer her mother had taught her.

"Do not waste your breath on prayers."

Rosa startled almost jumping off the bench, but caught herself and turned only to find no one standing there. Suddenly the night shadows seemed ominous and she grew anxious. Esteban was somewhere in the shadows. How long had he been there watching her?

This time it wasn't the chilled wind that caused her to hug herself as she peered into the surrounding darkness.

"You should have a shawl," he scolded as he stepped out of the shadows and slipped off his jacket. He went to her and draped it over her shoulders, his strong hands giving her shoulders a firm squeeze, though he would much rather take her in his arms and let his heated body warm her. The thought aroused him and he wisely took a step away.

She was struck speechless by his appearance. His dark shoulder length hair was in slight disarray and only added to his sinfully handsome features. But it was his body that more caught her eye. He stood poised, his muscles taut as if he was always ready to defend. Or perhaps attack? She was sure whatever the case, it would be an instinctive reaction.

"Prayers are never wasted," Rosa said, the scent of him drifting off his jacket to torment her senses. He always smelled of the earth after a rainstorm when its scent was most potent. And tonight there was a hint of grapes added to it, which meant he had been in the vineyards.

"I would argue that point most vigorously."

"I can understand you feeling that way with what you have been through."

"Your situation wasn't ideal, and yet, you still pray?" he asked wondering how she held on to her faith when the Curros had treated her so badly.

"If I had surrendered my faith, then the Curros would have robbed me of everything, and there was no way I would let them rob me of my soul."

His hand snapped out, grabbed her arm, and yanked her up so fast that her gasp caught in her throat for a moment before it rushed out of her.

"Pacquito whipped my soul out of me. It would be wise of you to remember that."

Anger, hate, and hurt filled his dark eyes and Rosa's heart went out to him. She had suffered many a beating but nothing that could compare to what he must have endured.

She placed a gentle hand to his cheek and her cool palm sizzled from the heat of his skin. "No, Pacquito did not take your soul." She moved her hand to rest against his chest, the heat radiating through his shirt. "It's inside you locked away waiting."

"For what?"

"For you to free it."

A smile more sly than pleasant worked at the corners of his mouth as he leaned down to whisper, "No, it remains locked out of fear, for if it ever surfaces it will be consumed by evil."

"You are not evil," she whispered, as if it was a secret.

"Let me prove how foolish it would be for you to believe that. Let me tell you what I'm thinking at this very moment," —his whisper grew harsh— "I want to strip you bare, bend you over the bench and jam myself into you over and over and over.

And if that isn't enough to satisfy me, then I'll see you down on your knees in front of me so that you can bring me to pleasure with your mouth."

If Esteban hadn't been holding her so firmly by the arm, she would have collapsed, her legs having turned weak from the shock of his blunt words and the vivid images they had produced. But if he had thought to repulse her, he was quite wrong. It actually had the opposite effect on her. She found her passion aroused. Was she as sinful as him? Or did she find her husband far more appealing than she ever thought possible? And if so could she possibly completely surrender to him and do those things that sounded so wicked but had aroused her?

She hadn't realized that her head had drooped as her mind had grown heavy with thought and when she slowly raised it... his mouth was a breath away from hers. In the next instant, his lips laid claim to hers like a man staking his territory.

He kissed her with such resolve that a tingle rushed through her and settled between her legs, leaving her throbbing. He pulled his mouth away, his teeth nibbling along her bottom lip, tugging and nipping with an eagerness that tantalized. Then he traveled down the side of her neck savoring every bit of her warm skin, a nip here, a faint lick there, and then a sharp nip that sent a passionate shiver through her. He retraced his path returning to her lips. His kiss turned hungry as did her need to feed on him. It was as if she couldn't get enough of him. The more the kiss lingered, the more she wanted. And it was easy to see that he felt the same.

Esteban felt his need grow harder and harder. If he didn't stop soon, he would do exactly as he had told her... he'd stripe her, bend her over the bench, and...

He yanked his mouth away from hers and stepped back, his hand shooting out to steady her swaying body.

Rosa stared at him confused.

"You don't want to step into my hell," he warned and disappeared into the darkness before she could stop him.

She had to sit, her legs weak, and his support gone. She pulled his jacket tighter around her and peered into the shadows. Was Esteban there somewhere watching her? She didn't care for the fact that he could approach undetectable until he was practically on top of her. She would never know when he was near or if he watched her. The thought unnerved her and she got up and hurried off seeking the solitude of her room. There she had a degree of privacy, though how private was anyplace on the hacienda when Esteban seemed to appear out of thin air.

Rosa sat on the end of the bed, Esteban's jacket still around her. How could passion for him strike her one moment and fear the next? She shook her head annoyed. She had been devastated when her parents died and even more distressed when she had been placed with the Curros and discovered the type of people they were. But she had been taught to survive and always remain strong. Her mother had told her that her prayers would not fail her and in a way they hadn't. She had prayed daily to be removed from the Curros and into a loving home.

And her prayers had been answered. Don Alejandro and Dona Valerianna were good and loving people and treated her well. Her life had improved tremendously being wed to Esteban. What more could she ask for?

I want more.

Esteban's words resonated in her head and she nodded, agreeing with him. She wanted more herself. She wanted a good and loving marriage and she wondered if they could have one. Passion certainly sparked easily between them but what good was passion without love. The young *ninas* had always paid the price for letting passion rule. And then they were left with nothing, not an ounce of respect.

She sighed and reluctantly removed Esteban's jacket and draped it over a chair. She wasn't sure what to do. She did want to learn more about him, for she felt it would help her to better understand her husband. The passion, however, was a different matter. She wasn't quite sure how to deal with it and that left her feeling vulnerable.

But no matter what, there was one thing she was certain about... she would survive. No matter what happened, she would survive.

Chapter Thirteen

Rosa sat in the garden, her drawing tools lying untouched next to her on the bench annoyed that her husband had kept his distance from her these last couple of days. How could they have any kind of marriage if they barely spent time together? And the more she had thought about it the more she realized that she wanted a chance at a good marriage. After all, she was stuck with him for the rest of their lives.

Stuck.

She had been stuck with the Curros. She didn't want to be stuck with a husband. She had to smile. She wanted more just as he did, but how to have more was the question.

The sound of laughter caught Rosa's attention. She stood and turned quickly, thinking she recognized the voice. But it couldn't be, though she hoped it was. A smile spread across Rosa's face as soon as she saw her friend Marinda talking and laughing with Dolores. When her friend caught sight of her, she hurried to Rosa and they threw their arms around each other and hugged tightly.

Rosa took hold of Marinda's hand and walked her to the roughhewn table and two chairs that were shaded by a large oak tree. As they sat, Rosa said, "I'm so glad you've come to visit."

"I've been wanting to, but Paco said that I must wait for an invitation. It is what the nobles do and now that you are one of them..." Marinda shook her head. "I told him that he was crazy. You are who you are and no one would ever change you. Then this morning the Cesare carriage arrived at my humble abode and I was told that my presence was requested at the hacienda." Marinda's smile grew alarmingly wide. "I tell you, I hopped in that carriage so fast that I had heads spinning. And the looks I got riding through town." She clapped her hands. "It was wonderful. I felt like a noble. I even waved to our friends just as you had done." She laughed. "They were too shocked to wave back. And oh how I'm looking forward to the ride home. Then I arrived here and Dolores was waiting and brought me to you."

Rosa wondered who had sent for her friend, perhaps Don Alejandro or his wife had taken pity on her. Or could it have been her husband? Whoever it had been, she was grateful. Marinda was the distraction she needed from her worries. Her friend always had funny gossip to share or stories of her and Paco that never failed to warm Rosa's heart.

They were soon deep in conversation, Marinda telling her all the latest news from town. The only time Marinda turned speechless was when two servants arrived and placed a bountiful meal on the table.

Rosa knew what her friend was thinking. This would feed her and Paco for a week or more, though knowing Marinda, she would share with others.

"You will take some home with you," Rosa offered and waited for Marinda to protest.

She looked ready to, and then stopped. "I would refuse your kind offer, but I know of some who could use this food."

"Then if not for yourself, take it for others, though I would recommend that you keep some of the fruit tarts for you and Paco, they are delicious."

Marinda laughed. "That's if I don't eat them all now."

The two friends talked in between enjoying the meal. It was when they finished and were enjoying the last of the pitcher of lemonade that the conversation turned to Esteban.

"There are whispers in town about your husband," Marinda said.

"That is nothing new, there are always whispers about Esteban," Rosa said. "He is a far better man than most think of him."

"The people are afraid that he will rejoin Pacquito's band of renegades?"

Rosa could not hide her shock. Her eyes turned wide and her hands began to tremble. "He would never return to that life," Rosa said, not doubting her words for a minute. "You don't know what he suffered at their hands."

"Then why did he stay with them? It is the question on everyone's minds. The renegades trained him to fight, so why not leave when he was strong enough to? Paco spoke with someone here at the hacienda that has seen Esteban practice with his knife and pistol. Paco got chills when the person told him how Esteban hit his target dead center at every try. And the speed in which he drew his knife was beyond anything he had ever seen. So with such skills why did he remain with the renegades?"

Rosa didn't have an answer for her friend and she wasn't sure how to defend him against such an accusation. She could understand everyone's concern and curiosity, for she wondered herself. What could have kept him hostage to Pacquito when he had been skilled enough to break free?

"I wish I had an answer for you, Marinda," she said. "I can only tell you that I believe my husband is a good and honest man."

"You barely know him, though,"—Marinda hesitated—"much can be learned about a man by the way he treats a woman in bed."

Rosa stared at her friend not knowing what to say. She did not want anyone to know that her vows had yet to be consummated. People would wonder why and when she attended mass there would be whispers and stares and evil looks from the Curros.

Marinda took her silence as fear and demanded, "Has he hurt you?"

"No. No, Esteban did not hurt me."

"Then what is wrong,"—her hand flew to her chest—"oh Lord, don't tell me you have yet to seal your vows."

Rosa clamped her mouth shut refusing to say a

word, though she didn't have to, her actions sealed it for her friend.

"Oh my, has he not sealed his vows because he wants no part of this marriage?"

That thought had never entered Rosa's head. Could it be possible? Or had it been her fault?

Rosa felt the need to offer some type of explanation. "I drank too much at our wedding and he left me to recover and sleep."

"This is good," her friend encouraged. "It speaks well of his character that he considered you were in no shape to make love. But since then?"

The memory of waking to him holding her in his arms brought a smile to her face. "He comforted me from a bad dream." She refused to think on what had followed or her cheeks would burn red.

"He does sound considerate," Marinda said, as if it was difficult to believe. "You have to stop falling asleep, unless... don't you want to make love with him?"

I'm a savage and will take you like one.

Not his exact words, but what had been implied. Making love had never been mentioned and she couldn't help but wonder if love would ever be a part of their marriage.

"You hesitate in answering," Marinda said. "Perhaps I ask too many questions. Paco warns me it will be different now between you and me."

"Never," Rosa said, reaching out and taking firm hold of her friend's hand. "Never will it be different between us. We have been friends too long, really more like sisters and I could not bear to lose you."

Tears came to Marinda's eyes. "I feel the same way, but you live this grand life now and—"

Rosa squeezed her hand. "That changes nothing. I will visit you and you will visit me and our children will be friends just as we are."

"That would be nice," Marinda said. "I would love for my children to be able to play here in such a lovely garden while we talk."

"And so they shall," Rosa assured her.

Marinda grinned. "Not if you keep falling asleep."

They both laughed and talk turned to babies.

"I'm hoping to have news to share with you soon," Marinda said, smiling. "And who knows we may find ourselves pregnant at the same time."

Rosa smiled, though made no comment. She had to first make the prospect a possibility and the thought did intimidate her.

They talked for another hour, and then Dolores interrupted to let them know that the carriage was there to take her home.

Rosa gave her a hug. "I'll visit you soon."

Marinda grinned. "I don't mind visiting you."

Rosa laughed. "I'll send the carriage for you, Dona Marinda."

"How lovely of you, Dona Rosa."

The two women laughed, hugged again, and as Rosa waved to a fading Marinda a sense of loneliness washed over her. She missed her best friend and wished that she could see her more often as she once had.

With a sigh of resignation, Rosa turned and returned to the garden to gather her drawing tools. Drawing lost all its appeal as did approaching suppertime. At first she thought it would be nice to finally share a meal with others, having eaten alone for so many years. She had thought there would be talk, laughter, and smiles. It was nothing like that. A lingering tension existed, making the meals uncomfortable. How could anyone eat under such unpleasant conditions? She wondered if she could feign a headache or something, then she could have a meal brought to her. She could even take it out to the garden and enjoy the lovely scent of flowers.

Fate seemed to be on her side when she entered the kitchen planning to feign a headache and ask for her meal to be served in her quarters.

Dolores smiled when she saw her. "No one will be present for the evening meal tonight."

"Why?" she asked curious over everyone's absence.

"I do not know why Dona Alejandro and Esteban will not be here, but as for Dona Valerianna... her head aches and she requested her meal to be brought to her quarters. So you are free to eat wherever you choose tonight."

Rosa didn't hesitate. Her choice came easily. "I'll have supper here with you."

Dolores shook a finger at her. "How many times must I remind you that you are part of the Cesare family now and do not belong in the kitchen?"

Rosa smiled. "Then we shall eat out under the stars." Before Dolores could protest Rosa got to work snatching up a gaily colored tablecloth from the stack kept in a large basket and hurrying outside with it. In the next few minutes she had the long wood table appearing as if there was about to be a party. Glass jars held candles while others overflowed with flowers. Baskets held fruit and bread and plates sat stacked in case anyone else wished to join them.

Rosa's enthusiasm soon had Dolores joining in and others as well. Soon the table was laden with *Tortillas*, *Torrejas*, corn dough fritters that Rosa's mother had often made and *Relleno de Carne* a chopped beef mixture that was a favorite of her father's and only made on special occasions. One of the girls squealed with detail when Dolores added a bowl of *Jiricalla*, delicious custard, to the table.

Soon there was laughter and talk and Rosa finally felt at home here with the other peasants. They had also forgotten her status and spoke with her as if she was one of them. To Rosa it was what she had longed for since her parents' death. It was as if she was with family once again.

Rosa learned who was wed to who, who was expecting a baby, who was not feeling well and needed help with their workload. It was the most pleasant evening she had spent since her arrival here and she wished that the Cesares could see what a meal should be like.

Silence suddenly struck the few who had lingered at the table after the meal was finished, and then they hurried off without a word. Rosa didn't have to turn around to see what had caused their reaction. She knew her husband stood behind her.

Dolores was the only one who didn't leave, though she stood. "May I get you something, Don Esteban?"

"I'll have a glass of wine with *my wife*." The strength of his voice made it clear that he wanted to be alone with her.

Dolores was quick to pour him a glass of wine and hurry off.

"You will cause undue stress on my parents if they were ever to find out that you had supper with the servants."

"I meant no disrespect, and I so enjoyed it. I hadn't realized that some who work here are relatives of people I know in town. It was so nice to speak with them as it was to visit with Marinda today." If she hoped by mentioning her friend that he would admit to being the one who had arranged the visit, she was disappointed when he made no reference to it.

He sipped his wine and kept a steady eye on her. "Do you like it here on the hacienda?"

"It is a much more favorable one to life with the Curros."

"That's not what I asked. Do you like it here?"

Rosa reached out for the decanter of wine to fill her empty glass.

Esteban grabbed the crystal decanter before she could reach it. "You need fortification before answering me?"

She smiled and shook her head. "One of the things I favor here is the wine."

Esteban didn't hide his smile. He removed the stopper and filled her glass. "And are there things you don't favor?"

She nodded and considered her response.

"Tell me," he said sharply when she hesitated.

If he wanted the truth, she would give it to him. "The place lacks smiles and laughter... and the cherished comfort of a loving family."

"There is no family here. There hasn't been in some time." He took a sip of wine and appeared deep in thought, or perhaps memories, then he finally spoke. "I wasn't surprised to learn that my sister Crista got sent away. After my capture my parents sent her off to Spain to be educated, or so they led everyone to believe. But it was fear for her safety that had them rushing her off and leaving this place empty."

"But you have returned and so shall your sister. It will be a home once again."

"You forget the one thing that makes a home a home," Esteban said.

Rosa didn't forget and she didn't think Esteban did either and so she waited for him to answer.

"Love," he finally said. There is no love here."

"There is plenty of love here, though people fear to show it."

"Love should not let fear stop it."

"Fear can do much damage."

"A strong enough love can conquer fear."

"But fear can overpower and leave even the strongest love vulnerable," Rosa said and wondered over their difference of opinion. He felt love should conquer all and she had learned that fear could be a deterrent to love.

"In the end though, would love succeed?"

She pondered the question but more so why he asked it, yet she responded instinctively, "That would depend."

"On what?"

"On how strongly *two* people loved."

Esteban leaned closer. "And what if one loved strong enough for the both?"

What was he truly asking of her? Did he expect her to love him, yet not return it? She answered without further thought. "It would take great foolishness or tremendous courage for one to love strongly and not have that love returned."

He stared at her, as if her response was not what he expected, and then he asked the very question that she thought to ask him. "Are you foolish or courageous, Rosa?"

Foolishly courageous. The answer had popped quickly into her head and she caught it before it could tumble past her lips.

"No answer?" he stood abruptly. "If you ever find an answer, let me know."

Rosa watched him disappear into the shadows and could not help but wonder how he would have answered the question.

Chapter Fourteen

Esteban rode along the ridge at the far end of the Cesare property. It was an overcast day and the smell of rain hung in the air promising more than a simple rain shower. He didn't know what brought him out here today, this far from the hacienda. Or did he? He gazed over the land—his land—and felt a tug in his gut. This was the first time he had felt a connection to it since his return. It was the first time he felt he had a future here.

Rosa.

He had grown annoyed with her last night when she had not answered him. But then what had he wanted from her? Had he wanted her to be strong enough to love him regardless of how he felt about her? Or had he hoped that her love could spark even the smallest bit of love that Pacquito had failed to beat out of him? Or was it hopeless? Would he never be able to love?

He shouldn't have been surprised, though he was, this morning when he had found that Rosa had breakfast set out on the terrace for his family to enjoy. She had even had the table set more gaily, similar to last night's table. Though instead of jars filled with flowers, crystal vases overflowed with freshly cut ones. A basket of grapes, still on the vine, sat in the center of the table and a bright yellow tablecloth struck the eye and should have brought a smile to everyone's face, but it hadn't.

Conversation had remained stilted, his mother and father as restrained as ever. By the end of the meal he wasn't surprised to see his father and mother go their separate ways, though at one time his father would have asked her to join him to inspect the vineyard that produced her favorite wine. And she would have accepted. Now it seemed that his mother and father rarely went anywhere together.

He wondered if Rosa could change life here on the hacienda or would she become as remote as the others in his family. He hoped she didn't. He had looked forward to seeing her smiling face each day. It had sparked an ounce of hope that life could possibly turn good. With hope, however, came concern that it could be snatched away from him in an instant, just as he had been snatched away from his family.

He knew Pacquito all too well. There was no way the man would allow him to walk away without retribution. He would be deemed weak in the eyes of his men and that Pacquito would not tolerate. It was only a matter of time before he came after Esteban... or someone he loved.

He tensed, every muscle growing taut. He would kill, and not quickly, anyone who would dare harm his family. It had been one of the reasons why he had considered not returning home, though in the end the tug to reunite with his family had been too strong to ignore. He had wanted, had ached, to return home ever since his capture. And he was glad he had.

He continued to glance out over the land and wondered if there would come a day that he would take this ride with his son alongside him. He had long ago dismissed the thought of children in his future, but with Rosa that was now a possibility.

He scowled. Of course he'd have to make it a possibility first, and that would mean...

He grew aroused and his mood darkened. How could he touch his wife after all the evil and vile things he had done? The spark of hope and joy the morning meal had brought faded quickly and he turned his horse around and rode back to the hacienda annoyed that he had allowed himself such foolish thoughts.

He arrived at the hacienda to find Dolores rushing his wife along one of the garden paths toward the hacienda, neither woman wearing a smile.

"Is something wrong?" he asked stepping in their path and bringing them to an abrupt halt.

Dolores explained. "Padre Marten is here and wishes to speak with Rosa."

"Did he say what he wished to speak with her about?" Esteban asked, stretching his hand out to his wife.

Rosa went to his side and took his hand, grateful he was there, since she worried over the padre's presence. Could he have possibly found out that their vows had yet to be sealed? Could he somehow nullify the marriage? She was surprised by how fearful she grew at the thought. She had not wanted to wed Esteban, but now that they were wed... she didn't find it all that terrible. And besides, she had come to care for her husband and...

She almost blushed at the sinful thoughts that filled her head and rushed a tingle between her legs. She turned her attention back to the matter at hand and tried desperately to ignore the spark of desire that seemed to ignite whenever Esteban was near.

"I only know that it is very important that I bring Rosa to your mother's parlor," Dolores said.

"Then let's see what the good padre wants." Esteban tightened his grip on his wife's hand and led the way.

Padre Marten paced the parlor where Dona Valerianna sat, her stitching resting in her lap. Esteban did not like the man's nervous strides or how he paled when he caught sight of him in the doorway. He had a feeling that the padre was not there to deliver good news.

Don Alejandro entered just as Esteban eased his wife down to take a seat and placed a firm hand on her shoulder.

Don Alejandro acknowledged the padre with a nod, and asked as he went to stand beside his wife, "How can we be of service, Padre?"

The padre wrung his hands as he took a step forward. "I never thought I would have to divulge a secret I have kept these many years, but circumstances have changed and the truth must now be told."

Rosa felt a chill rush through her and she shivered. Her husband's hand gave her shoulder a reassuring squeeze, the strength of it helped calm her.

The padre continued. "Many years ago baby, twin girls were left at the mission in Los Angeles with a letter instructing that the girls were to be found good homes and that the church would be compensated monthly."

The padre shook his head. "I was visiting the mission at the time and I and the padre there discussed the matter. Since the letter wanted the girls separated, we thought it was best that I take one of the babies and place her with a family in St. Lucita." He looked to Rosa. "That baby was you, Rosalita."

Rosa was too shocked to speak and had no time to digest the stunning news since the padre hurried on.

"It has recently been discovered that the twins were actually the daughters of Spanish nobles and their parents are in Los Angeles with the one twin Gabriella and have requested that the other twin,"—the padre gave a nod to Rosa— "that would be you, Rosa, join them there."

"My wife isn't going anywhere," Esteban said sharply.

The padre spoke with nervous patience. "While I advocate a wife obeying her husband, in this special circumstance, I believe it should be the wife's decision."

"No, what you're saying is that the church must now answer to the mysterious man who has been supporting it all these years," Esteban corrected. "That, Padre, is not going to happen. My wife is not going anywhere."

"No, Esteban, what I'm saying is that perhaps Rosa would like to meet not only the sister she never knew she had, but her true parents as well."

"I will say this only one more time," Esteban said his eyes focused directly on the padre. "My wife isn't going anywhere." He then stepped in front of Rosa and extended his hand.

Rosa was still shocked by the news, though she wanted desperately to speak to the padre, ask him questions, but most of all she wanted to go meet the family she never knew she had. However, she knew it would not be wise to disagree with her husband in front of everyone. She would talk with him privately and let him know how she felt. She only hoped it would make a difference.

She took his hand and walked out of the room with him.

They didn't exchange one word until they reached their bedchamber.

"You're not going," Esteban said releasing her hand and taking a step away from her.

She wasn't sure if he was angry or upset and at the moment it didn't matter to her. What mattered was why he would deprive her of meeting a family she never knew she had.

"Why not?" she asked firmly.

"Don't question me on this," he warned

sternly.

"How can I not question you?" she said with a sense of disbelief. "I have just been told that my parents who I loved dearly are not truly my parents. That my parents are of noble birth and that I have a sister and that they wish to meet me. How can you not let me go and meet my family?"

"You have a family here."

"Do I?" she asked, her temper beginning to rise. "Families care and love, share laughter and sorrow, I see none of that in this house. You are all distant, rarely smile, and barely spend time together and when you do, you are all so stiff and proper. Where is the love?"

"And you think the family you have never met will give you all that?"

"I don't know, but I would like to find out. I would like to meet my twin sister and see if there is a bond there between us even though we have been kept apart all these years."

Esteban knew he was being unfair, but he couldn't take a chance, not now. Pacquito could be waiting just for such a moment. And it wouldn't matter if he took a dozen or more vaqueros with them, Pacquito's men would easily conquer them and take him and Rosa prisoner. He needed to see this ended with Pacquito before he took such a chance.

He doubted Rosa would understand and he would give no explanation. "You are not going anywhere."

She wanted to snap at him and tell him that she

certainly was going to Los Angeles, and then a thought struck her. "Then let me invite them here."

"No," he snapped. He had enough people to keep safe. Adding more would only make it that more difficult to protect his wife.

His absolute refusal had her finally spitting out her anger. "You have no right to make this decision for me. I will go to Los Angeles regardless of what you say."

He stared at her a moment, and then he smiled, though it was not a friendly one. Then his dark eyes narrowed as his brow knitted tightly, and he took a step toward her.

Rosa did not know how she held her ground, though it probably was because her legs grew weak with fear and she would not be able to move them if she wanted to.

His hand reached out slowly and though it was obvious that he had no intentions of striking her, she felt the need to cringe, not that she did. She tucked her fear away and stood strong, though she worried that her trembling legs would give out any moment.

He ran his hand down her soft cheek and took hold of her chin as he stepped even closer to her, their bodies faintly touching. "It would be a mistake to defy me."

She responded with more bravado than she felt. "And what would you do to me, Esteban... whip me?"

She wished she could take the words back as soon as they fell from her lips, especially since he drew back for a moment as if she had slapped him.

He recovered quickly enough, his smile disappearing and his expression turning harsh. "Why would I mar your lovely skin when there are better ways to inflict punishment?" He lowered his lips to hers, though before he kissed her he whispered, "Much better ways."

Rosa shivered and if his arm hadn't coiled around her waist she would have collapsed. His kiss was gentle and yet beneath it she felt a tremor, almost as if he restrained himself.

As he ended the kiss, his hand slipped around her throat and though he caressed it, she sensed the tension in his touch.

"Don't ever defy me, wife, or you will regret it."

He moved so fast that her breath caught as he scooped her up and had her on the bed before she realized his intentions. His next move shocked her. He stripped the black sash from around his waist and quickly wrapped it around her wrists and then tied the end to the headboard, forcing her arms to stretch up above her head.

Fear trickled over her as he sat on the bed beside her.

"You would make a perfect sex slave."

Rosa gasped and Esteban laughed.

"Pacquito kept them to please his men. I became quite proficient at making a woman an obedient slave to serve my needs." He braced his hands on either side of her head and nuzzled her neck, kissing and nipping along her delicate skin, then settled his lips near her ear. "I'll strip you naked and keep you tied to this bed, and then I'll take you over and over and over again."

"You wouldn't." She hadn't intended to sound as if she pleaded, but her words rang like a plea to her ears.

His hand gently slipped over her breast and gave her nipple a taunting pinch. "Try me."

She stared at him in disbelief, knowing he would. And worse, wondered why the image his words evoked had brought a tingle between her legs.

She hadn't realized that she was squirming and wasn't sure if it was a feeble attempt to free herself or that the ache between her legs needed attention.

Esteban became aware of it himself and he sat up and ran his hand down her body to settle much too intimately against her. "Shall I give you a taste of what your defiance will cost you?"

He rubbed the palm of his hand against her mound and she gasped at the bolt of pleasure that shot through her. Before she could recover, his hand had slipped beneath her dress and his finger slide effortless between her legs to settle inside her.

"Wet and ready," he murmured seeming surprised.

And then he began to... torment her. It was the only way she could explain it for she felt as if she wanted to explode with pleasure and yet he stopped her just as... he continued the torment until it became so unbearable that she had to bite her lips to stop from crying out.

He stopped suddenly and brought his face inches from hers. "Defy me and the next time I'll have you begging for mercy."

He untied the sash and striped it from her wrists, then walked out of the room slamming the door behind him.

Rosa sat shaken, not sure which she should be more upset about, her husband's threat to make her his sex slave or her reaction to it? Whatever was the matter with her? Would she need to go and confess her sins?

She blushed at the thought. Never could she tell the padre what had happened here. He would not only think the worst of Esteban, he would warn her that she was being corrupted by evil. There was no one to turn to, no one to help her understand the right or wrong of it.

Would her twin understand?

The thought had her jumping out of bed. It was imperative that she go meet her true family. It could make all the difference. She straightened her dress and ran her fingers through her hair to tame the wild strands, then she hurried off to find the padre.

It took only a moment to learn from the servants that Don Alejandro had offered the padre a meal before he took his leave. He took the meal in the kitchen so that he could spend some time with the servants.

Rosa hurried along, hoping he was still there. She was relieved when she saw him sitting outside at the table enjoying his food with a couple of servants and Dolores.

Padre Marten smiled when he spotted her and waved. "Come join us."

Rosa didn't hesitate. She took a seat.

After several minutes of pleasant conversation dotted with laughter, Dolores ordered everyone back to work, leaving Rosa alone with the padre.

As soon as she did, the padre turned to Rosa. "You want to make the trip to Los Angeles to meet your family, don't you?"

"Very much," Rosa admitted, trying to keep the eagerness out of her voice.

"Has your husband changed his mind about allowing you to go there?"

Her shoulders slumped and she shook her head. "Unfortunately, no."

"I don't think Esteban realizes the importance of you going and what it means."

Rosa turned a confused look on the padre.

"My dear," he said like a patient father speaking to his daughter. "This means that you are not just a mere peasant, but of noble birth. And he cannot refuse nobility."

"That would not matter to Esteban," Rosa said.

"Perhaps but it would matter to the wealthy hacienda owners in St. Lucita. No longer could they look down on you. Actually, you would be far superior to them."

Rosa shook her head. "That doesn't matter to me, Padre. What does is meeting my true parents and my twin sister." She smiled just thinking of the idea that she had a twin. "I'm so excited at the thought that I have a sibling."

"Then you must go to Los Angeles," the padre insisted.

"But how when Esteban refuses to allow it?"

"Pray," he instructed. "God will find a way to reunite you with your family whether Esteban agrees or not."

~~~

Rosa's prayers were answered much sooner than she had expected. She took it as a good sign. She was doing the right thing by going off and meeting her family, at least that's what she kept telling herself. Besides if her husband could go off for a few days and not even tell her that he was leaving, why shouldn't she be able to do the same?

A shiver ran through her recalling Esteban's warning of what he would do to her if she defied him. And though it definitely should have been a deterrent, it didn't stop her. She would face her fate upon her return.

It was Teresa, the young servant girl who when asked if she had seen Esteban informed Rosa that he had left early that morning. When she had asked when Esteban was expected to return, Teresa had lowered her head and suggested that Rosa speak with Don Alejandro.

It was after her brief talk with her father-in-law that her decision had been made. Esteban would not be returning for a week or more, though Don Alejandro did not explain why or where his son had gone. He had purposely steered the conversation away from such questions. Annoyed that her husband had left without a word or explanation, she decided to make plans.

That night at supper she mentioned that she was thinking of spending a few days at the mission sequestered in one of the rooms the padre kept for prayer retreat. She knew about the private rooms kept ready for the privileged women of the haciendas since the Curros had been hired to provide meals for them. She had been the one who had cooked and served the meals, though she had never seen any of the women. The trays were left outside the door, and she would pick up the empty ones later.

The isolated retreat would serve as the perfect concealment for her trip to Los Angeles. No one would question her absence and if she was lucky no one would need to know that she had ever gone in the first place. Not until it proved necessary.

The more she had thought about it, the more perfect her plan sounded and when Dona Valerianna heard, she gave Rosa her blessing.

"How wonderful of you to pray so diligently for your husband," she said with teary eyes.

Rosa felt a pang of guilt and silently promised that on her journey she would offer numerous prayers so as not to disappoint Esteban's mother.

Don Alejandro seemed agreeable and slightly relieved, as if a burden had been taken off his shoulders. "I am sure Esteban would appreciate your sacrifice and also would be pleased that you are safely tucked away at the mission. When would you like to go?"

"Tomorrow morning."

And so she found herself deposited at the mission. The vaqueros escorted her to her room and saw her settled before taking their leave and returning to the hacienda to report to Don Alejandro that she had been safely ensconced in her temporary quarters.

They no soon as left then Padre Marten and she collected what they needed for the two days it would take them to reach Los Angeles. The only person the padre confided his departure in was Anita, the woman who had tended the mission for the last ten years. He informed her that he had been summoned to another mission to help and would return in a few days.

No one saw Rosa join him in the wagon and together they rode off, Rosa praying that she wouldn't regret her decision.

Chapter Fifteen

Esteban went straight to his quarters upon his return. He needed to wash away the sweat and grime he had accumulated on his prolonged journey before letting his wife know of his return. He had been away longer than he had anticipated and hoped his efforts would prove worth it. He had set a plan in motion and now all he could do was wait.

The day was warm so he decided to take a dip in the pond where he had enjoyed carefree times as a young boy. He hadn't been there since his return, hadn't wanted to go there, but now... he hurried along the winding path.

After leaving his bundle of fresh clothes and towel under one of the numerous oak trees that gave the spot a modicum of seclusion, he hurried and stripped off his clothes. He ran to the water and was soon swimming out to the middle as he had done as a boy, though now his strides were more powerful and it took him less time to make it to the middle.

He had expected to be assaulted by memories of wasted years with Pacquito's band and how often he had thought about this place and wished he was here. Instead his thoughts focused on Rosa, the taste of her so sweet, so innocent, and so inviting.

He floated on his back gazing at the clear blue sky sprinkled sparingly with white clouds. She constantly invaded his mind. No matter what his thought, she would pop in and interfere with it. He hadn't expected to be so attracted to his wife—he frowned—that was a lie. He had been attracted to her from when he first saw her, and his thoughts about her had been anything but pure and continued to be anything but pure.

Spending time with her had made him realize how much he enjoyed her company, and he was surprised to learn that she wasn't as docile as he had first thought. There were many things about her that had actually surprised him.

The most startling one was that she didn't seem to be adverse to his kisses or his touch. He had expected her to cringe especially when he had tied her to the bed—he grimaced—something he shouldn't have done and yet...

She had grown wet and he had grown hard.

He turned and began swimming, needing to erase the image the memory had brought. If not, he'd be finding her and finishing what he had started.

I want more.

The haunting words had him stopping and treading water. Damn if he didn't' want more from Rosa. He hadn't realized it himself until after the words had run unexpectedly from his mouth that day. When he had finally returned home after all those years of capture, it was with the intention of seeing that his mother and father were safe and to stay for a while, though not permanently. He would have to finish things with Pacquito before he could do that. Then he had seen Rosa in town and had not been able to hide his interest in her from his father or perhaps he hadn't wanted to.

He could have left then and there but there had been something about the petite woman that kept him there and though he had railed against their marriage, there had been a part of him that wanted it, wanted something permanent.

She was his now; she belonged to him.

Not until their vows were consummated.

The thought had plagued him and continued to plague him. He started swimming again, his strides strong and rapid as he tried to rid himself of the image of her tied to the bed. He had had no right to treat her like that and yet his anger had taken hold and he had reacted, reminding him of who he was... a renegade.

He had spent more years with Pacquito's band than he had with his parents. Yet those early fourteen years had been indelibly etched in not only his memory but his nature as well. His father had taught him well the way of a man and he had not forgotten... he hadn't wanted to forget those lessons. He had felt that if he had, he would have surrendered completely to the hell that had become his life.

Now there was Rosa and somehow she seemed to make a difference or was it that he was thinking differently? But she was not truly his until they joined as one and Esteban wanted to make certain that when he did it wasn't the renegade who sealed their vows, but the man his father had taught him to be.

After making sure he was thoroughly washed and dried, he slipped into fresh clothes and made his way back to the house. He wondered what his wife was up to and if she would be annoyed with him for having left without a word to her.

She wasn't in her quarters or the gardens she enjoyed frequenting, and then he realized that it was suppertime. He entered the dining room expecting to see her at the table with his mother and father. His parents were present, but his wife was not.

Esteban ignored his parents' startled expressions and demanded. "Where is *my wife*?"

"Rosa has been at the mission since your departure, safely sequestered in prayer for her husband," Don Alejandro said, "at her own request."

She prayed for his soul and Esteban wasn't sure whether he should be annoyed or pleased since his thoughts of her were much more sinful.

"I hadn't realized you had returned," his father said.

His mother smiled. "It is good to have you home again, please sit and join us."

"Yes, do join us, Esteban," his father said, hoping to find out where his son had been, though he dared not ask him directly.

His parents appeared eager for his company

while he was eager to retrieve his wife. "Another time, I want to go bring Rosa home."

"They serve an early evening meal at the mission for those in prayer and bedtime soon follows," his mother explained. "By now she would be asleep after a full day of prayer. Why not fetch her tomorrow? She will rise early to start another day of prayer."

Esteban didn't want to wait another moment to see his wife, but he also didn't want to disturb her sleep. He would be there when the sun rose to bring her home. For now he would please his parents and join them.

It wasn't until later when he found himself restless in bed, slipping in and out of sleep that he was suddenly struck by the question...

Why?

Why had Rosa decided to seek solitary prayer at the mission as soon as he had left? The question nagged at him. And when a possible answer finally came to him, he jumped out of bed, dressed, went to the stables, saddled his horse and took off for town.

He arrived just as the sun rose bright and strong, Padre Marten taking a quick step back inside the entrance of the church as Esteban brought his horse to an abrupt halt only a few feet away. He dismounted so quickly and approached with such a determined gait that Padre Marten stepped further back, seeking the safety of the church.

Esteban walked right up to the padre keeping

step with him as he kept retreating further down the aisle of the church until he bumped into the wood altar railing.

"Where's my wife?" Esteban demanded.

The furious look on Esteban's face had the padre blessing himself and silently asking for forgiveness for the lie he was about to tell. "She's in prayer and should not be disturbed."

"You're telling me that if I go search the prayer rooms that I will find her on her knees praying for my condemned soul?"

The padre attempted to take a firm stand. "You will not disturb those who have sought solace here."

Esteban snickered. "And who will stop me, Padre?"

The padre tried a different tact. "You would embarrass your wife after she has spent time in constant prayer for you?"

"Then bring her to me and that is not a request, Padre."

"She finishes her prayer vigil in two days. Come back for her then," the padre said hoping that Rosa would return by then, having left her with her newfound family with a promise they would see her safely home.

Esteban leaned his face closer to the padre's. "Bring her to me now or I will tear the mission apart searching for her."

The padre was well aware that Esteban would do exactly as he said and so he had no choice but to tell him the truth. "Rosa has gone to Los

Angeles.

He kept his hands tightly fisted at his sides for fear of reaching out and strangling the padre. "When did she leave and who went with her?"

The padre's mouth went dry and he had difficulty answering. "She left the day after your departure and I took her."

"No one else accompanied you?" he asked stunned that the padre and his wife had traveled without any protection. He kept a tight grip on his fists or else... he'd kill the foolish man. "And did you expect her to return home alone?" He grew even more furious at the insane thought.

The padre shook his head. "I would never do that."

He felt a sudden punch to his gut as another thought hit him. "Or perhaps you don't expect her to return home."

"No, no," the padre rushed to assure him. "Rosa has every intention of returning. She is your wife and takes her vows seriously."

That she would return out of duty annoyed him, but what did he expect... for her to miss him?

"Rosa got along well with her sister, and her parents assured me that they would see to her safety."

"You left her with strangers who guaranteed her safety but not her return home?" Esteban had to step away from the padre. He was that close to raising his fist to the man.

The padre tried to reassure him. "Rosa will return home to you, my son."

Esteban glared with fiery eyes at him. "You're right, Padre, she will because I'm going to go get my wife and when I lay my hands on her... God won't be able to help her."

Esteban turned and hurried out of the church, the padre rushing after him. He mounted his horse with such speed that it startled the padre and he quickly blessed himself.

"Blessings won't stop me from making you suffer if anything has happened to my wife," Esteban said with such cold resolve that the padre shivered. "Now tell me where you took her."

~~~

"I can't believe the padre would take that upon himself to do and not tell us," Dona Valerianna said, a hand to her chest after hearing the news.

"And I can't believe my wife defied me," Esteban said. "Where is Father, I must talk with him before I leave."

"I heard what you said to your mother," Don Alejandro said to his son as he entered the parlor. "Take as many men as you want with you."

Esteban shook his head. "The vaqueros will do me no good."

"You will go alone?" his father asked concern in his aging eyes.

"No, I will take men with me," Esteban said.

"You cannot mean to—"

"I will do anything necessary to get my wife and bring her home."

"Safely," his mother said firmly.

"That remains to be seen."

"Esteban!" his father said.

Esteban hadn't heard that warning tone since he was a child. "I'm not a little boy anymore, Father. I will deal with my wife as I see fit."

"It will do you well to remember who you are, my son."

"No, father, it would do you well to remember who I've become." With that Esteban left the room.

Dona Valerianna hurried out of her chair and went to her husband, taking hold of his arm. "Is he going to the renegades for help?"

"It seems that way, though I cannot believe that my son would be that foolish."

Chapter Sixteen

The Los Angeles area wasn't new to him. He had been on raids there with Pacquito. He had left much destruction in his wake and Esteban had been part of it. The memories still haunted him and probably always would.

He had made only one stop after he left the hacienda and now eight renegades rode with him and while the small group didn't appear threatening, it would be a foolish mistake to assume so. They were far more lethal than a large contingent. There was another man with them, though he was what the renegades referred to as a ghost, a tracker who was never seen or heard until it was too late. Esteban knew the skill set all too well, since he had acquired it himself. The ghost would keep watch of the surrounding area and report back news, by then it would be too late for unsuspecting souls to do anything but... die.

They rode hard. He wanted his wife back where she belonged... with him. He wouldn't fully rest until she was in his arms. And he intended to make certain that she understood that she was never to go anywhere without his permission again.

The more he thought about her alone and at the mercy of strangers, the harder he rode and the angrier he grew. And he wasn't sure if he would strangle her or kiss her when he finally got his hands on her.

~~~

Rosa sat with a cool cloth resting gently to her swollen cheek and listened to Gaby and Rafael. She had come to love the woman like a sister, though they had discovered that they were not twins—not even sisters—it didn't matter. They had bonded upon first meeting. And Rosa had learned much watching the spirited Gaby deal with the powerful and domineering Don Raphael, just as she was doing now.

"What do you mean you *forbid* me to go riding ever again?" Gaby demanded.

"You heard me," Rafael said, adding more sticks to the campfire.

"I'm not deaf—"

"Just obstinate," he finished.

"You're being unreasonable."

"I'm being a good husband."

"We aren't married yet."

"We will be soon enough."

"You can't—"

"I can."

"I won't—"

"You will."

"Why are you being so unreasonable?"

"Because I love you," he shouted.

Silence descended over the camp.

"And I love you, Rafael," she said for all to

hear. She leaned over and kissed him and he kissed her back.

The vaqueros cheered and Rosa cried, happy for Gaby and Raphael. She couldn't help but wonder if Esteban would act as lovingly as Raphael had upon finding out that she had disobeyed him and taken matters into her own hands much like Gaby had. Somehow she didn't think so. She pictured a far different scene and resolution. But she couldn't worry about that now. She had come to Los Angeles to find out about her true heritage and what she had discovered had left her with a broken heart.

The late night interrupted her musings with its familiar sounds; the fire crackled, a twig snapped here and there, and an owl gave a lonesome hoot.

Rosa clutched the blanket wrapped around her to her chest and glanced across the fire at Rafael and Gaby. His long legs were stretched out in front of him and his back was braced against his saddle. Gaby sat cuddled next to him in his arms, a blanket wrapped around her. They were a perfect couple.

Rosa closed her eyes for only a moment thinking of the man who believed he was her true father and wondered if he was as blind to the situation as he appeared to be. "Does Don Felipe know what his wife did?"

"No," Rafael answered. "He doesn't know anything. When I left he was joyously making plans to leave for Spain with his *family*."

"He had no idea we were in danger?" Gaby asked.

Rafael shook his head sadly. "He is blind to so many things. He assumes all people have a place in life and they must do what is expected of them. As his daughters, he assumed that of both of you. You would do, without question, as he directed."

"Just as his wife had done all those years," Rosa sighed, finding it hard to believe that a mother would want her own newborn twin daughters dead.

"You mean as she led him to believe she did," Gaby corrected.

"She was a cruel woman," Rosa added.

"You take after your true father," Rafael said, sensing her concern. "You're kind and thoughtful like him."

"Thank you. Is—is he all right?" Rosa asked, reluctant to hear the answer. She had barely gotten to know her real father, yet in the end he responded as only a true father would... he had protected her and Gaby with his own life.

"I don't really know. His wound was serious and I had to leave. I left him in capable hands. My people will see that he is well cared for."

"He's probably fine. We'll find out as soon as we return tomorrow," Gaby assured her.

Rosa prayed that he would survive, for she desperately wanted to get to know her father.

Rafael suddenly sat up straight and looked about, his brows drawn in a frown and his lips set tightly.

"Is something wrong?" Gaby asked, feeling the tension in his body.

"I thought for a moment..." He let his words trail off. "It's nothing."

"Your instincts are as good as ever, Rafael."

Rafael remained still at the sound of the deep voice that seemed to echo out of the darkness.

His men instantly aimed their rifles into the blackness that surrounded them.

"Hold your fire!" Rafael yelled. "And put the weapons down."

"Wise decision, my friend," the voice said.

"I know you too well. Your men surround my camp. We have no chance against you."

"This is true."

Rafael released Gaby and stood. He spoke into the darkness, as if the strong voice had the power to be everywhere at once. "What is it you want, Esteban?"

A dark figure emerged from the shadows of the night, but kept on the outskirts of the campfire's light so as not to be seen.

"You have something that belongs to me."

Rafael stared at the black figure, puzzled. "I have something that belongs to you?"

"Yes, although through no fault of yours, but I must insist you return it."

"I don't know of what you speak, but if I have it in my possession and am free to return it, I will gladly do so."

"Good, then you'll receive no trouble from me."

"I'm glad to hear this. Now, what is it I have?"

"My wife."

"Your what?"

"Wife!"

"I don't have your wife. Gaby belongs to me and Rosa—"

"Is my wife and belongs to me."

Rafael turned and looked at Rosa as if it could not be possible. This sweet young woman could not be married to such a monster.

Rosa stood slowly. She had known he would come for her once he found out she was gone and had anticipated this moment, growing more anxious over it each day. She had disobeyed him and now must face the consequences. "I'm sorry. I should have told you."

"I can understand why you didn't. Esteban isn't known for his kindness," Rafael whispered, feeling sorry for the young woman. "Do you wish to go with him?"

No, Esteban wasn't known for his kindness but he could be kind, for he had showed her kindness many times. And while she had missed him, she had also enjoyed the freedom this time had afforded her. She was tired of feeling a prisoner and couldn't help but voice her frustration, "Do I have a choice?"

"Of course you have a choice," Gaby said, standing and joining them by the fire.

Rosa smiled at Gaby, as if she was a child unaware of the danger that surrounded them. And they very well could be in danger, for she had no idea what Esteban would do if she refused to go with him. "It is best I go."

"Rafael, tell her she doesn't have to," Gaby insisted.

"No," Rosa said. "I will not place any of you in danger."

Gaby turned and stepped away from the fire. "Rosa is staying here with us," she shouted.

Rafael ran his hand over his face in frustration and Rosa cringed.

"You control your woman good, Rafael," Esteban said with a laugh.

"She is my sister," Rosa yelled to protect Gaby. "You will not hurt her."

There was a heavy silence. Rafael reached out and pulled Gaby back behind him.

"Rafael may not object to his wife speaking such, but you will hold your tongue or suffer the consequences."

Gaby opened her mouth and Rafael quickly clamped his hand over it. "Shut up," he ordered sternly. "You will only make it worse for Rosa."

He released her and she remained quiet.

"I will go," Rosa said.

"But—"

"No, Gaby, I must go," she insisted before Gaby could object any further. "You have given me strength and courage, and I am grateful."

Gaby threw her arms around her and hugged her tightly. "I shall miss you."

"And I you," Rosa said with tears pooling in her eyes."

"Will I see you again?" Gaby asked.

"I will be in touch with you somehow. I must

learn how my father is. Take care and thank you for all you have done for me."

Rafael stopped her from going any farther with his hand to her arm. It got the desired response.

A fierce growl sounded before Esteban warned, "Let go of her."

"I will, but understand she has been through much. She has a bruise on her face and I imagine on other parts of her from the fight she took part in."

"Who inflicted this bruise?" Esteban demanded angrily.

"The man is dead," Rafael informed him.

"Then I owe you a favor, my friend."

"Not necessary, Esteban, just be gentle with her. As I said, she has been through much."

"Thank you," Rosa whispered to Rafael before walking away from him toward the dark figure, her heart beating madly in anticipation.

As she approached a hand reached out and quickly snatched her into the mouth of darkness.

She found herself pressed hard against her husband's body.

"I should punish you here and now for disobeying me," he whispered harshly.

Rosa tried to explain.

"Not one word," Esteban warned with a finger to her lips.

She shivered. He was angry, very angry. She could feel it in every coiled muscle of his body and she wasn't sure what he would do to her, so she remained silent.

He turned and started walking, tugging her along behind him. He fought the urge to stop and strip her bear and check every part of her body to make certain she was unharmed. But he couldn't do that here and now. He and the others had to be on their way. He wanted to get her home as quickly as possible. He also owed Raphael for killing the man who had dared to lay a hand on Rosa. The thought that she had been in danger and he hadn't been there to protect her made him furious. He kept walking, relief beginning to overcome his anger. He squeezed his wife's hand. She was safe, and he would make certain she stayed that way.

Rosa didn't know how her husband could manage to find his way through the woods in the dark, but he did. She kept pace with him all the while wishing that instead of her stomach churning nervously over their eventual confrontation that she could talk with him and tell him all that had happened since her arrival here. What she had learned had stunned her and made her feel as if she didn't truly know who she was.

Esteban stopped suddenly, jolting Rosa out her thoughts and catching her around the waist so that she wouldn't collide with him. She moved closer to him, pressing herself to his side when she caught sight of several men surrounding them. It was easy to see that they were renegades and Rosa grew fearful.

Not a one of them said a word. They all mounted their horses tethered nearby and with firm hands on her waist Esteban lifted her to the saddle, and then mounted behind her. With his arm snug around her waist and one hand on the reins they took off at a slow pace.

The silence, curiosity, or perhaps it was fear had her finally speaking up, "I—"

"Not a word," he warned with a quick squeeze to her waist.

He was still angry and she was still anxious. Had he gone back to the renegades? Where was he taking her?

Her chest grew tight and she felt a well of tears threaten to choke her. What she had hoped would be a happy journey in discovering a family she never knew she had, had become a heartbreaking disappointment. And only now was she beginning to realize once again how much she had lost. Would heartache never stop? She swallowed hard, trying desperately to stop the tears from falling. It would do her no good to cry now. She had to stay strong, as she had watched Gaby do. But she didn't feel strong, no matter how much she told herself that she was. She wanted to break down in tears and cry for all she had lost.

Her heart ached along with her body and the day finally took its toll, and Rosa was never so happy to welcome the oblivion of sleep.

Esteban felt a squeeze to his heart when Rosa rested her head to his chest. Her body grew limp with sleep soon after and he tightened his hold on her. He wondered what had happened to here since her arrival in Los Angeles, especially what led to her having been involved in a fight. He would not think her capable of that, and so his wife surprised him again.

He wished they were home where he could make certain she was all right. By morning they would reach the designated stop and they would switch horses and be on the road again. The next stop was where his stallion would be waiting for him and they would not stop again until they reached the hacienda.

Esteban had grown accustomed to traveling for days without rest, but it would be a grueling journey for anyone who had no experience with it. He had no choice in the matter though. It was either that or take the chance of Pacquito possibly finding them.

He shook his head to clear his mind. He had to remain focused. It would be a long night and even longer day before they finally reached home.

"Wake up, Rosa."

Rosa winced at the pain from being jostled awake. It hurt too much to move. She much preferred the warmth of the comforting blanket. But the persistent voice continued to irritate her.

"Wake up!"

She reluctantly opened her eyes and they popped open even wider when she stared into her husband's dark eyes. She recalled then where she was and it wasn't in bed wrapped in a warm blanket. She was in her husband's arms on a horse.

"You have a few minutes to see to your needs and grab what food there is before we're on our way again," Esteban said and eased her away from him to dismount.

Rosa felt the pain of his absence, having to support her aching body herself, and she couldn't help but wince again.

His hands were suddenly at her waist and he eased her off the horse to rest her sore body against his. "You had no business going off on your own."

She did not want a confrontation here and now in front of these *renegades*, but she couldn't stop from asking, "Where are you taking me?"

"Home, and I intend to make sure you stay there," he snapped angrily, though he hadn't intended to. Her suffering upset him, but then so had her question. Why would she think he would take her anyplace else, but home?

She took a sharp step away, forcing herself out of his embrace... a mistake. Pain shot and stabbed at her in so many places, she wondered how she was able to stand. And then she realized that Esteban had taken hold of her again.

He leaned his head down and whispered, "Defy me in front of these men again and I will have no choice but to punish you."

Rosa recalled Esteban telling her how women were claimed in Pacquito's group. She didn't want to imagine how they were punished. She lowered her head to rest on his chest as if surrendering to him.

"Wise move," he whispered. He then walked her to a secluded area. "Hurry and see to your needs."

She did so quickly, ignoring her persistent aches. Afterwards he gave her a piece of dried beef , ordering her to eat. After she finished she went to the stream and drank handfuls of cool water, and gave her face and neck a quick scrub.

Esteban hunched down beside her and drank as well, then turned to her. "You would not ache so badly if you had obeyed me." He took her arm and with a rough tug pulled her to her feet.

She tried not to wince, but couldn't help it.

Esteban spewed a litany of oaths as he marched her to his horse. He hated to see her suffer and hated even more that he would add to her suffering. He had her up on the horse quickly and joined her just as quickly. He settled her against him and without a word took off, the other renegades following behind them.

The sun grew hot and so did Rosa. It was an exhausting day that never seemed to end. When dusk settled on the land, they finally stopped. And Rosa was ever so grateful, though her relief didn't last long. Fresh horses were made ready, only this time Rosa recognized Esteban's stallion and she wanted to cry out with joy for she knew that the animal would take them home.

Sleep claimed her during the night as they traveled and when she woke it was to find that she and Esteban were alone. She was curious about the renegades, who had only spoken to Esteban in whispers, but dared not ask him. They stopped only once for the horse to have water and then they were back on the road again. It wasn't until dusk that they rode over a rise and spied the hacienda.

They were home and while Rosa was overjoyed, she was also concerned, for now she would face the consequences of her actions. And she wondered if Esteban would do as he had threatened... tie her to the bed and... tears pooled in her eyes.

She fought back the tears and prayed, prayed that he would take her in his arms and hold her, comfort her... and love her.

Chapter Seventeen

Esteban wanted time alone with his wife, and he wanted answers to the endless questions that had manifested in his mind on the return journey home. So after his parents enthusiastic welcome, he offered a reasonable and truthful excuse for Rosa and he to retire to their bedchamber.

"It was an exhausting journey and we need to rest," Esteban said.

"I will see that Dolores has baths prepared and food sent to your quarters," his mother said. "We will see you tomorrow after you have rested."

They had barely entered the room when Dolores came in with several servants carrying a copper tub. She directed it to be placed before the fireplace and a fire to be lit.

"See to everything and then leave us," Esteban ordered.

The servants worked fast filling the tub and bringing in a table and two chairs and covering the table with a white linen cloth, plates, platters of food and two decanters of wine.

Rosa watched them, waiting for the moment they would leave and her husband would turn to her and... do what?

When the door shut behind the last servant, Rosa stood where she was waiting, her stomach knotted with worry while tears struggled against her fragile constraint.

Esteban removed his shirt slowly all the while not taking his eyes off her. He tossed his shirt to a chair, and then went to the table and poured a glass of wine.

He held it out to Rosa.

She shook her head.

He took a sip. "You disobeyed me."

Rosa remained silent, her focus on his bare chest and muscled arms. She wanted desperately to rest her head on his chest and have him wrap those powerful arms around her and hold her tight. Then she could pretend that he loved her, truly loved her, for at the moment she needed to know that she was loved.

He took another sip of wine before demanding, "Tell me, did you find a loving family to greet you with open arms?"

His words broke her crumbling control and she could no longer hold back her tears. They burst out in a torrent, rushing down her cheeks and she stood there, weeping uncontrollably.

Esteban let loose with a curse, slammed the wine glass on the table so hard that the stem broke, and rushed to his wife. He scooped her up in his arms and hurried to sit on the bed. He hugged her tight, her wet cheek pressed against his bare chest that continued to get soaked with her never-ending tears.

Her crying tore at his heart. He couldn't bear to see her suffer. He took hold of her face, tears running down her cheek and brushed his lips over hers. "Don't cry, *Caro*, you're here with me now and everything will be all right."

The strength of his arms, the brush of his lips, the endearment spoken with such heart all served to only make it seem that he loved her and it made her cry harder.

"Don't, *Caro*, don't," he whispered kissing her softly.

But she couldn't stop and she couldn't stop from bearing her heart to him. "Why? Why is it so hard to find and hold onto love? I thought my family would love me as I would surely love them." She shook her head. "How does a mother want her twin daughters dead?"

His brow knitted. Had he heard her right? "Your mother wanted you and your sister dead?"

"Gaby is not my true sister, my twin died when she was just a baby and the padres replaced her with Gaby." Rosa heaved a heavy sigh.

"Easy, *Caro*, I am here. Tell me. I want to know everything."

"My mother was a horrible woman. She plotted to have me and my twin killed shortly after we were born. If it hadn't been for my true father taking us to California we would have been killed in Spain. My mother intended to finish what she started after arriving here. My true father tried to protect me and Gaby, but he was..." She shook her head, her tears still falling. "I don't know if he survived his wound."

"Don't worry, we'll find out," he assured her,

praying that the man survived and his wife would get to know her father.

"Men, my mother hired, took me and Gaby, though we struggled. They killed my mother and the man who claimed to love her. Gaby helped keep me strong and made a plan for us to escape. It didn't work out as well as she had thought, but by then Raphael came to our rescue."

He definitely owed Raphael and one day he would pay him back.

"Don Felipe, the man who thought he was my father, was a fool. He knew nothing of his wife's deviousness or that she also planned on having him murdered while on their trip." She shook her head again. "He didn't even care about me. He only cared that I would do my duty as his daughter. Always duty... what of love?"

He felt a jolt to his heart and he knew at that moment that he loved his wife. He didn't know how he knew or why he loved her, he just knew that he did and the realization astonished him. He had never thought he'd ever be capable of loving anyone. And yet here he sat knowing without a doubt that he loved this woman.

Admitting it to her was another matter, that might take time, but they had time. They had the rest of their lives together.

Since he couldn't express what he felt with words, he did so through actions. He stood, with her in his arms, and carried her over to the tub. He eased her to her feet and then began to strip her gently. It didn't surprise him that she submitted to his tending without protest. What choice did she have when she didn't have an ounce of strength left?

He grew hard as he stripped away her clothes slowly revealing every part of her. He ached to harden her soft nipples with his tongue and to run his hands over every inch of her silky soft flesh.

He shook his head trying desperately to shake the enticing images away. Now was not the time. Rosa needed his help, his aching need would have to wait. Though he would have loved to have lingered in his task, he knew it was wiser to finish and get her in the water before it turned cold or before sanity failed him and he surrendered to his growing desire.

She sighed with pleasure as the warm water caressed her body and Esteban quickly turned away from her to collect himself, her soft sighs much too inviting. He had intended on washing her, but he realized it was not a wise idea. He'd never be able to stop himself from...

He heard the water splash and turned to look over his shoulder. He almost sighed with relief when he saw that his wife had scooped up the soap and was beginning to lather her hair. That was a task he could safely do... or so he thought.

He hunched down and took over scrubbing her hair, his strong fingers digging into her scalp and she sighed once again. It wasn't only her sigh that affected him, it was seeing her now hard, wet nipples just waiting to be licked, nipped, suckled.

Esteban abruptly stopped scrubbing her hair

and ordered, "Hurry and be done before the water grows cold."

"How selfish of me enjoying the bath when you must wash too," she said gently.

He wanted to kick himself. He hadn't thought any such thing and yet he couldn't correct her. He needed her out of that tub and dressed so that her naked body couldn't tempt him anymore. Not that clothes would matter, her naked body was branded on his mind. Just the same, he hurried to fetch her nightgown.

When he turned around she was standing in front of the fire drying herself, the flickering flames casting a shadow of lights across her lovely body. He stood staring at the exquisite creature that had captured his heart so irrevocably.

She turned just a fraction and his eye caught sight of... he marched over to her, dropped the nightgown to the chair and startled her when his arm went around her waist and he turned her backside to the fire's light. He ran his hand gently down her round bottom and stopped when he reached a dark spot.

"Who touched you?" he demanded, though he didn't realize how harshly he spoke.

Rose was quick to answer feeling all too vulnerable naked beside him. "No one, I fell when struggling with the men and hit a rock."

He squeezed his eyes shut for a moment annoyed with himself. The endless ride home had to have caused her pain but yet she had said nothing. But how could she have when he had warned her again and again not to say a word.

He spotted another bruise near her shoulder. How had he missed seeing these? He had been too intent on his own need to focus on her. He turned her around in his arms and took a step back to glance over her and see if he had missed any other injures she had suffered. He dropped down in front of her, his hand going to her knee where a large bruise began and his hand followed it up her leg along her thigh.

With a turn of his head, he was about to ask if it hurt when his eyes caught with the dark mound of hair between her legs. He stilled and took a deep breath, a mistake since his flared nostrils captured the fresh scent of her. Damn if he didn't want to bury his face there and taste her until he made her cry out with pleasure.

He stood quickly, grabbed her nightgown and slipped it over her head and when she winced he cursed. He'd been rough in his hurry to cover her and she suffered for it. Damn his miserable soul or damn himself for growing so hard that he could think of nothing else but taking his wife to bed and making love to her all night.

He didn't offer an apology. If he opened his mouth he just might kiss her, and then he wouldn't stop. He turned his back on her before even dare saying, "Eat." Then winced at his own word since he damn well ached to feast on her.

Whether it was wise to strip bare or not he didn't care, he did so, needing to dunk himself in the tub water that had turned cold by now. To his relief, the water was cold enough to help somewhat and he immersed himself in it. What he didn't count on was his wife standing beside the tub when he emerged, her naked body silhouetted beneath her nightgown by the fire's light.

"You need hot water," she said with such sincere concern that it squeezed at his heart, though didn't temper his response.

"No, go eat," he snapped and cringed as she turned and hurried to the table. He could see tears pooling in her eyes when she gave him a quick look after sitting, then turned away.

He mumbled several oaths directed all at himself and after a quick wash, he toweled himself dry and slipped into his robe that a servant had draped over a chair. He wanted to take his wife in his arms and... once again there would be no apology coming from his lips. He had been taught—no—he had been beaten anytime he had apologized after first being captured. Until he finally learned that he was never to apologize for anything he ever did. Old habits die hard as do memories of endless beatings.

He joined her at the table, her tears having been wiped away, though fresh ones lingered and she bravely fought them back. He poured himself a glass of wine and said, "Tell me more about your family, Gaby, and your father."

She sighed and closed her eyes for a moment, as if what she was about to say was difficult, and it was. "My family proved no family at all. My mother cared only for herself and never wanted my twin sister and me from the beginning. She wanted us dead, but my true father had the courage to rescue us and bring us to California. To make certain no one would ever find us, he had us separated." A tear slipped down her cheek. "My twin died when she was just a baby."

Esteban said nothing, knowing she had to talk and he had to listen. And he wanted to, he wanted to know it all, everything she had been through.

"After all the years of being hunted, we were tracked to the mission and in the end my father, my true father, saved mine and Gaby's life. I do hope he survived. I so want to get to know him. He seems such a good man."

Esteban saw how exhausted she was and suggested they get some rest. "You can tell me more another time."

Rosa didn't argue, she eagerly climbed into bed, but was shocked when her husband wished her a good-night and walked into the next room. She sat up in bed and stared at the closed door. She could not believe he left her there to sleep alone. She had thought— no she wanted— him there beside her in bed. She wanted his strong arms around her, his warm body pressed to hers and why... why didn't he seal their vows? What was wrong with her that he didn't make love to her?

She dropped back on the bed suddenly too upset to sleep. She had missed him so very much while she was away. It made her realize that somehow she had fallen in love with her husband. She wasn't sure how it had happened, it simply had, but wasn't that the way of love? It struck in its own good time. And tonight when he had been so tender and caring with her, she had thought that perhaps he was beginning to have feelings for her.

He could have left the servants to care for her, but he hadn't. He had seen to her care himself and had been so tender with her. He still issued orders and snapped now and then but how could anyone expect him to completely shed the renegade that was part of him now. It wasn't fair of anyone to think he could simply return to who he had once been. It would take time to reclaim parts of who he once had been, as it would take her time to deal and heal with all she had just learned about her true family.

Memories of her true father being so badly wounded while trying to protect her and Gaby came unbidden. She quickly shut her eyes against the images and fought back tears that once again threatened to spill.

All she knew of her father was that he had risked his life and given up all he knew to save and protect his twin daughters. He had told her that he had cared for her and her sister on the ship that brought them to California and how much he had enjoyed his time with them. He had known that the only true way to keep them safe was to separate them and keep his distance in case anyone from Spain tracked him here. His unselfishness had saved them even at the very end.

She prayed that her father had survived and that they would get to know each other for she already loved the man who had given her life and saved her life.

Her eyes sprung open and she couldn't stop the tears... she wept.

~~~

Esteban paced in his room. As tired as he was, he knew sleep would elude him tonight. Surprisingly, it wasn't images of his wife naked that filled his head but the thought of all she had been through while in Los Angeles and all she had learned about her true family.

He wished he had been there with her. He should have been there with her. He was her husband and should have been there to ease this heavy burden for her. Instead he had showed up and swept her away without any knowledge of all she had endured. He had thought to protect her and he had only made it worse for her.

A sound interrupted his pacing and he paused to listen. It took only a moment for him to recognize it. He went to the door that separated their bedrooms, swung it open and his heart felt as if it broke when he heard his wife's heartbreaking sobs. He hurried to the bed, shedding his robe along the way and slipped beneath the covers and took her in his arms.

He wrapped her close, laying his leg across hers to inch her even closer. Her slim arms went around him and she pressed her face against his chest and continued crying.

He kissed the top of her head, then whispered,

"I'm here, *Caro*, I'm here and I'm not going anywhere." She cried harder and he wondered if his words had upset her even more, but then she pressed harder against him and her arms tightened around him and he knew. She did want him there with her and he wanted to be there... always.

He knew the tears were necessary. They would help heal her and so he held her, stroked her back, and let her cry. He didn't know how long she cried. He only knew when she stopped, her breathes coming in short spurts. Then he felt her body ease and was relieved that sleep had finally claimed her.

Shortly after, he fell asleep himself, though was woken often throughout the night by his wife's fitful sleep. His hands stroked her gently and he reminded her in soft whispers that he was there with her. She calmed and once again slept peacefully.

It made him recall his own fretful sleep after he'd been captured. The worst part was waking the next day to discover that he truly was living a nightmare. He wouldn't let that happen to Rosa. She would wake in his arms knowing she was safe.

Chapter Eighteen

Rosa snuggled in the warmth not wanting to leave it. It felt much too wonderful and she felt much too content, more content than she had been in a long time. She shifted a bit to relieve the annoying pain in her shoulder and that's when memories of yesterday returned. She had cried herself to sleep in her husband's arms.

She raised her head to find him staring down at her.

"How are you feeling this morning?" he asked.

His concerned tone warmed her heart. "A bit sore."

"I will make certain that you remain in bed and rest today."

A tingle ran through her. Would he join her? Did she want him to? The tingle spread giving her the answer, though her heart had known the answer all along. It was just that she was nervous, unsure of how it would be between them. Would he treat her well or was there too much of a renegade in him still?

She wasn't sure if it was relief or disappointment that struck her when he eased her away from him and slipped out of bed. She stared at him as he walked naked to the chair to retrieve his robe. He was powerfully built... everywhere.

And it was when he turned, slipping into his robe, that she realized how hard he was, and the sight of him aroused with such passion, further aroused her own desire. So why was he leaving her? Why not stay and make love?

"I will see that breakfast is brought to you," he said and walked to the door.

Rosa sat up staring at the closed door he had disappeared behind just as he had done last night. Why would he not make love to her? She almost laughed aloud at her own thought. She had first feared intimacy with her husband and now here she was aching for it. How strange, but then she had never expected to fall in love with him and yet she had... and it made all the difference.

~~~

Esteban dressed quickly and left his room, giving orders to a passing servant as to Rosa's breakfast, and then left the hacienda. He couldn't trust himself to remain near his wife or else he'd... he shook his head. He headed for the orchards to clear his head and ease his ache, though he wondered if that was possible. He wanted his wife with an intense passion that he had never known, and it worried him. It had been ingrained in him to claim his woman and damn if he didn't want to claim Rosa. Just the thought of her on her knees and he driving into her with a force that would brand her his made him...

He shook his head again chasing away the image. He couldn't do that to her. It wasn't right.

She was his wife and should be treated with respect. He reached and picked an orange off the tree, and then froze as he turned to look over the orchard. He felt someone approach before he saw him.

He recognized the man right away, one of Pacquito's men, Carlos. He was of no great importance in Pacquito's camp, but then few were. What mattered was serving Pacquito, doing his bidding, and above all making no mistakes that would cost you your life.

Esteban said nothing even when Carlos stopped in front of him. He waited, rolling the orange around in his hand, as if the man's presence meant nothing to him.

"A gift, how nice." Carlos grinned and reached for the fruit.

"If you value your hand, you'll keep it at your side."

Fear sprang in Carlos's eyes. He had seen what Esteban was capable of whether he carried a weapon or not and he lowered his arm, making certain to keep his hand away from his sheathed knives.

"Pacquito says it's time for you to return home."

"I am home."

"Pacquito never released you. He's giving you a chance to return on your own and suffer no consequences."

Esteban took a quick step forward, causing Carlos to stumble back in fright. "I am done with

Pacquito."

"No one is ever done with Pacquito unless... death claims you."

Esteban knew all too well how true that was, which was why when he left he knew it wasn't over. It was just a matter of time. "I'm done."

"That you are, my friend." Carlos sneered and turned to walk away.

"Carlos."

He stopped and turned his head.

"If you dare step foot on my land again, I'll kill you."

The man hurried off and Esteban knew he couldn't wait, there was too much at stake now. He had to move his plan along. And as much as he didn't want to leave his wife just now, he had no choice. It was imperative that he see to this immediately.

He quickly gathered what he needed and without a word to anyone he was gone.

~~~

Rosa couldn't bear another minute in bed, especially since it had been hours since Esteban had left and he had yet to return. He had been so concerned about her that she thought he would have surely come to see how she was feeling.

She hurried into her skirt and blouse, slipped her sandals on, ran a quick comb through her long hair before twisting it up and securing it with an ivory comb, and then went in search of her husband.

The day was beautiful, the sun bright, the air warm and she felt more alive than she had in some time. Even though the visit with her true parents hadn't turned out as she had hoped, meeting Gaby and becoming friends with her had made it all worthwhile. She had learned much from the talks she had shared with Gaby and from watching her deal with Raphael, a powerful don. It had made her realize much about her own situation with Esteban. And of course missing him as much as she had was a realization in itself. That he had come for her hadn't been a surprise, but that he had listened so intently to her last night had been. And that he had held her in his arms while she had cried had endeared him to her even more. Now however she had questions for him. The one that troubled her most was... why had renegades been with him?

After making the rounds of the hacienda and not finding her husband, Rosa began to worry. Dona Valerianna didn't seem to think anything of it when she found her in the small parlor working on her embroidery.

"He's probably busy with his father in the vineyards," she said stopping work on her stitching to look up at Rosa. "How was your visit with your parents?"

"It did not go as well as I had hoped," she said, not wanting to go into detail about the ordeal.

"And your twin sister?"

"Unfortunately, I learned that my twin died when she was just a baby, the padres having replaced her with another baby girl." Rosa couldn't help but smile. "Gaby is wonderful and though she isn't my sister by blood, she is a sister to me. She will soon wed a powerful don... Raphael Cabrillo."

Dona Valerianna gasped and her hand rushed to press at her chest. "He is a powerful don, or so I've heard."

"He can be commanding, but it is obvious how much he loves Gaby." Rosa laughed recalling the pair. "And Gaby is so full of life and laughter, and she is so much in love with Raphael. They make a perfect pair."

"And Raphael's parents," —Dona Valerianna asked nervously— "they treated you well?"

"His father has passed, and his mother had been in frail health until Gaby became her companion. Now the woman appears well healed and enjoying life."

"Raphael weds his mother's companion?"

Rosa's shoulders went back, her head up. "He weds a peasant just as Esteban has done."

"You are no longer a peasant, Rosa, you never actually were," Dona Valerianna reminded her.

"I may have been born of noble birth, but I was blessed to have been raised by two kind and loving peasants. To me, they are my true parents and therefore I am a peasant as well. And I have no doubt that when Gaby and Raphael come to visit you will treat her as graciously as you have me."

"They are coming to visit... when?" Dona Valerianna asked anxiously.

"I hope soon, though I don't know when exactly."

Color suddenly drained from Dona Valerianna's face and Rosa hurried to her side. "Are you all right?"

"A bit lightheaded."

"Rest your head back while I go fetch a cold cloth."

"No, it will pass in a moment, and then if you wouldn't mind helping me to my room where I can rest."

"Of course," Rosa said worried, "but perhaps I should find Don Alejandro."

"No, he will only worry needlessly. It is nothing more than my sleepless nights finally catching up with me. A bit of rest and I'll be fine."

Rosa wasn't sure of that, what if she was ill and not telling anyone? She decided she would keep a closer eye on her mother-in-law and see for herself. With an arm around her waist, Rosa helped Dona Valerianna to her bed chamber.

Dolores came across them on their way there and hurried to turn down the bed. While Rosa helped Dona Valerianna into bed, Dolores hurried off to fetch a small glass of brandy, insisting it would help her to sleep.

Rosa wouldn't leave her mother-in-law, though Dona Valerianna insisted she would be fine, until she was certain she was well settled and her eyes heavy with sleep. She closed the door softly behind her and took a step, then stopped. She wasn't sure where to go or what to do now. It seemed that nobody was around and she thought it odd. Determined to find out where everyone had gone off to, Rosa hurried off to search and explore the hacienda.

The day wore into evening without any luck of locating anyone. The hacienda seemed eerily silent as if there was no life at all to it. Something wasn't right, and Dolores confirmed it when Rosa stopped by the kitchen.

"Something has happened, though no one knows what yet and many grow fearful. Heavy smoke has been seen in the distance and a group of vaqueros left here riding hard and fast while another group took up guard around the hacienda." Dolores shook her head. "Not good, not good at all."

"What could it be?" Rosa asked anxiously, having her own thought and praying she was wrong.

"No one wants to say it, but with the smoke," —Dolores quickly blessed herself— "one of the hacienda's could have been attacked."

Rosa didn't ask who it could have been. She knew it would be renegades. What frightened her most is that all would believe that Esteban rode with them. She could not believe that of her husband, but the renegades had been with him when he came to Los Angeles to get her. And while she refused to believe that he had rejoined with them, she wondered why they had been with him.

She wasn't hungry, but went to the dining room for supper anyway, expecting to find it empty. Dona Valerianna probably had decided to have supper brought to her. So she was surprised when she entered to see the woman sitting there alone.

"Alejandro has always sent word if he was to be late for supper," she said, her eyes darting about the room, as if expecting her husband to enter at any moment. "I don't know where he could be."

Rosa had no comforting words for the woman, her own concern having grown after speaking with Dolores.

"I am glad to see that you are feeling better," Rosa said taking a seat opposite Dona Valerianna.

"Yes, rest was just what I needed."

Conversation continued between the two women throughout the meal, though at times it was forced. It appeared as if they were both biding time, hoping their husbands would appear and bring an end to their worries. Their heads shot up and turned toward the door when they heard heavy footsteps approach.

Don Alejandro entered the room, smudges on his face and white shirt and a worried look on his face that alarmed both women. Never had either of them seen him so disheveled or upset.

He walked over to his wife with an outstretched hand and Dona Valerianna reached for it, her hand trembling.

Rosa braced herself for the news while silently praying that Esteban was safe and unarmed.

Don Alejandro squeezed his wife's hand. "The Garavito hacienda has been attacked by renegades. Don Manuel was shot, though the wound is minor.

Unfortunately two of his vaqueros were killed and there is extensive damage to some buildings, including the hacienda. "

Dona Valerianna gasped and Rosa paled, her heart going out to the families.

"I will go tomorrow and see what help Dona Elena needs," Dona Valerianna said.

"No," Don Alejandro snapped. "You must stay away... for now."

His wife turned a puzzling glance on him.

Don Alejandro took his wife's hand. "There are those who believe they saw Esteban riding with the renegades."

All color drained from Dona Valerianna's face and she looked about to faint.

Don Alejandro leaned down and wrapped his arm around his wife. "Vicious rumors. There is not one who could say they actually saw Esteban."

"He would not do that," Rosa found herself saying and believing it or perhaps she needed to believe it, needed to know that he would never do such a horrid thing. But he had done such evil things and she didn't want to think of the terrible things he had done.

"Where is he?" Dona Valerianna pleaded.

"I wish I knew," Don Alejandro said. "I haven't seen him all day, nor has anyone I've asked. He's vanished and it worries me."

Could Don Alejandro truly believe that his son had been part of this raid? Her stomach roiled, she didn't want to hear anymore. She stood quickly and excused herself, hurrying from the room before Don Alejandro or Dona Valerianna could object. She wanted to be alone to think, though her thoughts were jumbled. One thing that she knew for certain though was that Esteban had not been part of the raid on the Garavito hacienda. He had escaped that horrid life and would not return to it.

But he had ridden with renegades. You saw it with your own eyes. She wanted to yell at the warning voice in her head. Instead she shook away the thoughts or at least tried to. Her husband would return and she would have her answer. Right now he needed a friend who believed in him and that's what she would do... believe in him.

A rumble of thunder interrupted the silence, though it was in the distance. A storm was brewing and would bring a good drenching to the land.

Rosa entered the garden just outside her bedchamber and jumped when a strike of lightning pierced the night sky illuminating the darkness for a moment. She rubbed her arms, a nervous chill racing through her. She cast a silent prayer to the heavens for her husband's safe return, and then hurried into the room, shutting the doors behind her.

With nothing left to do and the long day taking its toll, Rosa slipped into a sleeveless cotton shift and got into bed. She worried that she wouldn't be able to sleep, her mind too cluttered. But her eyes grew heavy in no time and she drifted off.

She didn't know what woke her. Had it been a loud clap of thunder? Or had it been the wind that rattled and blew the patio doors open, sending the curtains billowing? She had yet to fully open her eyes, though she knew she had to. She didn't hear it raining, but the scent of it was heavy in the air and once it started the room would get drenched if she didn't close the doors.

Not wanting to slip from the comfort of the bed, she had to force her eyes open once she turned over to face the door. When she did, her whole body froze and her eyes widened until she thought they would pop from her head.

There silhouetted in the doorway stood her husband... or was it?

The man who stood there was dressed far differently from Esteban, yet had his same handsome features, though they were more hardened. He wore all black, including black chaps and a black vest. A knife was sheathed in his belt. A black hat sat low on his forehead, though his chin was raised so that she could see without a doubt that it was her husband. Or was he? His clothes were not that of a nobleman, but rather a renegade. Esteban might have stood on the threshold to their bedchamber but it certainly wasn't her husband who took a step forward into the room... it was a renegade.

Chapter Nineteen

Rosa scurried up in the bed to brace her back against the headboard, pulling the blanket up along with her and holding it against her breasts. He strode into the room as lightning struck and rain slashed down on the land. He closed the doors behind him and tossed his hat to the chair. Then as he approached her, he began to undress. Not slow but quickly, as if in hurry to be done.

His intentions were clear in his smoldering eyes. He would take her tonight... but how? Like a savage renegade or a loving husband? The thought sent a shiver through her.

He didn't say a word as he shed each piece of clothing and when he finished he walked to the side of the bed, reached down, snatched the blanket out of her grasp, grabbed hold of her wrist and yanked her up to him.

She thought for a moment that he would kiss her. Instead he released her wrist and grabbed hold of her nightgown and pulled it up over her head. His actions so stunned her that she froze. She was even more surprised when he pushed her to fall back on the bed and came down on top of her. He kissed her then, a fierce penetrating kiss that shocked her senseless and sent a rush of tingles through her entire body.

He left her lips much too soon. They pulsated and wanted more, though she didn't mind where his mouth went next. It descended to her nipple and he teased it with his tongue and lips unmercifully, then he did the same to the other one. He continued to switch back and forth, as if he couldn't get enough of either of them. His hand grabbed hold of one and squeezed and not that gently as he suckled the nipple. But it didn't matter to Rosa. She was lost in the pleasure that consumed her.

Along with her lips that continued to ache for more, her rigid nipples now pulsed as his mouth rained kisses down along her midriff and over her stomach. He nipped now and again, and her body bowed as if offering herself to him for more. His mouth drifted lower, his nose settling just below her hairline, as if he was familiarizing himself with her scent, and then his finger drove into her and she let out a cry.

His mouth moved to lick at her sensitive nub as his finger glided in and out of her and she thought she would go mad from the intense sensation. *Never.* Never had she thought love making could be this exquisite or that she could feel so alive with passion.

She reached out feeling the need to touch him, to be part of their joining.

He shoved her hand away roughly. "Don't!"

She yanked her hand up to her chest, the harsh reprimand startling her.

He moved off her then and she thought he was

angry and intended to leave her. She wanted to reach out and stop him, but she didn't. She didn't want him to go, but his rough command had her holding her tongue.

She was pleased when he moved to kneel between her legs and nudge them apart. He splayed his fingers through the hair between her legs, his palm settling against her nub to massage it with a friction that had her soft moans turning louder.

He stopped a moment, took firm hold of her backside and raised it so that his thick hardness rubbed against her teasingly, before sliding down to rest between her legs.

And then she saw something change in his eyes. She didn't know what it was, but she didn't think her husband was there any longer... the renegade had taken hold of her.

He flipped her over on her stomach, yanked her to her knees and she braced for what was to come.

It never did. She suddenly found herself alone on her hands and knees.

She quickly jumped out of bed and saw that the doors to the patio stood open, the rain pouring down and thunder rolling in the distance. She cast a glance around and saw that his clothes were still where he had left them. And she grew angry.

How could he do this to her? How could he return to her, not say a word, turn her senseless with passion and leave her aching? He had worked her to a point where she had been mindless with the want of him, and she hadn't cared how he would have taken her as long as he had taken her, made love to her, satisfied this pounding ache between her legs.

Good lord, she had never felt such an aching need in her life. She wanted her husband to finish what he had started. She wanted to explode with pleasure over and over and over.

"Damn him," she muttered and marched out of the room and into the rain.

She saw him standing naked in the grass just passed the patio, rain pouring down on him. She was so angry that she didn't stop to think. She marched straight for him.

He turned just before she reached him. "Get back inside now!"

"No," she shouted and went to smack his finger that pointed at the patio doors.

He grabbed her hand before she could hit him, though surprisingly she was quick and her other hand slapped at his shoulder. His eyes sparked with anger and he shoved her away. "In the house or so help me I'll take you right here on your hands and knees."

She was drenched, but her unsatisfied need and love gave her a courage she would have never thought she had. "Why? Can't you make love any other way?"

His hand grabbed her wrist and yanked her against him so fast that their wet bodies slapped together. "You're playing with fire, *Rosalita*."

"I am on fire, Esteban!" She dropped her forehead to his chest. "And only you can put it out."

The roar that spilled from his lips had her eyes turning wide and her body shivering. And as she went to pull away from him, he scooped her up and had her down on her back in the wet grass before she could take a breath.

He was over her and in her in one swift movement and when she cried out from a brief moment of pain, he stilled and roared an oath to the heavens. Then he began to move inside her slowly, though not for long since Rosa could not keep still herself, and she moved against him.

The rhythm turned fast, as if both of them were starved for each other and they could not get enough. Rosa latched onto his arms that strained with muscles and held tightly as she welcomed the sensation that grew with every thrust.

The rain continued to pour down on them, the thunder rolled, and her moans rolled along with it.

Her fingers dug into his arms and she thought she called out his name, but she couldn't be sure, and then she threw her head back and cried out as she exploded in a never-ending release.

As soon as Esteban saw his wife in the throes of climax, he exploded himself and it rocked him to the core, shattering him senseless. It was as if he couldn't stop coming since Rosa was squeezing every last bit out of her climax that she could, making his climax more intense than he had ever experienced.

Finally, he shuddered with the last of it and collapsed over her. He realized then that he had taken his wife out on the grass in a rainstorm, and he silently cursed himself. He got up, scooped her up and carried her into their room. He stood her near the bed, shut the patio doors, and then got towels from the chest and hurried to dry her off.

She surprised him when she grabbed a towel herself and dried him as he dried her. He couldn't believe her actions when she had, at times, cowered in front of him. But at the moment she attended him with ease and a caring touch. He hadn't known such a tender touch or such caring comfort in a long time.

"You must sit so I can dry your hair," she said and pushed him to sit on the bed.

He spread his legs apart and she stepped forward, towel in hand to dry his hair. He couldn't help but breathe in her scent, the rain not having washed all of it away. Though it was not just her luscious scent, but a combination of them both, and he found himself getting aroused.

How that was possible, he didn't know. He had come so damn hard that he didn't think he'd have a need that soon. But it wasn't only a need he had, it was a desire to bury himself deep in his wife and get lost in her again.

But that could prove dangerous just as it had almost done. He had barely stopped himself before taking her like the men did in Pacquito's band of renegades. Instead he took her outside in the rain on the grass. Whatever had he been thinking?

Damn, he had been so eager to get home to her that he had failed to shed that side of him that lingered with the renegades. She deserved better than what he had given her. She deserved to be loved and cherished, and he wasn't capable of giving her that. And yet here she stood seeing to his care.

He wanted so badly to apologize to her, but he wasn't capable of that either. He had learned, while with Pacquito, that to apologize was a sign of weakness and one suffered for it.

He rested his hands on her hips and eased her closer, pressing his face against her belly, so flat and soft. It struck him then that there was now the possibility of a child growing inside her. He would not make a good father and yet the image of her growing round with his babe filled him with a joy he didn't think possible.

He hadn't realized that he was kissing her stomach until he felt her fingers working their way through his hair and massaging his scalp. He loved the scent of her, the scent of them mixed together.

She was his now and would always be, it had been decreed with their joining and he would make certain that no one ever tore them apart. He'd kill anyone who tried.

He lifted her then and laid her down on the bed beside him, his hands staying at her waist. He had been growing hard, but with her lying there, a soft smile on her face as if she waited for him to take her again, he found himself turning as hard as a rock.

"Are you sore?" he asked not wanting to hurt her, but wanting—no aching damn painfully— to bury himself inside her.

"No," she said so softly he barely heard her.

He leaned down and rested his forehead to hers. "I want you again."

She skimmed her lips over his and whispered, "And I want you."

"You'll tell me if you feel any discomfort," he ordered.

She nodded, though she knew her need for him outweighed any discomfit she would feel.

He pressed his nose to hers. "I mean it. You will tell me."

She frowned. "But then you would leave me aching like the last time and," —her cheeks flushed a light pink—"I could not bear that again."

He ran a finger over her heated cheeks. "You wanted me that badly?"

She nodded and in another whisper said, "As I do now."

Take her.

He shut his eyes against the thought. He had been apart from polite society too long. The renegade side of him—the ugly side—forever reared its head.

Flip her over. Show her you own her.

He shook his head.

"I speak the truth. I do want you," she said.

It took him a moment to realize that she thought he was shaking his head at her remark, not believing her.

"I will hurt you," he said. *Somehow, some way I will hurt you.* He knew it in his mind and heart.

She pressed her hand to his cheek. "You would

never hurt me."

Her loving touch pushed him over the edge, and he kissed her knowing that it would not stop there. And it didn't. He once again began his descent over her body, only this time with his lips and with his touch.

Rosa writhed with pleasure, though every time she went to touch him, he pushed her hands away and told her no. She so badly wanted to touch him, needed to touch him, give him the same pleasure as he gave her. In time she hoped it would be so, but for now...

"Please, Esteban," she found herself pleading and he slipped into her gently.

As before their rhythm turned hungry, and they soon joined in a climax that left them both breathless and exhausted. And they fell asleep wrapped in each other's arms.

Chapter Twenty

Rosa woke the next morning with a slow stretch, a smile, and a need. She turned expecting to find her husband next to her, but his side of the bed was empty. Her smile turned to a disappointed frown. She had hoped that he would be there so that they could... she grabbed her pillow and buried her burning cheeks in it, recalling her actions last night.

What had made her follow him out into the rain? *Uncontrollable passion.* Her cheeks burned brighter at the thought. There was no denying how much she had wanted her husband to make love to her last night and she had made sure that he did. *The rain slashing down, the wet grass beneath her, his potent hardness, thick and deep inside her.* A heated tingle rippled between her legs from the vivid memories and she grew wet.

Whatever was the matter with her? She had wanted no part of this marriage, but she had unexpectedly fallen in love with her husband, only to discover that she hungered for his touch, his kiss, and the intimacy they brought. A thought struck her then. Last night all that concerned her had been her husband making love to her. She hadn't given a moment's thought to where her husband had been or what had happened to him for him to return in such a state.

She sprang up and out of bed and hurried to dress. She had to find her husband and see if he was all right and find out what had happened to him. She slipped into her skirt, blouse, and sandals. She didn't take the time to braid her hair, though she ran the comb through it quickly, and then hurried off. She heard raised voices as she approached the main living area. She followed the sound of her husband and his father arguing. She thought they came from the dining room, but when she turned the corner she saw that the two men were in the small parlor along with Dona Valerianna.

"Let them think what they want," Esteban said as she entered the room.

"Do not be so foolish, Esteban," his father reprimanded. "If the rancheros think that you ride with Pacquito again, they will see you hung."

Dona Valerianna gasped and when she caught sight of Rosa she shook her head. "Good lord," she said, her hand going to her chest. "A daughter-in-law who dresses like a peasant when she is a noble and a son who acts like a renegade."

Esteban turned an angry glare on his mother. "My wife's roots may be of noble birth but her heart is with her peasant parents who loved her, and do you forget that no nobles around here would have me as a son-in-law? And as far as my acting like a renegade,"—he walked over to his mother and leaned his face close to hers— "I am a renegade. And my wife will dress how she pleases."

Dona Valerianna gasped again, paled, and reached her hand out to her husband.

Don Alejandro went immediately to her side and took her hand in his as he addressed his son. "Whether you like it or not, you both have positions to uphold." He turned to Rosa. "Dressing as a peasant will not help your husband, especially now when he needs you to remain strong and by his side."

"I need no one," Esteban said with a cold anger that shivered Rosa, and then he stormed out of the room without a word or glance her way.

She didn't think twice, she followed him. She nearly caught up with him when he suddenly stopped and turned, his arm going out and his hand up.

"Don't follow me," he ordered sternly. "Our vows are sealed. It is done. Keep your distance."

Rosa stood speechless staring at him. She had thought... what? Did she think he cared because he had finally made love to her? No, he hadn't made love to her. You had to be in love to make love. Wasn't that why she had enjoyed making love with him so much? She had fallen in love with him. Had he simply consummated their vows? No, she didn't believe that. She would be like Gaby, persistent, in this case—for her—it would be for the pursuit of the truth.

He turned and walked away. She wanted to shout at him to stop, but she held her tongue. Now was not the time. Besides, they were wed, good and solid now, and nothing could change that. She belonged to him and he belonged to her. She felt a catch to her heart. Just as she had from the very first time she had seen him riding through the center of town. Her heart had gone out to him, for he had seemed as alone as she had felt. No one had wanted him and no one had wanted her. They had wanted each other last night and try as he might he couldn't deny that, though it seemed as if he tried. She couldn't help but grin since she doubted that he would keep his distance from her.

"Rosa."

She wiped the smile from her face as she turned to face Don Alejandro.

He stepped close and kept his voice low. "I know this cannot be easy for you, adjusting to a new life that is so foreign to you. But it is imperative that you act according to your new position, if for no other reason than to help your husband. With the rancheros learning of your noble birth, it may soften their opinion about Esteban. He may dismiss how the rancheros feel about him but it is important, especially with Pacquito showing his presence once again, that the rancheros believe that Esteban is not a threat to them, but is one of them."

"I understand, Don Alejandro," she said. And she did. She had learned that nobles lived by foolish rules. Their stiff and proper nature kept them at a distance from one another, though their lies made it appear otherwise. She much preferred to hug her friends and share with them and know that they cared.

"I knew you would understand. Now let us have breakfast." He held his arm out to her and she took it.

Esteban didn't join them, but then she hadn't expected him to. The meal passed like all others with inconsequential conversation.

It was when Don Alejandro stood to leave that Rosa asked, "Would it be permitted for me to go into town today? I'd like to visit with my friend." Before Don Alejandro could answer Rosa turned to Dona Valerianna. "I will change into a proper dress."

Dona Valerianna smiled and looked to her husband. "It would be good for the people to see that we do not hide during this troubling time."

Don Alejandro agreed. "You are right and especially so for Esteban's wife. I will have vaqueros escort you."

Rosa thanked them and hurried out of the room, though she detoured to the kitchen.

"Good morning, Dolores, and how are you this beautiful morning?" she asked upon entering the kitchen.

Dolores planted her hands on her ample hips and smiled. "At least you ask how I am doing before asking me for something. Your husband enters, barely nods, tells me what he wants, and then he's on his way." She shook her head. "I miss the young, caring boy who would haunt my kitchen for treats and bring me flowers."

"Esteban would bring you flowers?" Rosa

asked.

"Wild ones from the meadow." Dolores smiled. "When he was little he'd bring roots and all. He had such a giving and caring heart." Again she shook her head. "Those animals stripped him of everything. He doesn't smile, doesn't laugh... doesn't care."

"He does care," Rosa insisted. "I have seen it in him."

Dolores reached out and placed her hand on Rosa's shoulder. "Then fight and chase away the demons in him, then you will find a truly good and loving husband."

"What did Esteban want and where did he go?"

"He took some bread and fruit and told me that he would not be here for the noon meal. He did not say where he was going, though when he was young he would often share his plans for the day with me, and I would make certain that he took enough to eat with him. He was satisfied with what I gave him, so he will return for supper."

Rosa was relieved to know that her husband had not taken off again. He would do what he needed and so would she. Tonight they would once again sleep together. She would make sure of it. "I have plans of my own. Could I have some fruit and some of your luscious treats to take to a friend in need?"

"You share just like Esteban once did," Dolores said, smiling. "You two are good for each other."

Rosa gave the woman a hug and she returned

it. They worked together filling a basket, Rosa adding two bottles of wine to it. She then asked Dolores to see that it was placed in the carriage

She took extra care dressing and braiding her hair wanting to make certain she presented a proper appearance. She knew there would be consequences for what she was about to do, but she had to do it. She had to show people that she believed in her husband and would not hide away afraid of their gossiping tongues. Besides any repercussions couldn't be as bad as what she had suffered at the hands of the Curros. No one here had raised a hand to her and she didn't fear anyone would.

Don Alejandro saw her off and it wasn't until they were out of sight of the hacienda that she called out to the driver.

"Don Alejandra did inform you that I would be stopping at the Garavito hacienda before going to town."

The driver eased the horse to a stop. The vaqueros that accompanied began to stop as well.

"I was told you were going to town," the driver said.

"Pedro, isn't it?" Rosa asked, smiling and the man nodded. "I knew Don Alejandro would forget. I should have reminded him before we left. Dona Valerianna asked that I take this basket to the Garavitos and express our sorrow."

"What's going on?" the last vaquero to approach asked sternly.

It was obvious by his authoritative manner that

he was in charge of the small group and took his position seriously. Rosa turned her smile on him. "I was just explaining to Pedro that I'm to stop at the Garavito hacienda and give them this basket before proceeding into town."

"That was not Don Alejandro's orders," the vaquero snapped. "We are to escort you to town and back again."

"It's a brief stop and means much to Dona Valerianna," Rosa said, "but you have your orders and I do not wish to tread on your authority."

The vaquero seemed to give it thought and one of the other vaqueros smiled and said, "Maria would be pleased to see you."

That certainly changed the man's mind fast enough. And in no time they changed direction and headed for the Garavito hacienda. Rosa prayed that proper manners would not allow the Garavitos to treat her poorly, but regardless, she intended to keep her chin up and show everyone that she was a good wife to a good man.

When the carriage drew closer to the hacienda Rosa's stomach began to roil. She had not expected to see such devastation. Half of the hacienda lay in ruins and a large barn had burnt completely to the ground. A smaller structure had also burnt to the ground. Wood fencing lay in ruins and the vaqueros were busy working hard to repair the damages.

She had heard of the renegade attacks and the damage left in their wake, but never had she seen it with her own eyes. She knew Esteban could not have been part of this attack, but had he taken part in other raids that had caused the same destruction? She knew in her heart he had, for he reminded everyone often enough that he was a renegade.

However, the question on everyone's mind was... why had he stayed with the renegades so long? Why hadn't he returned home as soon as he was capable of leaving Pacquito's band? The question was one that would need answering.

A slim woman of fair height suddenly appeared in front of the hacienda and stood waiting for the carriage to approach. Rosa could see by her harried appearance that it had not been easy for her. But she put a smile on her pale face, tucked loose strands of gray hair behind her ears and greeted Rosa cordially.

"How kind of you to stop by," Elena Garavito said after Rosa was helped down out of the carriage.

"I was on my way into town and I wanted to express my sorrow over your tragedy and see if there was anything I could do to help."

"You can keep that renegade husband of yours away from here!"

"Manuel, your manners," Elena Garavito reprimanded harshly.

"My manners?" Don Manuel said shaking his head at his wife as he walked out of the shadows. "What of her manners coming here when her husband was the cause of all this destruction?"

The Cesare vaqueros dismounted and stepped closer to Rosa.

Rosa remained calm. She could not imagine how horrible the ordeal had been for the Garavitos and she did not wish to bring them anymore pain. She could see by the way Don Manuel kept his arm close to his side that he still suffered pain from his injury. And he looked to have aged considerably since her wedding, his dark hair having more gray in it and his once broad shoulders now had a slight hunch to them. She did not intend to argue with him, for she knew it would do no good. She wanted to extend her friendship as best she could in hopes that it would show that she believed in her husband. And she hoped that somehow, even in some small way, that would help.

"I am sorry you feel that way, Don Manuel," Rosa said calmly. "Perhaps we could share a glass of fine wine that Don Alejandro has sent along to you and discuss the matter." She gave Pedro a nod and he lifted the basket out of the carriage.

The man bristled for a moment, and then acquiesced with a sharp nod.

Dona Elena smiled and seemed to relax as she hustled Rosa into the hacienda. Rosa was shown to a small parlor that had survived the damage. It was similar to Dona Valerianna's parlor. Crystal glasses were soon brought by the servants along with a tray of fruits and cheeses.

Don Manuel sipped at his wine and glared at Rosa. She could see the frustration in his eyes and the anger. She could see how badly he wanted to say something and yet he held his tongue. It wouldn't be proper for him to unleash his anger on her, though the man did look ready to burst.

She came here to help her husband, but she realized that the Garavitos also needed help. So she made it easy for him. "Tell me of this horrific attack."

His wife stared at him as if he was a complete stranger as he poured out all the details, snarling and nearly spitting with anger as he did. When he finished, he poured, with trembling hands, a glass of wine and drank it down, then he poured another and sipped at it as he stood at the window staring out at his loss.

Rosa hoped that the venting of his anger at her would help Don Manuel. She had wished many times that she could spew her anger at the Curros when she had realized what her life would be like with them, but she would have suffered greatly for it. She wanted him to know she was friend not foe and so she offered it in a way he would understand. "The vaqueros linger while they wait for me, perhaps they can be of some help to you until I leave."

Don Manuel turned and stared at her, his eyes shining with unshed tears. It took him a moment before he said, "There are a few things I need done that could use extra hands. I appreciate the offer."

"You are most welcome," Rosa said.

He went to leave, then stopped, and turned, his unshed tears close to spilling over. "Thank you and thank Don Alejandro for his generous gift."

Rosa nodded and choked back tears that threatened to rise in her eyes. She realized it had taken a lot for Don Manuel to thank the wife of the man who he believed had taken part in the attack that nearly destroyed his home. Her visit had gone well and no matter the consequences, she was glad she had come here.

Dona Elena turned to Rosa with a tear in her eye. "You are most kind and most brave for coming here today. And I must say I appreciate your bravery more than you know."

"Dona Valerianna would have come if—"

"If her husband would have let her," Dona Elena finished. "Husbands can be difficult as you probably know."

Rosa smiled. "And stubborn."

Dona Elena laughed. "You learn quickly." Her laughing smile faded. "Valerianna and I once visited often and talked and laughed as we do now. We would work on our embroidery while our children played together. I don't know what happened to our friendship. Now we only see each other at large gatherings or church."

"Good friends may drift apart at times, but they never separate." Rosa had learned that from experience. There had been times, months, the Curros refused to let her see Marinda and when they finally got together again it was as if they had only been separated a day. And then there was Gaby. Even though they would not get to see each other often, their friendship would remain forever strong.

"You speak too wisely for one so young."

"Life and circumstances has a way of aging

us."

"There you go again speaking as a woman who has lived many years."

"I will say no more," Rosa said clamping her lips tightly shut in a smile.

"No, please don't," Dona Elena said with a tinkle of laughter. "I enjoy talking with you."

"I will visit more often and bring Dona Valerianna with me the next time," Rosa said. "But while I am here perhaps there is something I can help you with, Dona Elena?"

The woman smiled and shook her head. "You have helped more than you already know."

But Rosa was determined or perhaps it was what she would do if it had been Marinda who needed such help. Soon the two women were going through a section of the hacienda that had been partially burned collecting items that had survived the fire. And Rosa listened with heartfelt interest to stories of some of those items that brought a mixture of laughter and tears to Dona Elena.

Pedro came to collect her several hours later, informing her that time had gotten away from them all, and it was too late to go into town, and they would be late for the evening meal if they did not depart now.

Without thinking, Rosa gave Dona Elena a hug that at first startled the woman, and then she returned it.

"You have restored my hope," Dona Elena whispered in her ear.

They parted with Rosa promising to visit soon.

The visit went far better than she had anticipated. And hearing how Dona Valerianna and Elena had once seen each other often got her thinking of ways to bring the two women together again.

They had barely crossed onto Cesare land when she noticed that the vaqueros had moved closer to the carriage and, as if by instinct, her glance drifted to the ridge. A chill ran through her when she saw a band of men on horses at the top of the ridge.

Chapter Twenty-one

Esteban washed up for supper. He had spent the day out in the vineyards seeing how the grapes were doing and trying to forget about last night with his wife. But it had done little good. He could not stop thinking about her. And damn if he didn't want a repeat of it. He didn't know why he had told her to stay away from him this morning, he didn't want her to. He hadn't wanted to leave her when he had woken and found her snug in his arms. But if he had stayed until she had woken he would not have been able to stop himself from taking her again. And she had to be sore, whether she would admit it or not. So he had reluctantly left her to wake alone.

Now all he wanted was to see his wife and take her in his arms. He missed her and the thought frustrated him. He was getting used to having her around, having her care. When had that happened? It was as if she had snuck up on him and insinuated herself into his life and now that she was there, he didn't want to let her go.

He had thought he had lost the ability to love or did he fear to love or more so to be loved?

He threw the towel down that he'd been drying himself with and grabbed the clean white shirt off the back of the chair. He had to be careful, very careful. Pacquito was in the area and he was looking for trouble, but then he was always looking for trouble. This time, however, he was not the young frightened boy he had been when Pacquito had first captured him, though now he had a wife.

Anger raced through him and he clenched his hands into tight fists. He wouldn't only kill anyone who hurt Rosa, he would make them suffer, and he knew how to make a man suffer. Pacquito had taught him well.

He suddenly needed to know where Rosa was. With his shirt hanging open, he rushed through the door into his bedchamber only to stare at the empty room. When he had arrived home he hadn't seen his wife, but then he had been trying to avoid her since his only thought had been of scooping her up and carrying her off to bed for the remainder of the evening. He had seen his mother in the small parlor, but had purposely not asked about Rosa. Now he needed to know where she was.

He hurried to button his shirt, though left it unfettered at the neck, and slipped the ends into his pants, then he grabbed his jacket before leaving the room. Supper was to be served at any moment, so she had to be in the dining room. His steps were quick, though silent so his sudden entrance startled his parents.

What surprised him was that his wife was not there.

"Where is Rosa?" he demanded.

His mother smiled. "She went to town to visit a

friend. I'm sure she will be here any moment."

Esteban turned to his father. "You let her go to town?"

"I sent six vaqueros with her," Dona Alejandro said confidently.

Esteban actually laughed, which stunned his parents. "Pacquito's men would finish them off before they could draw their weapons." His eyes heated with anger. "What right did you have to give my wife permission to leave the hacienda?"

His father had no chance to respond, raised voices caught all their attentions. Esteban hurried out of the room, his parents following behind him. The commotion took them to the courtyard where more vaqueros gathered with their weapons.

When Esteban saw his wife sitting in the carriage, bent from her waist, her head almost touching her knees and Dolores placing a wet cloth to her neck, his stomach knotted and his heart pounded viciously in his chest.

He rushed to her side, his face filled with such rage that everyone scurried out of his way. When he reached her, he slipped his arm across her waist and leaned down to ask, "Are you all right?"

She placed her hand on his arm, took a deep breath, and then raised her head to look at him. She wanted to cry with joy that her husband was there beside her. "I'm fine. I foolishly let the men on the ridge upset me." She had been more than upset. She had feared for her life.

Esteban turned to Pedro and didn't need to say a word. He immediately explained.

"A band of men, eight or ten, were up on the ridge when we crossed onto Cesare land. They followed, parallel to us, slowly, never taking their attention off the carriage and didn't leave until we reached the hacienda, and then—" He shivered. "They let loose with a God-awful roar as if they were going to attack, but instead rode off."

Esteban turned to his father. "Send some men to warn the other haciendas that Pacquito is still in the area and post extra guides here."

"You heard my son, Pedro, see to it," Don Alejandro said, his arm around his wife's waist, her face pale.

Esteban went to move his arm away from his wife, but her fingers gripped it tightly. He leaned in close, his cheek a faint breath away from hers and whispered, "I'll keep you safe."

She pressed her cheek to his and loosened her grip.

Esteban scooped her up and lifted her out of the carriage, and with a nod to his father, he hurried into the house.

He took her straight to the dining room where Dolores was filling glasses with wine.

Esteban placed his wife on a chair and handed her a glass of wine.

She reached for it with a trembling hand and he quickly hunched down in front of her and wrapped his hand around hers to help still her trembling so that she could take a few sips. He then took the glass from her, placed it on the table, and stood, turning to his father.

"My wife is not to leave the hacienda without my permission. And while I am gone a guard will be posted outside our bedchamber."

"You're leaving?" Rosa asked, her heart that had calmed with his presence now hammering wildly against her chest.

"I need to see to this," Esteban said with a determination that sent a chill through Rosa.

Her hand shot out and grabbed his, squeezing it tight. "You cannot go."

"You will be safe," he assured her, though part of him knew that he was the only one who could keep her safe from Pacquito.

"It is not me I'm concerned for... it is you."

He looked down as her other hand locked around the one that already held on to him. He almost laughed at her attempt to stop him. Her meager strength could not hold him there.

"Please do not go," she pleaded softly. "I do not want to lose you."

Her words were like a lasso that wrapped around him and pulled tight, not allowing him to go anywhere. Little by little her words and actions were binding him to her, and damn if this wasn't one binding he didn't mind. The thought disturbed him and he pulled his hand out of hers.

"You have such little faith in me?" he snapped. He got angry with himself as soon as he let loose with the remark, his wife drawing her head back as if he had just slapped her.

"Faith has nothing to do with it," his father said. "It's foolish for you to ride off now. If another hacienda is attacked and you are once again nowhere to be found, then the rancheros will believe that you ride with Pacquito again."

"I do not care what they believe."

"You should," his father reprimanded. "You are wed now and you have your wife to think about and how your actions will reflect on her. Manuel Garavito believes you responsible for the attack and refuses any help I offer him and no doubt will soon let everyone know how he feels."

"Don Manuel accepted the help I offered him today," Rosa said without thinking and all three turned to stare at her.

"You went to the Garavitos and not to town?" Don Alejandro asked, as if he could not believe his own question.

Time to face the consequences of her actions, but before she did she reached for her glass of wine. Her hand still trembled and once again she found her husband reaching out to help her and hunching down in front of her, though this time he wore a look that made her a bit leery.

With his hand closed firmly around hers on the glass, he said, "Tell me, wife, why did you go there?"

"To offer my help in their time of need," she said quickly and almost cringed, for it sounded like a practiced response.

"And were the Garavitos pleased by your visit?" Esteban asked.

Rosa smiled and color popped back into her cheeks. "Yes. Don Manuel extended his thanks for the wine I brought them and accepted the help of the vaqueros. Dona Elena and I enjoyed the fruit and cheeses I also brought, and then I helped her salvage some items from one of the rooms damaged in the raid."

Esteban returned the wine glass to the table, and then lifted the hem of her dress. "I was wondering where this soot had come from." His hand went to her face and his thumb swiped along her jaw holding it out for her to see. "And this as well."

She surprised all of them by laughing softly. "It was a messy chore, but worth it. We were able to salvage many cherished items." Rosa turned to Dona Valerianna. "I told Dona Elena that you would join me when I visit next. There is much she needs help with."

"She has servants to help her," Don Alejandro said.

"Dona Elena needs friends now, not servants," Rosa said. "And she told me what a good friend Dona Valerianna is and how much she misses her."

"We will go help her," Dona Valerianna said before anyone else could speak.

Esteban stood. "My wife goes nowhere without me."

"Good, then you'll be joining us," Rosa said, keeping her smile firm even though Esteban scowled at her. At least the turn in the conversation had kept her husband from leaving.

"Why don't we all sit and have supper," Don Alejandro said sending a nod to Dolores for the food to be served.

"I have things to see to," Esteban said and turned to leave.

Rosa grabbed for his hand," Stay." She didn't mean for it to sound like an order. It was worry for her husband's life that caused it to sound like a command. Surprisingly, he didn't seem to take offense.

He leaned down in front of her once more and pressed his cheek against hers. It was warm and so soft that he would have lingered there if he could. He whispered in her ear. "What would you do to keep me here?"

Her knees began to tremble and she gathered her courage and pressed her mouth to his ear and whispered, "Anything."

Chapter Twenty-two

His wife's one word shot to his groin hardening him in an instant. Images flashed through his mind of all the things he'd like to do to her. And with the way she had responded so willingly to him last night, he didn't doubt her when she said, '*anything*.'

Esteban stood, lifted and turned his wife's chair with her on it, to place closer to the table in front of her plate. Then he took the seat beside her.

Dolores hurried to move the place setting from where he usually sat opposite his wife, to in front of him.

Pedro entered the room shortly after they began eating to inform Don Alejandro, though he looked at Esteban when he spoke, that extra men had been posted around the hacienda and that there had been no signs of anyone approaching. Men had also been sent to spread the word to the other haciendas to be on guard.

The news seemed to relax everyone at the table except Esteban. He was aware of how Pacquito and his men could sneak up and strike without anyone spotting them. He had done it himself.

Esteban was well aware of what the attack on the Garavito hacienda represented. It had been in response to his failure to obey Pacquito and return to his camp. The day would come—he always knew it would—that he would have to kill Pacquito so that he could finally be free.

Civilized conversation went on around the table, as if nothing had happened. But then his father would warn him that it wouldn't do well to upset the women. After supper, he would no doubt suggest that he and Esteban retreat to his study for a drink. Only then would their discussion continue about Pacquito.

He didn't intend for it to be a long conversation and the chances of it turning disagreeable were high. Whether anyone liked it or not, he had to bring an end to Pacquito's evil. He had thought he had left the band of renegades behind, but it had been a foolish thought. There had been those who had warned him that death was the only way of being free of Pacquito.

"You're not eating," his wife said, her hand going to rest on his hand that held a fork but hadn't used it.

He stared at her hand. Did she touch him out of concern? Out of duty? Out of Love? He almost laughed aloud at the ridiculous thought. She did what she had to do to survive just as he had and continued to do. And yet her hand rested so easily on his and her voice was so tender that he wondered if perhaps...

He yanked his hand away. "I'm not hungry." He didn't need to complicate matters by believing that she could possibly fall in love with him. And what good would it do her? He had already placed her in harm's way by marrying her.

Esteban had delayed long enough. He stood abruptly. "We need to talk, Father."

He was surprised when his father didn't disagree and the two men left the dining room with nothing more than a nod to their wives.

Dona Valerianna sighed. "I am sorry, Rosa, but I regrettably must retire."

"Is there anything I can do for you?" Rosa asked concerned, the woman looking paler than before.

Dona Valerianna stood, tears filling her eyes and said, "Yes, please don't let Esteban be taken away from us again."

Rosa sat staring at the retreating woman. Why did Dona Valerianna think that she could stop that from happening? She had no sway over Esteban... no one did. He lived by his own rules. Rules she imagined that had helped him survive. The problem was that he was still trying to survive. He had yet to fully return to his life here at the hacienda. He was still part renegade and he couldn't seem to let go of that.

She feared for him—and of him—at times, and she understood why Dona Valerianna feared losing him again. He could step back into that world and never return, and it upset her to think that she would never see him again. She felt her breath catch and her hand went to her chest.

The more she thought about it, the more she realized how in love she was with her husband. He certainly didn't make it easy to love him. She recalled her mother telling her that love rushed in and grabbed the heart and senses, leaving one blind and giving thought to nothing else. But when love finally settled, it was then that you found its true worth. She intended to find its true worth.

She left the dining room and wandered through the hacienda, thinking of how her life had changed so suddenly. And unlike the last time her life had taken an abrupt twist, this time it was for the better. She hadn't thought so at first, but Esteban had been much different than she had expected and the more she had gotten to know him, the more she realized she favored what she was discovering about him. And the more she wanted to protect him as he did her.

Anything.

The word had slipped easily past her lips as soon as her husband had asked her the question, though now that she had time to give it thought... she shivered. Would she do anything to keep him at the hacienda?

She finally arrived at her bed chamber and her hand paused on the door latch. She shook her head. Esteban was talking with his father, he wouldn't be waiting here for her. She felt her stomach catch at the thought. Was that disappointment she felt?

With a hesitant step, she entered the room to find it empty. One glance at the bed and her cheeks glowed red. She pressed her cool hand to one and smiled at the memory that stirred her senses and the thought that she wouldn't mind making more memories with him.

Her smile faded slowly. She wondered if he wished to make memories with her. Did he even think of a life with her or did he simply regard her as a convenience, a woman whose legs he could slip between whenever the urge struck?

She shook her head. No, Esteban was not like that. He couldn't have made love to her as he had if he didn't have some feelings for her, could he?

She blushed again at the intimate memories last night had stirred. She hadn't acted very proper following him outside, almost demanding he make love to her. But what was or wasn't proper when it came to the intimacies of marriage? In the throes of passion, it didn't seem as if anything would be improper between a husband and wife.

Anything.

Again the thought crossed her mind and again she wondered if there truly wasn't anything she wouldn't do to keep Esteban from leaving and taking the chance that he would never return to her. Or was she simply grasping for the impossible? Was he too much of a renegade to ever truly return home?

"Thinking twice of your offer?"

Rosa turned with a flourish, her thoughts having been so occupied that she hadn't heard her husband enter the room. She stood speechless and breathless. He was once again garbed as a renegade and that persona always managed to startle her, though this time there was no sheathed knife and he wore no hat.

"Are you leaving?" she asked worried over his

response.

"That depends on what you're offering," he said, waiting.

Rosa stared at her husband for a moment. There was something about the way he looked at her. It wasn't a plea. She doubted he ever pleaded for anything. She thought, though she could be wrong, perhaps crazy was more accurate, but she thought she saw a spark of hope in his eyes.

Was he hoping that she would give him a reason to stay? That *she* would be the reason he stayed? The thought that it was even a possibility had her turning her back to him, lifting her long hair out of the way and saying, "Help me undress."

He was at her side so fast and spun her around even faster to face him that she grew dizzy.

"Not necessary."

He grabbed her around the waist and lifted her several feet off the ground. And as he walked her to the bed, his mouth swooped down to overpower hers with a penetrating kiss. His tongue demanded she respond, though it needn't have, she was as feverish to taste him as he was to taste her.

Her eyes widened in surprise when he unceremoniously dropped her on her back on the bed, then spread her legs and positioned himself between them. But what he said next stunned her the most.

"Show me how much you want me to stay, free me."

Did he mean what she thought he meant? Or did his words have more meaning than he even realized? She gathered her courage, sat up, prayed her hands would not tremble, and reached for his belt buckle.

Her hands betrayed her, not that they trembled, but they didn't have the strength to pull the leather far enough back to unbuckle the belt. She startled when his hand settled over hers and with the strength of his hand wrapped around her small one, helped unleash the buckle.

She glanced up at him with the foolish thought to thank him, but her words died on her lips when her eyes caught with his. They smoldered with a fiery passion that sent her senses soaring. She pulsed between her legs and felt herself grow wet with the want of him. She had never thought that she could desire this man with such intensity. And her need to touch him, to place a loving hand on him, had her reaching out to touch his face.

He locked his hand around her wrist and with a roughness in his voice said, "It isn't there I want your hand." Then he pushed her hand down to rest against the bulge in his pants.

Why she startled, she didn't know. She was familiar with his impressive size, having seen and felt it, and yet the thick bulge stunned her for a moment until she realized it was the anticipation of knowing he would soon be inside her once again that had startled.

The thought, along with the image of him driving into her over and over, had her fingers eagerly slipping down into his pants to hurry and free him.

"Anxious?" he asked with a sinful smile.

His smile disarmed her since he rarely smiled and she couldn't help but return it as she whispered, "Yes."

His smile vanished and he stared at her as if he didn't believe her.

She pulled her hand out of his pants and his breath caught as if disappointed. Then her hands eased his pants down over his hips and it took only a moment for him to spring free. She stared at the full hard length of him and she had the sudden urge to taste him.

Could she? Should she? Would it be improper for her to dare place her lips on his... the image fueled her desire to do just that. And without thought or consequence, she leaned forward and slipped him into her mouth.

She heard him gasp and she smiled before her tongue began to lick him. She was surprised at how much she enjoyed the taste of him and how natural it felt to be so intimate with him. She soon became lost in play, teasing and tasting, and not being able to get enough of him.

Esteban shut his eyes against the exquisite pleasure she was bringing him. Her licks and tugs had been hesitant at first, though they had certainly grown him larger. It was seeing that she had wanted to, and dared to, taste him that had enlarged him all the more. Of course that he was the only one she had done this with—and he would be the only one she ever would do it with—also managed to grow him thicker. And damn if she didn't learn fast and seem to enjoy it.

He wished she was naked so that he could reach down and cup her breasts in his hands, squeeze them and enjoy the feel of them. The thought nearly had him exploding, though it was more the fact that his wife's mouth had become much too eager and much too talented in such a short time. And then there was the sudden thought that she belonged to him and only him. He had never had a woman that hadn't been used and abused by other men. He never had a woman as innocent and caring as Rosa.

Damn, what had he forced her to do with his demand of *anything*?

"Enough," he yelled as he pulled away from her, yanked up his pants, and moved off the bed, turning away from her.

"Did I do something wrong?" she asked.

He turned and the sincerity in her eyes felt like a punch to his gut. He had to get out of there fast or he'd be dragging her to the edge of the bed to taste him again. And he'd be damned if it would only take a few seconds for him to come in her mouth and he doubted she would like that.

"I'm leaving," he turned again.

"You can't," she demanded so adamantly that it had him turning around slowly to glare at her.

"What did you say?"

"You can't leave." Her tone softened as did her expression. "I need you."

Esteban fought with himself. If he took one step toward her—one step—he'd be finished.

There would be no turning back... unless. But that would be heartless of him, but then he had no heart so what did it matter.

Rosa mattered.

The thought angered him. He couldn't let her matter, he couldn't. If he did she would suffer for it. And he would die before he would see his wife suffer for the likes of him.

His anger fueled his decision and with quick steps he was on the bed, his body forcing her on her back and with quick hands he freed himself and tossed her dress up and was inside her in one hasty thrust.

He took her fast and hard, both their passions so close to the surface that they exploded in unison, in climaxes that left them breathless and more than satisfied.

Esteban didn't wait for his breathing to ease. He was up and off his wife in a flash and fastening his pants just as quickly. He then walked to the door, though he ached to stay with his wife, hold her, stroke her, fall asleep with her in his arms and wake with her the same way. He almost hesitated, turned around, and returned to her. But then he would only place her in more danger and without looking back, he walked out of the room.

Rosa stared at the closed door. She had thought for certain her husband would have stayed with her. It was as if she could feel his want to do so. It shocked her that he left her there alone. It also made her wonder if she would ever get passed the barrier that he seemed to keep between them.

This marriage was nothing like she thought it would be. She had believed she had no choice but to accept her fate and make the most of it, especially in her marriage bed. But now she realized she wanted more, and she knew that she would fight for it.

Chapter Twenty-three

Rosa empathized with Dona Valerianna. The woman was torn between happiness that her daughter Crista would soon return home and worry that her son may not return home, Esteban having been gone two days now.

Rosa refused to believe that Esteban would abandon his family, not after the horrors he had suffered while with the renegades. She hoped that in time he would confide more in her, though that took trust and it was obvious that Pacquito had robbed Esteban of trusting anyone. Pacquito hadn't only robbed Esteban of things, but he had also robbed Esteban's parents of their son in so many more ways than any of them realized.

Rosa wished she could do something to help Dona Valerianna through her worries that Esteban might not return and she realized that the most helpful thing would be to take the woman's attention off her children. She thought a visit to her old friend Dona Elena would be good. But Dona Valerianna reminded her that she was not allowed to leave the hacienda without Esteban's permission, and that Don Alejandro would not go against his son's wishes.

Rosa had tried asking Esteban's father for permission but as Dona Valerianna said, he would not go against his son's orders.

With her plans thwarted for now, Rosa slipped into her skirt and blouse and hurried off to the orange orchard. She planned to collect the succulent fruit and bask in the beautiful sunshine.

She, too, was worried about Esteban, but he had yet to heal and forgive, though she doubted that he realized he needed to forgive himself for doing whatever he had to do to survive his ordeal with Pacquito. She knew how survival could take its toll. She had thought that her nightmare with the Curros would never end and after so many years she had simply learned to deal with it, though she kept hope alive. It was the only thing that truly kept her going day after endless day. She wondered what had kept Esteban going and how he had finally managed to escape his nightmare.

She chased the many thoughts and concerns away, wanting to enjoy the beautiful day. She would continue to pray and hope for her husband's speedy return. She missed him, all of him.

Rosa blushed at the memories of him naked and hard, and shook her head. She had never imagined that intimacy with her husband could be so—she smiled—unforgettable. And she wouldn't mind sharing many more *unforgettable* moments with him.

She shook her head again. Now wasn't the time for such intimate thoughts. There was the day to enjoy and with luck perhaps her husband would return today and tonight they would...

Rosa silently scolded herself and hurried to the

orange orchard to keep her thoughts and hands busy.

She grabbed a basket as she entered the orchard. She had stopped by the kitchen before leaving and had asked Dolores if she needed oranges and though the woman had scolded her about doing a servant's chore, she had finally admitted that she could use some. So Rosa intended to fill the basket, keeping some for herself and Esteban.

The sun grew hot as she toiled at her task, though it didn't bother her. The thought that she had her freedom to do this at her leisure made it all the more enjoyable. And the quiet surroundings made it all the more appealing. It was as if she was lost in her own world for a couple of hours and that was a priceless gift to her.

"May I have an orange, *nina*?"

Rosa was so startled by the unexpected male voice that she had to grab the top rung of the ladder so that she wouldn't fall. She was familiar with only a few of the vaqueros on the hacienda, and she hoped this man did not mistake her for one of the servants since he addressed her more as a servant.

She turned and her words died on her lips. Not far beneath her stood a renegade. It wasn't hard to recognize one now that she had seen a few on the ridge that day, though up closer he was much more intimidating. And the stench of him almost had Rosa gagging. His dark, narrow eyes settled over her, as if inspecting every inch of her body and sent a shiver through her. His grin and a quick lick of his lips made it seem that he was ready to taste her. Where just moments ago she had embraced the quiet solitude, she now felt trapped by it. No one would hear her if she needed to cry out for help.

She had to get off the ladder and give herself a chance to run. She nodded and pointed to the basket a short distance from the ladder. "Help yourself." And as he did, she scurried down. Before she could put distance between them, he stepped so close in front of her that he forced her back against the ladder, trapping her.

Fear prickled along her skin as his stench assaulted her nostrils and turned her stomach once more. That he had been riding hard and long on the trail was obvious, though she wondered if perhaps it was his natural state as some men seemed averse to washing.

Though fear continued to sting her perspiring skin, she kept her tone firm. "Take a few oranges and be on your way. I have work to do."

"I'll take my fill," he sneered and her fear grew as he inched closer.

Rosa raised her hand to push him away when he was suddenly snatched away from her, and sent flying through the air. She was stunned to see him flat on his back a few feet away, her husband's boot jammed against his throat.

"I warned you, Carlos, now you pay," Esteban said.

The man's hands frantically tore at Esteban's

boot, trying desperately to dislodge it, his breath trapped.

Rosa almost felt sorry for the struggling man, Esteban showing him no mercy, but then he wouldn't have showed her any. The next thing she knew, Esteban yanked his boot away from the man's throat, reached down and grabbed him by his shirt while his other hand pounded him in the face. He repeated this several times before he effortlessly tossed him to the ground again.

He gave Carlos barely time to recover when he grabbed him and pummeled him again. The man could barely defend himself and went down several times. Each time, Esteban brought him to his feet to beat him again until finally he tossed him aside, as if discarding him like a piece of garbage.

Esteban went for the knife sheathed at his belt. "Now you die."

Rosa rushed to her husband's side, grabbing his arm. She stumbled as he shoved her away, but she quickly righted herself and grabbed his arm again and whispered for only him to hear. "You are not like him... you are not a renegade."

He shook his head, his glazed eyes clearing as if he was emerging from a trance. Then he turned away from her.

Her arm fell away and this time she didn't reach out again, she knew she had reached him.

"Go near my wife again and the next time I'll kill you," Esteban said with a cold resolve that had Rosa shivering. "Now get off my land and stay off it."

It took the beaten man several attempts to get to his feet. He spit blood as he did and could barely see out of one eye as he stumbled away without saying a word.

Esteban turned on her with such fury that she fell back against the ladder.

He pinned her against it with his body, his hands grasping the rungs on either side of her head. "What did I tell you about leaving the hacienda?"

She swallowed hard trying to moisten her dry lips so that she could speak.

"Do you realize what kind of danger you placed yourself in?"

Her mouth remained too dry to form any words, and though a bit of fear remained to prickle her skin, she couldn't help but notice the fine film of dirt that covered his clothes and clung to him. He had traveled the trail hard and though it didn't show, she knew he had to be exhausted.

Her hand went to his face to touch it lightly, not sure if he would turn away from it. But he didn't turn away, nor did he stop her, surprisingly he turned his cheek to meet her touch.

"You are tired and in need of a good washing and much sleep," she said softly.

His hand shot out to wrap around her waist and yank her against him. "You will join me in both."

It was a command, one he would not see disobeyed and as his mouth came down to claim hers, she knew she would not disobey him, for she realized that he needed her.

His kiss may have been possessive, but there was an ache to it that tore at her heart. Could he have missed her as much as she missed him? His hungry kiss certainly made it seem that way.

With reluctance, he eased his mouth away from hers returning again and again to nip at her lips until he finally said, "You should not have been in the orchard alone."

She remained silent, letting him chastise her, not fearing once that he would raise a hand to her like the Curros had done. He would not suffer the punishment on her that had been inflicted upon him.

"I will lock you in our bed chamber the next time I am away."

"There is an easier solution," she said softly.

His eyes narrowed. What is that?"

"Don't leave me again."

Had she heard a catch to his breath or had she wished it had been his reaction?

"I come and go as I please, and you will do well to remember that." His tone was stern, his words curt, as if he scolded.

She wanted to tell him that she loved him and cared what happened to him, but her response caught on her tongue. She wasn't sure what had stopped her. She believed she had the courage or was it his response she feared?

"Come with me," he said in that commanding way of his and took her hand in his.

His hand was warm, his hold firm, as if he didn't intend on letting go and it rushed a tingle up her arm. She walked along with him in silence, wishing he would share his thoughts with her and wanting to share her own with him, but debating whether it would be wise.

Esteban was still trying to calm himself. Rage had blinded him when he had seen Carlos nearly on top of his wife. He would have killed the man. After all he had warned him about stepping foot on his land again, and if his wife hadn't been there... he would have. But her words had killed his intentions. She didn't believe him a renegade any longer and perhaps it was time for him to do the same. Pacquito not only expected him to kill Carlos, a man Pacquito always thought expendable, but he also wanted him to. Esteban's actions would have sent a clear message that he was still a renegade, still one of Pacquito's men. Rosa whispered words had reminded him of that. Now Carlos could return to Pacquito beaten but alive, sending him a message that he was no longer one of them, he was free.

He had also wanted to throttle his wife for disobeying him and going off on her own without vaqueros to protect her, though now he simply wanted to strip her naked and slip inside her and get lost making love to her.

She had been on his mind night and day since he had left the hacienda and all he could think about was returning home to her. He had only been away a couple of days and he had cursed and complained to himself every minute of the days he had been gone. The brief trip had been worth it and he was relieved to learn that Pacquito's men had retreated, for now. Pacquito would often do that, hit a place, retreat, wait, let the people feel safe again and let down their guard, and then hit with fury.

If there was one thing that Pacquito's men feared most, it was his unpredictable temper. One minute he could be laughing with you and the next minute he would shoot you dead. And there wasn't anyone who escaped his wrath, not even his family. And worse, he enjoyed tearing families apart.

Esteban squeezed his wife's hand glad that she was there beside him as he led her to their bedchamber. He intended to have time alone with her and he would let nothing, absolutely nothing, interfere with it.

"Esteban, you're back."

Esteban scowled, though when he turned to face his mother, he softened his expression. Not enough obviously, since she took a step back away from him.

"I am so pleased that you have returned," Dona Valerianna said, then took a breath and added a heartfelt, "I missed you."

Esteban had been all too aware that his mother had feared him since his return and not once had she told him that she had missed him. But then he had never told her how very much he had missed her, her gentle voice, her caring ways, and most of all her loving arms.

The words spilled from his mouth without him

realizing it. "I missed you as well, *Madre*."

Rosa slipped her hand out of her husband's and stepped back hoping one of them would take the first step and one did... Dona Valerianna went to her son and threw her arms around him.

Esteban's arms circled her and held her tightly.

"I love you so much. I am so happy that you are home," his mother said through a stream of tears.

He wanted to tell his mother that he loved her, but the words stuck in his throat. And he could not help but wonder if his mother would still love him if she knew of all the terrible things he had done. Still he hugged her tight, wanting to linger in her arms that had so often comforted him as a child and had hugged him frequently, simply because she loved him.

Rosa kept her tears at bay, though it wasn't easy. Esteban needed this as did his mother. He needed to hear her tell him that she loved him and that she was happy he was home, though Rosa got the distinct feeling that when she saw her son this time, she knew that he was truly home.

"Did you just get home?" his mother asked taking a step back, but leaving her hand to rest on his arm.

"Only moments ago and as you can see I am in need of a washing, clean clothes, and sleep."

"I will send servants with food as well."

"Not necessary, I'm not hungry and my wife will help me with the rest," Esteban responded hastily wanting nothing more than to be alone with

Rosa.

His mother patted his arm. "Then rest and we will see you at supper."

"Your mother loves you very much," Rosa said as they walked to their bed chamber.

"She loves the young son she knew, not the son who returned home."

Rosa stopped and stared at him. "How can you say that when you haven't even given her a chance to get to know the man you have become?"

Esteban tugged her along, his eagerness to be alone with her growing him hard. "And she never will." He couldn't take the chance, for then he would risk losing his mother's love forever.

"Your mother would never stop loving you, unlike mine who never loved me from the beginning. Your mother has cherished and loved you since the day you were born and nothing will change that."

They entered their bed chamber and Esteban stepped away from her, shaking his head. "You are a fool if you believe that. My past will prevent anyone from loving me."

Rosa raised her chin. "It hasn't stopped me from falling in love with you."

Chapter Twenty-four

Esteban was too stunned to respond or turn and face his wife. He let her words sink in and they trickled down deep, weaving their way inside him, spreading warmth until they touched his heart. He shut his eyes a moment savoring the sensation. Never would he have thought that she would love him and never would he have thought to feel such... *feel*. Her words had made him feel, something he thought he'd never do again.

After being with Pacquito a while and giving up on ever escaping, he had learned to lock every bit of emotion away. If he hadn't, he could have never survived his ordeal. But his wife's words had cracked that lock and forced their way in and brought a joy that continued spreading and opening places he had believed long dead, and it felt good, so very good.

The problem was that he didn't know how to respond. Or was it that he felt himself such a vile creature that he didn't deserve her love? One thing he had learned about his lovely wife was that she spoke the truth and often spoke it from her heart, leaving herself all too vulnerable... like now.

She laid herself bare to him, barer than if she stood naked before him. And she patiently waited for his reply, but how did he reply? Did he admit that he felt the same? Dare he even admit it to himself? When he had laid eyes on her for the first time he had thought his reaction nothing more than pure lust, for he had turned hard at the sight of her. It had been his heart slamming against his chest that had made the difference. Never before had he experienced that with a woman. And though he had fought against the marriage, and would not dare admit it, he had wanted Rosa as his wife.

His conscious, which he had thought had long deserted him, had reared its head and warned him of her innocence, though she was innocent no more. But he had yet to corrupt her, though he feared that somehow, someway he would.

Words continued to fail him, though he had learned that action could speak so much louder than words.

He turned slowly, and with unhurried, though strong strides, he went to her. She did not back away from his approach, she stood firm, her chin up, though her lips quivered ever so slightly.

His response was instinctive; he reached out, wrapped his arm around her waist, and brought her flat up against him... and kissed her.

She didn't give thought to her response. She acted instinctively. She wrapped her arms around his neck and pressed her body closer against his.

Her eager response fueled his arousal. He didn't think he could get any harder, but as her eagerness grew, so did he.

He had wanted to take his time making love to her, but he had gone too long without her and his need for her was too great. He was already grinding himself against her, though it was in response to the way she moved against his thick hardness. It seemed her need was as great as his.

Later he could take his time with her. Right now his need was beyond control. He was about to tell her that he couldn't wait when the words rushed out of her mouth.

"I can't wait. I need you right now."

Damn it, if he almost didn't come right there and then. He had her flat on her back on the bed in no time. And with just as much speed slipped off his boots and out of his pants, then threw her skirt up, and hurried into her with a swift thrust.

She cried out in sheer pleasure. Until he was inside her, she hadn't realized how much she had missed him, missed this intimacy, missed this man she loved. She wanted, needed beyond any rationale sanity to touch him, have him completely naked, be naked herself so that nothing, absolutely nothing, separated them.

"I need to be naked. I need you naked," she blurted out.

"And I need to be inside you," he argued with a smug grin, a quick kiss, and a hard thrust.

Dropping her head back, she moaned and brought her bottom up driving him even deeper into her.

He threw his head back and groaned, then lowered his mouth to her exposed neck, raining kisses and hungry nips along it. He never tasted anything so satisfying in his life. Her skin was warm, sweet, and intoxicating, and he was addicted to it.

He reared back and practically ripped his shirt off, then grabbed her blouse and pulled it up to bunch in his hands. She raised her shoulders and head and he hurried it off her, the skirt followed. Slipping his arm around her waist, he yanked her up, and then grabbed her bottom to push her close against him.

She pressed her cheek to his. "I love having you inside me."

"By the time I'm done with you, you may regret those words."

She brushed her lips across his and whispered, "Never. Ever."

Her words sounded like a whispered promise that she would always keep, and he couldn't stand it any longer. He was too near to exploding and he wanted her to join him.

He took firm hold of her bottom and urged her against him setting a rhythm, then issued a soft warning, "I'm going to make you come hard."

She tilted her head to look at him and with a faint smile asked, "How many times?"

"Challenging me?"

"Are you up to it?"

He grinned and set a faster rhythm.

They climaxed so fast that it shocked the both of them, their cries of pleasure echoing around the room and before it ended, Esteban slipped his hand between their bodies and teased her small already pulsating nub.

Her passion escalated again, her hands going to his shoulders to hold on tight as he once again drove her to dizzying heights of pleasure and once again she exploded in a mind-stunning climax.

Rosa was letting the exquisite pleasure rush through her when suddenly he shifted against her, lowered his mouth to her nipple and rolled his tongue over the hardened orb again and again and again, setting her passion to flaming.

He stopped and was about to ease out of her and she cried out, "No! No, don't stop, please don't stop. "

Seeing her in the throes of yet another climax, it wakened another arousal in him, and he soon had her lying back on the bed, her legs wrapped tightly around him, as if she feared he would slip out of her and both of them engaged in another frantic rhythm, racing toward a climax that rushed at them in a wave of never-ending pleasure.

Esteban finally rolled off her and they both lay flat on their backs, their breathing labored, though he locked his fingers with hers, as if keeping her from leaving his side.

Rosa lay there more satiated than she ever thought possible.

They lay in the large bed, the afternoon sun drifting through the open doors, admitting a soft breeze. Rosa was glad that this section of the hacienda contained a lot of privacy, for she did not want to ever stifle her cries of pleasure when making love with Esteban.

She lay there beside her husband completely

relaxed and happy. She was actually happy for the first time in a very long time. She would have never expected that Esteban could fill her with such joy but he did, not that he couldn't be difficult at times.

With a slow turn of her head, she gazed upon her husband. She wasn't surprised to see him sleeping soundly. Whatever he had been up to had left him completely exhausted. He would sleep for hours no doubt, but she wasn't tired, she felt more exhilarated than ever and the day was beautiful, and the gardens beckoned. She could fill a vase with freshly cut flowers and place them in their room. Then he would wake to the rich fragrance.

Convincing herself that it was a good plan, Rosa carefully and slowly inched her hand out of her husband's and just as carefully rolled to the edge of the bed and off it. She gave a tentative look his way, worried that she may have woken him, but he hadn't budged and her heart went out to him. He looked so peaceful and content and she smiled, knowing she had been the reason for his contented slumber. She wouldn't be gone long, though she had no doubt that he'd sleep for hours, perhaps even into tomorrow. However, she wanted to be there, in his arms, when he woke.

She quietly slipped into her skirt and blouse and grabbing her sandals went out the open doors. She gathered what she needed and the basket overflowed with sweet scents. She so enjoyed herself that she lost all thought of time and when she finally realized that the sun wasn't at its highest any longer, she grabbed her full basket and hurried back to her bedchamber.

She turned in through the open doors and stopped. Esteban sat naked on the edge of the bed, his eyes scanning the room. When he saw her, he stood, walked over to her, stepped around her to close the doors, took the basket of flowers from her hand to sit on the floor, and then he quickly stripped her naked and scooped her up and carried her back to bed, pinning her body with his, kissing her and entering her all at once.

She wasn't surprised at how quickly she came, having had grown wet at the sight of him naked and thoroughly aroused. And afterwards he wrapped himself around her, settling her comfortably against him, though his whispered words were not what she wanted to hear.

"You're mine and you'll go nowhere without my permission."

He was asleep shortly after and she lay there awake wondering what to do. She had a larger taste of freedom by going off with the padre to Los Angeles. And she had to admit that she had enjoyed the adventure. She grew restless, her thoughts much too busy to sleep. The sun still shined bright, a warm breeze drifted in the air and she couldn't help but think of how inviting the garden had been. Dare she attempt to leave her sleeping husband once again?

When she heard a light snore from Esteban, she smiled and slowly worked her way out of his arms. She slipped into her clothes quickly and just before she was about to leave the room, she stopped. She quietly tiptoed to the chest where her drawing material lay and carefully gathered it together and finally scooted out the doors, closing them silently behind her.

She chose the garden not far from her bedchamber, knowing Esteban would no doubt come searching for her once he woke. She settled herself beneath a large, double-trunk oak tree, its wide, lower branches providing adequate shade against the bright sun.

As soon as she began to sketch, her mind began to ease and it wasn't long before all thoughts faded and she became lost in drawing.

That was how Esteban found her a couple of hours later, sitting under the tree, several drawings surrounding her while she busily worked on another one. When he woke he had been disappointed she hadn't been there beside him. He had worried where she had gone off to and had rushed to dress and go find her.

He called out as he approached her. "I've been searching for you."

Her head shot up and she smiled. "And you have found me."

He sat beside her in the shade, picking up one drawing after another to admire. "These are beautiful. You are quite talented."

"Thank you."

"Didn't I tell you not to go anywhere without my permission," he said and rested his back against the thick tree trunk.

"I am safe, I am home and I will always return home."

"That's what I thought when I was captured, and it took me sixteen years to return home."

Chapter Twenty-five

Rosa turned quietly to face her husband, hoping he would talk about his time with Pacquito and hoping by doing so he would help purge his past and release his pain.

"Every day I thought about escaping," Esteban said, "but it was difficult when Pacquito kept a rope around my neck and led me around like some animal. Now and then he'd remove the rope and I would attempt to escape. It took several efforts and whippings for me to realize that I was doing exactly what he wanted me to do. Pacquito enjoys beating people and he does it until he has the person begging for mercy, though he rarely gives it."

He grew silent and Rosa worried that he would say no more. She almost sighed aloud when he continued.

"I also learned fast that if I showed the slightest inclination of attachment to anyone or thing, Pacquito would..." His features grew stern, as if he was steeling himself against the horrific memories, and he turned his head away for a moment.

Rosa did not want to imagine the endless cruelty that Pacquito must have put him through. It was no wonder he found it difficult to form any attachment. Caring had cost him severe pain.

"Pacquito's men are cold, heartless, bas—" he stopped. "His men obey or else."

She wanted to ask the one question that was on everyone's mind. Why did he wait so long to escape such a hell? But she didn't know if the time was right. He was just beginning to open up to her and share his past. She didn't want to take the chance that he would turn silent and say no more. So she kept the question to herself, for now.

He stared at her a moment, as if debating with himself to continue and, then said, "Pacquito provided his men with women, he insisted on it, and they weren't always willing ones. He would make each of his men take a woman, on her hands and knees, in front of everyone. Sometimes he would take the woman first, and then the man would have her afterwards." He shook his head. "Refusing wasn't an option, unless one wanted to be beaten unmercifully and forced to do it anyway."

The repulsive image sent a chill through her and her pain for him grew. "I cannot imagine the horror of being forced to go against one's nature to survive. It must have been horrendous for you."

Most women would have run away from him by now and would never want to be defiled by his touch again. It had been the very reason why he had no intentions of ever telling his wife about it. Yet somehow he had felt the need to confess to her. Perhaps he had wanted to give her a chance to run away from him. Or perhaps he wanted no secrets between them. He wanted her to know everything about him, no matter how high the cost. And yet here she sat not only offering comfort, but believing that he was a good man forced to do an evil deed to survive. But how long would she believe in him with the more she learned?

"The horror is that that isn't the worst of it."

She shocked him even more when she rested her hand on his and said, "Then it is good that you are finally home and away from such evil. Now you can finally be free to be the good man you truly are."

How could she still believe him a good man when he had done such horrible things? And yet here she sat with a look of sympathy for him rather than disgust. But what if he told her... "There was an old woman," —sadness filled his eyes— "Lequita. She tended my wounds, snuck me food, and encouraged me to be brave. She..."

This time when he paused, Rosa knew he wouldn't continue. It was as if he suddenly locked his memories away, and she wondered what had happened that caused him to not want to remember.

The urge to make love to her overwhelmed him or perhaps he simply wanted to know if she would now abhor his touch and the mere mention of intimacy. He was about to find out when she spoke and he felt a sense of relief. Was he that worried that she would deny him? Or was he more worried that he would not let her? His wife had become a tonic to his soul that he could not do without.

"May I draw you?"

"Have your way with me," he said and settled comfortably against the tree trunk.

"Later," she said with a slight blush, "for now I'll draw you."

Esteban never showed emotion, so it always pleased Rosa when she got an unexpected reaction from him. His brow scrunched and he tilted his head slightly, as if he wasn't certain that he had heard her correctly.

She quickly turned to gather her drawing materials, though mostly to hide the smile that she couldn't stop from surfacing.

She yelped when his arm coiled around her waist and he yanked her onto his lap.

"Give me a sample of later," he whispered in her ear.

The privacy of their bedroom was one thing, but here in the open where anyone could see them. She felt her body flush with heat that she should be so daring. Without further thought she turned her head to claim his lips in a hungrier kiss than she thought possible.

He returned it with just as much passion, his hand easing his way up her blouse to settle gently over one breast.

She startled at his tender touch, her nipple hardening as soon as his finger grazed it and she wished it was his mouth that teased it. As usual she was already wet and ready for him and he no doubt was the same since he grew harder and harder against her.

Light laughter and voices broke them

reluctantly apart, though Esteban kept a firm arm around her waist so that she could not move off his lap.

When Dona Valerianna and Padre Marten rounded the corner and caught sight of them, Rosa flushed with embarrassment. Dona Valerianna did the same while Esteban glared.

"Is there something I can do for you, Padre?" he asked curtly.

The padre cleared his throat nervously as if he was about to give a sermon, and then shook his head, thinking better of it and said, "No, nothing," —then with a sudden change of mind added— "though I would suggest that you do your wife and you a favor and seek confession so that Rosa and you may once again attend Mass."

"Believe me, Padre, there would be no absolution for my sins," Esteban said.

"As you say, Esteban." The padre acknowledged with a slight bow of his head. "Now I must be going."

Dona Valerianna ushered him away with a promise of a basket of fruit fresh from the orchards.

Esteban turned stern eyes on his wife. "Don't think to convince me to seek confession and save my soul. You will waste your breath."

"There is no point to seek confession... yet."

"Yet?"

She nodded. "God will know you are ready for absolution when first you forgive yourself."

"Forgive myself for what, for allowing myself

to be turned into a beast?"

Rosa placed a gentle hand on his cheek. "For surviving."

"At what cost? At least in death there would have been honor."

"You survived a brutal capture and returned home, you think there is no honor in that?"

"The cost was too great."

"If you truly thought that, then you would have perished many years ago."

His wife was far more perceptive than he realized. The same thought had haunted him through the years. Why had he fought so hard to survive? The answer had always been the same. No matter what it took, he had wanted to return home to his family. And he finally had, only to find the impossible... a wife that loved him.

The urge to make love to his wife returned with a vengeance, perhaps because it was the one way, or the only way, he had of showing how much he... damn, but he loved her. Yet he fought against it, knowing that in the end his love for her would only bring her pain. And that was an inconceivable thought to him. He would not see her suffer, and so he would not let anyone know that he loved her more and more each day.

Rosa broke the silence with a tender kiss to his cheek. "Let me draw you." She didn't wait for his consent. She slipped off his lap and he let her go.

He sat in silence listening to the sound of graphite against paper and the sometime rustle of leaves when a warm breeze swept down around them. He hadn't known such contentment in a long time and before he realized it, his eyes drifted closed and he fell asleep.

Rosa didn't disturb her husband. He needed to rest and she didn't need his eyes open to draw him accurately. She knew his eyes by heart, and so she continued to draw.

Esteban rode his horse hard and fast. He had to get to his wife. She was gone and he couldn't find her. No matter where he went, where he searched, he couldn't find her. His heart pounded in his chest and his fear mounted. He knew who had her and he knew he'd have to kill him to free her. He heard her scream his name over and over and he rode faster and faster getting nowhere.

"Esteban. Esteban," Rosa said, trying to wake her husband from an obvious nightmare, though having difficulty.

He woke with a start, springing forward away from the tree.

Rosa quickly placed her cheek to his and whispered, "I'm here with you. It's all right."

He buried his face in the crook of her neck letting the warmth of her skin erase the chilling fear that ran through him. The scent of fresh fruit tickled his senses and he smiled. She was forever in the orchard picking fruit and the sweet scent always lingered on her skin. But it was her words that had soothed him the most.

She was there with him and everything was all right... unless Pacquito got a hold of her.

He brought his head up and took hold of her

chin and was about to tell her that she would go nowhere without him when she kissed him. It wasn't a gentle kiss but a demanding one, as if her urge for him was too great to ignore and it more than aroused him. It turned him rock hard.

It took only a moment for him to realize that if he didn't get her to their bedchamber they would be stripping each other bare right here where anyone could come upon them.

He got to his feet taking her with him, since she refused to let go of him and as he did he caught sight of the drawing she had done of him. The full impact of it halted him in his tracks and with an arm around her waist he leaned down and scooped it up.

He couldn't take his eyes off himself. She had not only captured his features perfectly, but she had captured the war of emotions that lay so deep beneath the surface; pain, anger, guilt, misery, and what he had never let anyone see... a hint of hope. She had known it was there. She had seen it when no one else had.

"You are complex," she said on a wistful breath and smiled, "but I love you anyway."

She was aware of his faults, perhaps better than he was and yet she loved him in spite of them. Was this real or was he still dreaming?

He leaned down and kissed her and when their lips met with loving urgency he knew it wasn't a dream. He soon had her up in his arms and was about to rush off with her to their bedchamber when his father called out his name.

Esteban silently cursed the man and placed his wife on her feet, though kept hold of her.

When Don Alejandro came into view, Esteban knew that he was not bringing good news.

"Another hacienda has been attacked. You must come with me so that they see that you were home with your family and had nothing to do with it."

"They will blame me anyway," Esteban argued.

"Possibly, but if you make the effort there is a chance some may see it differently.

Rosa laid a hand on her husband's chest. "Your father is right. It is best you go and see what you can do for your neighbors and friends." She reached up to kiss his cheek and whispered, "I will wait most impatiently for your return."

"In bed naked is where I want to find you," he murmured in her ear and gave it a slight nip.

She shivered, and he kissed her quickly.

"Rosa, please see to Dona Valerianna. She is quite upset by the news," Don Alejandro said.

With that the three entered the hacienda, going separate ways once inside, though not before Esteban gave his wife another kiss. He didn't want to leave her, but he had no choice. He knew going with his father would not end the problem. It was only the beginning of troubles that lay ahead.

A few hours later suppertime came and the men had still not returned. Dona Valerianna excused herself from the meal saying she wasn't hungry, and Rosa could not blame her since she wasn't either.

Before going to her quarters Dona Valerianna uncharacteristically gave Rosa a hug and said, "Thank you."

"For what?" Rosa asked.

"For being you."

Rosa wasn't sure what she meant. Sometimes she had felt she didn't know who she was and having learned that she actually hadn't been who she thought she was helped explain that. But now, being Esteban's wife had changed things again and she liked who she was becoming.

Rosa meandered through the hacienda eager for her husband to return. She loved spending time with him. She had so enjoyed sketching him out in the garden today and she intended to sketch more portraits of him until she found one that suited him best, and then she would paint him.

She wandered back to the front parlor, but her husband had yet to return. She was about to retire to their bedchamber to wait naked in bed for him when she heard raised voices approaching. They quickly turned to shouts by the time Esteban and his father entered the house.

"It is common knowledge that you disappear at times," Don Alejandro said. "You could have made it easy on all concerned and when asked told everyone where you go."

"It doesn't matter what I tell them. They believe that I serve Pacquito and do his bidding."

"Then tell them they are wrong. Tell them the truth," his father argued.

"Do you know the truth, Father?"

"I know my son is a good man and would not bring harm to his neighbors and friends."

Esteban appreciated his father's confidence in him, though he doubted others felt the same. "But do our neighbors and friends believe that or do they believe that I still run with the renegades and help them wreak havoc on their homes?"

"Address their concerns so there will be no doubt. Tell them you are negotiating with Pacquito."

Esteban burst out laughing. "Negotiate with Pacquito? There is no negotiating with Pacquito. You do what he says or die."

His father paled. "Then why do you go see him?"

"I don't go see him."

"Then where do you go? Who do you see?" his father demanded.

"To find the only man Pacquito fears... *hijo del Diablo.*"

Dona Valerianna gasped as she emerged from an open doorway and blessed herself twice as she said, "Son of the Devil."

Chapter Twenty-six

"You cannot think to seek help from the devil," Don Alejandro said helping his wife to the parlor to sit and where they all could talk. "He will want your soul for it."

Rosa reached out to take hold of her husband's arm and was relieved when he slipped it around her waist to tuck her against him. He was finally beginning to heal from his descent into hell and she would not allow him to be swallowed by it again.

"Your father is right, Esteban," his mother said. "The devil will claim your soul."

Esteban looked to his father, and then his mother, and with a coldness that chilled the room said, "I lost my soul a long time ago."

He waited to see his wife's reaction and tightened his arm around her when she drew closer against him, as if letting him know that she would not leave his side, though he couldn't help but wonder if she would regret it.

His mother gasped and blessed herself again.

Don Alejandro shook his head. "There must be another way to deal with Pacquito."

"Pacquito is a loathsome and cunning man. He's impossible to track or to find, as you well know, Father."

Don Alejandro's head drooped in despair. "I tried so hard to find you."

"I never doubted you did, but Pacquito knows this land better than anyone and he blends with the land like nothing I've seen before. You never hear or see him approach until it's too late. There is only one man whose skills far surpass his and when *hijo del Diablo* appeared that day in camp—"

"You saw *hijo del Diablo* with your own eyes?" Rosa asked her face paling. "No one has ever laid eyes on him and lived to talk about it."

"I never saw his face. It was as if he was a massive black form consumed by shadows wherever he went. Pacquito did not even look upon him. He was on trembling knees, crying in front of him. And he kept nodding, agreeing with the devil."

"So Pacquito is one of the devil's own. Why then would he help you destroy him?" his father said.

"When the devil's own disappoints, he suffers for it. Pacquito has disappointed the devil, only he doesn't know it yet, and when the devil finds out... he will help me."

"Help you do what?" his father asked.

"Find Pacquito so I can kill him."

Rosa was annoyed when Don Alejandro insisted that the conversation wasn't suitable for the women to hear. That it was late and they all should retire and he and Esteban would discuss what would be done tomorrow.

Having gotten to know her husband, she knew that no further discussion would change anything. He would do as he planned... kill Pacquito. And nothing would stop him not even the devil. He had been consumed by evil and the only way to completely free himself of it was to destroy it. She couldn't help but fear for his life and worse, she didn't know how to help him.

Esteban took her in his arms as soon as they entered their bedchamber wanting nothing more than to lose himself in making love to her and escape the madness of his situation.

Rosa pressed a hand to his chest, worrisome questions running wild in her head. "There must be another way to stop Pacquito."

"Do not concern yourself with it." He tried to pull her close, never expecting resistance since she always seemed to melt at his touch, but this time she slipped away from him, and he didn't like it.

"How can you say that?"

He had to smile at her demanding tone, for he had never heard her so adamant.

"Do not smile at me as if I was some child that you intend to placate. I am your wife and expect to be treated as such."

"Good, then be a dutiful wife and shed your clothes and get in bed," he said teasingly, though with a tone that was meant to be obeyed.

She slapped her hands on her hips and tossed her chin up. "No, not until I have some answers."

He gave an irritated laugh as he said, "You think to dictate to me?"

"Think of it whatever way you will as long as I have my answers."

Damn if her boldness didn't excite him and grow him hard. He had no intention of discussing anything with her. He wanted her in bed, and now.

He took a quick step toward her, but her hand shot up so fast in front of him that it actually stopped him from taking another step.

"No. We will talk first."

"You dare say no?" he snapped, then ordered, "You will do as I say."

She got so angry at his adamant response that she didn't stop to curb her tongue. "We talk or you can sleep in the other room."

His eyes narrowed, his nostrils flared, and he appeared to leap at her, though it was only a quick step toward her that he took. Still it frightened her that he moved so fast or perhaps it was that she was too frozen to move.

He didn't reach out to touch her or take another step closer, he simply stood staring down at her and she never felt so small or vulnerable. That he was angry was obvious, but then so was she. Didn't he understand how much she feared for his safety as he feared for hers? Her own question had her grasping the absurdity of it all and as he went to speak, she pressed her fingers to his lips.

"Forgive me, I spoke from helplessness. I will not have you sleeping anyplace but beside me."

That she apologized for her hasty threat stunned him, but more so it pleased him to hear that she wanted him in bed beside her.

"I feel helpless to help you and I feel even more helpless when you keep things from me, for then my thoughts take flight and I cannot stop from worrying about you."

Damn if his wife wasn't ripping his heart from his chest and claiming it with every word she spoke.

"While I have every confidence that you can best Pacquito, I fear for your life. I do not want to lose you." A smile crept over her. "You are turning out to be a better husband than I had expected and it would be wise for me to keep you."

He laughed softly after taking her hand in his. "Believe me, wife, when I tell you that you will never be rid of me. You're stuck with me."

"I don't mind being stuck with you. It is no chore, though..."

His arm went around her waist and he eased her against him. "Though?"

"Please, Esteban, share your thoughts with me, all of them. Do not think me too sensitive or incapable of dealing with any matter that comes our way. I am here for you and always will be."

That was it... she stole every single piece of his heart. It now belonged to her completely, without her, his heart would not beat. His first thought was to scoop her up, hurry her to bed, and make love to her, but that would be what he needed, badly. Instead, he would give her what she needed.

He took her hand and she went to walk toward the bed. He surprised her when he walked toward the patio doors. She followed without question, though it was there in her inquiring eyes.

They went out beyond the stone patio, mixed fragrances drifting along the warm night air, to sit on the wooden bench.

"You ask me to share my thoughts, but beware," he warned with a smile, "most of my thoughts are about you naked in my arms."

She chuckled. "That is good to know, since most of mine are of you."

"Naked in your arms?" he teased.

She was glad the night hid her blush as she softly confessed. "No. You deep inside me, making me come more than once."

"This conversation will not last long with you admitting that, though I do love hearing it."

"I will be good and say no more even if it pains me."

"You tempt my soul, woman."

She couldn't help but tease, it felt so natural to do so with him. "I thought I tempted a different part of you."

He took her hand and settled it between his legs. "Does that answer your question?"

"Most definitely," she said and gave his hardness a squeeze. "And once we finish talking I would be most happy to rain kisses on him for being so patient."

"Damn it, Rosa, how the hell do you expect me to concentrate on talk when all I'll be able to think about is you—" He shook his head.

"Then settle my worries so I may settle yours." She removed her hand and waited.

"Can mere words settle your concern? I can make no promises to you. This is something I must see done and Pacquito knows it, wants it as much as I do."

"Then why does he hide from you?"

"He doesn't hide. He'll draw me out when he is ready and that is what concerns me, for he will use someone close to me to do it."

"So you try to protect all of us."

"I could not stand for any of my family to suffer the hell that I did."

She had to ask the question that had tormented her. She placed her hand gently on his arm. "Surely, you could have left sooner. Why did you wait so long?"

Esteban knew it was the question on everyone's mind and that he would have to answer it one day. There was no longer any point in keeping it a secret and if anyone would understand, it would be Rosa.

He took hold of her hand and she squeezed it lightly.

"When I was first captured I was brave and foolishly thought I could withstand anything until I was rescued. I learned right away how dreadfully wrong I was. As days turned into weeks the only thing I prayed for was death.

"After weeks on the trail, we settled into one of Pacquito's home camps where an old woman befriended me. Lequita was her name and if it hadn't been for her I would have never survived my ordeal. She taught me patience and the art of survival, but most of all she taught me the true meaning of courage."

Esteban turned his head away for a moment and Rosa could tell that this was not easy for him to speak about. And she appreciated all the more that he was sharing it with her.

"When I turned seventeen, I was skilled enough to escape and Pacquito knew it. One day he called everyone together in the middle of the camp. It was never good when he did that for it meant that someone was about to suffer. But no one, least of all me, expected it to be Lequita. He announced to all that if I attempted to leave his group of renegades that Lequita would suffer for it. He then had several of his men grab hold of me before I could get to her, and he proceeded to beat Lequita within to an inch of her life."

Rosa cringed at the thought of the old woman's suffering.

"I couldn't leave her knowing that he would beat her to death if I did. She had been so kind and good to me. So I stayed until..."

"She died," Rosa finished. He didn't answer and the longer he didn't respond the more she wondered. "What happened?" she asked softly.

He choked on his words. "She took her life so that I could be free."

Rosa gasped. "Oh my God, I'm so sorry, Esteban. How horrible and how unselfish of her to do that for you."

"I left shortly after she was buried. Pacquito knew I would leave. He wanted me to so that we would finally have the showdown he'd been aching for. But it had to be under his terms. He wanted to make me pay for Lequita's death."

"He was angry at you for the old woman taking her life?"

"She wasn't *any* old woman... she was his grandmother."

Rosa gasped again. "He beat his own grandmother and would have killed her if you had escaped?"

"After I saw how he beat her I couldn't take the chance that he wouldn't kill her. She was a good woman, offering help to any who needed it. I often wondered why she remained in camp. Why she didn't go live elsewhere, away from her malicious grandson. She told me that he would be far worse if she didn't stay with him, and she was right. I saw her calm him many a time and save many a life."

"She sounds like she was a remarkable woman. But if you know that Pacquito expects to meet up with you why not wait for him to do so instead of getting involved with *hijo del Diablo*?"

"Pacquito will continue to attack, loot, burn, and kill while he gathers information before he finally comes after me. I don't want any more innocent people to suffer because of me."

"But *hijo del Diablo* will want something in return for his help."

"I will bargain with him."

"You cannot bargain with the devil," Rosa argued.

"*Hijo del Diablo* is nothing more than a man."

Rosa shook her head and took hold of her husband's hand. "Do not make the mistake of thinking him merely a man. He is called *hijo del Diablo* for a reason."

Esteban wondered if his wife knew how hard she gripped his hand. It was almost as if she had no intentions of letting him go. Not that she could stop him, though could she? He missed her desperately when they were separated and damn if his heart didn't ache for her, not to mention other parts of his body. But he had no choice in this matter. He had always known it would come to this. What he hadn't known was that he would have a wife he loved more than anything in the world. And it made the task that much more troublesome and difficult.

He attempted to reassure her. "I have become personally familiar with evil and know well what I deal with." Before she could continue debating the matter, he leaned down and kissed her.

"You are attempting to distract me," she said between kisses.

"Is it working?" he asked with a laugh and a nip at her neck.

"You know full well that your kisses never fail to excite me."

"You mean they make you wet?"

She swatted his arm. "You are wicked."

He took hold of her chin, his eyes settling on hers. "And still you love me?"

She had meant to tease him, but her words had

struck him differently, giving suspicion to his own misgivings. She could repeatedly tell him that she loved him, but her words meant nothing if he did not believe her. The truth was that she had hardly believed it herself at times. But she had learned soon enough that her fears and doubts had been misguided. Esteban was a good man with a good soul, even if he thought he lacked one.

"You hesitate to answer me," he said harsher than he meant to, his hand falling away from her chin.

"Do you not trust my word?" she asked softly.

"You haven't given me any reason not to."

"Then why question my love for you?" When he didn't answer, she bravely said, "Perhaps it's your love for me you question?"

He flew off the bench, turning his back on her, regretting his response before the words left his mouth. "I love no one."

Rosa stood and gathered even more courage to say, "I don't believe that. You could never make love to me the way you do if you didn't love me."

He turned around slowly. "I've always made the women that I have claimed feel as though I cared. It made their surrender that much easier."

His words angered her, and she believed that was exactly what he had intended to do... anger her. Not for once did she believe he didn't love her. And it was time to confront the issue. She took a sudden step toward him and demanded, "Tell me that you don't love me."

His eyes flared with anger and his lips

tightened, as if he fought against responding. And he did. His heart refused to lie, yet the truth could prove deadly for her.

"You can't say it, can you?" she said taking another quick step toward him.

He didn't move, though she was near on top of him.

She tilted her head to the side and whispered, "Show me."

Chapter Twenty-seven

Esteban scooped her up in his arms, though didn't move. He stood staring at her, amazed at her perceptive nature, or could it be that she understood him, believed in him and knew exactly how he felt no matter what foolishness he spouted.

"I'm growing impatient," —she lowered her voice— "for you to be inside me."

"Then I will stay inside you and satisfy you over and over and over."

"I never doubted you would."

He knew all too well that they weren't speaking about making love. They were speaking of just how much he loved her. And one day he would confess his never-ending love for her. Until then...

Esteban hoisted her up further in his arms and stole her breath along with a kiss as he walked to their bedchamber. He set her on her feet just inside the room, closed the patio doors and began to undress after seeing that she was already shedding her clothes.

Her eagerness spurred his and they were soon naked in bed. His hands quickly began to caress every curve and angle and she squirmed in pleasure. When his mouth began to follow the same path, she moaned and tugged at his shoulders.

He looked up at her.

"I can't wait any longer."

"I've only just begun."

"But I want—need—you inside me now."

"I won't deny you," he said and slipped off her to spread her legs and position himself between them.

Her eyes closed shut as her ache grew and she could feel herself grow wetter as his tip poked at her as if knocking and seeking permission, though he needed none. He was and always would be welcome inside her.

She wasn't surprised when he slipped an arm beneath each knee, then lifted her slightly making it easier for him to enter her not to mention allowing him to go that much deeper. Any moment now he would plunge into her and she would come in an instant, and then he would make her come again and again and...

He entered her slowly and not all the way before he eased out again and repeated the tormenting action a few times.

Her eyes flew open and on a moan begged, "Stop teasing me. I want to come now."

He pushed a bit further into her and pulled out again. "You'll come when I let you."

"You can't stop me. I'm too near."

"Is that a challenge?"

Her eyes suddenly turned wide realizing that this was a challenge he was far better suited for than she was. "You wouldn't."

"You wanted me inside you and it is exactly where I want to be, and I'm in no hurry so..."

He entered her with a swiftness that had her crying out with pleasure, though established a slow pace that drove her absolutely crazy with even more pleasure. He not only drove in and out of her, but he moved so that it felt as if he went round and round inside of her tormenting her senseless.

Every time she thought she would come, he stopped all movement and she groaned with disappointment. She didn't know when he had slipped his arms out from under her legs and settled over her. She gripped his muscled arms to hold on tight as he drove her to the edge over and over. It took her much too long to realize that her grip tightened on his arms whenever she was just about to come and so she wisely removed her hands to grip the sheet instead.

Not that it mattered, he seemed to know when she was near and once again stopped her from going over the edge into oblivion, which is where she so wanted to go and for him to go with her.

Esteban wanted to linger in the delicious torment forever. She moved against him in such frantic passion that it grew him harder than he thought he'd ever been. And he knew that when he finally let her come, it would not be just once but multiple times and he would explode with just as much pleasure seeing and feeling her burst in climax over and over.

Rosa pressed frantically against him. She would come. She wouldn't let him stop her. She heard his soft laughter and when he smiled she grew annoyed.

"You'll come when I let you."

Instinct took hold and she wrapped her legs around his locking him against her and at the same time drove herself up hard against him. The jolt sent him slamming deeper into her and with two more quick thrusts, she felt herself tumbling off the edge and sustaining the motion... took him with her.

Esteban threw back his head and roared an oath as he exploded in a climax that seemed never-ending, thanks to his wife. Her petite body continued pummeling his, her hips slamming against him in climax after climax.

He was spent before her, though he did his best to help her finish and when she cried out, "one more, just one more' he slipped his hand between them to massage her sensitive bud until she screamed out her final surrender.

They both lay on their backs utterly spent, their bodies wet with perspiration and their breathing far from normal. They didn't snuggle or touch each other, not even hold hands, so hot were their bodies.

When her breathing had calmed enough for her to speak, Rosa said, "I'm wet."

"Again?"

They both laughed and Rosa playfully swatted his arm. "From sweat and it's your fault."

He laughed again. "You challenged me."

"I'll remember that."

"Please do. I'd love a repeat challenge."

She smiled and turned on her side. "And I love when you show me how much you love me."

Esteban did not want to return to that conversation so he said, "We need to a bath."

Rosa wasn't upset by his lack of response to her remark. One day he would tell her and until then she would be patient, or at least she would try to be. "That would be nice, but it's late and I don't want to disturb the servants."

"We don't need them," he said and climbed over her, giving her a quick kiss as he got out of bed.

She sat up. "What do you mean?"

"There's a small pond not far from here. We can bathe there."

It sounded delightful and Rosa couldn't resist the thought. She hurried out of bed, grabbing the sheets and tossing them to the floor.

"What are you doing?"

"We can't return all clean and fresh and sleep on sweaty sheets."

She went to the chest where the extra linens were kept and in no time had clean sheets on the bed."

"You know how to keep a bed?" he asked, coming up behind her and wrapping a large towel around his wife.

"I had to do it for the Curros."

He turned her around to face him. "You'll do it no more. It's the servants' job."

"I don't mind doing it for us, especially since

this might not be the only time it's necessary."

He had been about to insist that she would do it no more and that was the end of it when he smiled at her explanation. "Only for us."

"Only us," she repeated and kissed his cheek.

He took her hand and led her from the room, out through the patio doors. It was a short walk, the path curvy and Rosa wondered if she would ever be able to find the place on her own.

The pond was small and secluded and the two shed their towels and were in the cool water in no time. They scrubbed themselves with the soap Rosa had brought with her and Esteban helped her wash her hair. They didn't hurry out after they finished. They bobbed in the water and Rosa listened to Esteban tell her about how his father had taught him to swim here, and how he and his family enjoyed picnics here.

She couldn't help but think of how she and Esteban would do the same with their children, though she didn't dare say it. There would be time to discuss children and the future.

When Rosa raised her hand to stifle a third yawn, Esteban announced that it was time for them to return and get some sleep. Esteban toweled her dry, refusing to listen to her protests that she could do it herself. When he was done he wrapped the towel snugly around her and sat her on a bench while he dried himself.

She didn't bother to protest any further. It wouldn't get her anywhere and besides, their frenzied lovemaking had finally caught up with her and all she wanted to do was crawl into bed and sleep.

He squatted down in front of her and gave her a gentle kiss. "Tired?"

"More than I realized," she said lowering her head to his chest. He smelled so fresh and felt so comfortable that she could have fallen asleep right there and then.

Esteban felt her fatigue slip over him and mingle with his own. He needed to get her back to their room and in bed where he could wrap himself around her, and they both could fall into a much needed sleep.

He lifted her into his arms and she snuggled comfortably against him. After only a few steps he felt her arms around his neck go limp and he knew she was asleep. God, how he loved this woman. And he wondered there under the night stars if the heavens had sent her to him. He wasn't one for prayers since they had failed him all those years ago, but he felt compelled to at least offer his thanks, to the stars, if nothing else, for sending her to him. He would be forever grateful and would forever keep her safe.

He stopped suddenly hearing something. It was faint but he had detected it. He wasn't far from their room, though with her in his arms he would be hard-pressed to protect her. He kept a steady pace and after a moment he realized that whoever followed him did not wish to attack or he would have done so already.

A few more steps and he entered their

bedchamber. He tucked his wife into bed, then tossed his towel with hers on the floor and pulled on a pair of trousers, grabbed his knife, and closed the patio doors behind him as he went to meet with whoever it was who wished to speak with him.

He listened carefully and hearing the rustle of branches, he stepped beyond the outskirts of the patio and into the shadows.

"I'm here. What do you want?"

"I've a message for you," the deep voice said.

"Deliver it then and be on your way."

"The devil will meet you."

"When and where?" Esteban asked anxious to see this task done and see his family finally safe.

The man gave him the details.

He didn't like the thought of leaving Rosa, but he had no choice. "I'll be there," he assured the man.

"You know that you will owe the Devil."

"I know."

"Remember that when your debt is called in."

Esteban heard his retreating footfalls, though he doubted many would. The man was skilled in keeping his footing light. What was more disturbing though was that the man had gotten passed the posted guards. His family was not safe and he would have to discuss what precautions needed to be taken to amend that.

He returned to his bed chamber, slipped out of his clothes and joined his sleeping wife in bed. He eased himself around her, settling her close against him, her warm backside tucked snugly against his groin. He would miss her and worry over her safety, knowing there wasn't anyone who could protect her as well as he could. But this meeting had to take place. It was the only way he could get to Pacquito before he did even more damage.

He fell into a restless slumber, not looking forward to leaving his wife, but looking forward to meeting the devil.

Chapter Twenty-eight

Esteban decided that it would be best if he didn't tell anyone that he had to leave until it came time to do so. He didn't want to cause his family needless worry, though he also did not want to simply leave without a word as he had been doing. He would not do that to Rosa again, especially after he, himself, had experienced how it felt to return home and find his wife gone. He would not have her waking one morning to be told that he had left. He would discuss his departure with her beforehand. He smiled, knowing she would argue with him about leaving and in the end—they would make love—and he would take his leave.

His smile faded. It was more difficult now to leave her than ever before and to leave his home, but then she had made a home again for him. He had been spending more time with his father discussing the running of the ranch and quite enjoying it. It reminded him of when he was young and his father would take him with him when he inspected the many sections of their land and explain how one day this would be all his.

The land, his inheritance, it all hadn't mattered to him after a while, now it mattered again and it mattered because of Rosa. He wanted a life with her, he wanted children with her... he wanted to grow old with her.

His gut tightened at the thought, for now, what he had once thought he'd never have, had become possible and he'd be damned if he let anyone rob him of it this time. He hurried his pace to join his wife for breakfast. She had woken before him and was dressed and about to leave when he had stretched awake.

She had smiled at him and hurried over to give him a quick kiss before telling him to take his time that she intended to go see that breakfast was served on the patio. He had had a different idea and she hadn't objected, but then she never objected or rejected his touch or kiss. She always responded so willingly. She actually wanted him as much as he wanted her or perhaps it was that she loved him just as much as he loved her.

He smiled at the memory of her tossing the covers off him, hoisting up her skirt and easing herself down on him with a passionate sigh that had him nearly coming there and then. Fortunately, their little tryst lasted longer and she had left him quite satisfied when she waved to him before hurrying out the door.

He walked through the hacienda, his pace slowing as he took note of changes he had not noticed before. Vases of fresh cut flowers were everywhere and some of Rosa's drawings hung in plain frames on the walls. No longer did the servants run in fright from him, they smiled and bobbed their heads his way. Some even sang softly as they worked. It was as if the place had sprung to life after lying dormant far too long.

Laughter interrupted his thoughts and he followed the happy sound. He stopped just before stepping out to the patio and watched his wife scooping up a young boy no older than four years who had climbed on one of the chairs and had grabbed a handful of fresh cut fruit from a crystal bowl.

"If you are hungry, Emil, ask me and I will see you are fed," she said smiling.

The little lad nodded vigorously. "I hungry."

Esteban smiled. Rosa would make a good mother, always smiling and tolerant of her children's antics. They would love her as much as he loved her. He stepped out onto the patio just as a servant woman came running into view.

She froze as soon as she saw Esteban, and then rushed forward, her head bent as she approached. "Please, Don Esteban, forgive my foolish son, he means no harm." She reached out to take her son from Rosa.

"Of course he didn't, Carlita," Rosa said handing the boy over to her.

"I turned away only a moment to hang the wash and he was gone," Carlita said as if trying to explain.

"Emil is a fast one. I've seen him run." Rosa reached out and playfully poked the boy. He laughed. "He was hungry and no doubt drawn to the delicious scent of the food."

"Does he get enough to eat?" Esteban snapped and realized he had responded too harshly when both women turned wide eyes on him.

Rosa laughed and shook her head. "He's four, Esteban, he's always hungry."

Carlita nodded. "That he is."

Esteban walked over and patted the boy on the head. "You come to Dolores whenever you're hungry, Emil, she will always have a treat for you just like she did for me."

Carlita's mouth dropped open, though Emil smiled wide and nodded happily.

"Thank you, thank you for your generosity, Don Esteban," Carlita said and turned and hurried off, Emil waving at Rosa and Esteban from over his mother's shoulder.

Esteban reached out, his hands going to his wife's waist and drawing her close. "Do you know all the servants' names?"

"I know many, especially Emil, for he's a curious little fellow, which leaves his mother always trying to find him or in search of him."

"You do well with children."

"I do enjoy them, but how can you not? They are so innocent and find such joy in so many things."

"Until life steals their innocence and they learn how harsh life can be."

Rosa was aware that he spoke about himself and her heart went out to him. She could not imagine living through what Esteban had endured and still continued to endure. He was free, yet he wasn't free. And he continued to keep himself removed from those he loved, but no more. She wouldn't let him. She had admired Gaby's strength and fortitude, especially when it came to those she loved. The spirited woman had let nothing stand in her way and Rosa was glad that she had managed to gain some of Gaby's resilience while there.

She pressed her cheek to her husband's and whispered, "We will teach our children well and they will know joy and much more."

Damn if she didn't know just how to squeeze at his heart. That his wife thought of having children with him thrilled him and made him more determined than ever to see this done with Pacquito.

He turned his face to capture her lips in a possessive kiss. She was his and his alone. Her body melted against his and he wished their clothes could fade away so that he could feel and touch her warm flesh. He couldn't get enough of this beautiful woman who he had been lucky enough to have as a wife.

A gentle cough brought an abrupt stop to their kiss, and they both turned to see Dona Valerianna step out onto the patio.

"It's a lovely morning. I am so pleased to be enjoying it out under the sun and with my loving family. I only wish Alejandro wasn't delayed in joining us," Dona Valerianna said as she went to take a seat.

Esteban went to his mother's side and pulled out a chair for her, though before she sat he kissed her cheek and said, "You're more radiant than the sun today, *Madre*."

Dona Valerianna's hand went to her chest and her eyes glistened with tears and with a tender smile, she said, "I have so missed hearing your never-ending compliments."

Esteban kissed her cheek again and hesitated, though only for a moment before saying, "And I have greatly missed saying them."

Dona Valerianna stepped around the chair and hugged her son, as if he had finally, at last, fully returned home to her.

Esteban hugged her tightly, so relieved to feel his mother's arms around him after all these years.

Dona Valerianna took her seat with a joyful smile. "What a lovely and colorful table you have had set, Rosa."

The three were soon engaged in a lively conversation, the first since Rosa's arrival there. Meals had always been so rigid and formal and much too uncomfortable to be able to fully enjoy a meal. It was beginning to feel like a family and Rosa was beginning to feel that Esteban hadn't been the only one to have come home... she had as well... at least she hoped she had.

The alarm bell tolled, startling the three of them.

Esteban was out of his seat in a flash and warned, "In the house and stay there until I come for you both."

"Be careful," Rosa said but her husband had already turned the corner and disappeared.

"Come, Rosa," Dona Valerianna said holding out her hand. "We must do as Esteban says and remain safe in the house."

How could Rose simply wait in the house until someone brought news to her? She wanted to know what was going on. "You go, I'll be right along. I want to make sure Dolores is all right."

"She will be fine. You must listen to your husband."

Rosa was growing tired of commands, always listening and following orders. Having had a taste of true freedom on her trip to Los Angeles, she had since found it difficult to be so compliant. Gaby had amazed her in the way she dealt with people, a smile and a nod, and then usually getting her way in the end.

"I will join you as soon as I see to Dolores," Rosa said and turned to hurry to the kitchen, though watching from the corner of her eye to make certain that Dona Valerianna went inside. The woman did, closing the patio doors behind her.

Rosa entered the kitchen to find a frantic Carlita and Dolores searching the kitchen.

"*Madre de Dios*," Carlita said through tears. "I cannot find Emil and renegades have been spotted on Cesare land. "What if they took him?"

Though Rosa's stomach roiled at the possibility that Emil should suffer as Esteban had done, she kept her calm and attempted to reassure the fearful woman. "He probably hid as soon as he heard the warning bell."

Carlita nodded. "He does know what the bell means." She wrung her hands. "Oh, God, please let it be so."

"Go to your other children," Dolores said and get them settled. I will go see if I can find Emil and bring him to you."

"*Gracias, gracias*," Carlita said hugging the woman, and then hurried off.

"Do you know where he could be?" Rosa asked.

"He loves to go to the orchard when his mother picks the fruit and fill himself with what he can get. I wouldn't be surprise if that's where he is."

"He did try to grab a handful of fruit from the bowl on the table earlier."

"Since he wasn't successful, I'd say he's at the orchard." Dolores pushed Rosa out the door. "You take shelter in the house and wait for the all clear. I'm going to find Emil."

"Not alone you're not," Rosa insisted and before Dolores could argue, Rosa headed for the orchard.

Rosa heard the screams as she approached the orange orchard. Her heart began to beat wildly and fear prickled along her skin. She stopped and turned to Dolores, a few feet behind her. "Hurry and get help."

"You go. I'll help the boy."

Rosa's noble birth surfaced. "I gave you an order, now hurry and do as I say."

Dolores stared wide-eyed at her for a moment, and then with a nod she turned and hurried off.

Rosa didn't hesitate, she charged straight ahead, scooping up oranges as she went. She caught sight of Emil squirming and fighting to get away from the man who held him firmly in his arms. It was the same man who had almost assaulted her in this very orchard.

She didn't waste time thinking over what she should do. She ran full speed screaming, "Put him down." Then she started throwing oranges, her only weapon, at the man.

A couple missed, then one after another caught him in the shoulder and the face. Emil wisely kept himself scrunched down over the man's arm to avoid being hit. Rosa didn't stop the bombardment. She ripped oranges off the trees as she went and continued her assault. The man didn't have a choice. He dropped Emil and shielded himself with his arms.

"Run, Emil," she shouted, but the little boy stopped, grabbed an orange and flung it at the man. His skinny arms lacked the strength to give it a good toss, but he was so close the it was enough force to stun and it did in just the right place... right between the man's legs.

He doubled over in pain, going down on his knees.

Rosa scooped Emil up and took off, not looking back. She prayed the man wouldn't regain his strength, though after only a few steps she heard footfalls behind her. But it was the shout that followed that sent a chill through her.

"You're going to die, bitch!"

Carrying Emil slowed her pace and she worried over his fate as well as her own. He was fast on his feet and no doubt could easily outrun the man, especially if the assailant was busy with her.

"I'm going to put you down, Emil, you're to run as fast as you can and get help."

He nodded. "I will. I will."

Rosa knew she was taking a chance of being caught, but better her than the boy. She stopped, put Emil down and he took off so fast that it startled her. She didn't waste any time in following him, though he soon disappeared from sight and she felt a sense of relief.

She didn't look back, didn't want to know how close the man was, though the pounding of footfalls behind her warned that he wasn't far. And within in minutes, he slammed into her back sending her hurtling forward and hitting the ground so hard that it knocked the breath from her for a moment.

He flipped her over and smacked her across the face with such force that it split her lip, the blood pouring down her chin. He hit her again, the sting to her cheek resonating through her head and stunning her senseless.

"Now I'm going to give you what you deserve, and then I'm going to take you to Pacquito and he's going to..." he laughed and started shoving her skirt up.

Rosa shook her head to regain her senses and didn't hesitate. She made a fist and with as much force as she could muster, and with Carlos too busy fumbling at his crotch that he didn't see the punch coming, she hit him square in the jaw and sent him tumbling off her.

She struggled to get her legs free, he having collapsed on them. She gave his limp body a shove and was almost free when he seemed to regain his senses. She hurried, knowing she had only seconds and once her feet were free she was on them ready to run. But she wasn't fast enough. His hand shot out and grabbed her ankle, sending her crashing to the ground again. This time she threw her hands in front of her face and tucked her arms against her body protecting herself as much as possible from the fall.

"Bitch!" he spat and grabbed Rosa by the back of the hair and yanked her to her knees. He kept a tight hold on her hair as his other hand fumbled with the opening of his pants until he finally freed himself. "Now you're gonna pl—"

Rosa's head was jerked forward for a second as Carlos's body was torn away from her, his hand breaking free of her hair.

Her husband stood with his hand around Carlos's throat and his feet dangling off the ground. He stared at her and his eyes filled with such a murderous fury that she moved back away from him.

"Go to the house," he ordered.

His fierce anger froze her. She couldn't move.

"God damnit, Rosalita," he screamed. "Go to the house... now!"

His threatening tone snapped her out her stupor and she scrambled to her feet and stumbled away. She had only gone a few feet when she heard the screams. She stopped and thought of returning, but her husband's menacing warning for her to leave had her staying on the path to the house. The screams grew so agonizing that Rosa clamped her hands over her ears to try and drown them out.

Rosa hurried her steps and was surprised to see Dona Valerianna pacing along the kitchen garden, while Dolores stood a few feet away. The two women ran to her.

"*Madre de Dios*," Dona Valerianna said and reached out to wrap her arm around Rosa. "Get the healing basket, fresh towels, and water, Dolores."

Rosa felt as though her legs couldn't go another step. "I must sit."

Dona Valerianna helped her take slow steps to an old worn bench beside the entrance to the kitchen garden.

Rosa took some much needed deep breathes, her breathing was labored from her ordeal. She hadn't had the time to be fearful, but now that it was over fear of what could have happened began to sink in, and she felt a chill start in her bones.

Dona Valerianna gently raised Rosa's chin to get a better look at her split lip and bruised cheek and winced. "You were very brave going after Emil."

"She was very foolish!"

Both women startled at Esteban's angry shout. It even stopped Dolores in her tracks as she approached with the requested items.

"I will tend, my wife," Esteban ordered. "Take those things to our bed chamber and bring a fresh bottle of wine as well." Then he turned to his mother. "Father needs help with the injured vaqueros."

Dona Valerianna cast a concerned glance at Rosa.

"She is mine to worry about."

"Then do well by her," his mother ordered sternly and walked away.

Esteban looked so very angry that it caused a nervous tremor to run through Rosa, and it intensified when he hunched down in front of her. He appeared as if about to say something, when his eyes drifted to rest on her split lip. He stood suddenly and scooped her up in his arms and though she winced from the pain, he said nothing. She knew then that he was more than angry... he was furious.

Chapter Twenty-nine

Esteban sat Rosa on the bed, took a couple of steps away from her, and then turned back to her again. His hands were fisted at his sides and his knuckles white in an effort to contain himself.

Rosa grew more upset, the chill that had started in her bones now spreading throughout her body, and she began to shiver. She couldn't stop tears from stinging her eyes, though she refused to shed them.

Esteban glared at her, shook his head, let out a growl, and walked over to her with such determined strides that she found herself easing back away from his approach. He reached past her, grabbed the blanket, wrapped it around her, and hunched down in front of her.

"Damn you for not obeying me, damn you for being courageous enough to risk your own life for that of a child, and damn myself to hell for not being there to protect you."

His strange way of saying that he blamed himself, not her, tugged at her heart and she placed a tender hand to his cheek. "Hell can't have you, Esteban, you belong to me now and I love you with all my heart."

He dropped his head to rest his brow against hers for a moment, and then he kissed her cheek gently. The words seemed to come to him as naturally as breathing as he said, "I love you, Rosa, I love you so very much."

She had been waiting to hear him admit what she already knew and it filled her with such joy that she forgot about her split lip and went to kiss him. As soon as her lips met his, she pulled back with a grimace and felt the blood start running down her chin again.

"Damn it, Rosa," he scolded and hurried to get a cloth and bucket of water. "We can't kiss until that lip heals, I will not see you suffer any more pain." He soaked the cloth, squeezed it, and then began to gently clean away the blood from her chin and lip.

She didn't care about that. What she did care about was that... "You love me."

His eyes focused on hers and this time his words surprised even him. "You have no idea how very much I love you."

Her joy grew in leaps and bounds. "I knew you did, I could feel it in the way you made love to me. And someday I knew you would tell me. I am glad that it was today."

He kissed her cheek. "Today and every day I will tell you that I love you"— he smiled— "though you did trick me into thinking that I wed a docile and obedient wife."

She poked his chest. "And you let me believe that I wed a cold, heartless renegade."

His eyes narrowed. "You did."

She went to disagree with him, but he placed a

gentle finger to her lips, avoiding her wound.

"The renegade in me will never go away, be cautious of him for he's a soulless bastard."

His warning sent a chill to invade the warmth that had finally settled in her. It had been the renegade part of him that had grabbed hold of Carlos and ordered her to leave. And it had been the renegade in him that had dealt with Carlos. Her curiosity urged her to ask about Carlos's fate, but he spoke before she could.

"You will remain abed today," he instructed, rinsing the cloth again and wiping away the last of the blood.

"Will you be joining me?"

"Don't tempt me," he said gruffly. "It's all I can do to keep my hands off you and reaffirm that you're mine, that you belong to me and no other, and that you will always be mine." He shook his head trying to chase away the vivid image of his wife on her knees in front of Carlos and what he would have forced her to do. The thought boiled his blood and he wanted to kill Carlos all over again.

Rosa stared at her husband, surprised by the pain in his eyes. He suffered more than she did. Her lip may hurt and she had a few aches, but she had no intentions of letting that evil man leave her in fear and suffering. She had learned many years ago, when the abuse started, that if she allowed herself to linger in it, it would forever keep her a prisoner. Every day she had told herself that somehow, someway she would be free of the

Curros and their cruelty and that day had come when she had wed Esteban. Now it was her turn to help Esteban and the only way she could do that was to love him.

"I am yours and always will be," she reaffirmed, though wished she could smile, her throbbing lip preventing it. "And you are mine. We are now one. And I will let no one take you from me... not even the devil himself."

A sting of fear caught Esteban unaware. It was a foreign feeling to him, having buried it long ago. But then he hadn't cared about anything then. It hadn't mattered to him if he lived or died, actually death had been a preferable choice. But he hadn't been that lucky and now he realized just how lucky he had been to live. Now he had Rosa, though the thought that something could happen to her just as it almost had today stabbed at his long suppressed fear.

He couldn't lose her. He wouldn't.

He cupped her chin gently. "The devil would run from you in fear."

Rosa raised a fisted hand and shook it. "He better."

Esteban laughed. "You are a treasure, *Caro*."

Rosa's heart fluttered at the sound of his laughter. He had begun to laugh a bit more each day and it was wonderful to hear him do so. She couldn't hold back a smile and once again her lip tore open and blood dripped down her chin.

Esteban swore beneath his breath. "That's it, no smiling, kissing, laughing, nothing that will cause that wound to keep bleeding."

"That will be difficult, since you make me smile so often and I want to kiss you all the time and there are times you make me laugh." She shook her head. "I am afraid I will once again fail to obey you."

"Does that mean I am also going to have difficulty keeping you in bed today?"

"Not if you stay with me," she said trying not to grin, but failing and of course blood trickled down her chin.

Esteban wiped it away with the rinsed cloth. "That wound will never stop bleeding if I join you in bed."

She laughed and winced and Esteban scolded her again.

"I don't want, nor do I need, to remain in bed all day. I'm bruised and a bit sore, but otherwise I'm fine, more than fine now that you've told me that you love me. Besides I want to know what's happening, what needs to be done, and most importantly what you intend to do. Otherwise I will worry endlessly."

He wasn't accustomed to sharing anything with anyone. That would require trust and renegades trusted no one, especially each other. So it was his nature not to share, but that had changed with Rosa. He wanted to discuss things with her, and it felt so right to do so.

He continued to clean the blood from her chin and neck as he spoke. "This was no raid on the hacienda. Pacquito was simply toying with me and letting me know that there was nothing I could do to protect the ones I love. That I was to return to camp or else."

"Why can't he just let you be?"

"No one ever walks away from Pacquito. It is the way he keeps his men in line. If his men think that I have succeeded in breaking free of him, then more may do as I have done and Pacquito's reign will be no more."

"That is good. It is time for his evil ways to end."

"The only way his reign will end is through death. Pacquito will have it no other way."

Rosa threw her arms around her husband's neck and pressed her cheek against his. "He cannot have you. I will not let him."

Esteban slipped his arm around her waist and shut his eyes for a moment lingering in her love. It was almost as if he could feel it seeping into him, comforting warmth that he didn't want to ever live without again.

He kissed her cheek. "You will need your strength to fight so much evil."

She poked his chest playfully. "Don't think that will get me to stay in bed and rest. The day is beautiful and meant to be enjoyed. And we must show everyone on the hacienda that we are strong and they are safe."

He shook his head. "You've just been brutally attacked and what do you talk about? The beautiful day and the care of others."

"That horrible man stole some of the joy from

this day. I refuse to allow him to take even more from me or anyone. I am fine, Emil is fine and with his family, the injured are being tended to and no one died, so it is a good day."

"I killed him," Esteban said so coldly that it sent a chill rippling through Rosa. "He deserved to die."

Rosa had thought that her husband had killed Carlos. The murderous look in his eyes when he had torn Carlos away from her told it all. She laid a tender hand to his cheek. "You did what you had to do. Now he will never hurt anyone again."

"I will kill anyone who touches you," he said.

Rosa shuddered, his words now ringing truer than ever, for he had proven he was a man of his word.

Esteban held her close, wanting her in his arms, always wanting her there. Today, more so than their wedding day, they had truly become one. And he would let nothing, absolutely nothing, tear them apart.

"Let me change," she said, "And then we will go and see if our help is needed."

Esteban stood. "I'll get Dolores to help you."

"That's not necessary. You can help me."

"No, I can't," he insisted backing away. "If I did, I'd have you naked and in bed in minutes. And you don't need that after what you've just been through."

She stood and closed her eyes a moment and when she opened them they were filled with sorrow. "You're wrong. Your loving touch and kisses are exactly what I need."

He was at her side in seconds, his arm coiling around her waist and drawing her up against him.

Her tears started then. She had been strong as long as possible, but what had happen had taken a toll on her. And she finally admitted it. "I was afraid, so afraid that Carlos would take from me what belonged only to you, my husband, that I gave freely and lovingly to and wanted only you to have. I don't know if I could have faced you if he had..." She shuddered at the thought of what could have happened.

He scooped her up in his arms, and then sat on the bed with her in his lap. "I'm grateful that I arrived when I did and was able to prevent you from suffering any more than you already had. But never, never think that I would love you or want you any less if something like that should ever happen. I was proud you fought so bravely, but always remember that I would want you to survive, no matter what, you must survive."

Words choked in her throat and she nodded while tears streamed down her cheeks.

Esteban held her and let her cry. She needed to cry. It would help release the fear that she hadn't realized lingered with her. The ordeal that she had been through could not be so easily dismissed and he would hold her and comfort her until her last tear was spent. And then...

"You should—"

Rosa pressed her fingers to his mouth. "Please don't tell me to rest. I don't want to be closed away in this room with nothing to do but think." She shivered. "Or fall asleep and drift into nightmares."

Nightmares he was all too familiar with and there was nothing worse than waking alone from one. "Let me help you change and we will do as you say... go and help others."

She swiped at her tears. "I would like that."

He expected to grow aroused as he helped her out of her clothes, and though he did, he found himself more concerned with tending her than making love to her. Especially so when he peeled away garments to reveal bruises he hadn't been aware that she had suffered. His temper rose as he silently cursed away his anger. Until finally...

"Damn it, Rosa, you took more of a beating than I thought."

"No, it's from the fall I took when I tried to get away from him and he caught me. I felt rocks jab at me when I went down."

Esteban shut his eyes against the image, wishing he could kill Carlos all over again.

She turned, naked in his arms. "Truly, I'm all right."

His hands went to her waist though he couldn't stop them from drifting further down over the swell of her hips and down even further to cup her backside. "I'm glad, but you will tell me if you grow tired or too uncomfortable and I will tuck you into bed to rest."

"You have my word."

He kissed the tip of her nose. "Don't dare smile," he warned as the corners of her mouth began to turn up. "You've bled enough today."

Rosa kept her smile from surfacing. "I will smile with my eyes," she said and spread them wide.

He laughed and hurried to help her finish dressing, afraid that her nakedness and dark smiling eyes would be his undoing.

"Do my eyes speak to you as much as yours do to me?" she asked softly.

"What do my eyes say?"

"That you want me as much as I want you," her eyes danced with a smile again, "though your roaming hands speak much louder."

He realized then that his hands were rubbing her backside and he stilled them. He brushed a kiss across her cheek and whispered in her ear, "There isn't a time I don't want you."

"It is good then that I feel the same way."

"Tonight... if you're feeling well enough—"

"I will feel well enough. Will you?"

Esteban smiled. "There you go challenging me again."

They bantered while he finished helping her dress in a skirt and blouse. He had insisted on her peasant dress, knowing it would be much more comfortable for her. She saw to her hair, quickly running a comb through it and twisting it to pin with a fan comb to the back of her head.

Once she finished, Esteban took her arm and wrapped it around his. "Now remember if you grow tired—"

"You will be the first to know."

Chapter Thirty

Rosa woke with a stretch and a wince, reminding her of yesterday's ordeal, and of how she had fallen asleep as soon as she rested her head to her pillow. She turned her head and wasn't surprised to see that her husband wasn't there. She knew exactly what he was up to. He had delayed coming to bed last night and now he was gone before she woke. He intended to avoid any chance of making love with her until she healed.

She didn't like that thought at all, even if he was being considerate. She was about to smile when she recalled the consequences if she did, so she smiled inwardly. She wondered if Esteban realized that renegades were never considerate. Little by little he was shedding his renegade persona and though he had warned that it would always be part of him, she was certain that someday it would fade into oblivion. And the reason was simple. He would no longer need it.

She eased herself out of bed and was surprised that her aches were far more minor than she had expected. Actually, the more she moved around getting dressed, the less she ached. She was also pleased to see that the bruise on her face had never turned that bad. It was already a pale yellow and would be gone in a couple of days. Her lip however was still swollen, though the wound had at least closed up some. She would have to be careful not to split it open again.

Dolores entered the room just as she was braiding her hair, having decided it would work best for today.

"You should have waited for a servant to help you," Dolores scolded with a shake of her finger.

"I have done for myself too long to be looked after by others."

"Your husband thinks differently. He had ordered that you are to do nothing but rest until he says otherwise." Dolores held up her hand when Rosa went to protest. "Would you make it difficult for the servants to carry out his orders?"

Rosa sighed. "No, I would never want that, but I feel fine. I don't need to rest."

Dolores pushed her hands away and went to work finishing her braid. "Esteban is worried about you and I have not seen him worry about anyone or anything since his return home. You have not only given him a reason to care, but also to live."

Rosa allowed herself a hint of a smile. "He told me he loves me."

Dolores grinned and blessed herself. "Thank the heavens. The man was carrying his heart for all to see, but he, himself, was blind to it." She tied the braid at the end with a yellow ribbon. "Now, the sun has been up for hours, the day beautiful so would you like to have breakfast on the patio or in one of the gardens since everyone has eaten already?"

"What is Esteban up to?"

"He's getting ready to go into town."

Rosa jumped up. "I want to go with him. I can visit with Marinda. No doubt she heard about the incident here and is worried about me."

"You are to rest," Dolores reminded.

"It will be restful to visit my friend," Rosa said and with a flourish was out the door.

She hurried through the hacienda, surprised that it was so quiet. She soon discovered from one of the servants that Dona Valerianna was busy checking on the wounded and Don Alejandro was with the vaqueros who were mending fences that had been torn down. Don Esteban was going into town for more supplies.

Rosa hurried to the stables and as she came around the corner she almost smacked right into her husband. Luckily, he was quick and grabbed hold of her before they collided.

Before he could say a word she said, "I want to go to town with you."

"What are you doing running around the hacienda when you should be resting?" he demanded, ignoring her remark.

"Why did you leave me to wake alone?" she asked with a slightest upturn at the corners of her mouth.

He leaned down almost pressing his nose to hers. "The same reason I delayed coming to bed last night."

"Which was?" She knew, but she wanted to hear him say it.

"You were exhausted and needed rest."

She placed her hand to his chest. "I need you more than rest, but since you so generously gave me time to sleep, I am now well rested. And I would love to visit with my friend Marinda."

"I can have her visit in a couple of days."

"Why can't I go now?"

"Because it isn't safe."

"I'm safe as long as I'm with you."

Esteban looked ready to argue, but her reasoning struck a chord. Even with guards posted around the hacienda Pacquito's men had managed to sneak onto the property and create havoc. And although his father was posting more guards, it wouldn't make a difference. If Pacquito decided to strike with all his force, nothing would stop him.

That thought alone had him saying, "You will come to town with me."

Rosa hugged him and fought not to smile, though her eyes turned wide with joy. "Do I have time to collect some fruit—"

"I will see to that. You go and find out from Mother what she needs from the Mercantile?"

"I'll be back shortly," she said, turned and hurried off.

Esteban stared after her smiling. She didn't even think that he might be sending her off so that he could leave without her. It amazed him that she trusted him without a doubt. She hadn't hesitated or questioned him... she simply believed in him.

He silently cursed her injured lip. He damn well wanted to kiss her—actually—he wanted to do more than kiss her, had since last night. But her exhaustion had been palpable. He had seen it in the way her shoulders had begun to droop and how her pace slowed and how she had repeatedly yawned. Not that she would have admitted it to him. She hadn't had to though. He had known once she had gotten into bed that she'd be asleep... and she had.

It hadn't been long after that that he had joined her. He had curled himself around her, her warmth seeping into him and though he thought that sleep would elude him, it hadn't. He had barely settled against her when he had fallen asleep. The worst part was waking to an aching arousal. He hadn't wasted a minute. He got out of bed away from her since if he had lingered, he wouldn't have been able to stop from making love to her.

Tonight, however, he would make love to her, gently, carefully, of that he was certain.

~~~

The town was abuzz with people. Many gathered in groups talking, no doubt about the renegades in the area. Rosa hoped that with the incident at the hacienda all would realize that Esteban was no longer part of the renegades, and they would be more accepting of him.

Esteban stopped the carriage in front of Marinda's small house, the six vaqueros with him remaining on their horses scouting the area with their eyes, while two dozen more vaqueros took positions throughout the town.

"You are to stay here until I come for you,"

Esteban ordered stepping down from the carriage and walking around to the other side to assist his wife. Her hands went to his shoulder as his went to her waist. It amazed him that she had grown so comfortable with him and so trusting. Where once he had seen fear of him in her eyes, he now only saw love. He placed her on the ground, brushing a gently finger over the bruise on her face.

"It's not that bad and it's already fading," she assured him.

"Be careful of your lip," he reminded, "you don't want to accidently open the wound again or it will take forever to heal. And it will be that much longer before I'll be able to kiss you again."

She lowered her voice to a bare whisper. "There are other places you can kiss."

Esteban smiled and though he didn't see it, Rosa saw the startled look of those around them. No one had ever seen Esteban smile. Now they would see that he was just like them... well somewhat like them.

He pressed his cheek to hers and whispered, "Tonight I'm going to kiss every one of those places."

"We will see," she said with a tap to his chest, "after all you did fall asleep last night."

"Who fell asleep first last night?"

Rosa didn't have a chance to answer. Marinda stepped out of the house with a broad smile and calling out her name. Her smile faded when she caught sight of Rosa, though she said nothing, for now.

Esteban grabbed the basket of fruit from the carriage while his wife hurried to greet Marinda with a hug.

"Don Esteban," Marinda said lowering her head respectfully when he stepped next to his wife.

"Marinda," he acknowledged with a nod, then turned to Rosa. "The vaqueros will be close by should you need anything. I will return for you when I finish, which should be in a couple of hours."

Rosa nodded with the slightest of smiles to let her husband know how pleased she was to be able to spend time with her friend.

No soon as the two women entered the house, then Marinda asked, "Did he hit you?"

Rosa was so taken aback by the question that she found herself speechless for a few moments. Then she shook her head. "Esteban would never hit me. Didn't you hear about what happened at the hacienda?"

Marinda lowered her voice. "There is talk that renegades where there, but no buildings were destroyed or lives lost. Some believe that the renegades were actually welcomed there."

Rosa gasped. "What fool would believe such nonsense. Several vaqueros were injured chasing the renegades off the property and I was attacked trying to rescue Emil."

"Carlita's little boy?"

Rosa nodded. "I was able to get him free of the renegade who had captured him, but if it hadn't been for my husband..." She shuddered unable to say anymore.

Marinda hugged her friend. "I am so sorry, Rosa, I didn't know. And when I saw your face..." She stepped back and took the basket from Rosa. "We will have a cool drink, and then go to the fountain and visit with the other women. Once they hear the truth, they will spread the news and the lies will stop."

"That would be wonderful, Marinda. Esteban is a good man and a very good husband, and I would like everyone to know that."

"Then you are happy with him?"

Rosa couldn't stop her cheeks from blushing. "Very happy—I love him and—he loves me."

Marinda yelped with joy and once again hugged her friend. "I am so happy for you. I have been praying every day for you and lighting candles. Paco says I will burn the church down I light so many candles."

The two women laughed, though Rosa was careful to laugh softly. She ached to kiss her husband again so she was vigilant about her lip.

"I have good news too," Marinda said with a smile so wide, it seemed to spread across her face.

"Tell me," Rosa said eager to hear.

"I'm pregnant."

Rosa screeched and threw her arms around Marinda. They hugged and laughed again and when they separated Marinda's smile faded.

"Your lip," she said and hurried to get a cloth. She ordered Rosa to sit and tended the wound. "It's not bad, just a little blood, but then you always did heal fast."

"Do not worry about that, tell me about the baby," Rosa urged. "When are you due? Have you thought of names?'

They were soon lost in discussing the baby. Time sped by and Marinda finally reminded that they needed to spend time at the town well with the other women.

Before they left the house Marinda said, "I am going to light more candles so that you will soon get pregnant and our babies are born close together and can be good friends like we are."

"That would be wonderful," Rosa agreed and they left the house arm in arm talking more about babies.

The women at the well greeted Rosa, pleased to see her. She knew that her peasant clothes made it easier for them to approach her, for it made it appear as if she was still one of them, and to her she was. It changed nothing that she was of noble blood. She actually didn't care.

After greetings were finished and family's asked about, it was Marinda who brought up the incident at the Cesare hacienda. The women listened intently as Rosa took it from there explaining what had happened. She made certain that everyone knew how much she loved her husband and what a good man he was.

After questions were asked and curiosities settled, talk turned to other things and Rosa was pleased. The women would spread the news and people would begin to talk differently about

Esteban.

The women parted to let Padre Marten into their circle when he made it known he wanted to speak with Rosa. His gasped when he took one look at her. And she was relieved when Marinda began to explain what had happened, then other women joined in and Rosa knew that by nightfall the whole town would know the truth.

The padre was soon enjoying a fat orange from the basket Marinda had brought to the well with them. She had kept enough fruit for Paco and her, and the rest she had insisted on sharing with the other women.

The padre blessed the women and left them to chat, taking another orange with him.

The women continued to talk and laugh and Rosa was ever so grateful for being able to share this time with them just as she used to. She had missed the friendships and she promised herself that she would visit more often once this ordeal with Pacquito was finally laid to rest.

"What is this I hear?" the booming voice called out. "You shame me?"

Rosa turned to see Roberto Curro and three other men approach.

"Move out of the way," he demanded of the women in his path.

They stepped aside reluctantly knowing Roberto would think nothing of squatting at them if they didn't. And none wanted to put their husbands' in the position of dealing with the harsh man.

Roberto came to a stop a few feet away from Rosa. "Your husband is forced to take a hand to you? Are you still a lazy sot? Have I taught you nothing? Or do you refuse to do your wifely duties?"

Rosa placed her hands on her hips and raised her chin a notch. "How dare you approach me and speak so discourteously to me. I am the wife of Don Esteban Cesare and the daughter of nobles, you will treat me with the respect deserving of my station. Now apologize."

Smiles popped out on all the women's faces and giggles could be heard behind her while Roberto looked about to explode, his face having turned bright red.

Roberto sputtered and spit as he tried to form an answer.

"You heard her. Apologize *now*!"

All eyes turned to the side to see Esteban standing there.

Rosa felt her breath catch. He had strapped on his sheathed knife and although his garments were that of a powerful ranchero, the weapon gave a hint to the renegade lurking inside him.

Everyone took several steps back and the three men with Roberto hurried off, though lingered nearby to see what would happen.

Not wanting to be made the fool in front of everyone, Roberto unwisely spoke up, "I taught her to be obedient—"

Esteban interrupted. "You taught her what cruelty was."

"I did no different than you, raising a hand to her so she knows her place."

Esteban took a quick step forward and Roberto stumbled back. "*Her place*? Rosa is not a servant, she is *my wife*. And I will not warn you again to apologize to her or I will show you exactly what happens when I take my hand to someone."

The threat was enough to have Roberto saying, "I am sorry."

"Not good enough," Esteban admonished, his dark eyes heated with anger. "You will acknowledge her properly and issue an appropriate apology."

Roberto did not look at all happy, though he did appear fearful, which no doubt gave him the impetus to say, "Dona Rosa, please forgive me for being so rude."

"Now bow your head and say it again."

Red splotches crept up Roberto's neck to stain his cheeks, but he did as he was told and bowed his head as he repeated his apology.

Esteban walked over to Roberto who stood visibly shaking at his approach. He leaned over and whispered to the man, "Don't ever talk to my wife again, don't even look at her or you'll be sorry."

Roberto tried for a bit of bravado. "Threatening to kill me again?"

"No, death is too swift a punishment. I'll turn you over to the renegades."

Roberto stumbled back away from Esteban and paled to the point that he appeared as if he would pass out. He turned and hurried off.

Esteban went to his wife. "Time to go home."

Chapter Thirty-one

Rosa took her time getting dressed for supper. Esteban had been summoned to the vineyards by his father shortly after they had returned home. Rosa had gone to see if Dona Valerianna needed help with anything and had spent the next few hours helping to deliver extra food to the families of the vaqueros who had been injured.

When they were finished, both women had gone off to change for supper and to Rosa's surprise and pleasure a bath was waiting for her. The warm water helped rejuvenate her, though she hadn't felt as tired as she thought she would after the active day she had so far.

Even with the incident in town, the time spent there had been enjoyable as was the ride home. They hadn't discussed Roberto and Rosa hadn't wanted to. She had wanted simply to enjoy the ride with Esteban and think of it as nothing more than a happy day spent with her husband.

She planned on the night being even more enjoyable, not once forgetting that he said he would kiss other places on her body. She shivered at the image it evoked and couldn't wait for later.

She had chosen a plain black lace dress that hugged her waist and had a lower neckline then she was accustomed to. She let her hair hang free cascading in waves down over her shoulders and back. And she hoped no one would notice that she wore her comfortable sandals.

With her appearance seen to, she hurried out of the room, looking forward to the evening ahead.

Esteban stood speechless when his wife entered the small parlor. Even with the swollen lip she looked radiant. And he loved her hair when she let it hang free. Then there was her dress that he wanted to get her out of as soon as possible.

He shook his head chasing away the images of stripping her out of it, but he couldn't shake away his growing arousal as easily. Damn if he didn't turn hard with just one look at her, especially when she looked so appetizing.

Realizing he was being rude just standing there, he went to his wife and took her hand leading her to a chair. He leaned down after she sat and whispered, "You look stunning."

She contained her smile, though he saw pleasure beam in her wide eyes and he smiled. He went and poured two glasses of red wine and returned to her side, handing her one. He then turned to his mother and raised his glass of wine. "I am most fortunate to have two beautiful and loving women in my life."

Dona Valerianna smiled broadly and Rosa noticed that the woman looked more radiant than she had in a while.

Dolores called them to supper as soon as Don Alejandro entered the room. They all took their seats at the table and were soon engaged in conversation.

Esteban rested his leg against his wife's, pressing it hard against hers now and again. He was eager to be alone with her, but he also wanted to make certain that she ate well since she had to take her time eating due to her split lip. So he attempted to be patient as he grew more tempted to grab her and hurry her off to their room.

"The vaqueros say there is talk in town that the renegades came here at your invite, which was why we suffered no destruction to any of our buildings," Don Alejandro said.

"It seemed to be the prevailing thought in town," Esteban said.

"Do you let everyone know how wrong they were?" his mother asked, indignant that people would even think such a horrible thought.

Esteban was annoyed that his father had brought it up at supper and he hoped to avoid any further discussion on the matter. "They will think what they wish regardless of what I tell them."

"By this evening everyone will know the truth," Rosa said.

Esteban turned to his wife. "Why is that?"

"I spoke with the women at the well and told them exactly what happened here. How vaqueros were injured, and Emil almost abducted, and how you saved me from the renegade. The news will spread quickly and all will know the truth."

"How do you know they believed you?" Esteban said.

"They are my friends. I grew up with many of

them and know their mothers and sisters. They know I would never lie to them. Padre Marten was there as well and never questioned my word. Besides, Marinda will tell them how much I love you and you love me and that will confirm the truth."

"You told her that you love me?" Esteban said as if he hadn't heard her.

Rosa stared at his odd expression. "Of course I told her I love you. She and I are good friends and share things like that. And I am proud of my love for you, so I want everyone to know."

"That you love a renegade?"

"Enough," Rosa scolded. "You are not a renegade. You are a good man and I will not hear you refer to yourself as a renegade ever again."

"Rosa is right," his mother joined in. "You are not or ever truly were a renegade. You were a captive of the renegades and you returned home to your family. You are my son and I love you and I am proud of you for surviving your horrific ordeal."

"Your mother is right," Don Alejandro chimed in. "It was no easy task to survive as you did, but like your mother, I am proud that you survived anyway you could and returned home to your family that loves you." He grinned. "And I am even more pleased that I picked the perfect wife for you."

"You didn't pick her," Dona Valerianna teased. "Esteban saw her and knew she was meant for him."

Rosa looked to her husband. "Is that true? Did you know I was meant for you?"

Esteban slipped his finger under her chin. "From the first moment my eyes met yours I knew you'd be mine."

He kissed her lips so gently that Rosa barely felt it, but that didn't stop a tingle from running through her.

"Another bottle of wine, Dolores," Don Alejandro called out when the woman entered the room. "We celebrate the love of family."

Dolores nodded, grinned, and hurried away with a tear in her eye to get the wine.

Rosa never felt so happy, never thought she would ever feel so happy again after losing her family. But now she had family again, family that loved her and she was overjoyed.

Esteban took hold of his wife's hand as his father offered toast after toast and as he did Esteban could see the future unfold. He and Rosa's love for each other would continue to grow and they would have many children and his mother and father would spoil them. His parents would age with time and he would one day take over the running of the ranch and the Cesare family would continue. It was all possible because a petite, dark haired, loving woman had the courage to fall in love with a renegade—no—with him, Esteban Cesare.

"I want to go visit Elena Garavito soon. It is time to renew our friendship," Dona Valerianna said. "Will you come with me, Rosa?"

"You can't go alone or with a few vaqueros," Esteban said.

"He's right," his father agreed.

"Good, then you'll come with us?" Rosa asked of her husband.

"That would be wonderful," his mother said with a smile.

"It might be a good idea," his father said. "Garavito land borders part of ours. We could have the vaqueros work together to patrol that area. You could speak to Manuel about it."

Since his return Esteban had kept himself removed from all the land owners, he had once thought friends. They certainly hadn't welcomed him home, but now seeing how things had changed with his family, he realized that he really hadn't truly returned home until recently. And it would be wise of him to once again connect with the other rancheros.

"We could do that, though it would be another neighbor of ours that Pacquito would go after next," Esteban said.

"Why?" his father asked.

"To show that he's got me surrounded on all sides and I have no way out, but his way."

"We will show him differently," his father said as if it was already done.

"We've been through this before, Father. I will do it my way so that it will be done once and for all."

"Then you still plan to meet with the devil?" his father asked.

"It's the only way for the playing ground to be fair. If I returned now to Pacquito, he would see me severely punished, and then I would have no strength left to fight him. If I wait too long to meet with him, he will escalate his attacks on the ranches and see that people died. The devil will see that we meet in a place where Pacquito cannot take advantage of me."

His father took a sip of wine before asking, "And you trust the devil to be honest and do this?"

"The devil has a score to settle with Pacquito."

"Then why doesn't he settle it?" his father asked annoyed.

"I believe it was due to a promise he made."

His father shook his head. "The devil keeps his word? I find that hard to believe."

"Perhaps, but I have no choice but to trust him."

Servants entered the room with a tray of sweet cakes and a bowl of fruit, ending the conversation. More wine was drunk and cakes eaten, but talk was not as enthusiastic as before.

Esteban was eager to retire to his bed chambers with his wife and get lost in making love. No soon as he eased back her chair then she popped out of it, and with a quick good-night to his parents, she was out of the room before he could take a step to join her. He mumbled several oaths as he walked along the corridor toward his bed chamber. His wife was annoyed and he knew why, though he didn't want to discuss it. He wanted her in bed and moaning with pleasure as soon as possible and as many times as possible. He was starving with a need for her and he intended to satisfy that need until he was fully quenched.

He entered the room and closed the door behind him, then slipped out of his jacket and tossed it on the chair. "Have your say and be done with it, quickly, for I have waited long enough to get you into bed."

Rosa's hands went to her hips. "Quickly? You expect me to be quick about how I feel with your decision to seek help from the devil himself?"

"The deal has been struck and nothing can change that. But if you feel the need to speak your piece, then do so. I will listen." His shirt joined his jacket as he waited for his wife to speak. He wasn't surprised to see a spark of fiery anger in her eyes and in a way he was pleased to see it. She had changed since they had wed or perhaps it was that her true nature was finally able to be free. And though he hated to admit it, the trip to Los Angeles seemed to have done her well.

So he was prepared for the lecture she was sure to unleash on him and since she would be fired up, their love making would be even more intense.

"My words would be wasted since they will change nothing," she said, her hands falling off her hips. "Perhaps action would speak much louder. Perhaps if I tell you that I will not make love with you until you see how foolish this plan of yours is, you will then seriously reconsider." She tossed her chin up in defiance.

Rosa waited, her heart thumping wildly, certain

that any moment her husband would explode with fury. It didn't matter though, she had to take this stance. She had to protect him from this foolish notion that the devil would help be his salvation.

It was as if a spark of fire ignited in his eyes and he walked slowly over to her and took firm hold of her chin. "We both know that will never happen."

She yanked her chin out of his grasp and walked past him with a flourish, needing to put distance between them. She stopped behind the chair where he had tossed his clothes and braced her hands on the top. Her legs trembled and passion churned deep inside her. She knew if he touched her that she'd be lost and would surrender to him. She couldn't let that happen. She had to make him understand how worried she was for his safety in hopes that he would change his mind and seek a different solution to the problem.

"You would force me?" she said and almost cringed, knowing full well her husband would never do that. And damn if he didn't laugh at her.

"*Caro*, we both know you just walked away from me because if I even faintly touch you, you will melt in my arms."

Rosa got angry, her eyes narrowing as she said, "I will not let the devil have you."

That she would defend him from evil itself gave his heart a lurch. It only proved how much she loved him, how much she would surrender for him and it gave him a fright.

"There is nothing you can do and you will do

nothing—I mean it, Rosa—you will let this be and I will do as I must."

"I cannot let you walk into hell alone."

His brow knitted and he shook his head lightly, as if not quite understanding her. "You can't mean that you would go to hell with me."

"I would brave the fires of hell for you."

He shook his head and snapped a finger at her. "Do not say that. You will not put yourself in danger for me."

"You do for me."

"A man protects the woman he loves, with all his heart. Besides this is my fight, not yours."

"You are my husband, the man I love. I will not let you fight this alone. You have battled by yourself far too long. Now I fight alongside you."

He stared at her in disbelief. How did this pint-sized woman think she could fight against such evil and win?

Rosa tossed her chin up again. "Don't you dare think I'm not strong enough to fight."

He had to smile at her audacity. "Well, you did have the courage to love me."

"It took courage to marry you, loving you came easily."

His heart swelled with love for her and all he wanted to do was scoop her up and carry her to bed. He went to take a step toward her.

Her hand shot up. "We have not finished discussing this."

His patience was nearly spent. He wanted her in bed... now. "Enough talk. I want to make love to you."

"And I ache for you to touch me and make me come," — she smiled— "repeatedly."

"That is not hard to do since you respond so easily to my touch."

Her smile tickled at the corners of her mouth. "And you don't succumb to mine?"

He took a leisurely step toward her. "Let's see who succumbs first."

She already knew the answer. It would be her. He would make sure of it and the thought sent a tingle through her. But that would have to wait. She shook her finger at him. "No, we will talk."

"It has gotten us nowhere," he said frustrated. His hands ached to touch her soft skin, his lips could almost taste her hard nipples and damn if he couldn't stop thinking about how wet she probably was for him already. "And must I remind you again that it will change nothing."

"It will change everything," she shouted.

He sent her a scathing look. "You raise your voice to me?"

"Since you fail to hear me I have no other choice," she said.

"No, you have no choice," he said, his own voice taking on a firmer timbre.

"Will I ever have a choice?"

"Yes, you have one now. Let me make love to you or continue to argue with me over something that you cannot change."

"You could die," she said on a soft sob.

"There is always that possibility."

"I would not want to live without you."

He stepped toward her and this time she didn't stop him. His arm went around her waist and eased her up against him. He brushed his lips lightly across hers so as not to hurt her wound and whispered, "Then tonight we will make a baby and you will always have part of me with you."

He scooped her up and carried her to bed.

Chapter Thirty-two

Esteban never made it to the bed, a pounding on the door and his father's frantic voice had him putting his wife down and hurrying to open the door.

"Renegades have been spotted headed for the Mercados hacienda," his father said.

Esteban muttered several oaths beneath his breath. Mercados land bordered their land. Pacquito intended to hit the place in the dead of night, and no doubt would inflict severe damage.

"Gather the vaqueros, though leave a contingent behind to guard the house. We ride immediately," Esteban ordered.

Rosa stood frozen as she watched her husband slip his shirt and jacket back on. No one would mistake him for a renegade. He never looked more like a powerful don of a hacienda than he did at this moment. And the potent sight of him had her limbs melting.

She laid her hand on his arm. "You will be careful."

He took hold of her chin and kissed her quick. "The thought of you waiting for me naked in our bed will guarantee my return."

"Naked, wet and oh so ready for you," she confirmed and ran her hand down between his legs to give him a squeeze.

"Damn it, *Caro*, you'll have me thinking of nothing else."

"Dispense of them quickly, then think of what awaits you."

He gave her another quick kiss and was almost at the door when he turned. "Stay put. I don't need to be worrying that you'll do something foolish."

"I will stay right here."

He nodded and was out the door.

She paced the room as soon as he left and the more she paced the more she worried. What if this was a trap to capture him once again? She shook her head. Esteban would not be that foolish. He would know what to do. Still, she could not stop herself from worrying.

A knock sounded at her door and she ran to open it.

"I wanted to make sure you were all right," Dona Valerianna said.

"Frightened and worried," Rosa admitted, knowing with how pale the woman was that she was feeling the same.

"This is such madness," Dona Valerianna said.

Rosa reached out and took the woman's hand to urge her into the room. "Sit while I get us some wine."

Dona Valerianna seemed relieved and with a firm nod sat in one of the chairs by the fireplace where a low fire burned.

Rosa sat in the other chair after handing the woman one of the glasses of wine.

"I thought when my son returned home that this would be all behind us and that he would be able to start a new life. I had never thought that that horrible man would inflict more pain and suffering on him."

"I hate to admit it but I wonder if the devil is the only one who can truly help Esteban deal with such evil."

"While I don't want my son involved with the devil, I have begun to wonder the same as you. Can the devil be the only one to help destroy evil? Then I worry that the devil will extract much more from Esteban than Pacquito ever did. There is no easy answer."

Long after they finished the wine and after Dona Valerianna left, unable to keep her eyes from closing, Rosa sat waiting. Her own eyes grew heavy with sleep and finally she surrendered and undressed, then climbed beneath the blankets naked to wait for her husband. She thought to stay awake but no soon as she laid her head on the pillow, her eyes closed and sleep claimed her.

Esteban stood over the bed watching his wife sleep. She appeared so content. Her arms snug around his pillow, as if she was holding onto him. The blanket barely covered her backside leaving a partial view that only managed to entice the hell out of him. And one breast lay bare, the nipple soft just waiting for his tongue to turn hard. Yet he stood there not touching her.

He had taken lives tonight, spilled much blood, inflicted much pain and still felt the intense heat of conflict. Every muscle in his body was as taut as a bowstring waiting to be snapped, waiting for that last ultimate target where the last vestiges of battle could be quenched.

He would assuage such heat with a willing woman when he returned to camp after an attack. But then any woman in Pacquito's camp had to be willing or she didn't survive. It was always a fast and furious mating and he didn't want to do that to his wife. He preferred to make love to her, but he wouldn't last long, not the first time anyway. He'd often come two or three times after a raid and damn if he didn't want to come inside his wife right now. All he'd have to do is slip into her and he'd be done. That wouldn't be fair to her.

Of course he could satisfy himself, and then climb in bed with her. It wouldn't take long. He would be done in no time with as hard as he was. The thought had him hurrying out of his clothes and he came to stand beside the bed, his hand easing between his legs to slide over the hard, long length of him.

He leaned over to ease the blanket off Rosa so that her backside was fully exposed. He couldn't stop himself from running his hand over the soft mound several times and down in between her legs to insert one finger just at her opening. It was warm and wet. Was she dreaming about him?

His finger played with her until she turned with a moan kicking the covers off and spreading her legs. He was tempted to slip into her, but he would spill himself too fast and that would not do. He reluctantly kept his hands off her and stroked himself. He'd be done soon, and then he would wake her slowly with kisses and intimate touches.

She touched herself then and he thought he would explode, but instead it grew him even harder. And the more she touched herself the more his passion grew, but he couldn't or perhaps wouldn't allow himself to come like this when he so wanted to be inside her.

He continued to stroke himself faster and faster wanting it done and over so that he could finally take her in his arms. He closed his eyes, though the image of her naked touching herself did not fade from his mind.

"Esteban."

His name whispered in a soft plea had his eyes shooting open.

She held her hand out to him and he could smell the scent of her on it. She was still drowsy from sleep, her nipples rock hard, and her legs further apart, invitingly.

"I want you so badly," she whispered and pushed herself up, brushed his hand away from his hard shaft and took him into her mouth.

He dropped his head back and groaned with pleasure.

She licked and sucked and he thought to spill himself into her mouth, but then he recalled not only her sore lip but what he had said earlier to her about making a baby. He took hold of her shoulders and shoved her gently back on the bed, slipped over her and into her with one quick, hard thrust that had her moaning.

"Harder, please harder," she begged and he obliged.

He drove in and out of her, every thrust driving him closer and closer to the edge and soon so very soon he would fall off and plummet into the abyss of pure pleasure... and take Rosa with him.

"We come together. Now open your mouth wide," he ordered and she did. He drove his tongue into her mouth, avoiding her lip as he drove ever harder into her.

She squeezed at his arms clinging to them like a lifeline.

He leaned up, bracing his hands on either side of her, his muscles taut and straining as he set a wild rhythm that had her moaning aloud for release.

"Together," he ordered in a harsh whisper. "We climax together."

"Yes, yes," she begged.

He slammed into her and ordered, "Now!"

Rosa screamed as she exploded in a blind climax that was never-ending. It rippled on and on and on.

Esteban felt the same. He thought he'd never stop coming. It shuddered him from top to bottom.

"Esteban," she pleaded softly.

He was familiar with that plea and he moved quick and hard inside her for her to climax again.

"Ohhh," she sighed as she drifted through another climax not as strong but satisfyingly delicious.

Esteban slipped out of her after he was certain she was done and collapsed beside her. He reached out and took her hand, brought it to his mouth, kissed it, and then laid both their hands on his stomach.

Her free hand went to rest on her stomach. "We made a baby. I know we did."

He released her hand and turned on his side to rest his hand over hers. "I agree. There was something different about it."

Rosa smiled. "Yes, so very strong and so very loving. I could feel it." She laughed softly. "Oh, and you can wake me like that anytime."

"Then we will have many children," he teased.

"I would like that."

"So would I," he confessed.

"Our children will bring many smiles and much laughter to the hacienda."

"They will add to what their mother brought here... happiness."

Rosa felt a tear tickle her eye and before it could fall she took hold of her husband's face and brought his lips to meet hers, though first she whispered, "I will love you forever."

They snuggled together, Esteban pulling the blanket up over them. They talked for a few minutes about family and the future. Rosa didn't ask what had happened with Pacquito's men and at the moment didn't want to know. She wanted this moment to be about them and possibilities.

Esteban felt the same. It was as if life had stood still for a few moments and let them be, just the two of them. And Esteban got a glimpse of what life could be like without Pacquito always being a threat.

Sleep finally claimed them and as Esteban drifted off, he vowed to end Pacquito's reign. And Rosa vowed to do whatever she had to, to keep her husband safe.

Chapter Thirty-three

Esteban searched for his wife. His promise to escort her and his mother to the Garavito ranch had been delayed several days. He and his father had been busy with the bordering neighbors in organizing a joint venture and in securing the area against further attacks.

This morning the visit had been delayed once again when one of the rancheros in the area arrived unexpectedly to speak with Esteban. The meeting had not taken long and not wanting to disappoint his wife again, he went to collect her, having already informed his mother that they would leave shortly.

He found her sitting alone on a bench in one of the gardens. He stopped a moment to watch her. She sat so silent, so still, and he wondered what deep thoughts had her appearing like a sculpted statue that graced a garden.

She startled when he stepped in front of her, and his arm went around her waist to lift her off the bench.

She smiled and playfully swatted his arm. "You snuck up on me."

"Your thoughts were too deep to hear anyone approach. Does something trouble you?"

She laughed lightly. "Wouldn't it be better to

ask what doesn't trouble me?" She laughed again. "This time, though, I must admit that there was no room for worry in my never-ending thoughts."

"Then you must have been thinking of me," he teased, pleased to know that she hadn't been troubled.

"Thoughts of you always fill my head and I am pleased, for when you are not around at least you are with me in my mind."

He leaned down and gave her a gentle kiss. "Then keep me there, for I am forever with you no matter where I am. But I am curious as to what had you in such a trance."

She blushed, Esteban laughed, and she swatted his arm again.

"Were you thinking of this morning when I hoisted your legs over my shoulders and had barely plunged into you and you came, and then came again. Or was it last night when we were both so eager that I took you against the door, your cries of pleasure so loud, the whole hacienda must have heard them?"

She gasped and her blush deepened. "They didn't."

"You were loud, though I didn't mind."

She swatted him again. "It is your fault that I scream."

"Shall I stop making you scream?"

"No—yes—no—"

His kiss devoured her confusing protest and it didn't take long before it grew much too passionate, though still a bit more gentle than usual since her lip was nearly healed. It took great resolve to tear his mouth away from hers. "We need to leave now or I will—"

"What? What will you do?" she asked a bit breathless.

He rested his cheek to hers and whispered in her ear, "I will drag you behind one of those trees behind us, hoist your dress—damn—I'm growing hard just at the thought."

"And I grow wet."

"Damn," he muttered, resting his brow to hers. "Mother waits in the carriage."

"Then make it fast," she murmured and ran her hand down along him and gave him an encouraging squeeze."

He grabbed her hand and did as she said, dragged her behind the tree, hoisted her dress and plunged in so fast and hard that with barely a few thrusts she exploded, squeezing around him so tightly that he bit at his lower lip from groaning aloud when he burst in an endless climax.

He rested his forehead to hers, his hand squeezing her bare bottom as the last of his climax rippled away. "Damn, but I love you."

She ran a fleeting kiss across his lips. "And I you, forever and always."

"Forever," he reaffirmed and they kissed as if sealing a vow.

They hurried to right themselves, and then hurried off laughing like two young children, happy and carefree.

A large troop of vaqueros accompanied them to

the Garavito ranch. Esteban rode in the front, though a few times he changed positions, his eyes forever on the landscape.

It wasn't long before they reached the Garavito ranch. Dona Elena was thrilled to see them. She and Dona Valerianna hugged like long lost sisters, tears pooling in each of their eyes.

Rosa was proud of her husband. He walked up to Don Manuel, extended his hand and asked what he and his vaqueros could do to help. Don Manuel was not as angry as the last time she had seen him. He spoke respectfully to Esteban and they walked off together.

Work had been done on the house and Dona Elena proudly showed it off. It looked lovely, and Dona Elena explained how she intended to embroider curtains for the repaired rooms. Dona Valerianna immediately offered to help and the two women were soon planning on meeting regularly as they once had done.

Rosa felt a bit of an outsider, since stitching wasn't a favorite chore of hers. And when the women's discussion changed to how they had drifted apart, Rosa knew it was time to leave the two women alone. She made an excuse about needing to get something from the carriage and left before either of them suggested that a servant fetch it.

She decided to wander around the hacienda with the purpose of seeing if she could be of any help anywhere. She didn't come here to be waited on or sit while others worked. She was much too used to keeping busy, to stay idle too long. She meandered off in search of a chore.

In the distance by the corral that had been repaired she saw her husband speaking with Don Manuel. The man appeared serious and her husband seemed to listen with intense interest. Curious, she would have liked to have gotten closer to hear what they were discussing, but if they saw her approach no doubt the conversation would end abruptly. She didn't want to interfere with what appeared an important discussion so she turned at the end of the house and headed toward the kitchen area.

Esteban never missed anything going on around him, even if it did appear as if he concentrated on only one thing. It had been a skill that he had acquired rather quickly when he was captured by Pacquito. He had realized that he needed to be aware of his surroundings so that no one could come upon him in surprise. He had learned to survey an area as he approached it and remember who stood where and did what and to listen to sounds so he would know if someone had moved or someone approached behind him. It had been easier than he had thought to see out of the corners of his eyes without anyone noticing, especially if he directed their attention elsewhere.

So when, out of the corner of his eye, he caught his wife walking alongside the house, he wondered what she was up to. She had hesitated a moment and he thought she intended to approach them, but then she kept walking until she disappeared behind the house. He didn't like her going off alone, but he had placed his men around the hacienda and on the outskirts. And he had told them to keep an eye on his wife if they should see her off on her own. His mother, he knew, would spend all her time with her friend. Rosa on the other hand, he had expected to venture off, though not this soon.

"You are one of us, Esteban, no one doubts that now," Don Manuel said.

Esteban returned his full attention to the man. He had been going on about how the rancheros had been discussing how he had saved the Mercados ranch from being attacked.

"Don Alfredo Mercados is grateful for your quick intervention in saving his home. We all see now how difficult your imprisonment with Pacquito must have been, but you remained faithful to your heritage and returned home to claim your rightful place." He smiled. "And you have taken yourself a beautiful woman to wed and no doubt will soon have a lovely family of your own."

"Rosa is beautiful and I am proud to have her as a wife."

"As you should be. She was courageous in coming here after my place was attacked. I am ashamed to admit that I was not as welcoming as I should have been and for that I apologize, though your wife did not let my poor manners upset her. She remained pleasant and helpful and by the time her visit came to an end, I found myself feeling as if she had helped in lifting my spirit."

Esteban grinned. "That's my Rosa... sharing her good-hearted nature." He felt his gut tighten, but then it always did when he realized again and again how lucky he was to have her as his wife. He had fought so hard against marrying her when he had wanted nothing more than to wed her. But he had feared he would corrupt her and instead—his grin grew—she had corrupted him with her loving heart. Damn, if he wasn't a lucky man. He almost laughed when Don Manuel repeated his thought.

"You are a lucky man."

"That I am, Don Manuel."

Don Manuel cleared his throat, his expression turning serious. "The other rancheros and I have been talking and we want to extend our apologies for mistrusting you upon your return home."

"While I had hoped for a different homecoming, I didn't expect it. How could I have when I had been gone so long? And no doubt if I was in your position I would have been just as apprehensive and cautious." His words were a revelation to him. He had been full of anger on his return home and it had grown as he continued to be treated so poorly. But now being wed, wanting children and safe surrounding for them to grow up in, he realized what had been at stake for the rancheros. And he certainly would have felt the same... he would have protected his family against the renegade that had returned home.

"Now that we have seen with our own eyes that you are truly one of us, we welcome you home with open hearts and arms. It is good to have you back, Esteban Cesare." Don Manuel grabbed hold of his face and kissed each cheek.

Shock turned Esteban speechless. Only a few days ago people were still apprehensive around him, but then his wife's words had stirred a different gossip. And going to his neighbor's rescue had helped as well, though truly it had been as Don Manuel expressed. He had become one of them again... he had come home... and he was ever so happy to be here.

"The rancheros have been talking and it was Alfredo Mercados who suggested, though we all agreed, that we should organize our vaqueros and join as one to keep our family and land safe."

"That is a wise suggestion," Esteban agreed. "There is strength in numbers."

"And in a leader, which is why we all agree that you should be our leader."

Esteban stared at him not sure he had heard him correctly.

"You have the most experience and you are... fearless. We would feel safe with you as our leader."

"I am not fearless."

"You are fearless, Esteban," Don Manuel said with pride. "For you to survive the tortures of hell with that madman Pacquito, you had to be fearless. How else would you have survived and returned home the good man that you are?"

Esteban was not used to praise, didn't feel he deserved, and so it was difficult for him to accept it.

"Even without Pacquito tormenting us, the rancheros believe it is a good time for us to unite. You never know what the future holds and as you reminded, there is strength in numbers. Together we can protect our families and land, separate we could lose the good life we have built here for ourselves and others."

Esteban thought about Rosa and imagined her growing round with his child. And he also thought about his sister returning home and his parents growing older. The rancheros were right. They needed to band together and be prepared for whatever may come their way.

His response was issued with strength and conviction. "I would be honored to lead."

Don Manuel broke into a smile. "Good. Good. This is what we all prayed to hear. Now did your father send some of that fine wine so we could celebrate?"

Esteban shook his head, though smiled. "That is why he sent so much wine? My father knew of this?"

Don Manuel nodded. "He also assured us that you would accept. He knows his son well."

"No, my father taught me well."

Cheers were heard when the news spread through the ranch. Cesare vaqueros boasted of Don Esteban's strength and courage and wine was passed around to all. Tears tickled Dona Valerianna's eyes when she heard and Dona Elena let a few tears fall claiming the news wonderful and how now they would all be safe.

Dona Valerianna nodded, though could not help but worry over the price her son would pay to see that not only his family would stay safe, but others as well. Now more than ever he would keep his appointment with the devil. And she could do nothing but pray for his soul.

Dona Valerianna went to her son and hugged him when he entered the room with Don Manuel. And as she did, she whispered, "I am so proud of you."

Esteban kissed her cheek. "Your words touch my heart, *Madre*."

She hugged him again.

"Where is my wife?" Esteban asked as his mother took a glass of wine from the serving tray on the table and handed it to him.

"I believe she graciously slipped away to give two old friends time alone," Dona Elena said.

Esteban nodded. "That's why I saw her disappear behind the house."

"The kitchen and servants quarters are there," Don Manuel said.

Esteban was about to excuse himself and go fetch his wife when Don Manuel motioned to one of his servants.

"Go fetch Dona Rosa and tell her we celebrate her husband."

The servant smiled, bobbed her head, and hurried off.

Esteban would have preferred to retrieve his wife himself and impart the news to her, wondering if it would upset her. While no doubt she would be thrilled that the rancheros now trusted and treated him with respect, she would worry for his safety, but then she would probably forever worry over his safety.

He was finishing his second glass of wine and wondering what was keeping his wife. His impatience was growing along with concern as he downed the last drop of wine in his glass.

"Another," Don Manuel said, though didn't give him a chance to decline, he filled the glass.

Esteban was about to take his leave and find his wife when the servant returned... without Rosa.

"Dona Rosa is helping to deliver a baby."

"Take me to her," Esteban ordered.

Dona Elena nervously stepped forward. "I will go see and send Rosa to you."

Esteban realized he had been harsher in his order than intended, and he also realized that it wasn't a man's place to be around a woman, especially one he wasn't familiar with, when she was giving birth. But he didn't care. He wanted to make certain his wife was all right."

"Thank you, Dona Elena, but I will collect my wife and return shortly." He turned and left the room before anyone could object.

He followed the servant through the hacienda and through the back of the house, passed the kitchen, to the small huts that housed the servants. He didn't have to be shown which hut it was. It was obvious. Women gathered round the place talking and waiting, though they grew silent as he approached.

He knew it wasn't his place to enter the hut where the birth was taking place, but he didn't care. He intended to make certain his wife was all right.

Rosa stepped out of the hut, a huge smile plastered on her face and called out, "It's a boy. Rita and Jose have a son and Rita is doing fine."

The women cheered and called out blessings to the new baby before drifting off.

Rosa was about to go back inside when she caught sight of Esteban and hurried over to him.

Her face was flushed and her hair, that looked to have hastily been pinned up, had loosened with strands falling haphazardly around her face and neck. Her sleeves had been pushed up and she wore the brightest smile. To Esteban she had never looked more beautiful.

When she reached him, her hand quickly went to rest on his chest. "Oh, Esteban, you must see him. It is so adorable; a thick head of dark hair and such full cheeks."

He covered her hand with his, wanting to keep it there for as long as possible. "And the mother is doing well?" He worried that perhaps the trauma of childbirth would cause her to worry about giving birth herself. He knew he was worried about the prospect. He had seen too many women die in childbirth while in Pacquito's camp.

"Rita is well and so happy. I must go finish helping and you must wait here so I can show you the baby." She hurried off before he could say another word.

He stood staring after her and worry descended over him.

Fearless.

It had taken a certain amount of fearlessness to survive his ordeal, but he didn't know how he was going to survive his wife giving birth to their children. He had heard the endless screams of the women who had given birth in the camp and he remembered the cries of the other women when death would claim one and often the child along with her. He didn't want to see his wife suffer in such agonizing pain, and he couldn't bear the thought of possibly losing her and his child.

He tried to remind himself that it was different here from the camp. That his wife would have good care and be with loving people who would tend her well. Still, the thought of her suffering and what possibly could happen, plagued him.

Esteban didn't know how much time had passed. He had been too lost in his worries to realize, but Rosa was suddenly there with a small bundle in her arms.

"Isn't he precious, Esteban? I can't wait until we have a son or daughter, but then we'll have plenty of both."

Plenty of both.

Would she survive them all? Would he?

Esteban finally took a look at the small bundle and he couldn't help but smile. A bush of dark hair atop his head, chubby cheeks, and sleeping peacefully, he really was adorable. His small mouth puckered once, then twice, and then it opened and puckered again.

"He's hungry," Rosa said with a laugh.

"How do you know?"

"I've helped birth babies before."

"I thought unmarried women weren't allowed to help birth babes?"

Rosa shook her head, smiling. "There are some that feel that way, but there are times when one has no choice. Marinda and I had to help deliver a babe one day when no one else was around. The woman had four children already and so she explained to us what we were to do."

The baby gave a cry, a soft mewl almost like that of a kitten.

"I better get him to his mother."

"Will you be long?"

"I'll be done in a few minutes, so please wait for me?" she asked with a smile.

"I'm not going anywhere," he confirmed determined to wait as long as it took.

It didn't take long, she returned in a few moments, the sleeves of her dress once again down along her arms and her hair still pinned to her head but the lose strands now tucked away. Her cheeks remained slightly flushed and once again he thought how beautiful she looked.

As they walked back to hacienda he told her his news.

She stopped and stared at him.

He couldn't tell if she was pleased or upset, her face showed not a sign.

Then she burst into a huge grin. "This is

wonderful news. The rancheros have finally seen and admitted how badly they have treated you and realized you are and always have been one of them, as for being their leader... it causes me concern, but they could not have chosen a better man to lead."

Esteban scooped her around the waist and lifted her to plant a firm kiss on her lips. When he set her down, her cheeks were flaming red. And he heard the servants around them giggling.

"Tonight we celebrate," he said.

"With family, good food, fine wine, and—"

He kissed her again and whispered, "Making love."

Chapter Thirty-four

Rosa kept herself busy as routine settled over the hacienda in the days that followed their visit to the Garavitos. Meetings with the various rancheros were held, either taking Esteban away for a few hours or being sequestered away in the study for hours. He always found time, however, to seek her out even if it was only for a moment and only for a stolen kiss, and she loved him even more for it. But it was the nights she enjoyed the most with him. And it wasn't that they would make love every night. Some night they would simply lie in each other's arms and talk and drift off to sleep. It was having him there beside her that mattered the most to Rosa, for she feared soon the day would come when he would leave to meet the devil. And she worried over the consequences.

She jumped when arms circled her waist as she arranged flowers in the vase in the parlor. "You forever sneak up on me." She swatted her husband's arm.

"You should be more attentive to your surroundings," he scolded playfully and turned her around to face him. "I am free the rest of the day, what would you like to do?"

"Truly?" she asked excited to have him all to herself.

He nodded. "I am all yours."

"Hmmm... and you'll do whatever I want?"

He cupped her bottom and pressed her against him. "I grow hard with anticipation to hear your desires."

She laughed softly. "What if I want to pick oranges?"

He nuzzled her neck. "A good place to make love."

"A picnic in the garden?"

He nodded and grinned. "A place to make more memories. I'll take you against the tree as I did that day, perhaps twice."

"A ride through the vineyards?"

He brushed his lips across hers. "Even better, I know the perfect spot near the vineyards where I can ride you like a stallion does a mare."

Rosa shivered at the image and was oh so tempted, but she had a different thought in mind. With the day hot, she longed to strip and— "A swim in the pond."

He grinned from ear to ear and gave her a kiss. "Oh, *Caro*, that's perfect."

"Let's hurry," she said grabbing his hand and tugging him along. "I want as much time with you as possible."

They made a quick stop at the kitchen for a picnic basket, and then made their way to the pond. They didn't wait to strip and hurry into the water. It was cool and refreshing against the hot sun, but then the many trees surrounding the pond offered shade.

They splashed and enjoyed like two children, though it wasn't long before they were in each other's arms, eager to make love... and they did.

Esteban lifted her and ordered, "Wrap your legs around me."

She did and he easily slipped into her.

They stayed that way for a moment, their arms wrapped around each other.

"I love the feel of you inside me," she said in a soft whisper and then laughed. "You fit perfectly."

"You were made for me and only me."

She saw in his dark eyes that his renegade side had surfaced and waited for it to slip away, retreat somewhere deep inside him as it had done of late.

"You're mine, *Caro*, mine and mine alone. No other shall ever touch you."

He took her mouth in a hungry kiss, and then lifted her to bring her down hard on him.

She gasped as he drove deep inside her, and he did it again and again. She braced her hands on his shoulders to lessen the impact, but he was too strong for her. She landed harder and harder on him until she cried out, "Esteban, stop!"

He stopped immediately and looked at her with such horror, as if just realizing how harsh his love making had been that her heart went out to him.

"A bit softer," she said and before she could kiss him, he went to lift her off him. "No!" she cried out, her hands going around his neck and holding tight. "I want you inside me."

"I've hurt you."

The pain in his eyes tore at her heart. "No, you

didn't."

He gritted his teeth for a moment before he spoke, "I treated you savagely."

"You would never do that," she assured him and kissed his cheek. "You were overly eager."

He shook his head. "No, I wanted to plant myself deep inside you, make you mine, only mine I—"

"I am yours and only yours and always will be. I love you and that, my dear husband, will never change."

Esteban rested his brow against hers, and though he would speak these words to no other, he owed them to his wife. They not only spilled easily from his lips, but came deep from his heart. "I'm sorry."

His sincere apology momentarily startled her. She couldn't recall ever hearing him apologize and yet he did so to her. She hurried to say, "No need to be. You stopped when I asked, a savage wouldn't. You are no savage. You are my loving husband who I trust without question."

"But I could have—"

"You didn't. You wouldn't."

"But—"

She kissed him silent. "You have never hurt me and you never will, unless..."

His eyes widened.

"If you don't finish what you've started here, then you will have caused me to suffer greatly."

A smile tipped at one corner of his mouth. The way it once had when she had first met him.

"I won't see you suffer," he said.

The sincerity in his eyes made her heart ache for she knew he referred to much more than what she was asking of him.

His hands went to her waist and he lifted her and brought her down gently. "You'll tell me if—"

"Yes, yes," she urged bouncing up and down on him.

He smiled this time and set a rhythm, though after a short time Rosa took over, urging him to go faster and he strained to hold her and not bring her down too hard on him. She would have none of it. He realized then just how hard he had forced her to ride him and he got angry.

"Stop frowning," she ordered curtly. "You make me think you don't want to be inside me."

That was it. He lifted her off him, scooped her up and carried her out of the water. He laid her on the blanket they had spread out for the picnic and lowered himself over her.

"I'm going to show you just how much I love you."

He started with a kiss to her lips, and then he began to travel down her body.

It was as if the world stood still for her. There was nothing but his lips on her flesh and his hands touching her so intimately that she thought she would die from the passion that shot through her.

He made her come with his tongue, and then his fingers, and then he entered her and made her come again. By the time he was done, he had accomplished what he had first wanted to do... he had made her completely, entirely, utterly his. She had surrendered completely to him.

It took time for her to return to normal, not that she wanted to. He had made her feel so... so... there was no word to describe it. She only knew she wanted to linger in it.

They lay naked beside each other, their hands joined, the leaves on the tree branch overhead fluttering in the warm breeze.

She laughed, her hand flying to her stomach. "I think you may have given me twins."

He laughed along with her. "And here I thought I had spared you from suffering."

"It is with joy I will bring your children into the world, though there may be a few screams first."

He winced. "If I could take your pain I would."

She turned to him. "Nonsense, it is my duty to birth the babes and your duty to make sure I enjoy making the babes."

He laughed again and brought her to rest on top of him. "I promise you I will do my duty."

"Good, now let's eat, I'm starving."

It was late afternoon by the time they returned to the hacienda. If things had been different Esteban would have spent the night there under the stars, with her. But present circumstances did not allow that.

They had barely arrived home when news was received that a nearby hacienda was in danger of being attacked. Esteban was quick to leave while his father remained behind. It was a plan all the haciendas had implemented under Esteban's direction. No hacienda was to be left completely without protection.

Rosa stared in the distance after her husband who had long since disappeared. Pride swelled in her chest for the man he had become since his return home and tears threatened her eyes. It had been only an hour since they had been alone, making love, enjoying their time alone, and now he was gone and she worried if he would return safely.

She wished this ordeal was at an end. She wished Pacquito would go away. She wished Esteban wouldn't meet with the devil. She wished life would finally settle and hold only little worries.

With a sigh of resignation and a determination to see this through with her husband, she turned and entered the hacienda. She would keep herself busy until his return and would pray that all returned home unharmed.

It wasn't until night had long since fell that Rosa discovered that her prayers had gone unanswered. Esteban arrived angry and injured, though his injuries were minor to Rosa's relief.

She paced the study waiting for him to finish speaking with his father. She had wanted to tend his wounds immediately, but he had adamantly refused. And she had wisely held her tongue, knowing he would have it his way no matter how much she protested.

His mother had left her healing basket for Rosa

to use to tend Esteban while she hurried off to tend the injured vaqueros. Rosa assured her that she would help her as soon as she saw to Esteban.

It was with solemn faces that the two men emerged from the study. Don Alejandro gave Rosa a sorrowful look and without a word walked away. Rosa's stomach clenched so tight that she thought she would double over with pain.

Esteban must have thought otherwise since he slipped his arm around his wife's waist and walked her to the parlor, her feet barely touching the floor. He sat her down and poured her a glass of wine.

She shook her head. "I need to tend you."

"Drink it," he ordered sternly, "or your hands will not stop trembling."

Rosa realized then how badly her hands were shaking. She took the wine glass with both hands and drank. Then she said, "Tell me."

Esteban poured himself a glass of wine and drank half of it before he answered her. "Pacquito has escalated his attack. We lost good men, many more were injured, and several buildings burned to cinders." He took another drink. "We saved a woman from being captured, though she perished from her wound a short time later."

Rosa's stomach roiled at the suffering.

"Pacquito is impatient now and when he gets impatient, he becomes very dangerous."

She jumped up after placing her wine glass on the small side table. "I must see to your wounds."

"Rosa—"

"Your wounds first," she insisted knowing

what he was about to tell her and not wanting to hear it.

He nodded.

"In our chambers," she instructed. "I have everything ready there."

"Including more wine?" he asked teasingly, wanting a smile to replace the frown that marred her lovely features, if only for a short time. He knew that what he had to tell her would steal her smile for some time.

But she didn't smile, not even a little. She grasped his hand tightly and led him from the room without saying a word. Once they entered the room, she made him sit on the edge of the bed, then she brought him a glass of wine.

He thought that she needed it more than he did, but he didn't say that. He took the wine and let her go about her business in silence. And with every movement she made, he could sense her worry growing.

She gently removed his shirt and began cleaning his chest and arms. There were minor wounds here and there, nothing serious and nothing that required bandaging. They probably came from altercations since his knuckles were scraped and bloody.

Rosa couldn't bring herself to speak as she worked. She feared she would break into tears if she did and she wanted to finish tending him. When she finished, he would tell her what she didn't want to hear and each time she thought of it her stomach clenched again and again.

When she was almost done, a thought came to her and she leaned down, gave a lift to his chin and brought her lips to his. She would put off the inevitable as long as she could by making love to him.

Her kiss grew more demanding and as it did she eased him back on the bed going down on top of him.

He in turn eased her off him to rest on her side and eased the kiss as well, until he brought it most reluctantly to an end. He went to speak, his lips a bare inch from hers.

She pressed her finger against them. "Please, no."

Her plea broke his heart, for he knew he would have to disappoint her. "We must talk."

"No," she said again with a shake of her head.

"We must, *Caro*."

Tears pooled in her eyes and she tried to fight them. She did not want to appear a whimpering wife. She wanted to show him strength, but it was so very difficult when her heart felt as if it was breaking in two.

"*Caro*," he whispered softly and kissed her gently. "If I could but change what must be done, I would. But no one will be safe until I see this through."

She understood that, but accepting it was another matter. "I know you must, but my heart breaks with the thought."

He rested his hand to her chest. "I would do anything not to break your heart, but I would do even more to keep you safe."

"You will not give your life for me," she ordered empathically.

He brushed her lips with his. "I never wanted to live as badly as I do now. I want a life with you, Rosa. I want to make babies with you and watch them grow. I want to grow old with you and see our grandbabies born. I love you beyond belief."

She couldn't stop her tears from falling. They trickled out one after the other flowing down her cheeks. "I did not want to cry, but I cannot help it."

"You can cry whenever, wherever, and for whatever reason you want, and I will always be there to comfort you."

She placed her hand to his cheek. "Then promise me one thing."

"Anything."

"You will return home to me. No matter what... you will return home to me."

"I will do whatever it takes to come home to you, *Caro*. I promise you."

"When do you go?" she asked, her voice trembling

He reluctantly answered her. "I must leave now."

She had known he would say that. She had known as soon as he had returned that he would be leaving again only this time on his own.

"I wish how I wish..." Her tears returned as her words ailed off. "How long will you be gone?"

"I'm t sure. It depends on what the devil has

to say."

She didn't want to think about what that meant, though it was obvious. If the devil told Esteban where Pacquito could be located, then he would go after him and bring this to an end. It terrified her to think of the dangers her husband was about to face.

"You must promise me something," he said.

"I will stay at the hacienda until you return, I promise," she said knowing what he was about to ask.

"You will not even venture to the orchards?"

"No, I will not go to the orchards. I will not cause you to worry over me while you are gone. I will keep myself busy here. I give you my word."

He kissed her. "Thank you, *Caro*, you have eased my mind."

He went to move off the bed and she grabbed him and hugged him tight. "Stay safe, my love."

He kissed her again and got off the bed quickly, as if he feared changing his mind and hurried out of the room.

Rosa laid there, tears streaming down her cheeks, her heart breaking, and her stomach tight with worry. She didn't know how she was going to survive this time without him, though after a few minutes of feeling sorry for herself, she sat up and wiped her tears away. Esteban was about to do what was necessary. She had to do the same.

She washed her face, pinned up her hair, and went to join Dona Valerianna in tending the injured.

The hacienda was busy with activity. Servants

rushed around, vaqueros were everywhere, and somewhere in the midst of it all Esteban was preparing to leave or perhaps he already had. She held her head high and went to do her part.

It was hours later, late into the night when she finally made her way back to her chambers. She was bone-tired and glad of it, for she would drop into her empty bed and fall fast asleep. Though she had been busy, her husband had never left her thoughts. She had continually prayed for his safety and for his speedy return.

She had walked around back to reach her chambers, the way she and Esteban so often did. With all the vaqueros around, she never gave thought to her safety. So when she was grabbed from behind, a hand covering her mouth, and dragged past the bushes and trees, she found herself too shocked to respond.

The man settled her back against a tree, his hand remaining over her mouth.

He was a tall, thick shadow in the black night and she feared his intentions.

"Listen to me," the shadow said sharply. "You can go with me willingly with no harm done to those here or Pacquito's men will be here shortly to take you and no doubt he will leave destruction in his path. If you come with me I will send word to Pacquito that we have you and he will leave the hacienda alone. You will give me your answer and ask no questions or others will pay for your disobedience. Do you understand?"

She nodded.

"Will you come with me willingly and in silence?"

Rosa didn't have to think about it. One way or the other she would be taken, but one way others would suffer and she could not let that happen. She nodded, though wondered who her captive was, since he obviously wasn't one of Pacquito's men.

Her suspicions grew as he led her to a small group of men waiting with horses. How did these men slip past the guards? And if they were not with Pacquito, then who had sent them and why?

She was placed on a horse and the shadow mounted behind her. More silent than she thought possible they made their way off Cesare land and disappeared into the night. As they got further and further away from the hacienda, she realized just why she had been taken. She was the bait Pacquito would use to bring Esteban to him.

The only question was... what would Pacquito do to her before Esteban could reach her?

Chapter Thirty-five

It took Esteban only a couple of hours to reach his destination. It was nothing more than a campsite, though heavily guarded. He was directed to the fire and given food and drink without a word being spoken to him. He accepted both, for not to do so would insult the devil and because he'd be wise to eat when he could. He needed his strength for what he was about to face.

The strange thing was that he had thought about the day he would kill Pacquito ever since the day he had been captured. It had been one of the things that had kept him alive... revenge. Now he wanted nothing more than to finally free himself from the evil man so that he could get back to his wife and live the life he had thought had been lost to him.

He had started missing Rosa as soon as he had left her. And leaving her had been more difficult than ever, especially when she had been so upset. He did not like leaving her like that. She had tried to be strong for him and had done so well, and then her tears had begun to fall and it had torn at his heart to see her so distressed. He wondered what she was doing now. She would probably be tucked safely in bed, sound asleep. No doubt exhausted from the busy and worrisome day. That was the image he held in his mind.

The thought brought a reminder to just how long and difficult the day turned out to be. He was feeling the fatigue himself and knew he would have to grab at least a couple of hours of sleep to make certain he was not worn down when he met up with Pacquito.

A man stepped out of the shadows and Esteban got to his feet to greet the devil. But one look told him this man wasn't the one he had come to see. He was short and solid with muscles and not a strand of hair on his head. He had fine features and dark eyes that seemed to have a perpetual squint to them, as if he forever had the sun in his eyes.

"The devil is delayed," he said abruptly. "He will be here at sunrise."

Esteban didn't like that news, but what could he say. He nodded and the man turned and the shadows once again swallowed him whole. He was annoyed, though he intended to use the time to his advantage. He would get much needed sleep and be well rested for what he was about to face. He stretched out not far from the fire, resting his head on a thick fallen branch. He stared at the numerous stars in the sky and thought about how he would much rather be sleeping with his wife by the pond under such a beautiful canopy. And one day soon he planned to do just that. He closed his eyes and thought about lying in bed cuddled around his wife and in no time fell asleep.

~~~

Every bone and muscle in Rosa's body ached. The first time they had stopped, her legs had almost given out from under her when she had been placed on the ground. It had taken all her strength to lower herself to the ground to sit, and it was only a short time after that that the man who had come for her—Jared—grabbed her by the arm and hauled her up. She was placed back on the horse and they continued to ride for hours.

She didn't know how she kept her eyes open, though she had nodded off a couple of times, her chin lolling on her chest. She was completely exhausted by the time they reached a campsite. At first she had thought that the men there were part of the band she rode with, but then she spotted the difference. The men who had come for her were far different from the grimy, worn-out looking men at the campsite.

And that's when she knew that they had finally arrived at Pacquito's camp. Fear trickled through her, remembering the stories Esteban had told her about what happened to the women Pacquito captured.

She had to stay strong. She couldn't let her fear show. Esteban would come for her. She had to hold on until then. One look at the way Pacquito's men leered at her and she knew it was going to prove difficult to hold onto her courage. The men whispered to one another, pointed at her, and then laughed. She didn't know how she would ever attempt to sleep tonight. She feared the thought of drifting off and being left vulnerable to these men.

Though the night was warm, a chill kept running through her. She kept her arms wrapped around her middle and her eyes focused on those around her. She wasn't foolish enough to think that she could defend herself against so many men, she could only hope and pray that she wouldn't have to try.

The other men scrambled to their feet at the approach of footsteps and grumbling. Then out of the shadows stepped three men. It wasn't hard to tell which one was Pacquito since the other two men walked a step or two behind him.

Rosa shivered at the sight of him. He was shy of six feet by a few inches and lean, but it was his face that, no doubt, struck fear. It was heavy with lines and a ragged scar ran down from just above his right eye to his jaw. Another scar cut across his left cheek to his nose. A small scar at one corner of his mouth made it appear as if he forever frowned on that side and one earlobe looked to have been bitten off. The worst part though was his brown eyes. They were so empty that you would think he was dead. His dark shoulder length hair was unkempt and tucked back behind his ears. His clothes needed a washing, but then he and his men looked as if they'd been on the road for some time, dirt and dust covering all of them.

Pacquito grinned when his eyes fell on Rosa and he walked over to her. "Esteban has found himself a beauty."

She suppressed the shiver that struggled to surface.

He walked slowly around her, inspecting her from head to toe, his eyes lingering in intimate places. "After I take you in front of Esteban, I will keep you for myself."

Her legs trembled and her stomach roiled at the disgusting thought and though words rushed to spew from her lips, she kept them tightly closed. Antagonizing him would do her no good. She must be patient and wait.

"You're a quiet one." He laughed. "I'll have you screaming in no time."

She bit at the tip of her tongue to keep from responding. It was better she said nothing or so she tried to convince herself.

He walked around her again, rubbing his chin. "I was going to kill Esteban fast and be done with him, but now," —he grinned wide—"I'm going to cut him so that he slowly bleeds to death and the last thing he will see as he lies there helpless and dying, is me riding you like a mighty stallion."

The image his words evoked was too much for her to bear. She couldn't hold back. Her words shot out like an arrow hitting its mark. "You are a hapless fool if you believe that."

Pacquito's hand shot out so fast that she didn't see it, but she did feel it. Her head snapped to the side so hard that she feared he broke her jaw.

"You will learn to obey me," Pacquito screamed at her.

Roberto screamed those exact words at her after having lived with the Curros for only one day. She had been a little girl unable to defend herself...

she wasn't a little girl anymore.

She tossed her chin up. "Never!"

He swung out to hit her again and this time she ducked and he missed her. He grew furious and lashed out at her again. This time Jared stepped between them, though not before Pacquito managed to catch the corner of Rosa's right eye and she stumbled from the blow.

"Enough," Jared ordered.

"You have no say in this. She belongs to me now. Take your men and leave," Pacquito ordered.

"My orders are to stay until the end," Jared said.

Pacquito laughed. "So you wish to watch me take her while Esteban dies?"

"What comes afterwards doesn't concern me."

"So you are to protect her from me until Esteban shows up?" Pacquito asked his laughter gone along with any remnants of a smile.

"I am here to see you get what is owed you."

The chill that had lingered in Rosa grew until she couldn't help but shudder. They spoke as if she didn't matter at all. She was nothing more than a pawn to them and it made her realize just how dire her situation was.

"Finally, he realizes this?" Pacquito snapped. "It is about time."

"Then do what you will with her tomorrow, but tonight she rests."

Pacquito's grin returned. "She'll need the rest for what I have planned for her."

His sneer turned her stomach and she was glad

that he walked away and joined his men at their campfire. They passed a bottle around, talking and laughing and jabbing fingers in her direction.

With trembling legs, she made her way to the campfire and collapsed close to it, her whole body chilled. She held her trembling hands out to the fire. She wished there was something she could do, but what chance did she have against so many men? And what chance did Esteban have?

The thought sent her stomach roiling so badly that she thought she would be sick, but she fought the waves of nausea, not wanting to show her fear to these men. But the more she considered the outcome, the more she worried that Esteban would have little chance against so many. Pacquito's men wouldn't simply let him walk away. The only thing that gave her some solace was that she would be there with him. Whatever his fate, was her fate too and they would share it together.

If her husband was to meet death, then she would greet it alongside him. With that thought in mind she began to nod off, though she'd wake as soon as her head bobbed too low. And so went her night, dozing and waking, making sure no one crept up on her until, with relief, she greeted the dawn and prayed that her husband wasn't far behind it.

~~~

Esteban rose with the dawn, eager to be on his way and see this thing done. He grew agitated when the sun was full up and the devil still hadn't made an appearance. He tried not to let his annoyance show, fighting to keep himself from pacing.

When the short, stocky man appeared Esteban wondered if he was the devil's emissary and that he wouldn't even get to speak with the devil himself. But then if that was so why wouldn't the man have spoken with him last night?

Esteban was about to approach the short man when he stepped aside and from behind a tree stepped a man so shrouded in black that Esteban took a step back. The man was covered from head to toe in a robe not that unfamiliar from what the padres wore. The hood hung over his head down to just above his chin and the wide sleeves fell past his hands making it seem as if he had none. He was tall, over six feet, and though the shroud covered him, from his imposing stance he appeared lean and muscular. He didn't appear to carry a weapon, but then his appearance so terrified that it was weapon enough to stop anyone from approaching him.

"You requested a favor Esteban Cesare."

His articulate and deep voice surprised Esteban. He sounded more cultured than he had expected. He nodded, though it hadn't been a question.

"You are willing to owe the devil?"

"I am," Esteban said without hesitation.

"You plan to put an end to Pacquito?"

"I do and he deserves it."

"Are you playing God, Esteban?"

Esteban caught the vehemence in his tone and shook his head. "God had no use for me and I have none for him."

"Then why does Pacquito deserve to die?"

"Because he was the reason the old woman Lequita took her life."

"Lequita took her life?"

Esteban shivered from the stone cold tone of his voice. "She did."

"Why?"

"Pacquito threatened that he would beat her again if I ever attempted to leave. She knew I would never let that happen. She had been so very good to me since the first day of my capture. I do not think I would have survived the ordeal if it hadn't been for her kindness and love. I would not see her beaten again because of me. I planned to wait until her death to leave." Esteban paused a moment before recalling the heartbreaking memory. "She was familiar with every plant, shrub, and tree in the area. She knew what could be eaten and what never should be touched. One day she ate berries she knew would kill her, though would give her time to speak with me first."

"She spoke with you?" the devil said and then demanded, "What did she say to you?"

"She told me it was her time to go. She was too tired to live any longer and that I wasn't to blame myself."

"That was all?"

"No, her last words were, 'Tell the devil I love him and to forgive me and not to forget his promise.'"

Esteban jumped back as did the short, stocky
man when the devil let loose with a terrifying roar.
The short man shuddered and Esteban felt his
blood run cold. They both stood still, not moving a
muscle or saying a word, waiting for the devil to
calm down and speak.

After several silent minutes, the devil said with
a growl, "You remained with her until she died?"

"Lequita died in my arms."

"You will kill, Pacquito."

It was not a question or a statement. It sounded
more like a demand. And since the devil wanted
Pacquito dead, Esteban wondered if perhaps it
would be more a favor to the devil and it would
negate owing him anything.

"You seem to want him dead as well. Will it
then be a favor I do for you and owe you nothing?"

"You owe me more than you know, and I will
extract payment when the time comes."

A chill ran through Esteban again, the devil's
voice ominous in his promise. He did not like, at
all, owing this man. He feared the payment might
be too high, but he could think of no other way.

"Then I will be on my way and see this done,"
Esteban said wanting away from the devil. "Where
can I find Pacquito?"

The devil turned and nodded to the short man
who proceeded to give Esteban the directions.

Once finished Esteban turned to leave when the
devil called out to him and he reluctantly turned
around.

"I had my men take your wife to his camp. She waits there for you."

Esteban clenched his fists, his fury mounting. If Rosa had been in Pacquito's camp since last night there was no telling what he had done to her. He shut his eyes against images that rushed into his head to torment him. He wanted to lash out at the devil, but instead he did what he never expected to do... he prayed for his wife's safety.

Before Esteban turned to go, he took a step forward and the short man blocked his path to the devil. With his fists clenched at his sides he stared straight at the black shrouded figure. "Know this and know it well. Devil or not, if anything has happened to my wife, I will hunt you down and kill you."

Chapter Thirty-six

The sun had been up for several hours and Rosa grew worried, not that her husband had yet to show up, but with the tension growing in the camp. Pacquito had been talking to his men in whispers since after sunrise and it seemed obvious to her, and she hoped to Jared and his men, that Pacquito was planning something.

She had noticed the whispering after returning from the nearby stream where she had gotten a chance to refresh herself. Her reflection in the water had startled her. Her jaw was bruised and swollen as was the corner of her eye. And her hair was a wild mane of tangles. She had quickly washed her face, and then had combed her hair with her fingers, getting the knots and tangles out as best as she could and hurriedly braided it. She hadn't wanted to greet Esteban looking a sight. It would make him think she had suffered worse than she had, and he didn't need to be worried about her. It was Pacquito he needed to focus on.

Now, however, she wondered if Pacquito had a change of plans. It certainly would seem that way with all the whispering and maneuvering his men were doing. So when the attack came, she shouldn't have been surprised. But she was, though only for a moment.

The melee gave her a chance to escape. She didn't stop to think, she ran; darting around fighting men, falling over wounded ones and ducking when she heard a shot ring out. She didn't stop to look behind her, she kept going. The edge of the camp and the safety of the trees were only a few feet away. She would make it. She would be free and when she was she would keep running.

She was almost there, another step or two and...

She was yanked back by her braid, swung around, and tossed to the ground. She grasped for air, the breath having been knocked out of her from the fall and tears stung her eyes from her braid having been yanked so hard. Her first thought was to urge herself to get to her feet, but her breath had yet to fully return to her.

It was too late anyway, a body suddenly straddled her and the sharp slap to her face startled the breath from her again. She felt and tasted blood pooling in the corner of her mouth.

"You're not getting away from me that fast," Pacquito said and leaned down to roughly press his lips against hers.

Unable to breathe, instinct had her raking her nails done his cheek. He jerked back away from her cursing and slapped her again, her head snapping to the side.

"You'll pay for that," he growled, "many times over."

He got off her and grabbed her arm, pinching it painfully as he forced her to her feet. His hand left her arm and wrapped quickly around her braid, then yanked it back.

"I'm not going to kill your husband yet," he said, planting his cheek forcefully against hers. "I'm going to enjoy you for a while, and then I'll return him to you well used. He won't want to touch you, but he will be bent on killing me. And an angry man is a foolish one, who makes foolish mistakes. Esteban will be easy to kill then."

Rosa almost got sick at the thought of having to endure Pacquito's touch. She prayed that Esteban would get to her before that could happen.

Pacquito dragged her to a horse and two of his men helped get her on it, Pacquito climbing on behind her

"Finish here, then you know where to join me," he ordered.

"Let us go with you," one man pleaded. "We may not be outnumbered, but the devil's men are beating us."

"All the more reason you are to stay and fight," Pacquito ordered. "Let no one follow me."

"We will die," the man said.

"I don't care." Pacquito laughed and rode off.

Panic rose in Rosa. She couldn't let him get too far away with her. Her husband no doubt would track them and find her, but it was what would happen until he did find her that worried her. She had to do something, especially before they reached open range where the horse could quicken his gait.

She had only one option open to her, and she had to be quick about it before Pacquito could stop her. She didn't wait to think about it... she threw herself from the horse, Pacquito caught in her swift momentum going with her.

~~~

Esteban came upon the fight. He scanned the area for his wife and when he didn't spot her or Pacquito, he cut a swath through the fighting to reach Jared. He kicked the man in the head that Jared was fighting, sending him sprawling to the ground.

"My wife?" he demanded.

"Pacquito just took her." Jared pointed past the two of them. "In that direction. On one horse. We'll finish here and be right behind you."

Esteban turned and with a few forceful kicks and solid punches, he made it through the melee. It didn't take him long to find the horse's tracks. They were deep since two people sat the horse.

He concentrated on the tracks, if he didn't, his anger would consume him and that would not help him reach his wife. He knew what Pacquito intended and if he didn't reach him before he retreated to one of his many hiding places, it would be difficult to find him. Esteban had no doubt he would eventually find him, but it was what would happened to Rosa if he failed to reach her now.

The thought sent a bolt of anger shooting through him and he almost roared with fury. He would not let her suffer a worse hell than he had been through. He had seen Pacquito do horrible things to women. Some were never right in the mind after he got through with them and some took their lives rather than suffer his cruelty. He would not let his wife suffer such a fate.

He followed the trail, his eyes and thoughts steady on it. He would find them and he would put an end to Pacquito's reign of terror.

~~~

Rosa hit the ground hard along with Pacquito. They rolled a few feet, Rosa scrambling to her feet before Pacquito could. She scanned the area quickly, hoping to spy anything she could use as a weapon. She grabbed a large rock and threw it at him as he stumbled to his feet. It hit him in the head and he stumbled again.

He swiped at the wound and his eyes glared with fury when he saw blood on his hand. "Another thing you'll pay for."

He rushed toward her and she threw another rock she had scooped up, hitting him in the neck.

It stopped him in his tracks and he gagged for a moment, his hand at his throat. Then his hands went to his belt, the one that held his pants, not the one that held his sheathed knives, opening it, and pulling it from around his waist. "That's it. *Now* you will pay."

Rocks were no longer a viable option and running would get her only so far before he caught her. What other choice did she have? She stared at Pacquito, her eyes widening, and then she went down on her knees, bending her head, and grasping her hands together. "I'm sorry. I'm sorry. Please don't hurt me," she pleaded.

"Too late," he grinned and brought the belt down on her shoulder. "You will learn to obey my every word."

She cried out, and he brought the belt down on her again. Her cry was louder this time, the blow harder and she realized that he was like the Curros. He took pleasure from causing pain. And she had learned that the more she had pleaded with Roberto or Lola to stop, the more they would swing the strap or their hands.

She gathered her courage and cried out for him to stop, she begged, promising she would do anything for him to stop. Her frantic pleas worked him into a frenzy and he brought the belt down on her back again. She cried out, pleading with him again and again as she grabbed onto his leg.

"Undo my pants and take me into your mouth, and I might stop," he ordered, though brought the belt down again on her.

She fumbled with his pants, continuing to beg him.

"Do it or I'll beat you until you bleed and still force you to take me in your mouth," he screamed.

He was beyond reasoning and the bulge in his pants confirmed that he was beyond hard. She shut her eyes for a moment and prayed that she had enough strength to do what she must. Then she reached for it.

~~~

Esteban heard his wife's terrifying screams and

he dismounted his horse, knowing he'd reach her faster on foot. He jumped over rocks, swerved around trees, ducked beneath branches and stopped in shock when he came upon the scene.

His wife was on her knees in front of Pacquito, her face in his crotch and he was about to bring his belt down on her back. Esteban raced toward him.

Pacquito's eyes turned wide with shock when he spotted him, at least that's what Esteban thought, and then he saw his wife scramble to her feet and back away from Pacquito. The man stared at her, his eyes turning wider, his face paling, and blood dripping from his groin.

Esteban saw the knife in his wife's hand and watched as she lunged again at a startled Pacquito and drove the knife into his heart, her words ringing clear.

"For my husband, you bastard."

She stepped back, leaving Pacquito to stare at the knife protruding from his heart. He yanked the knife out, blood pouring from the wound, and his mouth fell open as if about to speak, and then he fell over face first to the ground.

Esteban rushed to his wife's side, throwing his arms around her.

Pain rushed through her back, but she didn't care. She wanted him to hold her and never let her go. She buried her face against his chest for a moment, taking in his scent, feeling his warmth, and then she looked up at him. "I'm so glad you're here and you are never to leave my side again," she scolded.

Esteban touched her cheek gently. Seeing her injured face he wished he could kill Pacquito again and again and again for what he had done to her. "I will be by your side so much you will grow tired of me."

"Never, Esteban, never will I grow tired of being with you. I love you so very much."

He brushed his lips over hers. "I should have been here sooner for you. You should have never suffered such a beating. Seeing him bring that strap down on you—"

"No, no," she interrupted. "It was my plan for him to do just that so I could get close enough to grab one of his knives and stab him before he realized it. He reminded me of the Curros. They enjoyed beating someone who begged them to stop. That's why I begged him. I knew it would work him into a frenzy and give me time to grab the knife. And I did and now he's dead and you're free, Esteban, you're finally free of him."

Esteban hadn't even given that thought. He'd been too concerned for his wife to think of anything else. But she was right.

"You freed me. Good God, Rosa, you are courageous," he said with pride in his petite wife and hugged her tight, though loosened his grip when he heard her wince.

She wanted to tell him that the pain didn't matter, she preferred his arms around her, when suddenly a chill ran through her and she shivered. "I'm cold," she said finding it odd to be chilled on such a warm day.

Esteban saw how she had suddenly paled and realized that her ordeal was taking its toll. He reluctantly took a step away from her. "Listen to me, *Caro*, I want to hug you tight and chase away your pain, damn if I could only take away your pain, but your injuries won't let me. I must see how bad your wounds are and get you warm. Do you understand?"

She shook her head at first, and then she nodded, and then without warning tears began running down her cheeks.

Esteban cupped her face gently in his hands. "Cry, scream, do whatever will make you feel better. Whatever you need to do to release the pain of what you've been through."

She didn't get a chance to do anything. They both turned to the sound of horses as Jared and his men rode into the clearing. Jared was the only one to dismount. He walked past them and kicked Pacquito's body, then with a hard shove of his boot he turned him over.

"It is done, this is good," Jared said. "We will take his body." He motioned to his men and two carted the body to Pacquito's horse and draped him over the saddle. He nodded to Esteban. "You don't know what a lucky man you are," Jared said with a shake of his head. "You owe *Diablo,* you will hear from him."

With that he and his men left.

Rosa turned to Esteban, her shivering having grown worse. "I want to go home."

"You're in no shape to travel on a horse,

especially for several hours and that's how long it will take us to reach the hacienda. I'll build a fire and get you warm and you can rest. We'll return home at sunrise."

Rosa laid a trembling hand on Esteban's chest. "Please, Esteban, I want to go *home*. I want to sleep in *your* arms in *our* bed tonight and know *we* are safe."

He had to agree with her. He wanted to go home... *their home, their bed.* Besides, he didn't know if any of Pacquito's men survived the fight and if any would care enough to retaliate. He truly doubted it, but he couldn't take the chance. He would have to keep watch and that would prove difficult when his wife needed tending.

He took her hand. "This will not be an easy ride for you."

She squeezed his hand. "I will be with you and that is all that matters."

A single tear trickled down her cheek and he kissed it away, "I'll take you home."

He whistled for his horse and the animal appeared. Then as gently as he could he lifted his wife onto the saddle. She whimpered, but otherwise made no other sound. Tears running down her cheek told him that she was suffering more than she intended to let him know. He took the rolled blanket from behind his saddle, mounted his horse, and then draped the blanket around her.

"Get yourself comfortable against me and if you feel you cannot go on, let me know."

She nodded and eased herself against him,

winced and switched position. It took a few attempts until she finally settled in reasonable, at least he hoped it was, comfort against him.

"All set," she said and he could see that she was already fighting against the pain.

He wanted to curse the heavens, but instead he sent a prayer for a swift and painless journey. After all, this time God had heard him and answered his prayer. His wife was safe in his arms.

Chapter Thirty-seven

"What are you doing on that ladder?" Esteban demanded.

Rosa peered down from under the branches of the orange tree and smiled. "It has been two weeks; bruises, aches, pains are all gone. I feel fine."

"And you look beautiful," he said pleased to see how well and fast his wife had healed. But then between him, his mother, and Dolores, Rosa had been well tended. When they had arrived home that night two weeks ago everyone was happy and relieved to see them and eager to see to Rosa's care.

He had finally chased them all away after his wife was settled comfortably in their bed, and then he had joined her. He didn't think that either of them had ever slept so well that night or the nights that followed. He had worried that she would be plagued with nightmares from her ordeal, but not once did she sleep fretfully. Life had actually fallen into a peaceful routine and he cherished every minute of it.

She smiled at him and extended her hand for him to help her down.

His hands, instead, went to her waist and he lifted her off the ladder. He kissed her lips lightly before placing her on the ground.

She surprised him when she stepped away from him, planted her hands, and scolded, "When are you going to stop treating me like some fragile flower. I have told you repeatedly that I am fine and still you treat me as if I've yet to recover."

He went to say something and she held up her hand.

"I'm not finished." She ignored the way his eyes darkened and narrowed and continued having her say. "You kiss me as if my lips will break and your touch," —she threw her hands up in the air— "I barely feel it."

He went to speak again, his temper on the point of erupting, and she shook her finger at him.

"Not a word until I finish," she warned. "And when you're inside me you barely move and—"

"Enough," he bellowed and scooped her up and tossed her over his shoulder.

"What are you doing?"

"I'm doing exactly what you intended me to do, *Caro*, though God knows I'm going to have to go to confession again when I'm done."

"What? You went to confession? Put me down," she demanded and squirmed until he finally did. She faced him. "You truly took confession from Padre Marten?"

"I did. It was time," he said, tucking a strand of her soft dark hair behind her ear. "When our child is born I want to be able to stand beside you in church and see our baby baptized."

"You know I'm with child?"

"You're with child?" he said so shocked that he

took a step back.

"But you said..." she shook her head.

"Sooner or later you would have to be with child with how often we make love, but I didn't," —he stepped forward and placed his hand on her stomach— "know that the babe already nestled inside you."

"I have only realized it myself and I wanted to make sure before I said anything to you."

"You're sure now?"

"Very sure," she said with a wide grin, which faded quickly. "That doesn't mean you have to treat me like I'm fragile."

"But you're with child. It won't be proper to make love until the babe is born."

"What?" she said her eyes turning wide. "You can't mean that. All those months without you touching me," —she shook her head—"no, impossible I can't do that. I cannot live without your touch, without making love with you—" She stopped as soon as she caught the smirk in his eyes and slapped his arm. "That was mean."

He scooped her up in his arms. "Not as mean as telling me you barely feel anything when I'm inside of you."

She cringed, though with a smile. "I didn't know how else to get you to stop treating me as if I'd break each time you touched me." She chuckled. "Besides, this way worked faster."

He stopped just outside their bedroom door. "I'm going to make love to you and believe me you're going to feel it. Then we're going to gather the basket I've had Dolores fill and go to the pond, which had been my intention, and spend the rest of the afternoon there, eating and making love again, and then—"

"We'll return home and fall in bed exhausted, though make love again." She laughed.

"And fall asleep in each other's arms as we will do every night even when we are old and gray."

He kissed her with such passion that she sighed with the pleasure of what was to come and, with his wife pressed snugly against him, he walked into the bedroom and kicked the door closed.

THE END

You can read Gaby and Raphael's story and Rosa's adventure in Los Angeles in *Untamed Fire*.

Titles by Donna Fletcher

Single Titles

San Francisco Surrender
Rebellious Bride
The Buccaneer
Tame My Wild Touch
Playing Cupid
Whispers on the Wind

Series Books

Untamed Fire (Rancheros Trilogy)
Renegade Love
Book Three, Available 2014

The Wedding Spell (Wyrrd witch series)
Magical Moments
Magical Memories
Remember the Magic

The Irish Devil
Irish Hope

Isle of Lies
Love Me Forever

About the Author

Donna Fletcher is a *USA Today* bestselling romance author. Her books are sold worldwide. She started her career selling short stories and winning reader contests. She soon expanded her writing to her love of romance novels and sold her first book SAN FRANCISCO SURRENDER the year she became president of New Jersey Romance Writers. Donna is also a past President of Novelists, Inc.

Drop by Donna's website www.donnafletcher.com where you can learn more about her.